Praise for H

"*Beverly Roberts displays a rare depth of insight into thinking patterns, behavior and the emotions of her characters. She shows the heart of God to lovingly call us to see through His eyes and be transformed from the world's darkness to His light, a place of healing, wholeness, forgiveness and peace. Hillbrooke The Healer vividly portrays the power of God, through our faith in Jesus, our love and prayers for one another to bring about miracles!*"

--Marianne Siefert

"*In the first book of the Hillbrooke series as well as her second, Beverly Roberts paints a picture of the city of Hillbrooke, Michigan that I can actually see in my mind. People and places come alive. The characters have become my friends. In Hillbrooke The Healer, Beverly reminds us that healing always comes in the end! To God be the glory!*"

-Mary Kaye Foster

Be warned! Hillbrooke The Healer is not a book you can just pick up and lay down. Picking it up is no problem but laying it down---that's a problem. Beverly Roberts uses a vast array of literary methods to bring out an enchanting plot flitting from one fast-moving scene to another. The Pentecostal flavor is consistent and true to that outlook on life throughout the book. The characters are so real you either love them or grossly dislike them."

--Alton C. Smith, PhD

"*Hillbrooke The Healer, as well as Beverly Roberts' first book Hillbrooke New Beginnings, inspired me. The powerful prayers of the characters crying out to God in their time of need and on behalf of others caused a stirring in my soul to put the book down and pray. From cover to cover this book spoke of the power of God to intervene—when called upon.*"

--Brenda J. Lee

Other titles by Beverly Joy Roberts

Hillbrooke New Beginnings—2016

"My wife read the book Hillbrooke New Beginnings and found it very interesting. Biblical truths were presented in a way that captured the interest of the reader proclaiming truths from the Word of God, to create a desire for closer relationship with the Lord. The power of prayer was shown so clearly, and the need for the baptism of the Holy Spirit was emphasized. Excellent book! I am sure Beverly Roberts' next book, Hillbrooke The Healer, will be equally as interesting."

----Thomas E. Trask, former General Superintendent
of the Assemblies of God

"WOW! Lots of surprises! I loved it! I could not put this book down! This book not only was a great story, but it gives a very realistic picture of the issues that we face in this world and gives an accurate picture of how the enemy will try to sow discord among God's people. It also reveals God's mercy and faithfulness to His Children when we remain transparent to one another and faithful to HIM! LOVED it! Can't wait to read the next one!"

--Candace S. Korpi

"When I was done reading this book I was devastated. It was like a piece of my family was moving on without me. I was so sad to be done escaping to Hillbrooke after putting the kids to bed. I had times of compassion and times of tears as I read through so many spiritual encounters the characters were facing.

-Ministry Lifer, comments left on Amazon

Sign up at www.beverlyjoyroberts.com
For weekly devotionals by Beverly Joy Roberts.

Hillbrooke The Healer

Beverly Joy Roberts

*In honor of the four godly women in my life
who received their miracle;*

*Gladys Marie (Farrand) Smith (42)-my mother
Bessie Ferne (Holmes) Farrand (69)-my grandmother
Margaret Mae (Farrand) Keller (45)-my aunt
Beverly Jane (Winans) Roberts (70)-my mother-in-law
And Norma* Ouida *(Youngs) Smith, my step-mom, who is
(90) and counting*

Acknowledgements

Dear Reader,

Thanks for coming back for round two in the fictional city of Hillbrooke, Michigan. In my first book *Hillbrooke New Beginnings*, Pastor Rey and his wife Callan, had a spiritual awakening when they received the baptism in the Holy Spirit. In book two, *Hillbrooke The Healer*, they will come face to face with the power of a healing God.

Physical healing can be difficult to understand. We pray, fast, pled, bargain, cry, read scripture, and ask—but sometimes our requests are not answered in the way we hoped. One person may receive a temporal healing *(healing on earth)* while another receives an eternal healing *(to be absent from the body is to be present with the Lord)*.

In Hillbrooke The Healer, there are several sick people—some are sick physically, some emotionally and some spiritually—each of these three sicknesses carry with it separation.

<u>Physical sickness</u>
has the power to separate us through death.

<u>Emotional sickness</u>
has a way of isolating the one afflicted.

And <u>Spiritual sickness</u>
separates us from God.

Only one of these sicknesses comes with a guaranteed, immediate cure. Romans 10:13 says, "*Whoever calls on the name of the Lord <u>will be saved</u>.*"

The world tries to offer many counterfeits to physical, emotional and spiritual healing, but there is only one way to the Father, and that is through the Son, Jesus Christ. In the town of Hillbrooke, and wherever you live, there is a Healer and His name is Jesus.

I want to say a huge THANK YOU to the *New Life Book Club* for helping me in the proof reading of Hillbrooke The Healer. You ladies are the best! You make me look better than I am. Also, a heartfelt thank you to my sister, Barb Cody, who read the manuscript out loud to me over the course of a week while I sat at the computer and made the necessary changes—sisters are amazing people!

Thank you to Melissa Welch, and her eight-year-old son, Kaleb, who dialoged together and recorded their conversations about salvation and physical healing all from the perspective of an eight-year-old boy. I used some of their conversation verbatim in the book. I wish each of you could hear the actual recording of Kaleb's sweet little voice quoting scripture and telling the world about the power of the God he serves. It was a blessed experience.

Thank you, Sharon Chambers, Diana Wiehe and a few others who were the final readers—you bless me.

And to my husband of 42-years, Bob Roberts, he listened to me read chapters of this book that were rough and raw. I saw him cringe (*occasionally*) when he saw me coming with ten pages of story in my hand. Still, he allowed me to read it out loud to him—and for those who don't know—I'm not a great oral reader. (*It's painful to listen to!*) It was a labor of love on his part. He is without a doubt my biggest fan!

Thanks for choosing to read Hillbrooke The Healer. I hope it will be inspiring and faith building. Be blessed.

Sincerely,
Beverly Joy Roberts

List of Characters

New Characters:
Dr. Stuart Hayes M.D.—new doctor
Samantha Hayes—doctor's wife
Children: Isabelle and Baylee Hayes
Victor Darwin—The Healer
Debbie and Kim—Tom and Jean Brown's daughters

Returning Characters:
Rey Douglas—Pastor Community Outreach
Callan Douglas—Rey's wife
Children: Zander and Ty Douglas
Tom and Jean Brown—small group leaders
Heidi Alden—former church secretary
Grace-church secretary
Snake—Zak Parker/Carl Fields
Fauna Reynolds—Snake's girlfriend

Minor Characters: (new)
Ms. Klingburg—Social Worker
Dr. Kaplan—Hospital Staff Doctor
Mr. Palomo—Private Investigator
Steve Orvis—lawyer/Community Outreach board member
BudBabin—E-commerce Businessman/Community Outreach board member

Places:
Community Outreach Church
Hillbrooke Medical Clinic (new)
The Healer's (new)
Train Depot Restaurant Diner on Main (new)

1

The Brown's Small Group

D eer Lake was a beautiful backdrop for the *al fresco* anniversary gathering of the Brown's small group. Jean Brown's bare feet pressed against the wood slats of the deck gently rocking the porch swing back and forth. She circled the straw in her iced tea in rhythm with the movement of the swing.

Marilyn Fields eased into the swing next to Jean while balancing a plate of food in her hand. She watched as Jean blankly looked across the lake at nothing. Marilyn touched her friend's arm and whispered, "Jean. Is everything okay?"

Jean jerked her head in the direction of the touch. "Oh! You startled me." A smile formed on her face. "I was deep in thought. I've been a bit tired. Things have been hectic around here." Marilyn listened.

Jean chattered on. "Did I tell you the girls and their families are planning to come for a big family get together in about a month? I love it when they come, but you know…company can take a toll on you." The old Jean resurfaced with each word— energetic and bubbly.

Marilyn slipped her arm inside of Jean's while balancing her plate on her knees. "You know you can call me to help with anything you need. In fact, count on me for at least one meal. I'll be hurt if you don't let me."

Jean eased out of Marilyn's arm and stood. "I better start cleaning up some of this stuff before the wind carries these paper plates away."

"Let me help." Marilyn laid her plate of food next to her on the swing and tried to stand.

Jean placed her hand on Marilyn's shoulder to stop her. "I'm finished eating. You can help later. Relax and enjoy this amazing spring day." Jean began collecting the used paper plates and plastic tableware left unattended. Tom had put the garbage container next to the glass sliding doors for easy clean up. Jean dropped the trash she collected in the container then disappeared inside the house.

Watching from her place on the swing, a nagging concern for her friend filled Marilyn's heart. She wanted to press the subject further with Jean, but before she could, her daughter, Emily Edwards, took Jean's place on the swing. "Mom, have you heard anything about that new doctor in town?"

"No. Dad and I haven't been to the doctor in over a year."

"I took the kids last week for their shots. I like him. His name is Dr. Hayes. He's younger—maybe in his 40's. He's a nice addition to the clinic."

"Good to know. Does he have a family?"

Emily turned toward her mother and spoke with surprise. "I don't know. I would never ask that kind of stuff to my doctor. It was strictly business." Emily paused then added. "I really don't want to know my doctor on a personal level. Seems kind of strange don't ya think?"

Marilyn laughed. "I guess so." She continued to listen to Emily talk about her day while her eyes stayed fixed on the sliding door. Something was going on with Jean. Marilyn knew it. She didn't like the way Jean looked or how she was acting. It was out of character for Jean.

Emily followed her mom's eyes to the glass sliding door. "Mom, what's the matter with you?" Emily's tone was one only mothers and daughters use with each other.

Marilyn turned to answer her daughter. "Nothing—just thinking."

Emily shared with her mom the latest adventures of her two children. There was never a dull moment in their house.

All around them friendly chatter and laughter was heard. It was reminiscent of a family reunion more than a religious gathering. As people finished their dessert the group made their way into the Brown's family room. Two new members had joined since the group began six years ago. Kota Edwards joined his wife, Emily, four years ago. Then one year ago James Fields joined his wife, Marilyn. When all members were present there were twelve in attendance.

The small group had proven beneficial to the spiritual growth of the two newest members. These two men were once arch enemies. Now, each accepted responsibility for the wrongs they had perpetrated on others. Their first step was to seek forgiveness from the Lord followed by making amends with those they had wounded. These two steps set them on a road to wholeness.

Kota Edwards, kind and gentle, had made some poor life choices. The day he heard James Fields making unthinkable cruel comments about his recently deceased father, something snapped in him—bitterness took ahold like a malignancy. That was the day he formed a plan for revenge. To an outsider looking in, one might say that Kota accomplished his plan when he won the heart of Emily, James' daughter. Kota succeeded in seducing Emily. However, the plan that the *enemy meant for evil*, God reconstructed. Kota and Emily pushed passed the pain and God turned them into a loving family.

Kota opened his heart to the Lord. Once he fully understood the price Jesus paid for him, and the forgiveness the Lord freely gave—he was ready to extend that same forgiveness to those who he felt wronged him; Pastor Rey Douglas and James Fields. The Lord exchanged a hate-filled heart with a heart of forgiveness. Now these two men were as dear to Kota as brother and father. This change could only be credited to the restorative touch of a loving Heavenly Father.

The next step for Kota was to win Emily back. Some people thought she should make him suffer for the way he treated her, but Emily understood forgiveness. Before their daughter was born, she welcomed Kota back into her life. The final stitch that mended Emily's broken heart was forgiving Kota and reuniting with him.

For James Fields the process was different. He carried painful baggage from his childhood that proved to be a challenge as he grew in faith. James had been controlling, unmerciful and unforgiving as the head elder of the church board at Community Outreach. Then six years ago, he came face to face with his estranged son at the altar. James' remorse was immediate, but his transformation was slow. With a committed group of prayer warriors and men willing to mentor with love and patience, James slowly changed. His son, Zak who James had alienated, turned out to be his biggest encourager. Zak, himself, was a walking testimony of God's amazing grace.

Harold and Esther Smith still attended the small group. Harold continued to serve on the church board of Community Outreach Church. The Michigan winters and short daylight hours made it difficult for the Smith's to attend the once-a-week small group meetings. The first week they missed, a plan was formed to take turns picking them up. Now that spring had arrived and along with it 16 hours of daylight, the Smiths were able to resume their independence and drive to the Brown's house on their own.

The Ph.D.'s, Henry and Dorothy Samson, had not given up on the group. The past years for them had proven to be a steady time of growth in the Word. They had a hunger for more knowledge and a desire to share what they had learned.

Under the Samson's direction, an outreach ministry to the college and young professionals was formed. This group met on Sunday nights. They began with a handful of students meeting in the Samson's home. The group soon outgrew their house. They moved to the church to accommodate the crowd that had grown to nearly a hundred students.

This outreach for the Samson's was both challenging and rewarding. Watching young people, some who were away from home for the first time, vulnerable and searching, come face to face with a powerful, loving God was electrifying. Those attending were almost exclusively college age. The group was peer driven with the Samson's taking on a role of mentoring more than leading. Still they coveted their time with their own small group at the Brown's house. They needed fellowship with people who understood life before smart phones, tablets, twitter, #hashtags, Facebook and the Internet.

Pastor Rey and Callan Douglas tried to visit each of the new small groups as they popped up, but the Brown's small group was home and family to them. This group had weathered the storms of life together. This set the bar high for all the groups that followed.

Six months ago, Tom Brown turned down a job transfer to Denver, Colorado. Jean and Tom prayed about it and felt strongly God wanted them to remain at this church, in this small group and in the community of Hillbrooke. This was home now. In the past, when opportunities to move came their way, they had always accepted the transfer as God's leading knowing that each move gave the Lord opportunities to use them in a new location. But this time, they felt compelled to stay.

In fact, the confirmation to stay was a sweet assurance from the Lord that they were entering a new chapter. They purposed in their hearts to trust Him, no matter what. The Lord had never failed them. Never! They didn't always get what they wanted, but they accepted His plans for their lives, trusting their Heavenly Father. There was still love to share, lessons to learn and lives to touch in Hillbrooke, Michigan.

The Brown's small group was still on the receiving end of numerous prayer requests from outside their group. They fervently prayed for each one. The prayer requests came to them in a variety of ways; some were called in to the church office, others were submitted by way of the church website, sent by email or given directly to members of the group.

Zak Parker, also known as Snake, the runaway, the prodigal son of James and Marilyn Fields, created a Facebook (FB) page called Community Outreach Prayer. This prayer page had exceeded everyone's expectations with requests being submitted from around the world with over a thousand "likes." Each Thursday evening, when the Browns' small group came together, they took turns praying for the needs of those in their group, community and around the world.

□□

Tom Brown opened the small group meeting with a song. Their voices blended in acapella perfection. Following the song Tom led in prayer.

"Lord, we worship and adore You. We come to You as children reaching out to their loving Father. We have so many requests…so many needs, but before we even ask for one, we want to express our love, adoration and worship, just for who You are." Tom stopped praying, opened his eyes and spoke to the group, "Can we take a moment to express our love and worship with a word, a phase or a sentence? Speak to the Lord your gratitude, praise or one of the Lord's many attributes."

James spoke first, "Thank you Lord for Your complete and total forgiveness."

Then one by one—words and phrases were called out…

"He is my peace!"

"His love is all consuming."

"His presence is a sweet aroma."

"He is more precious than gold."

"He is full of loving kindness."

"He is the Author and Finisher of my faith."

"He is my Baptizer."

"You are Redeemer."

"My best friend."

And then someone said it. Tom wasn't sure who, but the words held power. Someone began to softly moan. Another joined in as one by one the Spirit of the Lord washed over the group. Then a Holy Hush fell. The Spirit of God began to move in a direction this group was all too familiar with when someone said, "He is Healer!"

2

(Five months earlier)
Welcome To Hillbrooke Dr. Hayes

Dr. Stuart Hayes glanced out the window of his sports car at the *Welcome to Hillbrooke* sign. His GPS said he would arrive in less than five minutes. Christmas lights trimmed the houses leading into Hillbrooke. The holiday trappings closely resembled a Currier and Ives Christmas card. Stuart eased his foot off the gas pedal turning his head to the right and left—scanning the darkened road for oncoming cars. He seemed to be the only one braving the weather on this December night—except for the moving truck following close behind him.

Stuart listened to the GPS giving him directions to turn in 500 feet onto Lancaster Drive. His car lights briefly illuminated the neighborhood bringing more festive houses into view. An old Victorian home drew Stuart's eyes from the road. Memories of his childhood home flashed before him. Christmas had been a special time of year for his family. The fresh cut tree, the red holly berries, the smell of pine and the sound of a crackling fire. A warm sensation rushed in at the thought of happier days.

Wet snowflakes splashed on the windshield of Stuart's car until his view was impaired by a layer of white. He flipped his wipers on and erased the snow from his sight. The happy memories he felt moments ago—were gone. A sad sigh escaped his lips.

Stuart spotted his new house on the left side of the road. It looked different than he remembered. It seemed further back— off the road. The long driveway curved in front of the house making a horseshoe shape. The wet blanket of snow that covered the ground hid the exact location of the driveway. Stuart drove slowly guessing his way. The stately brick house was dark and silent. It was his house—their house—the only house in the neighborhood without any form of festive décor; cold and unfriendly mimicking Stuart's inner emotion.

Dr. Hayes pulled into the driveway. Following close behind, the moving truck rolled to a stop. He opened his car door and stepped out into the night—alone. His feet sunk into the moist snow—cold and wet.

Stuart's wife, Samantha, along with his two daughters, Isabelle and Baylee, would be arriving in a few days. After much discussion, he reluctantly agreed to oversee the unpacking of the moving truck before the rest of the family arrived. He would rather have paid for someone else to do this mindless job, but Samantha insisted it be one of them. The thought of staying with the two girls—alone—without Samantha made the decision an easy one. He would go—she would stay.

□ □

The weeks between Thanksgiving and Christmas were an odd time to relocate a family, especially one with school age children. But Hillbrooke, Michigan needed a doctor, and the Hayes family needed to move—rather quickly.

Old Doc Russell had helped the families of Hillbrooke for decades. He served everyone from birth to geriatrics and was the much-loved family physician. The news of Doc Russell's heart condition surprised everyone. It ended his long run as town doctor, thus bringing together the union of Hillbrooke and the Hayes family.

Dr. Stuart Hayes was a workaholic with a quirky bedside manner. Samantha, his wife stood a few inches taller than her husband's five-foot seven-inch frame. She still possessed her youthful beauty. On the inside, the continuous pressures of stress and heartache eroded her core. The idealistic life of a doctor's wife with the perfect family would never be her reality. A sober truth she still struggled to grasp each day.

The Hayes children, fourteen-year-old Isabelle and ten-year-old Baylee were like sunset and sunrise. Isabelle with her flashes of bold color followed by impending darkness was sunset. Baylee was sunrise. She brought with her the promise of a warm, sun-filled day.

Isabelle entered puberty in a fury and emerged a hate-filled teenager. She had her parent's intelligence but refused to apply this knowledge to useful things. She chose to move in circles outside her realm of understanding with a crowd that was older. Her choice in clothes shouted, TROUBLED TEEN. When Isabelle was young, her parents felt their daughter's strength was a positive and one day her firm-resolve would land her a leadership role in society. Now, they just hoped she would make it through adolescence without a permanent criminal record or doing her body irreversible damage.

Stuart and Samantha knew Isabelle had been pushed to the sidelines, between Stuart's medical career and Samantha caring for a sick child. This dad and mom had years ago moved from parental figures to co-existing within the same walls as their troubled teen—all trying to survive—one more day.

Baylee, the younger daughter, endured the pain of a birth defect; Lower Limb Reduction (LLR). LLR stunted the growth of her legs causing her bouts of excruciating pain. The family had run the gamut of doctors. One medical doctor had gone so far as to call Baylee a hypochondriac which brought a prompt reply from Samantha.

"How could a child of six-years-old be a hypochondriac? She has no idea what or how one would be such a thing..." Samantha stood up keeping her feet firmly planted. She didn't trust what she might do had she moved one step closer to that condescending doctor. She continued. "And for another thing, how did my six-year-old manipulate her body to stop growing? Just how does a hypochondriac accomplish that small task?" Samantha ended the speech with one hand on her hip while her head bobbed from side to side. Fighting the emotion rushing in, she scooped her daughter up and walked out of that doctor's office giving the door a loud slam.

Once in the safety of their van, Baylee asked her mom, "What is a hyper-contractor?"

Samantha laughed—then wept.

Baylee never did get a straight answer that day. Samantha was consumed with helping Baylee and in the process forgot she had a husband and another child.

Dr. Hayes immersed himself in his career. He had stopped giving any suggestions about either of his off-spring a long time ago. He left them in the care of their mother. The only problem was that one child received an abundance of care while one was left to survive.

In the entrance of the Hayes' house a display of family photos lined the walls. The array of photos showed a family with coordinating outfits and big smiles—but rarely do pictures tell the whole story.

□□

Stuart walked toward the house fumbling with his key chain looking for the new house key. The newly fallen snow helped brighten the otherwise dark path. A gust of wind pulled Stuart's coat open sending a chill from head to toe. He quickened his pace. The wet snow on the ground sloshed with each step. He shook his head at the thought of doing any unpacking in this kind of weather.

Stuart stepped up on the porch remembering the first time he looked at the property a few months back. The housing inventory was low with only six houses in the city worth looking at in their price range. This house was the least offensive. The property was over an acre giving them privacy from their neighbors. Still, there was a sense of community in this country setting. It gave the options to be isolated or neighborly—whichever they desired.

Stuart unlocked the front door and pushed it open. He stepped into his new house. There was a chill in the air. He flipped on the nearest group of light switches lighting the better part of the front yard as well as the entryway. He searched around for the thermostat and found it near the entrance to the kitchen. He pumped the heat up to 75.

The sound of the front door slamming caused Stuart to jerk his head in that direction. The moving van driver stood sheepishly just inside the entryway. His snow-covered boots formed small pools of water on the wood flooring.

The awkward man cleared his throat then spoke. "Ya plan for us to do the unpacking yet tonight?"

Stuart checked his watch. It was 7:00 P.M. "No. Be here at 9:00 tomorrow morning. We'll get started then. Don't be late!"

The driver nodded in the affirmative and vanished out the door.

Stuart strolled around the house picturing in his head all the work that awaited him over the next two days. His thoughts were his only companion. I wish we hadn't rushed into buying this house. We should have rented, but no, Samantha felt *this was the place*. She felt at home here. She even went as far as to say, at peace.

Stuart hated it when people said inanimate objects or random places made them feel at peace. Peace was a mind choice. It didn't have anything to do with external forces seen or unseen. People choose to be at peace or turmoil. He could feel his own peace fleeting with his increased heartrate.

He spoke with disgust in his voice—to no one. "This place doesn't hold a candle to our last house." Stuart flicked off the lights and exited the front door with a loud slam. He thought, I'll put in my few days of work and supervise the movers then it's all on Samantha.

Stuart started his car and headed for the hotel where he and Samantha had stayed when they came to pick out their home six weeks ago. He hoped the suite he reserved was clean this time.

□□

Stuart Hayes and Samantha Lewis met in college. Samantha was popular, outgoing and friendly. Stuart was reserved, quiet and studious. Their friendship blossomed at a yoga class. It started with casual conversations before and after classes. Then the yoga class offered a weekend retreat. At the retreat things changed.

Samantha was caring and genuine. Her heart was always open to people and ideas. She found purpose in the meditation classes and the daily discussion groups. Stuart felt all forms of religion were for weak-minded people. He looked at yoga as exercise and nothing more. For him it was more of a social experiment. He watched and took mental notes of people's comments and reactions to the forces at work. He listened carefully to what he believed to be manipulation by the instructors. The leading discussions were a joke. His interests were firmly rooted in medicine, but he also believed the human body had many powers of healing outside the traditional path.

Stuart and Samantha's friendship grew with their first dinner date at the yoga retreat. A few months later they were living together. In less than a year they said, "I do."

Samantha dropped out of college to support her husband's dreams. Even with his substantial scholarships her contribution was important. During Stuart's residency, Isabelle, burst on the scene before they could get to the hospital. Looking back this should have been Stuart and Samantha's first clue that *this daughter* wasn't going to do things the traditional way.

Baylee came four years later. She was overdue, turned breach during labor and was born by emergency C-section. After two traumatic births, Stuart and Samantha decided their family was complete. Other than Isabelle being strong-willed and Baylee being small, the Hayes home was uneventful until Samantha noticed something wasn't right with Baylee's legs. Soon after that, Baylee developed sudden and inexplicable pain.

"Growing pains; everyone gets them—some worse than others." This was the phrase Samantha heard over and over. "You can use pain relievers, massage and heat. She'll grow out of it—in time." The words weren't much comfort to a mother coping with a child in pain. This diagnosis first came from within the home. Then an assortment of pediatricians and later specialists all dismissed the pain away as a natural part of childhood.

The longer Baylee's health issues continued the more stress fractures became evident in the Hayes family. Then finally the dreaded diagnosis came—giving the illness a name did not bring relief—Lower Limb Reduction (LLR).

Stuart had tried early in the diagnosis to be helpful. The sting of not easing Baylee's discomfort left him detached and buried with guilt. He threw himself into his medical practice while Samantha was consumed with the care of a sick child. This left Isabelle to find new ways to attract attention; good or bad. It didn't matter. Attention was attention.

Isabelle's behavior was the reason the Hayes family needed to move to Hillbrooke. She was caught on surveillance tape destroying property at her middle school. This was not Isabelle's first offence which meant she might be spending time in a juvenile detention facility.

Dr. Hayes was able to persuade the school not to press charges by paying for all the damages. Isabelle was able to move forward without a criminal record. The judge did give her a stern warning along with Stuart and Samantha. They knew it was time for Isabelle to have a fresh start—far from old acquaintances. They took the first medical position that opened—Hillbrooke, Michigan.

The winter months passed quickly with the Hayes family looking inward with only Dr. Hayes and Isabelle routinely leaving the house. Dr. Hayes went to his office and Isabelle to school while Baylee was homeschooled. Her illness prevented her from functioning for extended periods of time away from home.

□□

Baylee sat in agony in the back of the family van. She gripped the arm rests as the pain shot through her legs like waves of high voltage electricity. She willed herself to remain quiet. The grinding pain in her legs had plagued her throughout her life with only brief periods of reprieve.

The van slowed and then came to a full stop in front of a small house. Baylee looked at the weathered-gray wood planked siding. On the covered porch there was a painted white swing hanging from the ceiling. The wind blew just enough to cause the porch swing to move slightly. Baylee liked the way the swing moved with the breeze. It was gentle like a hypnotist's pocket watch, back and forth, back and forth.

The front door of the van slammed shut bringing Baylee back to reality. Samantha, Baylee's mom, walked around the van, pushed the button on the toggle key and watched the door ease open. The hurt was evident on Samantha's face. Even as young as Baylee was, she understood pain. All she could see in her mother's face was anguish. Her mother had vowed to do everything within her power to make Baylee's pain stop.

The sound of her mother's voice brought a renewed courage to Baylee. "Sweetie, can you walk inside, or should I carry you?"

Baylee replied, "I'll try and walk." She reached out holding on to her mom for balance. She guided her legs out together, sliding out of her seat, down to the ground and fell into her mother's waiting arms. She leaned heavily on her mom, and together they walked. Each step caused Baylee's face to grimace from pain, yet not a sound escaped her lips.

The sign nailed to the front door of the business simply said, *The Healer.* Baylee paused and examined the four steps leading up to the front porch. She mustered up the strength to conquer what seemed like a mountain. The climb proved more than Baylee could endure. Without saying a word, Samantha scooped her daughter up in her arms and carried her.

Once the obstacle was behind them, Samantha set Baylee down and allowed her to open the door to the business. Mother and daughter stepped inside. A chime on the back of the door made a soft sound as the door eased open. An attractive lady about Samantha's age sat behind a small desk chatting on her cell phone. When she looked up and saw customers arriving, she abruptly ended her conversation.

"You must be the Hayes family." She approached Baylee and dropped down to one knee. She awkwardly placed her hands-on Baylee's shoulders and spoke in an unpleasant and high-pitched tone. "We're gonna get you all fixed up young lady. You just wait and see."

The cheery lady stood, curled her index finger at mother and daughter, motioning for them to follow. She led them down a hallway and opened the door to a small, dark room. The blackout shades were pulled with one single lamp sparsely lighting the room. The smell of incense was nauseating. The smoke from embers in a small stone cup curled up in ringlets and encircled a nameless statue that sat on the table.

Samantha knew the routine. She guided her daughter toward the table, effortlessly lifting Baylee's frail body up. Samantha laid her daughter on the colorful, woven blanket. Baylee fearfully gazed up at her mother. This was not Baylee's first time to visit a "healer."

From her earliest memory, Baylee obediently followed her mother from one medical doctor to another. Then the diagnoses came. Samantha studied all she could find on the disorder. It appeared to be caused by something the mother may have come in contact with during pregnancy. The most recent doctor had said that in a few years Baylee may need one, but likely two prosthetic legs. Walking was becoming more and more challenging with each passing month. Samantha wasn't ready to see her child face an irreversible surgery. With the blessing of her husband, she branched out into alternative medicine. This *Healer* was number six on the list.

□□

Baylee wanted to run away. She wanted to scream—*get me out of here*. She didn't say a word or make a sound. The man walked into the small, dark room and turned on music that sounded like water trickling in a brook. It filled the room bringing with it a false since of peace.

The Healer leaned in close to Baylee's ear and spoke softly, "I'm going to rub my hands together then touch your legs where it hurts."

Baylee squeezed her mother's hand but remained motionless on the table. She prepared herself for another hopeless ritual. Her eyes darted from her mother's face to the face of the man who rubbed his hands together like a mad scientist. Then he placed his cold fingers on her fragile leg— forcibly pressing his fingertips into her flesh while chanting. Tears formed in Baylee's eyes.

Samantha turned away.

3

(Present Time)
Who's the Healer?

The first nine months of Pastor Rey and Callan's ministry at Community Outreach left them wondering if they had made the worst decision in their lives. They had been unprepared and unaware that God had amazing things in store for two flawed individuals with pliable hearts. Rey had made mistakes, but he took ownership of his poor decisions and made the necessary changes. Callan took a bit longer, but it was all the sweeter when she finally surrendered to the Lord. Hillbrooke was their place of new beginnings.

□□

Callan and Rey sat in the white rockers on their front porch soaking in the warmth of the sun. Spring wasn't officially here but the weather was pleasant giving them a few moments to enjoy each other's company and watch their boys riding bikes in the driveway.

Zander and Ty were acting a bit reckless for Callan's taste. They were obviously trying to outdo each other while their favorite audience watched.

Callan scolded. "Boys! Slow down."

Zander pulled his feet off the bike peddles and angled them out away from his body. A loud, Wheeeeeeeeeeeeee!" echoed all the way to the porch where Callan and Rey watched. Zander followed that trick by pulling his feet up to the balance bar of the bike, and then he tried to stand on the bar. He raised one hand in the air like a rodeo cowboy.

Callan's warnings fell on deaf ears.

Ty watched his older brother and cheered him on.

Callan turned to her husband, "Rey, stop them!"

"No. Let them play. Don't you remember taking a spill or two from your bike?"

"Really? You think my sisters and I did that kind of stuff." Callan shook her head in disbelief. "Do you know me at all?"

A smile formed on Rey's lips. He kept his focus on his sons but reached over and held Callan's hand.

Callan took a deep breath and confessed. "It's hard letting them grow up. They aren't babies anymore. They think they own this town riding those bikes all over the neighborhood. I think they know more people in Hillbrooke than we do." Callan jumped out of her rocker cupping her hands around her mouth. "Boys be careful. You're going to get hurt." Callan looked at Rey with *that* face. "Callan, they're being boys and brothers. Brothers live to outdo each other."

She sat back down keeping her eyes fixed on the boys. She chuckled. "I was actually called Ty and Zander's *mom* the other day." Rey took his eyes off the bike show to look at his wife while she continued to share. "I love that we live in a safe place that allows them a childhood like this."

Rey's hand still rested on top of Callen's. She turned her hand palm side up and entwined her fingers with his. She gave his hand a squeeze. Rey looked at her with a contented smile.

"The Lord has certainly blessed us with a good life." Rey agreed.

The next seconds played out in slow motion and forever changed the course of the summer.

Going as fast as he could, Ty peddled toward the road. A second later, without warning his bike jerked to the right wedging his front tire between two rocks bordering the end of the driveway. The impact catapulted him over the handlebars into the air. He glided through the air then vanished into the deep ditch at the end of the driveway. A deafening, hollow thud followed. It played out in a matter of seconds—yet seemed like a nightmare with no escape.

Callan jerked her hand from Rey's and covered her mouth to muffle a scream. The tranquility of the previous moments suddenly was replaced with seizing fear. She bolted toward the ditch praying. "Jesus, Jesus, Lord, help him. Help us."

Rey's reaction time was quicker. He reached his son first and knelt by his side. Callan still running yelled. "Don't move him."

Zander was closest when the accident occurred. He jumped from his bike allowing it to fall in the driveway. He slid down the embankment, paralyzed with fear looking at his brother—not talking—not moving. Zander, just two years older than Ty, took a few steps back and watched.

Callan and Rey leaned in close to Ty. Callan spoke with a soft tone while she held her own fear at bay. "Don't move. We're going to get help."

Ty began to moan. His left arm rested at the side of his body in an unnatural position.

Callan went into emergency-mom-mode. The instructions began to fly instinctively. "Rey, run to the house and get a blanket. Call 911. We can't move him."

Rey responded, bolting in long strides across the ample yard to the house.

"Ty—baby, lay still. Try not to move. You've hurt your arm. Help is coming. Does your head hurt?" Callan waited for her son to respond.

Ty whimpered. Then his eyes flittered.

Callan could see the whites of his eyes. A bolt of fear shot through her whole body. She fought the urge to cradle him in her arms. Instead she softly patted his face. "Stay awake, Ty. Daddy's getting help."

Ty opened his eyes wide then shut them again without saying a word.

"Let's listen and see if we can hear the siren." Callan glanced in Zander's direction and could see the shock on her eldest son's face. One child moaned in pain and the other was silenced by fear.

She looked at Ty again. "Ty, can you hear me? We're going to pray. Zander come over here and hold my hand." Callan reached out in Zander's direction. He stood stationary—just out of reach. She wiggled her fingers encouraging him to come.

Hesitantly, he moved toward his mother and took her hand. Zander's face was void of emotion and for a moment Callan thought she may have two boys going into shock.

She took Zander's hand, laid her other hand on Ty's chest and prayed as the Spirit of the Lord guided her. "Jesus, I need Your help. Please touch Ty's body and heal him. Stop his pain and flood his heart with Your peace. I pray for Zander, that

You would speak peace to his heart as well. Chase worry from him. Lord, I trust in You. I know your plans for my family are good. They are plans not to harm us." Callan paused then added, "Use this for your glory." Her words of understanding were replaced with the language of the Spirit.

Callan's eyes momentarily opened when she felt the breeze of a blanket touch her face. The blanket drifted down to cover her son's motionless body. Rey tucked the blanket around Ty to keep him warm while they waited for help to arrive.

Callan added, "Lord, give everyone who touches our son wisdom to know what he needs and how to handle this injury. In Jesus name I pray. Amen!"

In the distance, the wailing sound of a siren sent a wave of emotion coursing through Callan's whole body. The urge to surrender to the moment pressed in. She fought off the chills that were causing her teeth to rattle. She silently prayed, *Lord help me be strong. Help me do this.*

Rey stepped out of the ditch into the road—ready to flag down the ambulance.

□□

The Emergency Department doctor was smiling when he stepped into room #24. In his hand was a large plastic x-ray. He slid the transparent film under a clip on the wall and flicked a switch illuminating the x-ray. Even to an untrained eye, the clean break in Ty's arm was visible.

The doctor pointed to the break and said, "He won't need surgery. We'll be able to put a cast on his arm and young Mr. Douglas should be back on his bike by mid-summer. His arm will be sore for a week along with a colossal headache. He does have a mild concussion."

A twinge of remorse shot through Callan's chest. She should have insisted the boys wear their helmets.

The doctor continued. "From what I can see, Mrs. Douglas, you handled this like a professional. You would be surprised how many people move children with these kinds of injuries, causing them more pain and further complications. Good job!" Rey looked relieved.

Callan breathed deeply for the first time in what seemed like hours.

Rey looked at Ty and gently tousled his hair, "Well, this isn't the best way to begin the summer young man."

Ty was groggy from the pain meds but mustered a half smile before he turned his head to the side and closed his eyes.

The doctor instructed, "You will need to follow up with your primary care doctor in a week to be sure his pain management is under control. Also, your family doctor will want to make sure no other issues arise. Your son will need another x-ray in a few weeks to see how his arm is healing. Tonight, you should wake him up every few hours and ask him some questions to be sure there are no complications with the concussion." The doctor handed Rey the paperwork then touched Ty's arm. "Okay, let's get you fixed up." He proceeded to wrap up Ty's arm like a mummy.

Zander watched from behind his parents, unusually quiet.

□□

Heidi Alden sat at the reception desk in the office of *The Healer* gazing out the window at the side of the neighboring building. Her thoughts raced. *Why did they build these buildings so close together? I feel like I can't breathe in this confined space. I love my job. The Healer's office is the best place I've ever worked. Victor Darwin, The Healer, values my opinions—he's nothing like Rey Douglas.*

Six years had passed since Heidi was released from her position as office manager at Community Outreach Church. She had six years to let it go, six years to process her feelings and still the pain was fresh and resurfaced at the oddest times.

Heidi's thoughts continued to accuse Rey Douglas. I know he's hiding something. I never trusted that man. The best day of my life was the day I left that church. They thought they could destroy me. I'm glad that old life is done—gone forever. That crazy church service where Rey confessed his wrongs in not visiting that man Bill Edwards who was sick and dying. No one even cared about that man dying, his family or his funeral. The next thing you knew Rey Douglas is one of those hyper spiritual nuts— all remorseful for his actions.

That started the dominoes falling—I just never expected to be caught in the avalanche of an unfaithful husband—good riddance to that two-timing cheat. A smug expression formed on Heidi's face—John probably learned how to be unfaithful from watching Rey Douglas. It was while he was part of that Community Outreach Church board that he pretended to be a Christian. What kind of pastor wouldn't know they had a team member like my X-husband? I think Rey knew about John's infidelity. He probably even was covering for him. Well, good bye to both of you losers. Who needs either one of you? Not me.

Heidi glanced down at the open appointment book on her desk. She ran her finger over the name of the next client. She remembered this lady had neck pain. Heidi saw her at the grocery store rubbing her neck. This woman was referral number twelve.

A smile formed on Heidi's mouth. She imagined the 'job well done' and 'I couldn't do it without you' comments from *The Healer*. Looking around the waiting area, she noticed finger prints on the glass topped coffee table. She opened her bottom drawer and pulled out the cleaning wipes and walked across the room to polish the glass top.

Most days there were only a few clients which gave Heidi way too much time to think. Her thoughts turned again to Pastor Rey. Her lips pinched tightly as she remembered how he came into town thinking he was all *spiritual and holy*. Seeking the Lord for this and praying for that. He was always praying, helping the poor, visiting the prison—like who cares about those people. Rey Douglas sucked all the fun out of church.

And James Fields—he was the biggest disappointment. Acting like a crying baby at the altar—he was supposed to be the leader, the man with the plan, but he turned out to be as ridiculous as all those religious idiots at that church. Just because his tattooed criminal, runaway son gets religion—and Marilyn, forever the drama queen, she acted out the story of the Prodigal Son in front of the whole church.

I knew the first time I invited that woman to church that she was a fanatic. Asking me, if I was saved and how does one get saved—what business is that of anyone? James and Marilyn both got theirs when their little do-gooder daughter, Emily turned up pregnant. I knew she was sleeping around—the tramp.

Heidi smiled at the pain she imagined this caused the Fields' family. She stood back and angled her head to see if the smudges were gone from the glass topped table. Satisfied with her work, she returned to her desk and looked out the window. The spring flowers were poking up along the edge of the brick wall at the business next door. Heidi studied the flowers unaware that Victor Darwin, her employer watched her from the hallway.

The phone in *The Healer's* office rang playing a scale of soothing notes like a wind chime. Heidi picked up the receiver and answered in a soft, breathy voice, "Peace and healing to all who call. This is Heidi. You've reached the office of *The Healer*. You're not alone."

"Hey Heidi, it's me." The me, on the other end of the line, was a familiar voice, one that did not need to be identification with a name.

Heidi responded. "What's up?"

"Just thinking about you wondering how things are going."

Heidi glanced around the empty office. "It can be a bit boring here but it's still better than the other five places I've worked since leaving Community Outreach. I can't believe you still go there. When will you wise-up?"

"It's not so bad. I never understood why you disliked Pastor Rey so much. He's not boring like other preachers."

"I can't stand hearing his name. I've been with *The Healer* for more than one year. *He* has helped me let go of all the hatred and pain of my past. I'm the *happiest* I've ever been. I would go so far as to say *tranquil*." Heidi hung on the last word allowing her tone to soften on the second syllables.

"I'm happy to hear that. Maybe I should stop by for one of those massages you're always bragging about."

Heidi smiled moving into sales mode. "You really should. I've had special sessions with *The Healer* and they've been therapeutic bringing true peace to the troubled places of my inner turmoil." She paused and looked side to side.

Victor, still listening in the hallway, took a step backwards a half smile formed on his lips. His tongue moistened his lips.

Heidi whispered. "It's like he can read my thoughts and knows my feelings. He discerns just what to say to bring me back to my center place. My life is nearly perfect now. What more could I ask for?"

Victor moved slowly down the hallway. The floor made an eerie creaking sound under his feet that echoed into the waiting area. Heidi abruptly ended her phone call and walked down the hallway. No one was there.

Victor stood in the darkness of the first examination room. His back pressed against the wall and breathed in the scent of the incense that still lingered from his last patient. Then he flicked on the lights and walked across the room to adjust the display of flowers on the table near the statue. He was careful to keep them angled toward the examination table and dressing area.

4

Dr. Hayes is IN

T he waiting room at the Hillbrooke Medical Clinic was exceptionally busy. Heidi Alden strolled in like royalty expecting people to vacate their seats to make room for her.

No one moved.

Heidi purposely kept her back to the other patients as she approached the sliding window where the receptionist sat. Heidi jotted her name down on the list. The receptionist opened the window and took the clip board out of Heidi's hand. No words were exchanged, nor eye contact made.

Heidi thought the staff could use some customer service training. She turned away from the counter and walked to an open area of chairs closest to the door purposely choosing a seat far from the coughing and runny noses of children.

She plopped down in the uncomfortable chair refusing to rest her hands on the side arms; Heidi folded them in her lap. The gossip magazines on the table next to her caught her eye. Using one finger she moved the publications around on the table until one captured her attention.

The caption revealed a deep, dark skeleton recently uncovered. The picture of a teary-eyed couple on the front cover was now fodder for public consumption. Heidi had seen the reports on the news shows. Everyone was discussing their personal business and judging them openly. Throwing caution to the wind, Heidi picked up the germy gossip rag. Even before reading the article, she thought, serves them right thinking they are above the rest of us. Look how the mighty have fallen. She flipped to the page that told every intimate detail of the young couple's private life and pending divorce.

The door leading to the hallway of the examination rooms opened. A middle-aged nurse stepped out and called the name, "Ty Douglas."

Heidi stiffened. Her shoulders bolted up like someone stuck a gun in her back. On the other side of the waiting room wall, she heard multiple people stirring. She looked in the direction of the waiting nurse. The family of three walked out from behind the dividing wall—Callan, Zander and Ty Douglas. Ty's arm was in a cast. Callan greeted the nurse with a smile and made casual conversation as the door to the examination area eased shut behind them.

As Heidi watched the scene play out a vicious hatred rose up within her. She wanted to jump up and shout—she's a fake, a liar, a fool. She could feel her pulse racing. Her heart pounded in her chest. She had to calm herself before she went in to see Dr. Hayes. Breathe, just breathe. She told herself. Breathe slower.

Get a grip. Be in control. Remember why you're here. This initial visit was contrived to get more information about Dr. Hayes' sick daughter, Baylee.

When the doctor's wife and daughter came to *The Healer* last week the mother gave Heidi a limited amount of information about Baylee's condition. Now, Heidi was on a fact-finding trip for Victor Darwin, *The Healer.* He sent her under the guise of a 'Meet and Greet' with the new doctor in town. Seeing Callan caused old hurts to resurface. A fresh wave of loathing for Pastor Rey and Callan settled on Heidi.

It had been years since Heidi was let go from her position at Community Outreach Church but at that moment the wound felt fresh. She tried to implement *The Healer's* techniques for peace, but her mind was void of remedies. The feelings of disdain for the Douglas family, and *that* church, had not diminished in the least. Seeing either Rey or Callan around town usually brought back the old feelings of being fired—let go for no good reason.

Heidi comforted herself with this thought; I did my job. One might say I even did it well. Pastor Rey had told her that the two of them weren't compatible. That she would be happier in another place of employment.

Heidi realized she made a grunting noise out loud and glanced from right to left. She thought, at least I socked it to him with six months of unemployment. He owes me so much more.

Then he replaced me with that cry baby Grace Babcock. That was insulting—like she could do the work required. All she could do is feel everyone's pain. Crying and praying with them like it was happening to her personally. Such a fake—no one cares like that. I wouldn't be surprised if there's a little somethin'—somethin' on the side between Rey Douglas and his new secretary.

Heidi turned her head to the side like an idea was just born. She smirked. Come to think of it—I saw it when I worked there. Callan is a fool.

□□

The door clicked shut behind the Douglas family. The nurse led them down the hallway maze to the pediatric examination room. It was a bit childish for a boy of eight, but Ty obediently sat on the blue ducky paper that covered the table. The two walls were decorated with woodland animals. The largest wall had a mural of the woods. It felt like you could step into the wall and be lost in a magical forest. Even though Ty would never admit it, he did like looking for all the hidden animals in the forest. He and Zander loved coming to this room.

A knock on the door drew all three sets of eyes in that direction.

"Come in." Callan replied to the knock.

Ty and Zander both sat up straighter as the doctor opened the door and entered the room.

"Hi guys. I don't believe we've met. I'm Dr. Hayes taking over for Dr. Russell. I see we have a broken arm here." He walked over and held Ty's arm. The one that wasn't broken and said, "Wow. It looks fine to me. Are you sure it's broken?"

Ty looked a bit worried. He glanced at the cast on his left arm then at his mom. She was smiling.

"It's this arm, Doctor." Ty pointed with a nod of his head at the arm wrapped in the bright orange cast.

"Oh. Are you sure it's not this one?" He pointed at the right arm again and laughed. Then Ty knew he wasn't the usual *get down to business* kind of doctor.

Dr. Hayes smiled. "Yep, I see it now. That cast should have been a dead giveaway. Let's get you set up for a repeat x-ray in two weeks. We want to make sure things are healing correctly. Hopefully, if all is well with the x-rays we can get that cast off in 2-4 weeks. Fingers crossed!" Dr. Hayes looked at Ty's chart on his open laptop. Then he looked at Callan and asked, "Do you live on Lancaster Drive?"

Callan answered. "Yes—yes we do."

"Mrs. Douglas, I think we're neighbors. We can't be more than a few houses apart. Is your house the white brick ranch with gray shutters and the red door?"

Callan looked surprised that the new doctor in town was her neighbor, and he described her home in detail. She resisted the pride that was trying to find a nesting place in her thoughts and responded, "Well, welcome to the neighborhood Dr. Hayes. Do you have a family?"

"My wife and I have two daughters. Isabelle is 14 and Baylee is 10. Isabelle starts high school next year and Baylee is homeschooled."

"Zander is almost 10." Callan motioned toward Zander who looked at the doctor like a deer in the headlights. Callan continued. "Are you enjoying the neighborhood?" Before Dr. Hayes could reply Callan continued. "We love it here. These two boys know just about everybody in a mile radius of our house. In the summer it's hard to get them to slow down and come home. They are moving from one adventure to another. We'd love to meet your family sometime."

Dr. Hayes looked at Callan and smiled. "That would be wonderful. Baylee could use a friend. We are relatively new here and she doesn't get out much." Dr. Hayes turned to the boys, "Would you mind stopping by to see Baylee sometime? I know it's a lot to ask seeing she's a girl, but she can also play video games with the best of them." Dr. Hayes looked at Ty. "I bet she'd like a chance to sign her name on that cast."

The boys smiled at the thought of a new challenger and nodded.

Dr. Hayes pulled his business card from his pocket and jotted down his address on the back along with his home phone number. He handed the card to Callan. "My wife's name is Samantha. She could use a friend, too."

□□

Heidi simmered at a low boil in the waiting room for her turn with Dr. Hayes. She moved to a different place in the office, one that was far from the view of those leaving. She fought to hold it together. If she had to see Callan face to face, she didn't know how she might respond.

"Heidi Alden?" The same nurse called her name. Heidi stood and hesitantly followed the full-figured nurse down the maze of hallways. Her eyes darted in every direction scanning the area for Callan. No Callan in sight. Perfect!

The nurse opened the door to an examination room. "You can wait here Mrs. Alden. The doctor has a few patients ahead of you. He'll be in very soon."

Heidi took the seat nearest the window. She fumbled around in her purse for her phone and pulled it out to check her FB account. She snorted air through her nose as she scrolled through her friends list until she landed on her friend who still attended Community Outreach Church. She felt justified in her actions. The facts were what they were. Pastor Douglas was a womanizing child abuser, and just like that her lie became truth—to her. She chose to make her post public. Hillbrooke really should know they have a wolf in their midst who is trying to pass himself off as a sheep.

Heidi scrolled through the comments on FB for a few minutes then put her phone away. She checked her watch. It had been about ten minutes. She figured she'd give him 20 minutes of her time, if he didn't show by then she was leaving. A few minutes later, there was a soft tap on the door.

Heidi cleared her throat then spoke softly, "Come in..." She could have added...*said the spider to the fly,* but she didn't.

Dr. Hayes opened the door slowly and poked his head into the room.

Very handsome, she thought. She sat up taller—a warm smile formed on her lips.

"Hello Mrs. Alden. What seems to be the problem today?"

"Dr. Hayes, nice to meet you. I'm here for a 'Meet and Greet.' Dr. Russell was my doctor for years and I wanted to come and meet you and introduce myself. Please call me Heidi. Mrs. Alden is a thing of the past, since Mr. Alden decided he didn't want to be married anymore." Heidi moved a bit uncomfortably in her chair and re-crossed her long legs. She moved her leg back and forth partly from nerves and partly because she hoped Dr. Hayes would notice.

"I'm sorry to hear that. I'll make a notation in your file. Do you have any questions for me regarding your healthcare?" The doctor's eyes were drawn in by the movement of Heidi's leg then he quickly refocused on the laptop on the counter in front of him.

He felt uncomfortable with this woman. She seemed about his age. He searched the file for her birthdate. Yep! She was two years younger but looked ten years younger and dressed twenty years younger. One could say on a scale of one to ten with one being flirtatious and ten being provocative— this woman was a dangerous twelve.

Heidi kept her eyes fixed on the doctor. "I work for *The Healer* here in town. I'm his receptionist. He is located downtown in the old gray house one block off Main Street. I'm not sure if you've heard of him?" Heidi waited to study the doctor's face to see if he and his wife were communicating.

"No. I can't say I have. Is there a reason I should know him?"

"Well, yes. I met your daughter, Baylee last week when your wife brought her in for a healing massage."

Dr. Hayes looked up from his laptop with a puzzled expression. "A massage for Baylee?"

"Well, *The Healer's* massages are different than the kind you go to for relaxation. He uses healing oils, music, incense and prayers." Heidi watched to see the doctor's reaction.

"Really? Was it helpful?" Dr. Hayes asked.

And there it was. Just what Heidi was hoping to hear— zero communication between the good doctor and his wife. Heidi responded, "I believe it was helpful. They set another appointment. Has Baylee been sick long?"

"Yes. It's been most of her life." Dr. Hayes stopped talking and stared at the laptop. His professionalism was gone—replaced with sadness.

Heidi not wanting to close the communication went a different direction. "I noticed Ty Douglas broke his arm. I used to work for his father. I was his office manager. He certainly is one mischievous little guy. I wonder how that *accident* happened."

Heidi put just enough emphasis on the word *accident* to cause Dr. Hayes to look up from the computer screen. The curiosity was easy to see in the doctor's eyes.

Heidi continued, "I've seen his parents pulling and jerking on those little arms more than once." Dr. Hayes looked directly at Heidi.

She knew she had his full attention.

"Are you saying that you suspect what happened to that little boy wasn't an accident?"

"Well, I can only speak to what I saw when I was working for his father, Rey Douglas. You can see I'm not working there anymore." She lowered her head like she knew more than she should tell. Her not working at Community Outreach Church had nothing to do with the treatment of the Douglas children and she knew it.

"Do you have any more questions about the practice or me as a doctor that you would like to ask? I have a few more patients waiting."

Heidi stood and smiled. She felt her work was done—for now. Speaking to Dr. Hayes with her over-the-top friendliest voice and a bit too close in proximity she said. "It was very nice to meet you Dr. Hayes, and we'll take good care of that little girl of yours at *The Healer's*. I've seen him work wonders on other clients. We are going to believe for the best possible outcome for your little girl as well."

Dr. Hayes returned her smile and handed her a paper for check out. "There won't be any charge today. If you have any health-related needs that arise in the future, you may call the office for an appointment."

Heidi's ankle turned slightly as she moved toward the door. She brushed against the doctor as she exited the examination room. "Oh, pardon me." She said. A satisfying smile formed on her lips showing self-approval. She only wanted to soften the doctor toward *The Healer*. She didn't realize she would also have an opportunity to give Rey and Callan Douglas a direct punch to the gut. She reveled in her good fortune as she exited the clinic. She was able to cast disparaging seeds about the Douglas family, and Heidi was sure Dr. Hayes took the bait. After all, he had a moral and ethical responsibility to report suspected child abuse. This was better than any scenario she could have planned. The doctor would have to report the abuse and he couldn't reveal it was she who implied it.

□□

Dr. Hayes walked down the hallway to the next patient's room. He wondered if he had been premature in inviting the Douglas children to his house, and what was he going to do with this information? Was this woman even credible? Maybe it was true, and by withholding it he could be endangering the children. He would review the boy's medical records before he went home. If there were any other suspicious injuries to either boy in the past few years—he would have to consider this information credible.

5

The Steps of a Good Man

Pastor Rey pushed the intercom button on his phone, "Grace? Grace are you there?" There was no answer. He waited a moment wondering if he should call again. Then he decided to walk down the hallway to the main office. He pulled back his shirt sleeve and checked his watch. It was 3:00 P.M. They still had 90 minutes before the church office closed.

Rey wondered. Am I missing something? Is it my birthday? No. Is it the anniversary of our arrival at the church? No. Was a group of people going to jump out from around a corner and yell, surprise? I sure hope not! I hate surprises. As he drew nearer to the office, he coached himself. Okay, prepare yourself. Act happy! Be pleased that people are prepared to scare you to death with loud shouts.

Rey rounded the corner into the office. No one was there— this only added to his paranoia. Then he noticed the workroom door was closed. He walked over and slowly opened the door apprehensive of what may be waiting for him in the darkness.

Grace stood alone in the dark. The light from her cell phone cast a soft haze across the otherwise dark space. She held the phone to her ear listening. Her eyes were wet from crying.

Rey knew he had interrupted something personal. He mouthed the word *sorry*. Then turned on the light in the workroom and closed the door.

Walking back to his office he easily dismissed the incident. Grace was sensitive to everyone's pain. If someone called the church with a prayer request Grace cried with them. If she heard a sad story, she cried. If she saw another person crying she cried. It was who Grace was, and Pastor Rey liked that her heart was tender.

Grace was kindhearted and sensitive. This was a stark contrast to the former office manager—who Rey inherited. Heidi had been inappropriate, indifferent, prying—even calculating. While Grace cared about each person individually that came into her life; Heidi only had time for those she felt advanced her position. It was a turbulent day when Heidi was dismissed, but soon after that the atmosphere in the church changed. Things weren't always perfect—but now everyone agreed. The objective was reconciliation not discord.

A few months following Heidi's dismissal from the church, news reached Pastor Rey that John Alden had served his wife of fifteen years with divorce papers. John had already stepped down from his position on the church board the week following the outpouring of love and forgiveness at the altars of Community Outreach Church.

When Heidi's employment with the church ended, she and her husband left the church. After the smoke of this fiasco settled, it was found out that John had been involved with a much younger woman for a while, and to add insult to injury this woman was expecting a baby with him. Something Heidi never wanted.

Pastor Rey and Callan wished Heidi no ill will, yet she blamed them for everything wrong in her life. All her fury was focused on them. The year following her dismissal, she was vicious toward them and the church. Now, they rarely saw her or felt any repercussions from their brief acquaintance with either Heidi or John Alden.

Rey knew when Grace was done sympathizing with whoever was in crisis that she would come to his office to see what he needed.

□□

There were five phones positioned in strategic locations throughout the home of Stuart and Samantha Hayes. Rarely was a phone ever returned to its holder once it was carried off. The symphony of phones in the doctor's house began ringing in unison. Samantha glanced at the empty charger in the laundry room and made the split-second decision to run to the kitchen to answer the phone. She could hear phones ringing along the way but didn't have time to stop and search for them. She knew her only hope was the kitchen phone. No one ever moved this phone from its holder. Rarely was anyone but her in the kitchen.

Samantha dashed from the top floor of her 4,000 square foot home to the kitchen located at the back of the house on the main floor. Rounding the corner to the kitchen she counted the last ring before the answering machine would pick up. She reached for the phone and breathlessly answered trying to sound professional and not like a crazy woman.

"Hello, Dr. Hayes residence." Samantha was never sure, if the call was of a personal nature or professional. So, she wanted to err on the side of professionalism.

"Hello. Mrs. Hayes, this is Callan Douglas, your neighbor. I live a few doors down. We are the house with the bright red door. You may have noticed it." Callan paused to see if her home made an equal impression on the doctor's wife as it had on the doctor.

Samantha Hayes interrupted Callan. "I'm sorry, Mrs. Douglas. Did my daughter do something to your house or property? We will pay for the damages. She is going through a difficult time right now. Please, don't involve the police." Samantha paced back and forth in the kitchen while she spoke.

It was Callan's turn to interrupt. "No! That's not it. I've never met your daughter. That's why I'm calling. My son who is eight years old broke his arm and your husband is his doctor. He noticed that we were neighbors and invited the boys to come over and meet your daughter. I was under the impression that she was homebound, not out doing vandalism." Callan followed the comment with a nervous laugh.

"Oh, I'm sorry." Samantha said with a hint of chuckle in her voice. "Baylee is our youngest daughter. She is ten years old, and yes, she is homebound for the most part. I'm sorry for the confusion. Isabelle is our little rebel. She is fourteen going on thirty. In our old neighborhood, most calls from our neighbors were related to her acting out in a number of unacceptable ways." Samantha paused and looked out the wall of windows into the backyard. A row of arborvitae trees walled her in, blocking the view beyond the yard. In the five months she lived there, she had never ventured out past the deck to see what was behind those trees.

Callan wondered if she should push through with Dr. Hayes's invitation. She said a silent prayer, *Lord, give me wisdom. I need your help*—immediately a peace settled on her. "If Baylee would be up to a visit from a couple of rowdy boys, we could stop by sometime." Callan left it very open ended to give Samantha plenty of wiggle room.

Without hesitation Samantha answered. "I think that would be wonderful. We've been here five months, and Baylee and I could both use some company. How does tomorrow sound? We could meet about 11 A.M. and I'll fix lunch."

"Great! Can I bring something?"

"Sure, how about a bag of chips, we'll keep it simple and make it a kid friendly lunch."

"Okay, that sounds perfect. We'll see you tomorrow." Callan ended the call feeling conflicted. She felt sorry for the plight of this woman with a sick child, but she also wasn't sure she wanted to mix her children with that older girl. The one Samantha thought, vandalized her home. Callan sighed and silently prayed. Lord, give me direction. Help me keep my children safe, but also be willing to reach out to others in need. Direct me.

An unexplainable excitement began to stir in her heart. How this related to meeting the Hayes family, Callan wasn't sure. What she did know was that the Lord had given her the green light to move forward. Callan knew this wasn't a chance meeting. Their families had lived two doors down for months, and *now* God ordained that they should meet, and the best part was she was invited in. She would be obedient to the leading of the Holy Spirit.

Callan prayed. "Whatever your plans are for this family, let me be led by You in everything I say and do. Also, Lord— please allow Zander and Ty to be an encouragement to Baylee, and the other girl—can't remember her name right now, but

You know her situation. Help her Lord. I pray for whatever she is struggling with. Put Your finger on that issue and bring healing to her troubled soul. I don't know the spiritual condition of this family, but You do. Lord, help me be sensitive to know what to say and when to say it. Silence every other voice that would try and distract me from being obedient to You."

Callan paused for a moment then ended her prayer, "I ask these things in the name of Jesus." She smiled thinking how differently she would have handled this situation six years ago. Her concern would not have been for the spiritual needs of the Hayes family. It would have been more about what to wear, whose house was nicer and the prestige of having the doctor's wife as her friend. She was happy that old social climber was gone forever.

Callan's thoughts turned back to the Lord. She wondered what His plans were for this family. A sweet presence of the Lord filled her heart as she resumed her chores. Later that evening Callan shared with the boys the plans to meet Baylee Hayes tomorrow.

Zander immediately had second thoughts. "But Mom, she's a girl and she's sick."

Ty piped in, "I want to go, and I want her to sign my cast." He paused, then added, "I think I can beat her at the video game— even one handed." He held up his right arm and did some karate chops in the air. He jumped straight up in the air then landed in a 'ninja pose' ready to strike if suddenly attacked by unseen marauders.

Callan shook her head and laughed.

Ty broke his pose. "Finally, I might have someone I can beat." There were only two things that Zander and Ty knew for sure. Baylee was sick, and she was a girl. Both boys assumed she wouldn't be much competition. But none of them knew that a special friendship was about to commence over a name written with a green permanent marker on the cast of a rambunctious boy.

□□

Baylee's older sister, Isabelle, sat in the window seat of her second story bedroom with her legs pulled close to her body in a fetal position. She scanned the vacant backyard through the pane of glass. The only thing in that yard that remotely resembled that children lived in this home was one lonely tire swing that moved slightly in the spring breeze. Neither she nor Baylee had ever swung in that swing—not once. Weekly, a local company in Hillbrooke manicured their perfect yard. Her father had little time to dawdle about doing yard work. He had few precious moments he was available to his family. Isabelle Hayes felt like a prisoner trapped in her tower—alone.

Heaviness pressed on Isabelle's chest. She couldn't breathe— trapped by her age and circumstances. Her mood turned dark at the thought of school letting out for the summer. In three weeks she would be cut off from the outside world. As wretched as middle school was it was better than the prospect of this mausoleum of sickness, depression, anger and hopelessness—these were her only companions. Isabelle rested her forehead on her knees then pressed her head— hard—into the bones of her knees. A wave of hate washed over her causing her heartrate to increase revving up her imagination. My parents only have time for Baylee. Poor Baylee—is Baylee, okay? Can you check on Baylee?

Isabelle locked her jaw until her temples pounded. She whispered. "I hate this house. I hate my life. I hate my school, my teachers and those pathetic middle school infants. I hate…" Her thoughts drifted off. She stood up and went to her desk. She pulled open the drawer and grabbed a fist full of ink pens. She slammed them on the desk. Taking one pen she broke the plastic case holding the tube of ink. She reached for the scissors in the cup on top of her desk and cut the pen open allowing the ink to drip onto a piece of paper. Things were getting messy, but she didn't care. She retrieved the needle from the sewing kit tucked away in her closet. Then she took a black ink pen and carefully wrote the word HATE in capital letters across the inside of her left wrist. She turned her left-hand face down and rested it on the desk. Slowly, she turned her hand toward her face bringing the underside of her wrist back into view. Her eyes connected with the word. A satisfied smile formed on her face. HATE, the word looked back at her with sympathy for her plight. It felt good.

Isabelle took the small needle and held it between her thumb and index finger. She dipped the tip into the ink. Then she poked the tip of the pin into the flesh of her wrist. The first poke wasn't bad. She felt alive. She did it again and again until there were droplets of blood dripping from her wrist. She went to her en-suite bathroom and retrieved a box of tissues. A huge pink flower decorated the side of the box. The pretty flower made her think of her mom picking this happy *box* of tissues for her bathroom. The sight of the flower fueled her dark mood.

She flung the box of tissues on the desk with enough force to crush the cardboard. It felt good to destroy something. Pulling out a tissue, she dabbed at the dripping blood as she repeatedly pierced her skin over and over until the first letter took shape. It looked good—H. This was going to be a longer process than she expected.

Her own thoughts reinforced her glum. Who cares? No one is going to call for me—check on me—I've got plenty of time.

She dipped the needle in the ink and poked her flesh again— and again—and again. The letter A began to take shape.

There were no interruptions. No one questioned her hours of solitude shut up in her bedroom most of the weekend. No one asked Isabelle, how she was doing, if she needed anything or if she wanted to go anywhere. The only time her name was called was to help with something regarding *Baylee*. Can you sit with Baylee for a little bit? She's lonely.

The thought of her mom—forever busy with Baylee's needs— brought Isabelle's anger to the boiling point. She focused on the ink dripping from the needle and pondered her invisibility. She picked at her flesh again. A small trickle of blood ran down her forearm. She sighed with contentment as a euphoric feeling swept over her.

Over the course of the weekend Isabelle found the time and ink to finish her tattoo. With minimal effort, she was able to keep it from her family.

6

Rooted and Grounded

J ean Brown's eyes fluttered open. The sun streamed in the window warming her face. Lately, Tom was up and gone to work hours before she felt like getting out of bed. She struggled to fully wake up. Forcing herself out of bed, she sluggishly walked to the bathroom. The scales lured her in like a fisherman's hook.

Jean cautiously stepped on the bathroom scales. A sinking feeling gripped her in the pit of her stomach. She stepped off the scale keeping her eyes downcast. She turned to walk away, then stopped, turned back and gradually eased her foot back on the scale for a second attempt at the number she desired. The scale made a beeping noise until the three-digit number appeared. She looked down at her feet, took a deep breath and deliberately exhaled. She had lost twenty pounds over the past six weeks. Normally, this would be reason to rejoice, but accompanied with her constant state of exhaustion, slight cough and stomach pain—concern was mounting.

At first, she thought the weight loss was awesome. What woman in her sixties doesn't want to drop a few pounds? She had always struggled with some extra weight. Her loving husband never failed to tell her daily—she was beautiful. Most of the time she believed him, but occasionally she believed the lies of the advertisements that tried to control all females from their earliest comprehension.

The print and television ads try to mold young minds telling them what to feel and how to think. Jean had bought into the pressures of her culture through her youth and even into her adult years, trying to take off those unwanted pounds. She would hold the pounds at bay for a year, but always without fail they would return one at a time until they were all back. She finally had reached the place in her life where she accepted her weight and was enjoying life—chocolate cake and all.

Jean held the phone in her hand and dialed the number to the Hillbrooke Medical Clinic. The recorded greeting was like a memory test; push one for this or two for that until she finally heard a human voice say, "Hello. How may I help you?" "Yes, I'd like to make an appointment with Dr. Russell." "Dr. Russell has retired. Dr. Hayes is taking over for him. Would you like to see Dr. Hayes?" The woman's voice on the other end was matter of fact and purely professional.

"Yes, that will be fine."

"May I ask what your medical need is?" Again, the receptionist was purely uninterested and had a job to do, the quicker the better.

Jean felt emotion pushing in, trying to take her down. If she told the receptionist what she suspected then the faceless, nameless person's demeanor may change from business professional to human and caring. Any kindness at this point would send Jean into a fit of tears.

Jean pushed on. "I've been having some issues with unwanted weight loss. I thought I should have it checked out by the doctor, just to be sure it is nothing to worry about."

There was a brief pause, and then the girl came back with a quick reply. "Okay, the Doctor can see you tomorrow at 4:30 P.M. Will that work for you?"

"Yes. I have it written down. I'll see you tomorrow." Jean hung up the phone. A wave of emotion swept over her. Fear was attacking her from every side, and she didn't like it. It was an unwelcome stranger.

She walked from the kitchen to the family room and turned on her iPad. With her index finger she swiped at the controls until peaceful music filled the room. The recording artist worshiped freely. Jean sat down in her favorite chair and looked out the window. Gloomy, negative thoughts pushed at her from within. On the table beside her, the Bible laid open. She slid the book into her lap and lowered the reading glasses she used as a headband. Her eyes focused on Ephesians 3. She silently read the chapter until verse fourteen then she began to whisper the words—personalizing the passage and making it a prayer.

"Lord, for this reason I kneel before You and pray that You would strengthen me with the power of Your Spirit. Penetrate me all the way to my inner being. That You may dwell in my heart through faith. I proclaim that I am rooted and grounded in Your love."

With each word, Jean's volume increased until she was declaring the Word with the authority and privilege of a daughter. "I know, Lord that there is nothing more powerful than Your love—it's the breadth and length and height and depth. I ask now, as a daughter of the Most High, that You would fill me up with Your love. Push out every thought that is not pleasing to You. Fill me with the fullness of Your presence."

She found her voice, lifted her hands in the air and began to sing praises to the Lord. Darkness fled, and peace returned.

□□

Pastor Rey heard a tap at his office door. "Come in."

It was Grace. He glanced at his watch. It was five minutes before they would leave for the day.

Grace answered the unasked question that filled the room. "Pastor, the call I received earlier was very disturbing. I need to speak with you, but I think Callan needs to be there when we talk. If she is home, I'd like to speak with both of you—together."

"Well, this sounds serious. You aren't quitting, are you?"

"No. I hope it doesn't come to that. Let's wait and talk when we're all together. I'll wait at my desk. Buzz me once you find out if Callan is available." Grace left the Pastor's office closing the door behind her. She went back to her desk and tidied things up while she waited.

The intercom at Grace's desk buzzed and she picked up the phone. "Callan said its fine. She wanted me to invite you to stay for dinner, if you can."

"Tell her thanks, but not tonight. We'll just talk. Then I need to get home." Grace hung up the phone and felt sick in her stomach. She thought of that childish rhyme, sticks and stones may break your bones, but names will never hurt you. What a lie. Somebody with their head in the sand must have come up with that trite, little saying.

Pastor Rey walked out to the parking lot by way of the front office. "Grace, I'm leaving now, if you want to follow me?"

"I'll get the lights and lock up. I'll be there shortly." Grace walked through the office, shut off the lights then locked the doors as she left the building. Pulling away from the church, she felt an overwhelming love for this place rise up in her. It wasn't just a job to her. It was an extension of her home. It was a calling. She loved the people she worked with like they were her family. Helping the body of Christ through service was a high calling, not just a job to her.

Five minutes later, Grace pulled into the long drive at the Community Outreach parsonage. She had been here many times for dinners, fellowship and special staff meetings. Today felt different. The information she was about to share could change her relationship with this family forever. Grace got out of her car and walked toward the parsonage.

Callan waited on the front porch with a concerned look on her face. "What in the world is going on with you, Grace?" She motioned for Grace to come in and gave her a hug before she was fully inside the house. "Now, sit down and let's get to the bottom of whatever is on your mind. It can't be all that bad. We can work this out."

Tears were already forming in Grace's eyes. Callan had the tissues ready to go and gave them a little push across the coffee table in Grace's direction. Grace didn't take a single tissue but placed the whole box of tissues on her lap. Then pulled out the first of many and dabbed at her eyes.

"I'm sorry for all the tears. You know me. Tears, tears and more tears. Sometimes I wish I could handle one crisis without the threat of dehydration." Grace tried to laugh at her own joke, but it fell flat.

Callan coaxed her along. "Come on, Grace. We won't judge you. What's going on?"

Grace kept her eyes fixed on the tissue box on her lap. "Today, at the office I received a phone call. I sat at my desk for a while until I knew I needed privacy." She glanced in Pastor Rey's direction. "That's when you saw me, Pastor, in the dark workroom crying." Tissue number two was pulled out of the box. "The call was from a friend of mine who goes to another church in town. We are friends on Facebook and know each other from high school. She was letting me know that there was a vicious rumor being circulated about me…" Grace stopped talking and the sobbing began—tissues #3 and #4.

Callan reassured her. "Take your time Grace. We're not going anywhere." She shot a worried look in Rey's direction. He shrugged his shoulders.

After what seemed like a long time Grace was able to spit out the words. "…me and you Pastor."

Rey shook his head in disgust, "Grace, people are mean and cruel. We know it's not true. We've dealt with rumors before."

Grace interrupted. "Pastor, Callan, its Heidi who's spreading the lies. She said that she saw Pastor and me…" Grace covered her face with her hands and shook her head. "I can't say it. It's bad."

Pastor Rey made a clicking sound in disgust and shook his head. "Tell us Grace. We'd rather hear it from you than someone else."

Grace kept her eyes closed. "She told my friend that she caught you and me kissing and hugging and spending hours together privately in your office. She told them she was fired because Pastor wanted me to be more accessible to him without Heidi's prying eyes." Grace opened her eyes feeling the worst was behind her. "…and that's why the church paid her six months' severance instead of the usual two weeks to 30 days."

Rey moaned. "We know the truth and besides that the board minutes recorded the decision, we only wanted to help them with six months' severance to be kind. We have nothing to hide. The truth has a way of coming out in the end."

"She told people that we've stayed in hotels in town and that she has the receipts. It's so horrible what she's saying. Of course, it's not true, but others will believe the lies, because they want to think the worst about good people like you, Pastor, without giving you or me a chance."

Rey affirmed what he said before. "We are not going to give this a moment's thought. We'll pray for her. God's Word says to pray for those who try to do you harm."

Callan responded to Rey with a hint of annoyance. "Rey, you think prayer is the answer to everything. You'll have to excuse me here, but I'm just a bit peeved right now. Heidi is talking about *my* husband! MY HUSBAND is being lied about and I'm supposed to pray." Callan gave a slight laugh at the end of the sentence to try and lighten the mood, but she couldn't lighten the heaviness in her chest.

Grace continued looking at Callan. "I know as this new gossip begins to spread that people are going to believe these lies are true. I want you both to know—I'm willing to step down from my position to silence the rumors. I love you both and Community Outreach Church. I won't do anything to bring dishonor to our church or to anyone."

Pastor Rey chimed in with an edge to his voice that was rarely heard outside the pulpit. "Absolutely, not! That would give credibility to the rumors, and that is not the way we are going to handle this. First, we will pray—Yes, Callan—pray. Then, I'll talk with the church board. Then, after these godly men give me counsel, I will address these lies from the pulpit and seek legal advice, if I feel it's necessary." His emotions had reached the righteous indignation level.

He spit his words out at no one in particular, "Pretending something is not happening doesn't make it go away. We need to take this bull by the horns and shut the mouth of the accuser." Rey breathed a short prayer. "Lord, Help me."

Callan moved from her chair to the sofa next to Grace. It was her turn to claim some tissues from the box on Grace's lap. She grabbed a handful then put her arms around Grace and drew her in. They comforted each other.

Rey bowed his head in his hands massaging his temples with his fingertips. In a low voice almost a whisper he spoke, "God is about to do something in our midst. That is why the enemy is rising up against us. Satan wants to distract us. He wants to divert our attention. Cause us to circle our wagons and look inward. Well that's not gonna happen, Satan! You are a liar, deceiver and accuser of the brethren! You are defeated! This is just a shot over the bow. Get ready! Something amazing is coming!

7

Being Neighborly

Zander and Ty followed their mom down the driveway and along the side of the road. A slight breeze cooled the morning air. Ty stuffed a green permanent marker in the back pocket of his blue jean shorts. Under his good arm he wedged the latest video game that was all the rage in the 7-12-year-old age group. The game had arrived in the mail a few days ago from his Grandpa and Grandma Douglas. It was a "get well" present, since they wouldn't be able to see him for a few weeks.

Zander complained a bit when he watched his brother open the gift. He made it very clear that it wasn't fair to get gifts for being clumsy and breaking your arm. The initial shock of seeing his brother wounded and lying semi-conscious in the ditch had worn off and sibling rivalry resumed.

Callan gave the boys some last-minute instructions as they approached the Hayes house. "Be polite, and Zander smile! You look mad. Ty don't talk the little girl's ears off. I don't know how sick she is, so let's all be on guard. We don't want to over stay our welcome. We may have to leave quickly, if she becomes ill. If you don't like her or you feel uncomfortable playing with a girl, I won't make you go back."

The boys marched along keeping pace with their mother. "Boys, how about if in this first visit we show them about the Lord with how we act?" Zander rolled his eyes.

Ty responded, "I want to meet her mom. Maybe God will heal her, if we pray."

"Ty, we'll meet them first. We don't want to scare them. You boys need to be nice and considerate. I want to see how the Lord directs me." Callan turned her head to look directly at Ty and pointed her finger at him. "Ty, I mean it. Don't pray for her today. We don't know what they believe."
Ty shuffled his feet kicking up a cloud of dry dirt.

Callan placed her arm around Ty's shoulders and drew him close to her. "I'll tell you what; we'll start praying for them tonight before bed. Would you like that?"

"Yes. I want to pray for them, Mom." Ty got a bit animated with his arms and dropped the video game as they turned into the Hayes' driveway.

Zander snatched the game up holding it in his hand like a captured prize. He glanced in his mom's direction then handed it back to his brother. Zander wasn't smiling. Callan wondered where her little boy had gone. She thought, for goodness sake— he's barely ten.

Callan did a quick inspection of her boys to be sure they were presentable. Her shoulders slumped as she looked at Ty with his broken arm and Zander who needed an attitude adjustment. She sighed in a whisper, "Well, what ya gonna do? It is what it is."

Callan reached out to ring the doorbell, but before her finger connected with the buzzer the large front door swung open. An attractive woman about Callan's age stood smiling at them.

Samantha was dressed impeccably. Callan fought off her old nature. The sinful nature that loved to compare—sizing people up to make sure she came out on top. She wished she could crucify these feelings once and for all, but her old nature resurrected at the oddest times.

She prayed silently. Lord, help me not to compare myself with anything but Your Word. Lord, I pray for this family and any needs they may have both seen and unseen. Give me the mind of the Spirit to see, hear and feel Your heartbeat of love.

Callan extended her hand to Samantha and smiled. And just like that, the old nature was once again put to death.

The hostess took Callan's hand while talking excitedly, "Hi. I'm Samantha Hayes, and you must be the Douglas family. Come in. I'll take you up to meet Baylee." Once they were all inside the house, Samantha looked back at Callan and whispered, "Is it okay with you, if the kids play in Baylee's room? It's more comfortable for her to be in bed, if possible."

Callan felt uncomfortable leaving her boys alone out of ear shot. She hoped they would not forget the little talk they had on the walk over. In her mind she saw her boys jumping on the bed while a sick child moaned in pain.

Callan looked at the boys and gave them *the look*. "Sure, I think that should be okay." Callan continued with a tone the boys knew all too well. "These two boys know *how* to behave as guests in other people's homes. Right boys?"

In unison they said, "Yes, ma'am." They all followed Mrs. Hayes up the stairs to Baylee's room.

Zander poked his head in the room and whispered. "It's pink." It was loud enough for Callan to hear and she jerked her head back. She tapped his arm with her index finger and gave him the *not-another-word* look.

Baylee's bedroom was pink but bigger than most living rooms. There actually was a sitting area. Two walls had floor to ceiling built-in shelving units. Bins of toys filled the shelves along with rows of books—lots and lots of books. A 60-inch television hung from the wall directly opposite the bed. The queen size bed nearly swallowed up the small girl propped up by pillows. Looking out from the pillows were two very big brown eyes surrounded by a mop of curly brown hair.

Callan glanced at her boys wondering if they would be comfortable not only playing with *a girl* but a sick one to boot. She fought back the tears. Her mother's heart was breaking for this little girl. As well as for her mother whose cheery voice and big smile couldn't mask the pain in her eyes.

"Baylee, this is Zander and Ty Douglas and their mom, Mrs. Douglas. They live just a few houses away from us. Isn't that nice they came to visit? Ty is one of dad's patients."

Ty smiled and pointed at his broken arm to prove the obvious. Baylee smiled back and greeted them all by name with a "very nice to meet you" attached at the end. Zander relaxed when he saw that she was friendly and had an awesome bedroom, even if it was pink. Plus, she didn't act sick or gloomy.

Ty pulled out his new video game and stuck it in Baylee's face. "Have you played this one, yet?" Baylee took it out of Ty's hand and looked it over.
"No, but I've been wanting to get this. Let's try it out."

Ty handed the game to his brother. "Zander, will you put it in for us?" Zander took the game from Ty and walked over to the machine and popped the disk in place. He looked like he'd been using their equipment for years. In a matter of moments, the game was up and running and the three were chatting like they were old friends.

"We'll be down in the kitchen, if you need anything. Lunch will be ready soon." Samantha motioned for Callan to follow her, and she reluctantly did. Callan took a few nervous steps then she slowly looked back over her shoulder. She was prepared for a Barbie doll to propel passed her head at rocket speed. Instead, she saw the beauty of children being children. They didn't know how to be unfamiliar with each other. They adapted to the situation and moved forward.

Ty and Zander were plopped down on the edges of the bed on either side of Baylee. All three kids held a game controller in their hands. Except Ty who worked his controller with one hand by balancing it on his cast.

Callan felt a peace stir within her. She exhaled a content sigh. A feeling of gratitude welled up within her for these two precious, crazy boys.

Samantha scurried around the kitchen preparing lunch.

"What can I do to help?" Callan offered.

"You can sit right over there at the island and we can talk, while I fix lunch." Samantha's cheery disposition from moments ago was replaced with slumped shoulders and a visible heaviness while she robotically moved about the kitchen.

Callan sensed oppression in and around Samantha. Callan fought back the tears as she watched. Then the Spirit of the Lord opened Callan's eyes. Samantha's lips were moving, and words were coming out, but Callan saw through the eye of the Spirit. There were two heavy looking rocks sitting one on each of Samantha's shoulders. It was humanly impossible for Samantha to function under the weight. But she did.

Callan silently prayed, Lord, help Samantha. Help her to trust me and help me to know how I can minister to her and to this family.

Callan got up from the bar stool, walked around the kitchen island and touched Samantha's hand. Samantha stopped moving and stopped talking. The touch of human kindness froze Samantha in place.

Callan kept her hand on Samantha's and spoke in a soft voice. "I want to help you. Let me make the sandwiches." Samantha's eyes started to blink, and tears began to form.

Callan continued with a calm voice. "It's okay, Samantha. You've been carrying things for a long time. Let me help you. We can start with lunch."

Callan stood next to Samantha at the kitchen island. She silently prayed for God's timing and direction as she spread peanut butter and jelly on the bread.

Happy voices and the sound of video game music drifted down to the kitchen from Baylee's bedroom at the top of the stairs. For the first time in a very long time Samantha didn't feel alone.

8
He Loves You!

School on Monday was a reprieve for Isabelle. As much as she hated it—it was also her out. School was her time to forget about the depressing walls of sickness that had become her abode. Isabelle was tall for her age and dressed older than the other 8th grade girls. These girls had mostly avoided her since her December arrival in Hillbrooke. She projected an attitude that naturally pushed people away. The isolation she felt at school mirrored her home life. No one tried to push past the boundaries that Isabelle firmly established reinforcing her despair.

Next year Isabelle would move to high school where the kids would understand what she was going through. She anticipated the opportunities to socialize outside home and school with people who wanted to commiserate.

□□

Most days, fourth period History class was a trial for any fourteen-year-old's attention span. Lunch was over, and the students still faced three more hours of school. It was also a tight rope walk for the teacher endeavoring to educate sleepy students about world history.

Isabelle fought to keep her eyes open. She tried doodling in her notebook. Occasionally, she turned her wrist to view *the word*—HATE. It had become a permanent part of who she was.

A loud screeching noise reverberated through the classroom bringing everyone to attention. A female voice boomed through the intercom, "Mr. Flynn, could you send Isabelle Hayes to the counselor's office?"

This was followed by the students making an "Oooooo" noise that indicated to all that someone may be in trouble. All eyes were on Isabelle as she picked up her backpack and leisurely loaded it with the items lying on the top of her desk. Isabelle would not dignify the boring-teacher, nor the students—all morons—with an ounce of emotion or a single word as she left the room.

Strolling down the deserted hallway toward the counselor's office, her thoughts reinforced her feelings of isolation. *I could just walk right out of this school, and no one would care. I'd be gone! GONE! Done with it all—this school, teachers and everybody in authority! They think they can just call, and I must jump.*

Isabelle, go to the office. Isabelle, did you finish the assignment? Isabelle, do you have the answer to #5? Stupid people! Stupid, stupid school! Stupid counselor!

Isabelle was looking down at the floor while she shuffled her feet in the direction of the middle school office. Rounding the corner, she looked up to see a young woman leaning against the open door to the counselor's office. The woman had long black hair. It hung over her shoulders on both sides past her waist. She was young, maybe mid-twenties. Isabelle thought she looked like a throwback to the hippies of the 1960's. All she needed was a patchwork skirt and a bandanna to complete the look. She certainly didn't look like the other professionals who worked in the school.

Who is she? Isabelle wondered. And why is she smiling at me?

"Hi. Are you Isabelle Hayes?" The woman turned her head slightly revealing on the side of her face a brightly colored butterfly tattoo. Isabelle didn't want to stare, but it was nearly impossible not to. That tattoo was like a powerful force drawing her eye in like a moth to light. No matter how much she willed to look away she couldn't.

The butterfly lady waited. Her expression was somewhere between a half smile and an all-knowing smirk.

Isabelle felt naked, her inner most thoughts revealed by the expression on her own face. She collected herself.

"Yes. I'm Isabelle, and I was told to report to the counselor's office."

"Great! I'm Fauna Reynolds. I'm the school counselor filling in for Mr. March until the end of the school year."

Ms. Reynolds extended her hand to Isabelle and her long-sleeved shirt pulled away from her wrist revealing what Isabelle guessed to be a sleeve of tattoos. She could only see the area of skin directly around Ms. Reynolds' wrist but usually if someone had tattoos there, then she probably had them all the way up her arm. Isabelle formed her opinion in one second. This counselor's night job was probably a biker-mama or tattoo artist. She thought about flashing her tattoo at the woman just to let this authority figure know that she wasn't the only one with a tattoo.

Isabelle rubbed her wrist. It was painful to the touch. On second thought a tattoo doesn't make someone like her a 'friendly.'

Ms. Reynolds stepped back to allow Isabelle to enter the counseling offices. The counselor motioned for Isabelle to move in the direction of an open office just to the left of the reception area. The name plaque on the door read, *Mr. March-School Counselor.* Isabelle walked into the small office followed by the tattooed hippy. The room was awkwardly small. She took her seat across from the desk. When she sat down her knees touched the cold metal of the desk in front of her. With the chair touching the wall behind her—she had no place to go.

Ms. Reynolds took her place in the seat of power behind the desk. Isabelle slouched in her chair trying to portray an image of, *you don't scare me.*

The counselor's face fought back a smile.

Isabelle felt like this woman could see straight to her heart and was reading her innermost thoughts. She fidgeted in her seat trying to find that sweet spot that allowed her some leverage. She coached herself—show-no-fear—you got this!

"Isabelle, I see from your records that you transferred here in the middle of the school year."

There was an awkward silence.

Isabelle knew the counselor was hoping that she would spill her whole life story. *That* wasn't gonna happen. She chose not to answer since it wasn't really a question. It was a statement of the known facts. She kept her focus on the counselor while attempting to keep her own face void of expression.

Isabelle did not reply.

Fauna continued after a long pause. "I see your father is the new doctor in town."

No response. No blinking. Steady gaze.

"And it looks like you had a few issues at your previous school." Isabelle hated that her life was written out for others to read. It disturbed her greatly. The image she was trying to project was polluted by another's description of her, written on paper and not one of her own making. She felt her life spiraling out of control, yet again.

Fauna could read the worry on Isabelle's face. "Isabelle, this is just a routine visit. We want to make sure you are adjusting well to your new school and that you're ready to transition into high school in the fall. Do you have any concerns or issues you'd like to talk about today?"

Isabelle kept her response curt, "No issues. I'm looking forward to moving on to high school." Isabelle decided to throw the hippie a bone. It appeared the tattooed woman really wasn't trying to dissect her dark subconscious or slice her emotions open for inspection.

The counselor kept her eyes fixed on Isabelle and waited. Then Isabelle added, "Can I go now?"

"Just one more thing." The authority figure reached across the desk and took Isabelle's left hand. She turned her wrist over to reveal the homemade tattoo. The word, HATE surrounded by red, puffy skin was in full view. Before Isabelle could jerk her hand away, she felt the first tug on her tightly laced world of hate began to unravel.

□□

Samantha Hayes stood at her kitchen island flipping through recipe ideas on her iPad. The phone on the counter next to her began to ring. She glanced at the caller ID. It said Hillbrooke Middle School. She cautiously picked up the phone debating whether to answer the call.

What had Isabelle done now? She wondered. With less than two weeks left in the school year.

She reluctantly pressed the phone key and with her usual cheery greeting she greeted the caller. "Hello, this is Dr. Hayes Residence."

"Is this Mrs. Hayes?"

"Yes. This is Samantha Hayes. Is everything okay with Isabelle?" Samantha pondered what her daughter might have done to provoke this call.

"This is Fauna Reynolds from the counseling office. I met with Isabelle today to discuss her plans for moving up to high school in the fall. I think there may be some issues that we need to discuss face to face. Is there a time that would work for you and your husband to meet with me tomorrow? I have an opening at 4:30 P.M."

"Miss Reynolds, my husband is a doctor and he only has one morning off each week. Could we just talk about this issue now— over the phone?"

There was a long pause while Fauna thought about Samantha's request.

"I think it would be best if we meet tomorrow. Speaking face to face is always the best. Meeting with both parents is a good idea too. However, I do understand work schedules. I would be happy to meet with just you, Mrs. Hayes." Fauna tried her best not to alarm Isabelle's mom. She needed to gage with her own eyes how these parents would respond to the information. She didn't want to read the headline *Tattooed Fourteen-year-old Murdered by Parents.*

Samantha silently calculated different scenarios juggling in her mind the needs of Baylee, Stuart and Isabelle. Isabelle refused to babysit Baylee under any circumstances, and Samantha had not formed the kind of friendships in Hillbrooke that would allow her to call someone to watch her sick child. She shook her head and inhaled. The words formed in her thoughts—I hate my life.

With as much control as she could find, Samantha blurted out, "Sure that would be fine. I'll see you tomorrow afternoon. Good bye." Anxiety attacked Samantha's thoughts like a spray of bullets. She wanted to believe the best hoping everything was okay. Deep down—logic prevailed. It was never a good thing when the school counselor asked to speak with both parents in person. Good news was rarely withheld for face to face meetings.

Samantha was still holding the phone in her hand when the back door slammed shut. Isabelle passed through the kitchen without a word. Samantha stood stationary and silent.

Isabelle breezed by—anger visible on her face. She headed to her domain on the second floor.

Samantha followed her and knocked on Isabelle's bedroom door. "Issie, can I come in?

There was no reply.

"I need to talk to you." Samantha rattled the door knob. It was locked. She rattled it again speaking at the same time. "Please, let me in. We need to talk."

Silence.

"Issie?" There was a pleading in Samantha's voice.

Inside the room Isabelle laid on the bed her left wrist pressed against her chest. Tears formed in her eyes while she listened to her mom's voice. There was still a child inside Isabelle crying for the comforting touch of her mother. The battle within her raged.

Samantha laid her head on the door and spoke softly. "Iss, Baylee's done pretty good today. We saw a new doctor yesterday called, *The Healer*."

And there it was…Baylee. The wall went up and all the feelings of being unwanted and unloved rushed in. Isabelle willed to stop the tears. They wouldn't stop. Something was drawing her to the door and to her mother. She swung her feet to the floor and instinctively walked toward the door.

Mother and daughter were only a few feet apart; Isabelle reached for the door knob.

A piercing scream reverberated through the upstairs. Isabelle quickly unlocked the door, turning the knob, she flung open the door. Her mother was gone. She could hear her voice comforting Baylee in the next room.

Samantha soothed her hurting child. "Lay still, breathe slowly."

Baylee was overcome with pain.

Samantha leaned over the bed. She stroked her hair—afraid her touch may inflict more agony. There was nothing she could do. Baylee's next dose of medication wasn't allowed for another hour. They would have to wait it out. The sound of her cries was heartbreaking.

Isabelle stood at the door of Baylee's room. Her mother's back was to her. Samantha comforted her hurting daughter unaware of the silent festering pain ready to explode only a few steps behind her.

Isabelle wondered how she could have believed even for a moment that her mother cared. Mocked and betrayed by her thoughts rage rose up within her. Just moments ago, she was willing to surrender to her mother's pleas. Her mother's actions were proof that her needs would always be secondary. She may as well be invisible. She turned away, ran down the stairs and out the front door.

For twenty minutes Isabelle ran without stopping. Panting, heart pounding she slowed down and looked at the unfamiliar deserted road. She spotted a shade tree a few yards off the road. She walked into the tall grass and plopped down under the tree completely hidden from the world.

She rested.

Isabelle's thoughts churned. I hope they worry about me. Maybe they'll think I'm dead. That would serve them all right.

Isabelle turned her tattooed wrist into her line of vision. She rubbed her finger slowly over each red puffy letter. H-A-T-E! It was painful to the touch, but it felt good. She wasn't invisible. She could feel the pain. It coursed through her body. She was alive.

Lying on her back she looked past her wrist toward the darkening sky. Thunder could be heard in the distance. Isabelle stood up, strolled back up to the road and continued to walk away from her home unconcerned for her own safety.

The first few sprinkles of rain began to fall. Thunder and lightning were in the distance but drawing closer.

Isabelle spoke out loud. "Who cares? I'm not afraid."

The sound of a car slowing down behind her gave Isabelle a moment of concern. She realized how vulnerable she was on this deserted road. Her pace increased.

The car pulled up beside her. The passenger window eased down. Isabelle kept her eyes looking forward for as long as she could.

"Hi. I don't want to scare you, but I saw you walking and wondered if you needed a ride somewhere. This storm looks like it could be a bad one. It's not safe for you to be out here alone." The woman behind the wheel flashed a big smile and extended her hand toward Isabelle. "My name is Heidi Alden. I work in Hillbrooke at the office of *The Healer*. I have a cell phone, if you want to call your parents."

Isabelle was relieved to see it was a woman about her mother's age. She remembered her mom had mentioned *The Healer* helped Baylee. She quickly calculated the risk of being struck by lightning compared to getting into a stranger's car. These were her only two options because she certainly wasn't calling her mother. Her mother would need to suffer a bit longer for making her care. She made a fool of me. Isabelle's eyes narrowed, and her jaw clenched tightly.

A boom of rolling thunder rumbled, followed by a flash of lightening not far from where Isabelle stood.

Isabelle opened the car door and slid into the front seat clicking her seatbelt on.

The woman kept smiling. "You know who I am. Now who do I have the pleasure of meeting?"

"I'm Isabelle Hayes. I live in Hillbrooke."

Boom. Another bolt of lightning followed, and the sky opened with a torrent.

Heidi raised her voice to be heard above the downpour. "You are pretty far from home. I'm going to turn around and take you back into Hillbrooke." Heidi took a closer look at the girl and thought she looked familiar. Hayes, Hayes she played the name over in her mind. Then blurted out, "Is your father the new doctor in town?"

"Yes. And my sister Baylee visited *The Healer.*" Isabelle freely offered the information.

Heidi glanced at the girl again looking at her eyes she could see she'd been crying. "You know when I was a bit younger I used to be in the Big Sister program. I took girls about your age to do fun stuff like going to the movies and out to eat." Heidi turned and looked directly at Isabelle. "Do you know much about this program?"
Isabelle shook her head in the negative.

Heidi educated her. "It's a safe time away from the problems teen girls face at home. You know, I'm a great listener, if you ever want to talk." Heidi paused to let the lie resonate with Isabelle. "Hey! How about if we stop for a bite to eat before I take you home?"

Isabelle thought it over for about a second and responded.

"Sure. I got no other plans."

"Do we need to call your parents?"

Isabelle answered with all the cockiness of a wounded fourteen-year-old, "Naah. They don't care what I do, where I am or who I'm with."

"Well, I'm sure that's not true. Where do you live?"

"I live on Lancaster Street in town. Do you know where that is?"

Heidi thought to herself, boy do I know where that is. I avoid that street like the plague. "Sure. Let me take you out to eat and then I'll drive you home."

Isabelle wanted to stay away from home for as long as she could. Mostly to make her parents worry but also not to hear her sister cry.

"I didn't bring any money."

"No problem. This time it's my treat." Heidi picked a fun little restaurant on the edge of town. She wondered how it stayed open. This secluded place was perfect for not being seen.

Within an hour of Heidi and Isabelle meeting she knew the troubles that lurked inside the walls of the Hayes house. She noticed the HATE both on the face and wrist of this little girl. Heidi even identified with Isabelle. They were both unappreciated and unnoticed. Yes, these feelings were familiar issues to Heidi. She wasn't sure how she would use this to her advantage, but she was happy to have this child in her pocket for now.

9

You're a Great Listener.

The Train Depot Restaurant was Snake and Fauna's favorite meeting place. Fauna led Snake by the hand into the restaurant. She chose a booth far away from the few customers. The couple had been dating for almost a year— both seemed smitten with the other, but any talk of marriage was off-limits.

"Isn't this the booth we sat in the first time we met?" Snake hoped his recalling this special place first would give him some brownie points for later.

"Yes. It is. Very good of you to remember."

They scooted into the booth and ordered their beverages from the waitress while looking over the familiar menu that hadn't changed in five years.

Fauna smiled. "Do you remember that first date was four hours long? We only planned to have a soft drink together, but ended up with dinner and dessert and, if I'm not mistaken, when we left they locked the doors behind us."

Snake smiled. "I think when they dimmed the lights we finally got the hint that the place was closing."

"They didn't know us then and probably judged us by all the tattoos. They probably were scared to tell us they wanted to close the place up."

Snake reached across the table and held Fauna's hand.

A feeling of contentment filled Fauna when she was with Snake. She was ready to move this thing to the next level. She wasn't content to be the girlfriend forever. She wanted it all. The husband, the house and the kids—this was all on her wish list. She tried on several occasions, without success, to draw Snake into conversations about the future. She even tried using her skills in family counseling, but when Snake saw the path she was on he was skilled at shutting her down.

Fauna had fallen for Snake—all six feet five inches of him— tattoos and all. He had treated her with honor and respect since the first day they met. Fauna felt like she was getting pretty good at reading him and for a few months something had been bothering Snake. She couldn't exactly decide what, but something wasn't right.

Fauna knew all about his past, the struggles he had with his judgmental father, and that he had run away from home at seventeen. He changed his name from Carl Fields to Zak Parker and spent the first four years of his twenties in jail, but that was all behind him now. He was reunited with his family, forgiven and was following the Lord. She saw firsthand that his Christianity was not in name only. He was a living testament of the Bible story of the woman pouring out the oil on the feet of Jesus. He had been forgiven much and he expressed it in giving back whenever he found the opportunity.

Snake volunteered on Saturday mornings at the juvey home in Hillbrooke. He taught the boys how to use the computer in a positive way and as a possible career opportunity for the future. He knew where most of these kids were headed, if someone didn't step up to help. He wanted to be a listener, not an accuser. Snake hoped his non-judgmental ways would make him a person the teens would trust and confide in. He knew only too well how quickly a life could spiral out of control. His moto was, "If I can help these kids now—they wouldn't have to live with regrets later—possibly forever."

Fauna had tried to find out what it was that was holding Snake back. She knew pushing too hard would only shut him down. She decided to give her hopes for a future with Snake a rest. She would not bring it up again. She would stop manipulating, scheming and maneuvering and release this to the Lord. She would trust Him with her future. She fought the temptation to yell, put a ring on it already!

The waitress took their meal orders, then Fauna shared with Snake about her day. "I had a student come into my office today and it was like déjà vu."

"What do you mean?"

"This girl was me—when I was her age. The difference, of course, is she comes from an intact family with two parents and a sibling."

"Then how is she like you?" Snake asked.

"She's carrying the whole world on her shoulders and thinks she has tons to prove."

Snake looked across the table at the beautiful person telling him about her day. He loved her expressions, the way she turned her head when she laughed and the concern in her voice when she told him about the kids she worked with. His heart hurt that they could never be man and wife. He knew he should end it—and soon. Dragging this out was only making it more painful for them both. He didn't say a word. Opting instead to listen intently to every word she spoke.

"I saw she had given herself a homemade tattoo. Of course, you know that's not safe to do at any age, but especially not at fourteen." Fauna stopped talking and flashed a mischievous smile at Snake. "I know what you're thinking. Who am I to point a finger—right?"

They both laughed while Fauna pointed at the butterfly tattoo on her face. Then she moved her hand like a game show model showing the next prize to the make-believe contestants.

"All joking aside—I saw the tattoo when I called her into the office for another reason. I called her out on the tat. It said HATE across the inside of her left wrist."

"That sounds like a sure cry for help."

"That's what I thought. I called her parents today to set up an appointment. Her mother is coming into the office tomorrow. I've got a feeling it's going to rock her world. Nobody wants to see their baby tattooed."

"Why didn't you just tell her on the phone? Then let them handle it at home."

"I could have done that, but I wasn't sure how the parents would react. It could be worse for the girl, if the parents are prone to violence. I'm hoping I'll be able to read the situation better in person."

Snake listened to this passionate woman pour out the details of her day. How he wished it could be across their table, in their home, as man and wife. He pushed the thought out of his mind. He wouldn't entertain painful, never-gonna-happen dreams.

Snake asked. "Is it possible that the parents already know? A tattoo is kind-a-hard to hide. I mean…" His eyes locked on the side of Fauna's face and gave a half smile. "...when they're in plain sight."

Fauna gave him *the look*, the one where she tipped her head to the side and twisted her lips sideways. She did that to show disgust in a fun way. "Okay, fine. Point taken! But the moment I saw it, I noticed it may be infected. I could see it was fresh maybe less than a week old." Fauna pictured in her mind what the tattoo looked like. "...and I'm concerned as much for her mental state as I am for her physical safety."

Snake leaned back and pressed his lower back against the vinyl booth. The booth was short for his tall frame. It felt like a lumbar support more than a seatback. "Well, I'm giving way to the professional on this one." He leaned forward again and rested his arms on the table. "How did this troubled girl react when you called her out on a tiny wrist tat—when the counselor is plastered with 'em?"

"Oh, she reacted. First—she came in the office all—give me your best shot—attitude, quiet and moody—superior and unaffected by this mundane world. Then, when I turned her wrist over to reveal the tat—wild anger rose up in her like a caged animal afraid for its life."

"Well, she showed her hand. Didn't she? There is obviously something deeper going on with that girl."

"Yes, she did—and yes, there is." Fauna reached across the table and held Snake's hand again. They chatted more about her day and his day like two old married people—only they weren't married. They lived in two different places. Each wishing they were together, but a great divide separated them. In Snake's mind it was insurmountable and in Fauna's it was unknown.

The counselor in Fauna knew if Snake would just talk about whatever it was—they could work it out. She was sure Snake cared deeply for her, still for some reason marriage was off the table. For Christian believers that also meant other things were off the table, like living together and having a family. Two things Fauna wanted. The companionship they shared the past year was wonderful, but Fauna was ready for the forever-committed relationship. Snake was holding back, and she had two options; fight back by scheming with her womanly wiles or submit it to the Lord in prayer—and wait.

□□

Doctor Hayes collapsed into his desk chair. He had just left his last patient and was ready to go home for the evening. There was just one more thing he had to do. He rolled his chair up to the desk, opened his laptop and scrolled to the file for the Douglas family. He searched the medical history of the children. There were a few trips to the ER with burns, another broken bone, one visit to the ER for stitches and the usual trips for childhood related illnesses like high fevers and infections.

Stuart leaned back in his chair and folded his hands behind his head. He made a sigh, almost a moan, as he contemplated turning the Douglas family into *Child Protective Services*. The question loomed, what if they were innocent? This family would be needlessly placed in the system, possibly for years. He stood up from his desk and decided to wait a day to think it over. Also, he was going solely on the word of one woman he didn't even know. He didn't want to react hastily. He left the Douglas file open on his computer screen and switched off his office light closing the door behind him.

Stuart drove home feeling exhausted. He thought about the twenty patients who rotated through his office. Two were referred out to a cardiologist, the Douglas boy with a broken arm, two 'meet and greets,' one of those was the Alden woman—pretty but something was a bit off there, three with diabetic complications, three yearly physicals, two sports physicals, two ear infections, four who needed a prescription for coughing and antibiotics and one unknown rash that turned out to be a reaction to glue from a previous test.

He loved being a doctor, but sometimes he daydreamed of coming home to a doting wife and problem free children. As he pulled into the driveway a warmth filled his heart when he saw Baylee sitting on the front porch. He didn't even pull into the garage opting instead to park in front of the house. Leaving his briefcase in the car, he hurried to his daughter.

"Look at you, beautiful girl. Are you getting some sun?"

"Yep. Mommy said that I could sit outside for a little while, as long as I didn't try and walk anywhere."

"Well, you have a very smart mommy. Is she in the house?" Baylee nodded her head in the affirmative. Dr. Hayes pulled up a patio chair and sat close to his daughter. These pain free moments were rare and cherished.

"Is Isabelle home?"

Baylee pinched her lips together and looked away. Then she answered like the information was being pulled from her. "Isabelle was home. I heard mom knocking on her door, just before I had an attack. Then she was gone. Mom is making phone calls inside."

Dr. Hayes patted the top of his baby girl's head. "I'll be back in just a minute." Stuart went into the house allowing the screen door to slam shut behind him.

Samantha stood in the kitchen, vacantly staring at the phone lying motionless on the kitchen island. She lifted her eyes from the phone long enough to see her husband standing in the doorway.

"Oh. You're home. Did you see Baylee? She had a bad episode a few hours ago, but now she's feeling much better."

"Where is Isabelle?" The tone in Stuart's voice was more concerned with what illegal activity his daughter may be engaged in than her physical safety. "You know we can't risk another situation with the police."

"Yes. Stuart. I'm aware of that." Samantha breathed in deeply trying to keep her composure while she explained. "She came home from school upset about something and locked herself in the bedroom. Then Baylee needed me. Isabelle just bolted out of the house. It's been nearly three hours. I'm hoping she is just blowing off some steam."

"Did you try her cell phone?"

Samantha forced herself to remain civil. Her words became slow and drawn out. "Yes. She didn't take it with her. I heard it ringing in her bedroom." Samantha paused. The feeling of being sucked into a vortex caused her to grip the countertop in front of her. Hopelessness was evident in her voice. "Probably wouldn't have mattered. When she's in one of these moods, she is vengeful enough to let it go to voice mail." Samantha's voice broke, "If she were in some sort of danger—I'd just feel better, if she had her phone." The thought of Isabelle in a precarious situation nested in Samantha's thoughts.

"We'll give her another hour, and then we're going to have to call the police." Stuart paused then added. "That crazy child, I think there is a key element missing in her make up. Why can't she understand the situation we're in with a sick child and me trying to set up a new practice?" While Stuart's words still hung in the air he looked at his wife and really saw her for the first time since arriving home. She was at the breaking point. He knew it.

He added with a bit more concern for her in his voice. "And you, trying to keep this house running smoothly. She is an unfeeling and uncaring child. Maybe we should consider a little stint away from home for her. There are great boarding schools to help set a rebellious child on the right path. Or we could ship her off to one of your relatives. We are going to have to do something." Stuart could see his wife mentally shrinking into the fetal position right before his eyes.

Samantha hadn't moved since their conversation began. The blank expression on her face spoke volumes and he knew his ranting wasn't helping.

Samantha looked up from the counter. "The middle school counselor called me just before Isabelle came home. She didn't go into details why, but she needed to talk to us. She wanted both of us to come in. I told her you wouldn't be able to make it." Samantha hadn't asked a question, but her tone implied plenty.

"If you can't handle it, I can try and make other arrangements at the clinic."

Samantha felt the implication. He thought she wasn't capable. "No. I'll go, but what about Baylee. Who will watch her?"

"Can't she go with you and just wait in the office."

"Yes, but if she's in pain or sleeping that would be difficult."

"Fine, drop her at my office. She can sit in there until you're done. When you pick her up I may have a free moment for you to update me on the meeting with the counselor."

"It's at 4:30 P.M. Do you think you could close up an hour early and come with me?"

"We'll see how the day goes. Bring Baylee to the office. If I'm too busy to leave, you can go to the meeting and leave Baylee with me."

"Mom." A small voice spoke from behind Stuart.

"Baylee. You might fall." Samantha hurried to her daughter, wrapping her arm around Baylee's waist; she led her to the family room sofa.

"I'll be upstairs in the office, if you need me. I'll be doing a little research on boarding schools." Sarcasm dripped from Stuart's voice. Then he headed up the stairs two at a time.

"Is Isabelle going away?" Baylee looked at her mother with concern.

"Of course not. Daddy is just kidding."

10
Evil Comes

Heidi felt a rush of adrenaline as she turned down Lancaster Drive. Isabelle directed her to the largest house on the block. Heidi glanced at Rey and Callan's house two doors down from the Hayes house. The sight of the parsonage caused her breathing to accelerate. Heidi gave a soft grunt through her nose at the thought of Rey Douglas. Isabelle looked at Heidi with a puzzled expression.

Realizing she made the noise out loud, Heidi gave Isabelle a warm smile dismissing the grunt. "I was thinking about something—that's all." Heidi never dreamed this week would present so many opportunities. "I'm glad we were able to do this today, Isabelle. Maybe we can do it again sometime."

Heidi put the car in park and opened her car door. Her long legs glided out of the car with ease. Heidi preferred dresses to pants. Her motto was—use what the good Lord gave you. Don't hide it—flaunt it.

Heidi confidently walked toward the front door of the Hayes house following Isabelle's lead. She planned to impose herself into this hurting family partly for *The Healer*, but mostly for the mischief she might cause. Also, Dr. Hayes may be a bit lonely being new in town. She might just have the solution for that little problem as well.

Before either Isabelle or Heidi touched the first step of the porch, Samantha threw open the front door. "Where have you been Isabelle? We've been so worried."

Isabelle pushed past her mom and ran up the stairs leaving Heidi and Samantha blankly looking at each other. Samantha remembered Heidi from *The Healer's* office.

Heidi lifted her eyebrows and smirked. "Bet you're wondering how I ended up with your teenage daughter?" Heidi followed the question with a clumsy laugh.

Samantha half smiled at Heidi. "Would you like to come in for coffee?" She was relieved her daughter was home and grateful it was not a complete unknown that came to her rescue.

Heidi quickly ran a few scenarios over in her thoughts. She wanted to play this to her own advantage. If she accepted Samantha's invitation, there may never be another one. It would be better if she decides when they meet again.

"No thank-you. It's been a long day for me. I need to get home. I would like to take a raincheck on that cup of coffee. I'd love to get to know your family better. Maybe we could do it another time and I can fill you in on all the details of how Isabelle and I met? We did have a nice connection today. I could tell she wanted to talk more. But I wouldn't want to do that without your blessing. You can think about it. I'll give you a call in a few days. Isabelle gave me the number. I'd enjoy taking her out for pizza and a movie sometime. If you think she'd like that?"

Samantha knew this woman had shown her daughter great kindness, but why would she want to be friends with her fourteen-year-old daughter? She pushed the thought aside, thankful that the day ended with Isabelle home safely and without police involvement.

"When you have time give me a call and we'll have you over. We can talk more about that then." Samantha said from the porch.

Heidi agreed and turned to leave. She glanced back and yelled a good-bye to Isabelle who was peeking out from the top of the stairs. Driving home she played over the events of the day. She couldn't believe her luck.

When she arrived home, she opened the door to her one-bedroom apartment. Shutting the door behind her, she kicked off her heels. They landed across the room. She had a daily ritual she performed. The first thing she did was light the candles peppered throughout her apartment. The ambiance of the candle light and the aroma gave the whole apartment a spa-like feel. She deserved to be pampered. If no one else would pamper her—she would do it.

She opened her freezer, selected from the assortment of frozen dinners and placed one in the microwave. Making the few steps from the kitchen to the living room, she turned on the cable news show. Her favorite one was the network that bashed anything and everything religious. Calling them weak-minded people, stupid sheep that follow their leaders without a mind of their own—she loved when the commentators diminished religion. Heidi personally had been bit—stung—attacked without cause by *Christians*. It was payback time.

The Healer had worked with Heidi to forgive the cruelty inflicted on her by Christians in general and the Community Outreach Church particularly. He also told her that until wrongs were made right, true forgiveness wouldn't come. Her path to find true forgiveness was for the betterment of all. *The Healer* had taught her that the best way to make a wrong right was to level the playing field by getting even. This was a concept Heidi could sink her teeth into.

Heidi poured herself a glass of wine, then eyed the glass and poured a bit more. She walked the few steps across the small apartment and dropped down into her sofa. She played over in her mind her remarkable good fortune. Dr. Hayes' family dropped into her lap like a gift from heaven. There was sick Baylee—needy and consuming all her mommy's attention. The older girl, Isabelle, was troubled. I'm reasonably sure I'll be able to stoke that fire in any direction I choose. Lastly, tired 'ol mommy, Samantha, is overwhelmed with her miserable life—she won't even see me swoop in.

Heidi reclined back on the sofa and rested her feet on the coffee table. She looked at her manicured toe nails with approval. Then glanced at the mirror to the right of the T.V. screen and saw her reflection. She smiled back at herself with satisfaction, raised her glass in a toast and turned her focus to the latest gossipy news story.

□□

Samantha settled Baylee in Stuart's office with an iPad, her cell phone and a snack. "I'll be back in an hour or so. If Daddy finishes early, then he'll take you home. You'll be okay." Samantha was trying to convince herself of this statement more than her daughter. "Are you comfortable?"

Baylee knew her mom was concerned, "Bye, Mom. I'll be fine." When Baylee was feeling good her tone sounded like a sophisticated adult more than an ill child. Leaving the office, Samantha glanced at her husband's messy desk. The family picture was pushed far to the side and barely visible with piles of folders blocking the smiling faces.

Samantha moved the files back and picked up the frame. Holding it in her hand, she examined the family imprisoned behind the glass. Looking at her image, Samantha felt like she was suffocating. She was in a three-way real life physical tug-of-war. There was the work-alcoholic husband who was emotionally not available, the rebellious, selfish teenager in crisis and the sick child in pain. The physical pull of Baylee's needs yanked on one hand and Isabelle's needs pulled at the other hand, with no more hands available for her distracted husband. She knew she was running on empty, and Stuart had gone past empty a long time ago. Something had to change and soon.

Samantha laid the photo back on Stuart's desk, turned back and kissed Baylee good-bye one more time. She hurried out of the office pushing past the emotions that tried to bring her to her knees.

□□

Fauna sat at her desk in the counseling offices at the Hillbrooke Middle School. She called the desk hers, the office hers, but the door held another's name. This temporary position in the public school didn't allow her to do the type of counseling she dreamed about. This was her second week at the middle school and in less than three weeks school would be out for the summer. At least her foot was in the door for now. Being a school counselor wasn't her dream job, but it was better than waiting tables. Waitressing had provided well for her all through college but opening her own family-counseling center was her life's dream.

The type of counseling she could do in the public school was primarily career testing and helping students select their yearly class schedules. Despite having her hands tied up with district restrictions, she was grateful for each opportunity to speak into the life of a hurting child.

Fauna drifted off in thought. *My dream-counseling center would be a place where the* Wonderful Counselor *would be welcome. The mention of His name would not be taboo, but the hope of all who came for help. My center would not be governed by the state, restricting me from praying with hurting people or openly talking about the power of Jesus Christ to transform lives.*

Fauna understood from personal experience what it was to be broken, damaged and living in a dangerous home situation. When given the opportunity she to share freely the redeeming love of Christ—this she would do. The healing touch of Christ in the life of a child was more precious to her than a temporary job. If the chance presented itself, she would tell the hurting what they needed to hear—come what may.

Fauna glanced at the clock; Mrs. Hayes would be arriving soon. This was a situation she needed to handle both professionally and delicately. What parent wants to hear that their fourteen-year-old child had done permanent damage to their body? Fauna could relate to the pain she saw in Isabelle. The 'tough girl' persona was performed with excellence. Fauna understood Isabelle's need to keep everyone from the raw pain she was hiding. Someone had to reach this girl before it was too late.

Fauna was only twelve when she felt this same raw pain and despair. She had watched her mother die a slow painful death from complications of drug abuse and other diseases brought on by hopeless life choices. Her only parental figure had lost the will to live—robbing Fauna of the only person in her life who cared even the slightest bit about her. She was without father, siblings, aunts, uncles or grandparents. She was left alone in a world of pain with no one that remotely cared if she lived or died. When *Child Protective Services* finally caught up with Fauna, she was thirteen, a child of the streets—wild, hateful and angry—nursing a death wish.

It would take five years, six different foster homes and one group home before Fauna believed *someone* cared. The Lord brought a teacher into her life that could see past the pain. Through the kindness and perseverance of one, Fauna opened her heart to the Lord. God touched the broken pieces of her life and put them back together again.

□□

The nurse for Dr. Hayes called the next patient. "Jean Brown?"

Jean stood up and followed the nurse down the endless hallway. Her eyes focused on the scales snuggly sitting against a wall. It was the newer model. The one with the digital numbers placed on the wall for all those passing to observe and take mental note of other patient's private information.

The nurse stopped at an open examination room and pointed. "You can put your things in here. Then I'll weigh you." Jean left her purse on the chair but kept on her shoes and jacket. She followed the nurse to the end of the hall and stepped on the scales. The nurse wrote down the number on a slip of paper.

Jean and the nurse returned to the examination room and she opened the laptop to register the weight. She looked at Jean and said, "Good for you. You've lost twenty-five pounds since your last visit a year ago. Now what was your reason for coming in today?"

Jean didn't feel proud only apprehensive. "I've been concerned about the weight loss. I haven't felt like my eating has changed and I'm tired all the time. I just thought I'd better come in for an exam to be sure everything is okay."

"Dr. Hayes will be in shortly. There is one patient ahead of you." The nurse hurried out of the room like she was embarrassed for making the congratulatory weight loss comment. Any other time it would have been an accomplishment worthy of praise—but not today.

Jean liked Dr. Hayes. His bedside manner was kind and compassionate. He treated her health concerns with respect. She knew she wouldn't leave his office with *all* her questions answered, but he reassured her that rarely were these types of things serious in nature, that she did the right thing coming in. The testing he scheduled would give them the information they needed to treat the weight loss. They did a routine blood test before she left the office. The results from that would be back in the office tomorrow.

Dr. Hayes said that he or his nurse would be calling tomorrow with the results. Jean tried to push away the nervousness that gripped her stomach.

Once inside the car, Jean prayed. "Lord, You know my coming and my going. You know when I am awake and when I sleep. What is happening right now is no secret to You. I trust you with my life. I know that I am getting older and this tent is wearing out at the seams. Whatever time I have on this earth—may I always bring glory to You. I love you Lord!"

□□

Fauna glanced at the clock. She had fifteen minutes before Mrs. Hayes arrived. She got up from her swivel chair and shut her office door. Resting her elbows on the desk, she laid her face in her hands and whispered a prayer.

"Jesus, help me." A mournful sigh eased from her lips. "Help me, Lord. Help me to say the right things. Help this family as they come face to face with the issues tormenting their daughter. Help Isabelle. Cut past her pain and touch her with Your healing hands. You know the exact place where she's broken—fix her. Help Mrs. Hayes not to be angry—no killing the messenger. Bring hope and healing to this family. Open the eyes of both mother and father to the pain buried in their daughter. Help them not grow weary in the pursuit of wholeness. Lord, I know You hear my prayer. Let Your will be done in this family. Protect them from the hand of the enemy. Hold them in the protective covering of Your hands. In the name of Jesus, I ask these things. Thank you, Lord."

Fauna lifted her head at the sound of voices outside her closed office door. Standing up she took a deep breath, pushed her shoulders back and opened the door. Samantha Hayes sat alone in the reception area. She looked just as uncomfortable as her daughter Isabelle had yesterday when they met.

"Are you Mrs. Hayes?" Fauna asked politely with her hand extended.

Samantha Hayes stood up and turned in the direction of the voice. With her mouth slightly open Samantha's eyes locked on the tattoo on Fauna's face.

An awkward pause followed as her brain registered the information her eyes sent; *a butterfly tattooed is on the counselor's face.*

Samantha tried to present an appearance of being unaffected by the huge insect, but it was impossible not to gawk. She forced her eyes to look away.

"Yes. I'm Mrs. Hayes. I'm sorry my husband won't be able to make it. I did tell you that he's a doctor and the sick don't like to be kept waiting." Samantha let out an uneasy laugh and accepted the hand of the counselor.

"No problem. These days we're happy if any parent shows up for special meetings like this. I'm Fauna Reynolds. You can call me Fauna, if you'd like. Come in." Fauna stepped back behind her desk and motioned for Mrs. Hayes to step inside the compact room. "I'm sorry about the size of the office. I hope you won't be too uncomfortable in these tight quarters."

Fauna couldn't help but notice the striking similarities between mother and daughter. Both were very lovely in appearance and equally uncomfortable sitting in the chair adjacent to her desk.

"Mrs. Hayes, I spoke with Isabelle yesterday and I believe there are some strong indications that she is going through a rough time right now." Fauna paused and kept her eyes on Mrs. Hayes who had failed to make direct eye contact with Fauna since coming into her office.

Samantha kept her focus on a poster that hung on the wall behind where Fauna sat. It was the one of the cat hanging on a branch. The caption said, Hang In There.

Samantha felt looking at the poster gave the general appearance that she was looking in the counselor's direction without having to connect with the flaming tattoo on Ms. Reynolds' face.

Samantha spoke to the wall behind Fauna. "Yes. I'm sure Isabelle's records show that she's been going through…" Samantha dropped her gaze to her lap and continued. "…some struggles the past few years."

Fauna looked directly at Mrs. Hayes, but Samantha did not lift her eyes. "My concern in calling you in today was regarding something I noticed while Isabelle was in my office yesterday. I felt it was imperative that we talk as soon as possible to be sure you were aware as well."

Samantha and Fauna looked eye to eye for the first time.

Fauna continued, "I noticed she has a homemade tattoo on the inside of her left wrist. It looks less than a week old." Fauna decided to give her the facts in small bite size pieces. No need to kick the poor woman while she was down.

Samantha looked shell shocked confirming Fauna's suspicions that the parents were not aware of their daughter's actions.

Samantha's thoughts raced wildly in her head. How did she do it? Why would she do this? What will people think? We've failed her, yet again. She finally spoke. Her tone was mournful, "Did she open up to you about the tattoo when she met with you?"

"No. I noticed it. Before she left the room, I reached across my desk, took her hand and turned her wrist over." Fauna acted out the steps as she shared the incident with Isabelle's mom. She took Mrs. Hayes' hand in hers and pointed at her wrist.

"The word HATE was written out in capital letters." Fauna touched the underside of Mrs. Hayes' wrist. She pointed to the place where the tattoo was located.

Samantha sucked in a gulp of air. She exhaled quickly with a sigh. Then she pulled her hand free from Fauna's and held it close to her own body. Fauna watched the woman across from her physically and emotionally withdraw.

"HATE? I just don't understand why." Samantha's pain was evident. She held her left wrist tightly with her right hand pressing both against her heart.

Fauna rethought the slow approach. Maybe she should have just ripped the bandage off all at once. The tattoo and the word HATE were two direct blows to Samantha's heart. The third one was coming. It was a bitter pill to swallow no matter how Fauna chose to dole out the information.

"Mrs. Hayes, I probably wouldn't have called you in for the tattoo alone. There was a more important reason. I think the tattoo may be infected. She may need medical treatment, and I wasn't sure if you were aware she had the tattoo. I was concerned that waiting any longer could affect her health."

Samantha's eyes filled with tears. Fauna pushed the box of Kleenex sitting on her desk toward Mrs. Hayes and silently prayed.

11

Peace in the Storm

Jean Brown reclined on the wicker chaise lounge and soaked in the sun. A book lay open on her lap. She had only read a few lines before her eyes grew weary. The warmth of the sun made her feel hugged. Her thoughts drifted from happy to dark. The more she thought about her sudden weight loss the more concerned she became. When she made the fateful decision to do a search on the internet she discovered her issues could run the gamut from diabetes to impending death. She had made the decision to let the doctors do the diagnosing, but the waiting was unbearable.

Jean's cell phone rang in her pocket sending a vibration from her hip to her knee. She pulled the phone out. She checked the caller ID—HILLBROOKE MEDICAL CLINIC. "Hello."

"Is this Jean Brown?" It wasn't the doctor but one of his staff. Maybe that was a good sign.

"This is she. Are the results from my blood-work in?"

"Yes, the blood work is in and Doctor Hayes wants you to see an oncologist as soon as possible. He can recommend one, or if you have one that you have seen in the past, you can make your own appointment with that doctor. If you need a referral from your insurance company, we can handle that for you. We'll get that taken care of as soon as you have your appointment."

Jean's head was reeling. She was hearing words, lots and lots of words, but one word was elusive until Jean asked, "Do I have cancer?"

"We don't know. Right now, it's just routine protocol. The doctor felt your blood test justified a closer look and more testing. He wanted it done by an oncologist. They are qualified to map out the best course for a proper diagnosis. Don't worry Mrs. Brown. We do lots of referrals like this and rarely does it amount to anything. We want to be sure we are giving our patients the best care."

Jean tried to keep her voice steady. Inside she could feel her heart rate soaring and a weightlessness in her arms. She spoke out loud, "Who is the doctor that you are referring me to?" Inside she prayed. Lord, help me be calm and remember that You are with me—now and forever.

"If you use our referral, I can call and make your appointment for you, if this will help?"

"Yes. I would appreciate that. Thank you."

"I'll get everything set for you and call you back later with the appointment time. Good bye Mrs. Brown."

Jean let her arm drop to her side with the cell phone resting in the palm of her hand. Suddenly, it was too heavy to hold. She was numb. The protective bubble she was in the past few weeks just burst. The "C" word was on the table. She had pulled the short straw in the family gene pool. Would she follow the path of two grandparents, both parents and one sibling? And they say cancer isn't hereditary. She picked up the phone and dialed Tom at work.

"Hey—Jean did you hear from the doctor?" There were no words that followed that question. "Jean are you there?" A soft "Yup" was all Jean could say.

"I'm coming home. Be there shortly." Tom hung up. He felt his whole world shift off the axis. His movements were slow and forced like he was moving through life in thick syrup. He was a realist and so was Jean. They had talked about scenarios like this throughout their forty-five years of marriage. Now they were living it out in real time and every moment counted.

□□

Samantha Hayes pushed open the middle school door and walked out of the building. Heading for her van in the parking lot, she was lost in thought. Her van sat eerily alone. She fumbled around in her purse for the toggle and pressed the button to unlock her door. The car alarm sounded, and Samantha trembled at the sound. The toggle fell from her hand unto the hot asphalt. She whisked the keys up turning off the alarm as she stood.

Silence.

Glancing quickly from side to side Samantha felt stripped naked fully exposed for the judgmental eyes of the world. Her imagination shouted; look at the horrible mother and emotionally unavailable wife. The car alarm had called out to the world; look at the carnival freak—come one come all. She felt the nonexistent pointing fingers, imaginary whispers of people and shocked expressions on the faces of the fictional spectators.

Samantha hurried the rest of the way across the empty lot to the safety of her van. Tears formed in her eyes as she used the steering wheel to pull herself into the front seat. Once inside she pushed the start button and listened for the hum of the motor. For a moment she thought she would be able to push through. Then she surrendered dropping her head into her waiting hands. She wept allowing the hopelessness to swallow her.

□□

Dr. Hayes finished entering information into the last patient's file then powered down his laptop. He looked over at Baylee sleeping. She was slumped over the arm of the chair. She moaned softly as she repositioned her small body. She was wrapped up in a blanket like a burrito with her sweet face resting on her arm. She was pain-free for the moment.

Stuart looked at his sleeping child and hated to wake her up, but he was more than ready for *this day* to end. Scooping Baylee up in his arms, he whisked her off to the car. Baylee remained sleeping as he fashioned her into the back seat and headed for home.

Stuart opened the garage door expecting to see Samantha's van. She wasn't home yet. He pulled in and closed the door behind him. Baylee was still sleeping in the back seat; he picked up his cell phone and called Samantha. It went directly to voice mail. He debated for a moment if he would leave a message. He decided against it. He turned his attention to Baylee.

"Sweetie, we're home. Can you walk into the house, or do you want me to carry you?"

Baylee looked at her father with sleepy eyes and a half smile formed on her face. "We're home already." She sat up straight and yawned. "I'll walk."

Stuart helped his daughter out of the car, and Baylee did well until she faced the three steps leading into the house. He effortlessly lifted her up in the air by grabbing both of her arms. Baylee let out a squeal of delight—until she landed abruptly on her feet in the mudroom. She yelled out in agony. Stuart immediately regretted his spontaneous decision.

Stuart, the doctor, called out to his elder daughter, "Isabelle! Are you home?" He repeated Isabelle's name three more times, each time his volume increased until Isabelle rounded the corner into the mudroom. She looked at her father slumped over Baylee who was sitting on the floor whimpering.

"What!" Isabelle's tone was sharp to the point of disrespect. She observed the situation and the guilty expression on her father's face. "What did *you* do?" Accusation dripped from her attitude. She casually strolled over to examine Baylee.

Dr. Hayes was out of his element kneeling on the floor next to one child while the other one evaluated the situation. He was ill prepared to help either daughter. Both were wounded— one on the inside and one on the outside.

The sound of the garage door opening helped everyone refocus. Samantha got out of the van red-eyed and burdened. She approached the open door and saw Baylee on the floor, Isabelle standing over her and Stuart with a very guilty look on his face.

Samantha immediately asked, "What happened?" Even while the question exited her lips, she was lifting Baylee in her arms and walking to the family room. Isabelle and Stuart followed behind like two guilty children.

Stuart clinched his jaw. He didn't need to explain himself to anybody. This was Samantha's fault. She probably was out shopping instead of picking Baylee up and keeping an eye on

Isabelle. What was Isabelle doing home alone? I'm sure that counseling appointment didn't take *this* long. Must be nice to be irresponsible and carefree, he thought.

Once Baylee was settled in the family room, Isabelle bolted out of the room without saying a word. Samantha asked to speak with Stuart in the home office. She started up the stairs. Stuart cut in front of his wife hurrying to get to the office first. He chose the big leather office chair that sat behind the desk. If she was going to scold him for something, he wanted to be in the power seat when it happened. Samantha took the chair in front of the desk. For the first time in the few minutes that Samantha had been home Stuart looked at his wife face to face.

"Have you been crying?" He asked with a hint of *again* in his tone. "It's time we stop pretending Baylee is going to improve. I know you don't want to talk about it, but she's ten now, still in pain and her chances of improving are null. It's time we talk about the amputation to improve her quality of life."

"Stuart. That's permanent. No going back. I can't do that. I just can't."

"Why do you fight against reality? She's sick. She's not getting better. She's in pain. This would be to help her have quality of life."

Samantha ignored his question while forming one of her own. *"You do* remember why I dropped Baylee off with you—right?"

There was a short pause while Stuart hit rewind in his cluttered mind. Then he answered, "Obviously, you went to talk to the school counselor about Isabelle. What did she do now?" Samantha forced her lips together fighting the temptation to explode. Her lips began to quiver. Stuart had good qualities, but patience was not one of them.

He sharply replied. "Did she kill somebody in 6th hour? What?"

Samantha wasn't sure how her husband would react. He was a doctor, but in this case, he was a father first. She opted not to drag it out like the counselor did with her. It was about time he felt the up close and personal side of parenting a teenager.

"Isabelle gave herself a homemade tattoo." Samantha pointed to the inside of her wrist while she talked. "It says HATE and it may be infected. The school counselor saw it when she had a routine appointment with Isabelle yesterday. You'll need to look at it." The words flowed from Samantha's lips without emotion. She could have been saying something as mundane as, stop on your way home to pick up milk and bread.

Stuart sat in his power seat. His face held no secrets. He looked like someone shot an arrow into his heart. Without saying a word, he stood, walked past his wife to the hallway and leaned against the wall outside of Isabelle's bedroom. He stayed there for a few seconds, then knocked.

"Issie, I need to talk to you." The door opened, and Stuart saw his daughter. He really saw her. She was a beautiful girl with empty eyes. He reached out and took both of Isabelle's hands. She winced and pulled them back. "Issie. We know. I need to see if it's infected."

Isabelle extended her left hand and turned it over exposing the ugly word tattooed on her soft skin. He gently touched the letters and then followed a faint pink line up Isabelle's arm about two inches from her wrist. "We need to go to the hospital, Issie. It looks infected."

Stuart focused on the upside-down word. He turned her wrist to bring the word in view. H-A-T-E. With pain evident in his face and voice he whispered, "Why Issie?"

□□

Zander and Ty Douglas shared a bedroom at the Community Outreach Church parsonage. There were plenty of bedrooms in the spacious parsonage, but they preferred sharing. When the family arrived in Hillbrooke five years earlier, the boys were young and still fearful at night. Leaving their bedroom doors open and strategically placing nightlights didn't help them adjust to separate bedrooms. Each morning Callan found her two sons in bed together. She stopped fighting it after a few weeks and allowed them to share, which made for many late nights of talking and laughing. The boys were building lifelong memories and for that Callan was grateful.

The Douglas brothers had been in bed at least twenty minutes. Sleep evaded them. Each thinking about the new little girl named Baylee that they met. It was Ty who broke the silence first.

"Zander are you still awake?" He whispered to his big brother.

"Yep! What do ya want?"

"I was just thinking about Baylee. Do you think she's going to die?"

"Of course not. Kids don't die." Zander's tone carried an authority that was reassuring.

Ty responded. "But—her mom is sad. I think she's really sick."

"You don't know that for sure." Zander was on the top bunk and leaned over to try and see his younger brother's face. "She'll be fine. Remember how she acted when we played with her. Why are you worried about her anyway?"

"You know, I was thinking next time we go over there we should pray for her."

Zander flipped onto his back and looked up at the ceiling for a moment before warning his brother. "You're just asking for trouble. Mom said that we can pray for her at home. They don't even go to church. They probably don't know anything about praying. People learn that kinda stuff when they go to church."

"I know that, but what if *we* prayed for her the next time we go over there." Ty held his index finger in the air while he spoke even though it was too dark to be seen. "I've been thinking about the stories Ms. Grace told us about Jesus healing people. She said that Jesus prayed, and we should be like him."

"That would be embarrassing." Zander rolled his eyes at the ceiling.

"No one would have to know. We could ask Jesus to heal her. I think He'll do it—I mean if we ask?" Ty poked his head out from the lower bunk. He squinted trying to see his brother in the dark room. All he could see was Zander's arm dangling over the edge of the bunk. He gave his brother's hand a good swat.

Zander pulled his arm back and turned on his flashlight. He pointed the light directly in Ty's eyes. "I don't think kids are supposed to pray for other kids. Adults do that kind of stuff." He spoke with a firm voice that held a certain amount of authority.

Ty knew the light shining in his eyes was a declaration of war. He covered his head with the blanket and searched for his flashlight. He was at a disadvantage since he only had one working arm. He finally located it near the bottom of the bed. Maneuvering it with one hand he flicked it on and the battle ensued.

Within a few minutes footsteps could be heard coming down the hallway. The flashlights clicked off, silence filled the room and the brothers lay motionless.

Callan opened the bedroom door. The room was dark and silent. She stood in the doorway trying to speak sternly. A smile could be heard in her voice. "I don't want to hear another peep from you boys. Now get to sleep—both of you." She shut the door and waited outside. There were a few more giggles and then all was quiet. Callan walked back to the family room with a grin on her face.

12
Maple Bacon Cake

Saturday morning Grace eased out of bed after a restless night. Her mind was in overdrive from the discussion with Pastor Rey and Callan a week ago. She still struggled with the question of staying on the church staff amidst the rumors that she and Pastor Rey were having an affair. Grace's first instinct was always to run. She hated confrontation in any measure or form. Over the past five years, she had swatted at rumors that came her way, but this time it felt calculated. Grace sat on the edge of her bed and thought how this seemed over the top even for Heidi. She decided to private message Heidi on Facebook refusing to allow bitterness to take root in her heart.

□□

Heidi's phone made a ping sound signaling an incoming notification on her Facebook account. It was a private message. She touched the screen of her phone and opened the icon. It was from Grace—the cry baby.

I loathe her. She is a light weight, easily led and no backbone. I can only imagine how that church is in shambles. There is no way Weepie could ever fill my shoes.

A satisfied smile rose on Heidi's face as she began to read the message.

Hi Heidi, While I was at work a few weeks ago I found out a rumor has resurfaced about Pastor Rey and me. I was sad to find out that it originated with you. You of all people should know the truth since we all worked together in the same office for over a year. I want you to know that I am praying for you, and the truth about everything will come out in God's timing. Be careful, Heidi. I know you don't want to be labeled a slanderer, malicious or a liar. Labels have a way of attaching themselves to people. They can stick around for a long time— even a lifetime. I want only the best for you, and I trust you will find your way back to the Lord's love and forgiveness very soon. –Grace

Heidi's chest heaved with anger. She resisted the instinct to throw her phone across the room. How dare Grace act all forgiving like I'm the bad one! She's the adulteress, not me. Heidi formed the thoughts in her head—believing her own lies. Grace deserves whatever she gets. I'd love to copy her message and repost it for the whole world to read, but she skillfully worded it to make me look like the bad guy here. Just like her to pass the buck.

Heidi opened her contact list and called *The Healer*. He answered the phone with his usual greeting, "Peace and wholeness to you. This is *The Healer*. I'm here."

Heidi didn't waste any time but got straight to the heart of the matter. "I'm so glad you picked up. This is Heidi. I'm having an issue with a past co-worker bothering me with

Facebook messages. She has me all upset. I could use a special session with you. Are you available?"

"Heidi, the office is closed today. How about if you come in to the office on Monday morning about thirty minutes early? We can talk then."

"Fine! But I'm not feeling any peace and wholeness right now." The sarcasm was evident.

"We will deal with that on Monday. Do deep breathing and meditation for thirty minutes. You'll feel much better. I'll see you then. Sweet peace and contentment be with you. Think good thoughts. Remember you are in control and don't allow others to control you. You are your own master. Be kind to you. You deserve it. You are a good person."

Heidi heard a click signifying the end of the call. She felt a measure of peace step into her turmoil. She loved the way *The Healer* told her nice things about herself. No one else seemed to manage to say one kind word to her. *The Healer* was right. She is master of her life. She is in control. She is a good person. She is kind.

Heidi continued to repeat these words as she prepared for her day.

□□

Through the years Grace had bumped into Heidi at several local stores. Whenever she passed her on the road she smiled and waved. Occasionally, Heidi responded in kind. She knew Heidi was hurt and angry over losing her job, but she never thought she was capable of such lies inflicted on her for the sole purpose of spite. These rumors were not even veiled like the ones that were circulated five years ago.

While Grace sat on the edge of her bed she massaged her forehead with her finger tips trying to erase the thoughts that continued to assault her mind. She prayed, "Lord, help me. What should I do?" A portion of scripture came to her mind. She mulled it over thinking about the words allowing them to take root. She was certain this portion of scripture was not a perfect quote, but the meaning was there. Still sitting on the edge of her bed she spoke the Word out loud, "Casting down imaginations and bringing into captivity every thought to the obedience of Christ." Taking a deep breath, she claimed the words again.

Then she stood up and headed to the bathroom. With each step she could feel her shoulders move upwards and her back straighten up. She looked at herself in the mirror and spoke, "The enemy comes to rob, steal and destroy, but the Lord has come to bring life abundantly." Looking back from the mirror were tired eyes, red from sleeplessness, a smile formed on Grace's lips. Her hands shot up in the air and praise began to pour from her lips. She was not defeated. God made her victorious through Jesus Christ.

Moments later, Grace sat in her breakfast nook. Her Sunday school lesson book lay on the table with her Bible. She had been teaching the 4th-6th grade class at Community Outreach for a few years. At first it was a challenge. She did not have children of her own nor did she have any training to teach children. She pushed past her inadequacies by asking questions, and she read books to educate herself on the teaching of elementary age children.

Now she was in love with each child that passed through the doors of her class. The naughty ones had a special place in her heart. She was on a personal mission to win them over to the Lord by teaching them the joys of serving Jesus. Each week, when Grace prepared her lesson, she would pray for her students by name. During class time, she believed with them for the needs they shared.

The cover on the teacher's manual showed a picture of Jesus laying His hands on the eyes of what appeared to be a blind man. Over the next three months all lessons were on healing at the 8-11-year-old level. Picking up the quarterly, she opened it to lesson number three. She laid it on the table in front of her. It was entitled, *Bringing Your Friends to Jesus*. It was the story of the paralyzed man who couldn't get to Jesus without the help of his friends.

□□

Stuart Hayes coveted his weekends. From Friday evening to Monday morning the family knew these were sacred hours of relaxation for a busy husband and father. None of the family had planned for the events that filled their weekend. Isabelle had been admitted to the Hillbrooke Medical Center for 48-hours of IV antibiotic. This left Stuart without a reprieve from the medical world for seven straight days. He was either at the hospital with Isabelle, or at home with Baylee. Neither one of these options were the weekend he had planned. From the moment he stepped into the house on Friday evening, it had been non-stop family issues.

Stuart left early for the office on Monday morning. He was ready to delve into medicine and out of the pool of raging female hormones. He would like just one day without an emotionally sensitive wife, a rebellious teenager and even a day without dealing with poor Baylee whose difficulties were not of her own making. He wished for a single day away from it all.

Stuart sat down at his desk and reviewed his schedule for the day on his laptop. On the desktop screen he noticed two medical files still open—the Douglas children. He gave an exhausted sigh. He really didn't want to deal with this today.

Everything in him wanted to remove them from his view. He double clicked on each file and opened them side by side. He scanned the information for a second time. He really hated this part of his job. He hit the intercom button on his desk phone and before the nurse could answer, he blurted out, "I need the number for Child
Protective Services."

"Yes, Doctor Hayes. I'll get that office on the line and put them through to you." The receptionist was a no nonsense, army drill-sergeant with exceptional respect for authority. She always called Stuart Hayes, Doctor or Sir and he liked it that way. In his last office things were getting too familiar with his nurse. He knew it and she knew. He was glad to be out of that complicated web.

He grunted in the affirmative and disconnected the call.

□□

Monday morning Samantha had a fight with Isabelle to wake up and get ready for school. Most mornings were a fight, but this day was worse. It was her last week of middle school and the thought of arriving with her arm in a sling was more than she could bear. The doctor at the hospital felt it would be best to keep the arm immobile for a few more days.

"Come on, Mom. I just got out of the hospital. I should be allowed one day off."

"Your dad and I both decided it was best for you to finish out the week. You're fine."

"I'm on pain meds. I could fall asleep standing up."

"Get ready. You're going to school."

"I hope you know that every nosey teacher and student is going to be in my business. Thanks a lot for that!"

"You can thank yourself for that Issie. I'm not the one that did that to your arm. You did it to yourself. We're leaving in 15-minutes."

"I won't go."

"Do you really want to begin the summer like this? You're fourteen. Everything you own is under our control...13-minutes and the clock is ticking."

Isabelle left for school in a fouler mood than usual.

With Isabelle off to school and Baylee reading in her bedroom, Samantha took a moment to herself. She missed having a friend, someone to confide in, who would listen and not judge her or her family—good or bad. Samantha recalled the kindness of Callan a few days ago. This woman was mere minutes away—two doors down. Samantha needed someone—right now. She remembered that Callan had said that she was a good listener.

Digging through some scrap paper by the phone Samantha located Callan's phone number. Before she could put her hand on the phone—it rang. Samantha cleared her throat then answered using her professional voice, "Hello. This is the Hayes residence. How may I help you?"

"Wow! You sound like the executive office of a major corporation." A forced laugh followed Heidi's remark. "Hi Samantha, this is Heidi Alden. We met at *The Healer's* office last week and briefly when I dropped your daughter, Isabelle, off." Heidi paused hoping she had name recognition.

"Heidi, nice of you to call. What can I do for you?"

"Great! I found you at home. I know Isabelle's in school, but I was thinking, I could drop by with lunch for you and Baylee. I was thinking about 12:30 P.M. I'd love to talk to you about the possibility of spending some time with Isabelle. She did open up to me when I picked her up on that deserted road last week." Heidi wanted to make sure Samantha knew that she owed her— big. "I thought you may want to get to know me better before letting your teenager go out with me. I could sense when I dropped Isabelle off that you seemed worried. I thought being new to Hillbrooke that you also might like a friend. So—how does lunch sound and some girl talk? I'm buying." Heidi tried to present herself as the girl next door, everybody's best friend. She needed Samantha to trust her— fully.

Samantha looked at Callan's number in her hand and tucked it back in the open drawer where she found it. "Heidi, this is such a surprise and so thoughtful—even timely. When should I expect you?"

"I'll be there after noon with food in hand. See you then." Heidi hung up the phone feeling victorious like she had been in a race nosing someone out right at the finish line. She fought the temptation to do a victory dance in *The Healer's* empty office. A triumphant smile formed on Heidi's lips. A feeling of contentment like the ones she experienced recently when she told Dr. Hayes about the suspected abuse of the Douglas children.

Telling the truth about Rey's fling with Grace had been equally invigorating. Doing the right thing felt good, just like *The Healer* had told her.

□□

The intercom buzzed in Dr. Hayes's office. He hit the speakerphone button. His nurse's voice bounced off the walls of his small office.

"Dr. Hayes, the oncologist copied us the report on Jean Brown. I thought you'd want to see that today. I'm forwarding the email on to you now."

"Thanks. I'll start seeing patients in about ten minutes."
Dr. Hayes sat at his desk working through the list of patients
on the day's schedule. It was going to be a full day. He had
two yearly physicals, a removal of stitches, two maternity visits,
five follow-up calls, two wound care check-ups and three
Monday call-ins for seasonal sicknesses.

Dr. Hayes opened his email and read the report on Jean
Brown.   The diagnosis was pancreatic cancer with a
recommendation for chemotherapy. The prognosis wasn't
good. He normally did not follow-up with the patients he
referred out, but when someone received a cancer diagnosis it
was his practice to do a follow-up call even if he would not be
the attending physician. He wanted his patients to know he
cared and was not abandoning them in their time of need. He
knew the first question, once the initial shock had worn off
would be—how much time do I have?

Dr. Hayes examined the report again focusing more on
what it didn't say than what it did. He knew she had mere
months to live.

□□

"Jean, we need to talk." Tom's eyes were red and swollen. He
had given Jean as much time as she needed over the past days
to process what was happening. She cried without restraint.
He comforted her. He listened. They sat exceptionally close
on the sofa and embraced for long periods of time. They had
both cried an ocean of tears in the past few weeks wondering
what might be ahead, and now they knew.

Neither Jean nor Tom spoke a word to anyone besides
each other—and the Lord. They had not told their daughters,
Pastor Rey, Callan or their small group anything—yet. Very
soon this desperately private matter would be public.   Their

family, friends and acquaintances would all know the intimacies of how the Browns were dealing with life and death.

Tom put his arm around Jean's shoulder while she stared out the picture window at the lake.

Through her emotion Jean forced out the words. "We need to call the girls." She rested her head on Tom's shoulder.

Tom was unable to speak. He drew her in closer and held her tighter.

"I feel numb at one moment then a wave of emotions will come and knock me off my feet. I'm trying to regroup. I'm trying to pull myself together. It's an agonizing thing to think about telling our daughters that I'm dying. I've always been the anchor for Debbie and Kim. I don't know how I'm going to bear it….my girls." Jean closed her eyes, shook her head and quoted a portion of scripture. "I know Who I believed, and I'm persuaded that He is able."

Jean prayed. "Lord, help me. Lord, help the girls and Tom and our friends. Lord, I can't walk through this in my own strength. I need You." Jean turned her face into her husband's chest and embraced him. Tears, more tears—so many tears. Tom held her tightly.

Neither Tom nor Jean spoke for a long time. Then in a broken voice Tom whispered. "Though the fig tree does not bud and there are no grapes on the vines, though the olive crop fails, and the fields produce no food, though there are no sheep in the pen and no cattle in the stalls, yet I will rejoice in the LORD, I will be joyful in God my Savior…Are you ready?"

Jean nodded but didn't move from Tom's embrace. It felt right.

Tom could feel her size was getting smaller by the day, but he could still feel her weight and warmth against his body. For now, he would hold on tight.

□□

Samantha poured water into the coffee maker and slipped the coffeepot back in place. The doorbell chimed. She glanced at her watch. It was only 11:15 A.M. She opened the front doors to see Callan Douglas smiling back at her with a cake in her hands.

"Hi. I hope this isn't a bad time. I know I should have called, but I could almost hear you screaming across the yards for cake. I hurried up this morning and made my favorite homemade Maple Cake with crumbled up bacon on top. I'm guessing you're one of the millions who believe—everything is better with bacon. Did I catch you at a good time?" Callan asked with a glint of mischief in her eyes.

Samantha's face beamed. "It's the best time and I just made coffee." Callan walked in carrying her *cake of obedience*. She rarely questioned the prompting of the Lord anymore. This time was no exception. She was watching one of the early morning news shows and the guest chef was demonstrating how to make a Maple Bacon Cake. Then she checked her Facebook page, and, in her news, feed was the same recipe. That was the first time she felt, coincidence—maybe. Then she opened another site on her computer looking for a recipe she was going to make for dinner and that website highlighted a recipe each day.

Guess what recipe? If you guessed Maple Bacon Cake— you'd be right! Twice might be a coincidence, but three times was enough to inquire of the Lord. She prayed, and a thought raced through her mind like an audible shout, *"Samantha needs you."* She didn't hesitate but went to the kitchen to bake the cake as fast as she could.

Callan followed Samantha to the kitchen and placed the cake on the countertop and took a seat at the kitchen island.

"Callan, something really strange happened this morning. I felt like I needed to talk to someone. I just needed a friend. Your name came to mind and I was ready to pick up the phone to call you when another person called and asked to come over for lunch." Samantha offered the information freely to Callan while she plated the cake and poured the freshly brewed coffee.

"Oh. I'm sorry. My coming over was very impulsive. I should have called first. I won't stay long. I felt strongly this morning that you needed a friend."

Samantha stopped what she was doing and looked directly at Callan. "You have no idea. That's why I was going to call you this morning. I don't have one person in Hillbrooke that I can call my friend. It's been a rough few days."

Callan replied. "I don't know the details of what you're going through, but I wanted to tell you that I believe in the power of prayer. If you would allow me to pray for you I'd love to do that."

"My life is such a train wreck—I'd have to be crazy not to accept any help I can get. This weekend our daughter, Isabelle was admitted to the hospital with blood poisoning from an infected tattoo she gave herself. She hid it from us. It's so embarrassing." Samantha swallowed a sob. "The school counselor told us."

"I'm sorry. Is she okay—right now?"

"Physically, she'll be fine. Emotionally is another story. We have tried so many things. We took Baylee to *The Healer* downtown and we are thinking about taking Isabelle there too." Samantha spoke without emotion like she was reciting an over rehearsed poem from memory.

Callan questioned. "I don't know anything about this *Healer*. Is he a pastor from a certain church?"

"Oh no. He's located downtown about a block off Main Street. It's an old gray weathered house. It just says *The Healer* on the door. I found him online. He does chanting and massage. He was pushing his health books, herbal remedies and music CD's on us when we were there. I didn't buy anything—yet. We'll probably go back and give it a try. At this point what do I have to lose—right?"

"Let me look into this *Healer* and get back with you. It sounds dangerous to me to dabble in that sort of thing." Callan felt a check in her spirit.

"Really?" Samantha seemed surprised by Callan's concern. "I did some of this in college. It's harmless—I'm just not sure if it's doing any good. Nothing really seems to be helping either one of my girls—I'm desperate."

Callan voice was confident. "Desperate situations are the ones my God specializes in. Can I pray for you right now?" Samantha nodded her head in the affirmative.

Callan reached for Samantha's hands and held them while she prayed. "Lord Jesus, I invite You to intervene in the lives represented in this family. There are problems layered on top of problems that have formed a sticky web. But this trap is not too complicated for you. You have the power to make this right. I pray for Baylee who is suffering with pain in her legs. Lord, you can bring physical healing to her little body. Lord, in your perfect time—heal Baylee.

Callan paused and swallowed. "Also, Isabelle whose pain is not from a physical illness, yet is equally painful and dangerous to her health. Bring healing to Isabelle's emotions; soothe the pain within her by touching the empty places and hidden hurts. Bring the right person into her life to guide her into truth. Don't allow any imitation or distortion of the truth to poison her. Prepare her heart to receive the truth."

Callan cupped both of Samantha's hands in hers and continued. "I pray for the marriage of Samantha and her husband. Place a guard of protection around this family and preserve this union. Our enemy, Satan, is the destroyer of homes. He is not welcome here. Place a guard of protection at the door of this home. Deception and lies are not welcome here." Callan stopped praying.

Samantha opened her eyes and looked at Callan's face. Callan's eyes were firmly closed. Her brow was furrowed. She seemed to be listening to an unheard voice. Then she began to pray again.

"And Lord, Samantha needs You to be her burden bearer. Someone to help her shoulder the weight—the load she is carrying is too heavy. Lord, will You be the one to lift her load? Allow her to discern truth from deception. Help her know who You are, how much You love her, and how much You want to help her—even when things seem hopeless." Samantha listened intently to the words Callan prayed.

"Lord, I ask these things in Your name. Your powerful name. That name that is above all names." Then before she could say amen the tenor of her voice changed—it was no longer as one asking for favor. Callan's speech resounded with authority. "Lord, cover and protect this family from evil. Preserve this marriage and this home. Protect these children from lies and deception that comes to rob, kill and destroy." Callan paused again as if waiting for clearance of some kind. Then she ended with, "I ask all this in the name of Jesus— Amen." Callan released Samantha's hands and opened her eyes.

Samantha spoke with brokenness evident in her voice. "No one has ever prayed for me or my family before. How did you know how to pray? Who taught you that prayer? It felt alive. Does that make sense?"

"Perfect sense. I know you must meet someone for lunch, so we can talk more later. Call me anytime you need to talk. I have so much more I want to tell you. We'll do it again soon."

Callan got up to go. She figured she already held Samantha's hands—why not go ahead and give her a big hug too. She embraced Samantha and held her tight for a moment knowing in her Spirit this woman had been giving and giving without the benefit of receiving.

Callan prayed silently as she walked home cutting across the yard between the Hayes' house and hers. Lord, protect Samantha from all attacks of the enemy. Put a hedge of protection around her. Keep her heart, mind and spirit sensitive to your voice. Awaken her Spirit to know what is *truth*. Don't allow her to be blinded by deception. Callan walked up the steps of her porch and opened the front door. As she stepped inside a car slowly eased up Samantha's driveway.

Callan felt a shiver as the screen door slammed shut behind her.

13

A Crack In The Armor

Fauna leaned against the wall outside the counseling office at the Hillbrooke Middle School. The deserted hallways gave her the exhilarated feeling of wide-open spaces compared to her claustrophobic office. She glanced at her watch. Second period was about to end. Fauna backed her heels up against the wall behind her in preparation for the onslaught of teens.

The bell echoed through the hallway. Fauna readied herself for the rush of students. The hallway erupted in a sea of voices and footsteps. The students came in every size, carrying books and backpacks. Some kids passed by in a hurry while others strolled by casually. Fauna scanned the hallways. Her eyes locked in on her prey. Finding an opening, she darted out into the sea of middle schoolers zig-zagging through the crowd toward Isabelle Hayes.

Isabelle increased her pace hoping she was not the focus of the nosey counselor Ms. Reynolds. Isabelle kept her eyes straight ahead. A hand reached through the crowd and touched Isabelle's shoulder. She stopped. Resistance was futile.

"Isabelle, I need to speak with you for a few minutes in my office. I'll send a pass with you to your third hour class when we're done."

Isabelle turned and met the counselor's eyes. She did not speak a single word.

Fauna could feel the heat and hate. "Please, follow me to the office." She added to make sure Isabelle knew this was not up for debate. Fauna walked back toward her office with less resistance now that the hallway traffic had thinned out. The bell rang announcing the beginning of third hour.

Inside her office, Fauna tried to make conversation with the angry teen. "What is your third period class?"

"English..." Isabelle mumbled without emotion and spoke soft enough to cause Ms. Reynolds to lean forward to hear. Isabelle enjoyed that moment of control. She knew it had to be Ms. Reynolds who told her parents about the tattoo. Isabelle thought; if she tries to be friendly with me or apologize for telling—well— don't even bother Ms. Butterfly Tattoo 'cause I won't forgive you—not now—not ever. She crossed her arms over her chest, clenched her jaw and narrowed her eyes. This time she didn't look away but kept her focus directly on the counselor.

"I spoke with your mother on Friday about your tattoo. I noticed it was infected. Did you see a doctor over the weekend? I see you have your arm in a sling today." Fauna tried to keep things cordial.

Another muffled one-word answer. "Yep."

Fauna decided to take another approach. "I know you're not blind, Isabelle. You probably wonder why I would even care about your little tattoo seeing I have so many on my body, even one on my face." Fauna paused. She gave Isabelle a moment. The teenage brain took a bit of time to filter things through hormones and emotions.

The pause was short lived. Isabelle inhaled quickly through her nose and snorted a burst of air back out of her nose keeping her jaw clinched. Then it happened. The spew of angry words verbally gushed from Isabelle's mouth all over Ms. Reynolds. This time there was no mumbling, no whispers and no restraint.

"You make me sick. Trying to be all *look at me.* I have a tattoo on my face, but I'm an adult so I can do whatever I want. Your arms are full of tattoos. You're a freak! And you act like you're all concerned about me. Hypocrite!"

Isabelle changed her tone to a mocking voice. "Oh, Isabelle, must have a problem. I'll help her because I'm a tattooed freak show. She'll trust me." Isabelle paused to breathe. Her volume increased, "Well, you don't know how I feel. You don't know anything about me. All you know is what's written down in that file. Words—just a bunch of meaningless words, and I don't trust you." Isabelle fought the emotions welling up within, but they were too strong. Her voice began to crack. "I'm done talking. I'd like that pass now to go back to class."

It pained Fauna to hear the hateful words directed at her, but this did not dissuade her from her job or mission. She prayed a silent prayer, Lord, give me divine wisdom. Give me favor with Isabelle. Help this wounded child.

Isabelle stood up demanding. "Can I have that pass? I'm done here." She put her palm up directly in Fauna's face.

Fauna opened her desk drawer and pulled out the tablet of hall passes. She wrote down the date, time and a quick reason for Isabelle's tardiness. Then she pulled the sheet from the pad. Fauna laid the pass on her desk and put her hand firmly on top of the yellow paper. She looked up past Isabelle's empty hand and met her glaring eyes.

This time Fauna narrowed her eyes. She stood up keeping one hand on the paper. With her free hand she reached over and shut her office door with a firm push. There was a large window in her office that looked out into the waiting area. It was for the counselor's own protection. Fauna sat back down and told Isabelle to do the same. Shutting the door had done the trick. Isabelle reverted to a caged animal mentality and obediently sat.

"Isabelle, I'm going to do something that most professional counselors wouldn't do. We are taught that we should never reveal anything personal to the ones we counsel, but I think you need to know this." Fauna moved in her seat to find a comfortable spot, folded her arms across the desk and leaned forward.

"You know, Isabelle, you're not the first kid who's had it rough at home, and you won't be the last." And with that Isabelle heard the story of Fauna. She didn't spare this fourteen-year-old girl many of the details of her life. Isabelle heard in detail the miserable childhood of Fauna Reynolds. She listened with a new-found respect for the tattooed authority figure. Ms. Reynolds told her the *whole story*— including salvation. She unfolded the gospel message of a Savior who redeems junk that nobody else wants. When she was finished there was a slight dent in the teens' armor.

"Before you go back to class, Isabelle, I'm going to pray with you. I'm going to close my eyes, but you can do whatever makes you comfortable." Fauna bowed her head and began to pray, "Lord, I pray for Isabelle asking that you bring healing to the pain she is feeling—touch her. Help her know that she is special and loved. You took her pain before she was even born. You carried it, so she wouldn't have to. Help her know how much you care about her and love her. Your Word says that you value her so much that you gave Your Son to take her place. Lord, tear down the walls that she has built. Help Isabelle see how much You value her. You have not forgotten her. Protect her I pray in Jesus name. Amen."

Fauna opened her eyes and looked up. Standing outside her office window was another school counselor. The expression on her face was one of confusion. Fauna slid the pass across her desk to Isabelle. "Anytime you want to talk, I'm here." Isabelle picked up the paper and walked out of the office without saying a word.

The other counselor poked her head in Fauna's office and said, "Were you praying with that girl?"

"Yes, and it felt great! If you want me to pray with you, just ask."

With that the other counselor arched her eye brows and tightened her mouth to a vertical line. "We only have a week left of school. You better watch yourself." Then she added with a laugh, "That kind of stuff could go on your permanent record." She turned and walked toward the school's administrative offices. Fauna whispered, "Lord, let your will be done."

□□

Debbie and Kim, the daughters of Tom and Jean, were both married living in different states. Debbie, the eldest, and her husband were active in their community church where they team-taught the elementary Sunday school class. They had two school age children. Debbie was a stay-at-home mom and her husband owned a construction company in their town.

Kim was married but had chosen to raise two rescued dogs instead of children. The idea of children was not completely off the table for Kim—just not now, as she often told the people who felt they had the right to know such personal information. The 'not now' comment gave Jean and Tom the hope that their family wasn't complete—not yet.

These two girls couldn't be more opposite. They were raised by the same parents, under the same conditions, but Debbie had the passive, sweet nature of her mother while Kim had the take-charge nature of her father. This trait served Tom well in the corporate world as well as Kim in the birth of her own business. She was driven, accomplished and wanted things done her way. Kim and her husband were church attenders, on the fringe, part of the crowd—marginally part of the church community.

The one thing both girls did share was an overwhelming love and respect for their parents. Thanksgiving, Christmas, Easter and one week in the summer marked the family's traditional gatherings. These occasions were held sacred and all schedules were cleared to make time to be together. Even in the mist of differences, love was present when they came together to celebrate.

□□

Tom sat on the sofa and Jean stood at the window, each looking out reflectively at the peaceful lake. Tom reached for the cell phone lying on the coffee table in front of him. It felt exceptionally heavy in his hand. For a moment, he imagined not making the call. He could stay in this moment forever. He would love to reject the diagnosis. Denying their time was ticking away moment by moment. Denying that it was time to tell the people in their lives whom they loved. He felt pent up rage for his situation. Tom felt the truth of Jean's sickness devour the dream of their future.

Tom patted the seat on the couch next to him motioning for Jean to come and sit down. Her thin frame moved away from the window toward Tom. Jean sat down so close to Tom that their sides were touching.

Telling their daughters this news was the hardest thing they had ever faced in their years together—*so far.*

Tom dialed the number and turned on the speaker phone. They would do this together as they had done all family related things together for the past 45 years.

Their eldest daughter, Debbie, picked up on the second ring. "Hi Mom—what's up?"

"It's me, Dad. How are things going?"

"Well, this is a surprise. You don't call very often." Debbie let out a little laugh. A serious tone followed, "Why *are you* calling? Is everything okay? Where is mom?"
Jean piped in. "I'm here too."

"So, what are you both doing calling me? Is Kim gonna have a baby—finally?"

"No, Honey, I have some difficult news I need to share with you. Is Gary home?"

"No Dad. He's at work. You're scaring me. Did something happen to Kim? Come on what's going on?"

Tom gave his daughter the grim diagnosis the best he could. He ended with, "We still have to call Kim."

Jean broke the silence. "Honey, I know this is hard and you have a lot of questions." She paused and looked at Tom for strength. He squeezed her hand and she continued. "We've talked and prayed about this. We've only known for a few days."

The sound of soft sniffles came through the phone. Debbie repeated one word over and over, "Mom—Mom—oh, Mom."

"Debbie, we love you. Dad's going to pray with you before we call Kim." Jean nodded her head at Tom to pray. She bent forward and buried her face in her hands to stifle the sound of her sobs. There was no fight left in her and she surrendered to the emotions that she had held at bay.

"Baby let's pray." In brokenness Tom poured out his prayer and their daughter tightened her grip on the phone feeling she would surely be swallowed alive. She tried to believe and agree with her father for a miracle. Her faith was being sorely tested. Father, mother and daughter said their good byes only to relive it all again with daughter number two, Kim.

Kim didn't initially cry. She took the road of denial and unbelief repeating the words, "No, no, no! I won't believe it. It's a mistake. They made a mistake. Did you get a second opinion? Doctors make mistakes."

Tom tried to reassure her, but Kim's denial was firm. She was immovable in her disbelief like Thomas in the Bible. She would have to see with her eyes, touch the medical records with her hands and hear the doctors before she would accept the report.

Kim ended the conversation with, "I'm coming as soon as I can make arrangements. I need to speak to the doctor in person!"

Tom prayed with Kim. Following the prayer, she remained determined to have the outcome she wanted.
It was done.

Jean and Tom embraced holding on far longer than the quick hello or parting hugs of the past. When Jean released her husband, she looked at his moist eyes and said. "I want to live Tom, but I'm not afraid to die."

"I know. But are you sure you don't want to at least try the medical treatment? Give it a fighting chance." He punched the air with his fist.

"My only chance is God. You heard the prognosis. I only have weeks, maybe months. Either God heals me, or I die and see my Savior face to face. I'm trying to look at that as a win/win. My only regret will be to leave you and the girls." Jean surrendered again to her tears.

Tom continued to hold her until she regained her ability to speak.

"Tom…promise me that you'll be okay. I need to hear it." A longing filled Jean. She wanted her daughters with her— one more time. Soon everything she believed would be fiercely tested. "I promise. Both the girls and I—will be okay."

14

Cast Your Cares On Me

Heidi turned her car into Samantha's driveway. A woman walking away from the Hayes house toward the parsonage looked a lot like Callan. Heidi felt a prickly heat on her arms. She cursed Callan Douglas, her husband, her children and her church. That woman deserves whatever comes her way, Heidi thought, wondering if Callan had been at the Hayes house. Heidi breathed in a deep cleansing breath followed by a quiver that passed through her whole body—just like *The Healer* taught her.

Heidi looked at her refection in the rearview mirror checking to be sure her makeup was applied with perfection. She wasn't sure who might be home for lunch. She gracefully eased out of the car, opened the trunk and took out a box full of takeout foods and headed to the front door. Balancing the food, she extended one free finger and pushed the doorbell.

Samantha opened the door and greeted Heidi with a smile. Heidi saw a much different face than she remembered from their last meeting. This Samantha looked content—even pretty. Her voice sounded less needy than it had a few hours ago when she imposed herself on Samantha for lunch.

"Come in. It was kind of you to consider bringing lunch for Baylee and me." Samantha stepped back and allowed Heidi into her home.

Heidi entered the Hayes house scanning the entry wall photos like a cat on the prowl. From the hallway, she took in as much of Samantha's decorating skill as she could. She did a quick inventory of the quality of the furnishings, art value and knickknacks. Heidi prided herself on her ability to do this on the few steps to the kitchen. She decided the family photos would give her the best bang for her verbal buck.

"Samantha, I love that wall of family pictures. What a beautiful tribute to a loving family." She watched Samantha closely for a reaction.

"Thank you. There's a lot of history on that wall. It reminds me of all the wonderful things about being a wife and mother but also that families aren't perfect. I remember the back-story to each one of those photos." Samantha paused and shook her head. "Some make me smile—others I would prefer not to dwell on. Still, together they make up the story of our lives."

Heidi kept her expressions neutral hoping her inward thoughts would not be revealed. The picture explanation was too sloppy and sentimental for her liking, but it did give her the confirmation—all was not harmonious in the Hayes house.

Heidi thought—fine. Two can play at this game—you want sloppy—I can give you sloppy. "Samantha, that was well said and so true. It's the good and bad times that make a family and help them endure through the tests of time." Heidi felt like throwing up in her mouth. A blissful family life for Heidi would be a rich husband who worked a lot of hours outside the home and stepchildren in boarding school. No family pictures necessary unless they were vacation photos of she and her husband on a cruise or at an all-inclusive resort somewhere wonderful! Her own humor brought a smirk to her face.

Remembering the purpose of the house call Heidi asked. "Will it just be the two of us or will Baylee or your husband be joining us?" Heidi slipped onto the nearest bar stool at the kitchen island.

"Stuart definitely won't be joining us. He hasn't been home for lunch in years. Baylee had a sandwich in her room earlier, so I guess it'll just be the two of us."

Her mouth said, "Awesome," but her heart said—that's a big disappointment. She continued with, "I was hoping it would be just the two of us. That will give us a chance to get to know one another better. There's so much I'd love to know about your family." Heidi smiled. She imagined a cat gulping up a canary and licking its lips as she watched Samantha unpack the to-go boxes.

Following lunch and a ton of personal questions, Heidi said her good byes to Samantha. Back in her car, Heidi recalled the highlights of their conversation as she interpreted them. There were no new revelations; pretty much the stuff she assumed from the first few encounters with the Hayes family. On the positive side she was finally able to pin Samantha down on the possibility of taking Isabelle out Samantha would check with Isabelle and if she wanted to go out—they would select a time and place. Taking a teenager out for dinner and a movie would be a small price to pay to find out how she should move forward for *The Healer* and for herself.

Samantha stood at the door and waved goodbye to Heidi. It had been a long time since Samantha had felt happy—truly happy. Over the past years, happiness had been fleeting, but today she went from no friends to two in a matter of hours.

She had always prided herself in being a good judge of character. There was something confusing to her about Heidi.

What it was exactly, Samantha couldn't put her finger on it. The moment she would feel a red flag on the play giving her second thoughts about Heidi, the woman would say the perfect thing to bring Samantha back around. She wanted to trust Heidi, but she also wanted to follow her instincts. Her daughter, Isabelle, seemed to like this woman so if socializing with Heidi gave Isabelle an outlet for her anger then, so be it. And if *The Healer* could help Isabelle and Baylee—Samantha wouldn't stand in the way of that either.

Callan had never given Samantha a reason to be concerned. She was attentive in a caring way knowing when to listen and when to speak. Samantha knew this type of friend was a rare find. The sight of the Maple Bacon Cake on the counter brought her thoughts full circle.

□□

On Wednesday mornings Pastor Rey prayed for the church membership, staff and other needs in the community. He walked, knelt, stood or sat. Occasionally, he even lay prostrate on the floor. He usually prayed in the privacy of his office. Sometimes he prayed in the well-appointed prayer room, where each wall held a banner giving suggestions who to pray for; missionaries, government officials, church ministries, the sick. The conference room also served as a place to meet for prayer for various groups in the church, but today Pastor Rey felt drawn to the church sanctuary.

The urgency to bury his face in the carpet at the altar propelled him to move outside the office—nothing I else would do.

"I'll be in the sanctuary praying." Rey yelled back to Grace as the office door shut behind him. That was all he had to say.

Grace knew the rest without Pastor saying a word. She would not disturb him unless Callan called. This was not his regular Wednesday morning prayer time but rather one of his impromptu prayer times. Pastor Rey obeyed as the Spirit led. He started out walking in the sanctuary in front of the altar. He ended up on his face at the door of the prayer room.

Twenty-five minutes passed before Pastor Rey stood. He looked at his watch. It was lunch time. Walking back toward the office he reached in his pocket pulled out his cell phone and called Callan.

Two rings later Callan answered. "I hope you're calling because you want to take me out for lunch."

"Well, okay—that sounds great! We only have a week before school is out for the summer. We'd better take advantage of lunches for two before they become lunches for four."

"You must have forgotten the boys only have one more day before their summer break."

"How did I miss that?" Rey shook his head in mock frustration.

"Oh—I don't know maybe between being a pastor, Ty's broken arm and being accused of having an affair with your secretary— you didn't notice it was June!" Callan cocked her head to one side to add emphasis to her words.

"Okay, message received. *Slow down.* I'll be there in fifteen minutes." There was a pause and then Rey added, "There is one more thing I wanted to tell you. I'm not sure how else to say this except to come right out and say it. When I was praying this morning, I felt the Lord speaking to me." Rey paused while he pondered how to put the next part into words. "I believe He was saying, *don't worry—it's all under control.*"

"What?" Callan felt a tightening in her chest. In a concerned tone she asked. "Is there something I should know?"

"No. I felt an urgency to pray that was all. My spirit felt heavy and I went into the sanctuary to pray. I feel like it was for both of us. It's a reminder from the Lord—we are not supposed to get worried about something that may be coming because *He has it all under control*. That's it."

"Do you think something bad is coming our way? I mean, Ty already broke his arm. Maybe the message was delayed or maybe it's in regard to that false accusation. What if something bad is coming because of that?"

Rey assured her with a calm voice. "I'm sharing this with you because if something does happen sometime soon—we can both be reminded that the Lord has already prepared us that He has everything under control. We need to trust him. He is not surprised by anything that's coming."

With a huff in her voice, Callan replied. "Fine! I'm not going to worry about something that hasn't even happened." After a thoughtful pause, Callan's patience returned. "I might need a gentle reminder, when and if something does happen, because— you know me—it's my nature to run back to my old ways."

Rey kept quiet. He knew Callan didn't need to be reminded of days gone by.

Following a moment where neither Callan nor Rey spoke, Callan said, "Are you on your way home yet?"

"No. I'm just walking out the church door."

"Okay—see you in a few."

"Callan. Wait! Before you go—what do you think about going to that little restaurant on the edge of town?"

"Sure. I want to drive by a place called *The Healer*. It's downtown."

"Are you looking for another church?" Rey laughed at his own joke.

"No. I visited with Samantha Hayes this morning and she mentioned this place. It sounds New Age and kinda creepy. I just wanted to check it out. She seems naïve about evil. I'm concerned. I'll just leave it at that."

Then Callan added. "I almost forgot to tell you. I was able to pray with Samantha this morning about the turmoil in her life. She seemed genuinely happy to see me when I stopped over. I think our time together was positive. I'm trying hard not to be pushy with her. I just want to lay one brick at a time."

Callan had straitened up the kitchen, freshened up her make-up and thrown a load of laundry in the washer all while talking to her husband. She ended the call with, "I'll see you in a few."

□□

Isabelle entered the code for the garage door and waited for the door to open. Moments later, she casually strolled into the kitchen. Samantha tentatively watched from behind the kitchen island trying to gauge Isabelle's mood. Her daughter made direct eye contact with her. Samantha slightly smiled at her daughter, and Isabelle returned the smile in kind.

Feeling brave, Samantha ventured a question. "How was your day Issie?"

"Pretty good." Isabelle laid her backpack on the floor and took a seat at the kitchen island. Samantha couldn't remember the last time Isabelle had sat at the island without being told to do so.

"Are you hungry?"

"What do ya have?"

"This is a delicious cake that Mrs. Douglas, from a few doors down, brought over this morning." Samantha pushed the cake toward Isabelle. Isabelle swiped her index finger along the side of the layer cake taking an ample finger of frosting and tasted the bounty.

"That's good. I'll have a piece and some milk."

Samantha moved quickly hoping she would not wake from the dream. She pushed the plate with cake and a mug of milk toward Isabelle and waited.

"Mom?"

"Yes."

"I talked to that counselor again today at school. You know— the one who you met last week. I think she isn't as awful as I thought."

"Really?" Samantha wanted to keep the conversation going if she could by allowing Isabelle to lead the way.

"You just never know what people are going through when you first meet them. Sometimes a person can appear to be just what you think you want or need, but then later they turn out to be the worst thing possible for you or vice versa." Isabelle took a bite of cake and savored the flavor then washed it down with a gulp of milk.

Samantha attempted a question. "Were you thinking of anyone specific?"

"No, not really. Just people can fool you. You really have to be careful not to judge good or bad too quickly."

"My—my, aren't you wise beyond your years today. Was it Ms. Reynolds who helped you see this?"

"Sorta." Isabelle replied.

"Well you can spend as much time with her as you want. I like this new attitude. Oh, by the way, Heidi Alden, the lady who drove you home last week in the rain storm, stopped by

today and we had lunch together. She wants to take you out
Friday to dinner and a movie. Do you want to go with her?"

"I don't know. That seems kinda weird. Why me?"

"You don't have to go out with her—only if you want to."

"I'll think about it."

Isabelle finished her cake and pushed the empty plate back
toward her mom. "Thanks Mom." She grabbed her backpack
and headed upstairs.

Samantha stood in the kitchen, a feeling of joy swept over
her. This must be how moms with happy, healthy and well-
behaved children feel daily. She closed her eyes and breathed
deeply, savoring the moment.

A piercing scream invaded her happy moment followed by
the familiar call for help.

Samantha rushed up the stairs to Baylee's room. She was
not prepared for what she saw. Knelt next to the bed, Isabelle
stroked Baylee's hair and spoke softly, even kindly, to her little
sister. "Mom's coming. It'll be okay, Sissy."

It was a picture Samantha had longed to see and it proved
more than she could endure.

□□

Callan had an hour before the boys got off the bus. While
downtown with Rey they drove by *The Healer's* place of
business.

"Rey, there it is." She pointed at the weathered building.

"Could we stop for a minute for me to get some
information?" "I'm sorry. I must get back to the church. I
have an appointment."

Callan studied the business as Rey drove by. "I'll look it
up online when I get home."

Rey reached over and took Callan's hand, holding it in his. His eyes still on the road and his thoughts consumed with the issues he faced.

Callen placed her hand over Rey's and they drove on in silence until they turned into the parsonage driveway. Callan waved good-bye to Rey and headed into the house. She grabbed her iPad lying on the family room sofa and sat down in the recliner, propped her feet up and did an Internet search on *The Healer.* A question popped up on the screen asking for permission to use her location. Callan chose the box marked "yes." The first place on the list showed an address located in downtown Hillbrooke with a picture of the place they had driven by minutes ago.

Callan clicked on the link to open the website. The webpage was obviously homemade with an array of snapshots arranged like they were casually laid on a table slightly overlapping. The top picture showed a turn-of-the-century home with gray shingled siding. A crudely, carved sign hung on the door with the words *The Healer* burned into the wood.

Callan navigated the few tabs on the website. What she read was scary and alarming. The comments and testimonials caused the hair on the back of her neck to prickle.

"The touch of *The Healer* sent waves of peace rushing through my body."

"*The Healer* is skilled in relieving pain and the room where he healed me was serene."

"I was full of hate and anger until *The Healer* placed his hands on my head and chanted over me. Then my mind felt like it was being bathed in a vat of warm oil. My anger was gone. My hate turned to love."

Callan had felt some of these same things when she encountered the power of the Baptism in the Holy Spirit, but the words she read on this website were empty, giving credit to someone other than God. It seemed counterfeit and empty. These comments did not bring peace or reassurance to her heart, but rather an urgent call to pray.

Callan laid her iPad on the end table and closed her eyes. A sense of impending danger swept over her. She bypassed her known language surrendering to the wooing of the Spirit by praying with groans and in an unknown tongue. She knew as she prayed that an unseen spiritual battle had ensued between a known victor and a defeated foe.

The sound of the backdoor slamming ended Callan's intercession. Glancing at the clock she was surprised how much time had passed.

Zander rushed into the family room, dropped his backpack at his mom's feet and yelled in a song like chant, "We're almost out of school! We're almost out of school!" After delivering this important news in song, he turned and headed for the kitchen. He yelled back over his shoulder, "Can I get a snack?"

"Dinner will be ready in an hour so only fruit or a cheese stick."

A groan of disapproval came from the kitchen.

Ty was moments behind his brother. He walked up to Callan and examined her face. "Mom, have you been crying?"

"I was praying."

"Oh." Ty moved his mouth to one side and nodded with understanding. "*That* kind of praying."

"What do you mean, *that* kind of praying?"

"You know, Mom. The kind where you and Jesus hold hands."

"What?"

"Like the time you prayed over me when I fell off my bike and broke my arm." Ty raised his arm in the cast as a reminder, just in case his mom had forgotten the incident. "When you prayed for me you weren't alone."

"Huh?"

"You know. Jesus was with you, and you guys were partners. It was like when you pick someone to dance with. You hold out your hand and your partner takes your hand. We did square dancing in school like that and when the person takes your hand then you're partners."

Callan felt her heart rate increase. "I think you're a bit confused about what happened that day. You did hit your head pretty hard. Zander and I held hands and I prayed for you."

"No Mom. It was Jesus. You prayed, and He held your hand." Ty's voice was full of emotion. "I knew I was going to be okay because you and Jesus were dancing. He was your partner. He was singing over me."

Callan decided not to press the subject anymore. She could see Ty's jaw tightening up. She knew that look of frustration—when he felt he was not being understood. She remembered that same look from past disagreements with this strong-willed son. In his childlike way, his description was actually a pretty clear picture of prayer.

The picture of the 'prayer dance' suddenly became clear in Callan's mind—her reaching her hand out to the Lord and Him in return accepting it. Then the beautiful dance begins. The picture brought a smile to her face. Immediately the words formed in her mind. *I am the Lord your God. I am with you. I will bring victory. I will create calm in the midst of the storm, and with My love I will dance over you and rejoice in song.*

Ty still stood in front of his mom. His face relaxed into a knowing smile. "You get it, now don't you? I was right. It was Jesus. He's your partner."

Callan sat—speechless—tears formed in her eyes.

Ty walked toward the kitchen saying to no one in particular, "I think I'll have a banana for snack."

The sweet presence of the Lord surrounded Callan. It was gentle but fierce. It was peaceful yet empowering. It brought clarity during confusion. She glanced over at the iPad sitting next to her and touched the screen awakening the homepage for *The Healer*. She touched the phone number on the screen and the sound of the dialing number was heard through the speaker.

After two rings a recorded female voice answered. "Peace and healing be with you. You've reached the office of *The Healer*. Our office is closed at this time. Please leave a detailed message following the chime. We will return your call soon. Be whole."

There was something discomforting and familiar about that voice. A feeling of dread gripped Callan. She ended the call without leaving a message. She opened *The Healer*'s website again and found the name of the owner, Victor Darwin.
I'll look that up later—maybe after dinner.

A loud crash in the kitchen brought Callan back to mom mode. "Hey, boys what's going on out there?"

"Zander broke the fruit bowl." Ty reported.

Callan signed loudly as she walked to the broom closet. She repeated a familiar phrase that she had been saying daily for years. "I love my boys. Boys are awesome. Boys are fun. I love my boys. Boys are awesome. Boys are fun."
Zander yelled in defense. "It was an accident."

When Callan arrived in the kitchen the fruit she had bought was covered with shards of glass and the bowl given to them on their wedding day was beyond repair. She paused for a moment calculating the risk of trying to remove the glass from the fruit. She realized it would be pointless and pulled the waste basket over to clean up the mess.

"Boys go eat your snacks in the family room. You can watch a show until dinner." The boys scurried off. Callan bent down and began cleaning up the mess. "I love my boys. Boys are awesome. Boys are fun. I love my boys. Boys are awesome. Boys are fun."

15

No News Is Good News

Callan finished cleaning up after dinner then joined Rey on the back deck to watch the boys toss the softball. It was one of those rare nights at the parsonage when they were able to be together without a kid's sporting event or church activity.

Callan sat in the porch swing with Rey. "I didn't tell you yet the whole story of praying with Samantha today. Do you want the detailed story or the condensed version?"

"Give me the detailed version with just the facts." Rey glanced at his wife for a moment to read her mood. Then added, "Do over! Tell me the story however you want. I'm listening."

"Good choice!" Callan lowered her eye brows. "From the time I woke up this morning until now, I have felt the presence of the Lord in a powerful way..." It felt good to share her day with Rey. They usually couldn't talk about daily activities until the boys were in bed.

Callan unfolded the events of the Maple Bacon Cake, the visit with Samantha Hayes, *the Healer's* website, Ty's revelation of *the prayer dance*—all the way to the broken fruit bowl.

Rey focused on his wife with amazement. "I guess I should ask you more often—what you did?"

Callan confessed. "I'll admit all my days aren't as full as this one."

Rey looked out in the yard at his sons. "What about that Ty— isn't that insightful? That's my boy!"

"I know—pretty amazing coming from an eight-year-old, and he was firm on what he saw." Callan stopped and pointed to her jaw. "You know how he sets his jaw when he's about to go into defense mode. Well, when I saw that—I knew it was a *'pick-your battles'* | kind of moment." They both laughed.

The phone sitting on the table between them vibrated then busted into a praise song. Rey picked up the phone to check the caller I.D.

"It's the Brown's. Should we take it?"

Callan rolled her eyes. "Well—of course."

Rey answered the phone.

Callan listened to Rey's side of the conversation. His face looked concerned.

"You probably figured out by that conversation that Jean and Tom are stopping over. Something is going on with them. Not sure what, but I think we're about to find out. They'll be here in about 15-minutes."

Callan called the boys in and got them settled in their room with a video game. Tom and Jean arrived twenty minutes later.

□□

Fauna saw the "*Help Wanted*" sign in the restaurant window. She pulled into the parking space at the back of the building and entered the restaurant from the parking lot. It was a Mom and Pop operation at best. The tables were all square with four chairs per table—no booths. The menu was carefully written on a chalk board over the counter. The cooking was done in full view of all who entered.

An L-shaped counter area separated the kitchen from the restaurant and had seating for twelve people. There were five customers in the whole place. Tips would be minimal here, plus it was a huge step down from school counselor to waitress in a dive diner. She swallowed hard and stood at the counter until the cook walked over to take her order.

"What'a ya hav'n?"

"I was interested in applying for the waitress position. Is it still available?"

"Yeah. It pays $3 an hour and you bus your own tables. I need ya mostly during rushes at breakfast, lunch and dinner. You can have off time when the traffic is low. You don't split tips either. What you get is yours."

"I can't begin until my current job ends in one week. And I can't work Thursday nights or Sunday mornings. If that works for you then I'm interested."

"Sure. Come back when you're ready to start and we'll do the paper work then." He walked back to the grill and flipped a few burgers.

Fauna wanted to order food but didn't want to disturb his concentration. She left feeling content to be employed, at least while she waited to see what would happen with her counseling job. She did have a few leads, but until something permanent opened she was back to waitressing.

□□

Callan wiped the countertops while she paced in the kitchen waiting for the coffee to brew. The sound of the doorbell gave her a start. She felt blasts of nervousness rush through her body.

Rey answered the door and welcomed Jean and Tom in with the usual hugs. The two couples settled down in the formal living room. A tray of coffee and a plate of cookies sat untouched on the coffee table. Tension hung in the air— something Rey had never sensed before in the presence of this godly couple.

Rey broke the silence. "Tom, I've felt you and Jean have been exceptionally quiet the past few weeks. Is there something Callan and I could do to help?"

Six years ago, Tom and Jean Brown became their spiritual parents. Directing them into a deeper, fuller relationship with Christ, one they never imagined possible. Tom and Jean walked with them through a dark time in their personal lives. Since that time, they had been the go-to couple for Rey and Callan. It was unsettling to see these giants in the faith going through their own personal battle.

Tom took Jean's hand and blurted out the news. "We received some bad news recently. We are still processing it and praying. We've had to make some difficult decisions and we felt we needed to let you both know what's happening."

Rey's throat immediately felt dry. He glanced at Callan who wore her feelings on her face. She looked like her whole world was crashing down.

Tom cleared his throat again giving the facts without frills. "Jean has been diagnosed with pancreatic cancer. The prognosis is grim, and she has chosen not to have any traditional treatment. We have made the difficult decision to step down from our position as small group leaders. We do have a recommendation for who could take our place. I thought we could announce it this week on Thursday at our regular meeting." It was a mouthful, but Tom got it all out in one breathless statement.

No one spoke for a moment, then Tom added. "That is if you approve, Pastor."

Callan pulled a tissue from the box that still sat on the coffee table from a week ago when Grace stopped by. She moved next to Jean on the sofa. She put her arms around her dear friend and held her tightly. No words passed between them.

Callan wanted to be the one to bring comfort to this amazing woman. She wanted to say the right thing, do the right thing and be there for Jean in her time of need. In her heart she wished it was Jean who would embrace her as she had done so many times before when Callan was sad, worried, hurt or spiritually in need. She needed this godly woman in her life.

Then Callan felt Jean's hand slip to her back and begin to comfort her with soft pats. "It's okay, dear. We're a bit ahead of you." Jean paused then added in a whisper. "We know Whom we have believed and are persuaded that He is able."

Callan laid her head on Jean's shoulder and wept freely— for the second time that day.

The Browns and Douglas's prayed together asking God to step into the situation in all His might and power to bring physical healing as His Word proclaimed. After their prayer time there were many questions about the what, when, why and how of the situation.

A break in the conversation gave Rey the opportunity to ask Tom, "Who did you want to recommend to fill-in for you and Jean. I can't bring myself to say replace. Is that okay with you?"

"I pray it's just a fill-in. I know some people think this might sound cliché, but Jean and I are praying for healing—with the add-on—God's will be done."

"Then we will stand and believe with you for both healing and God's will." The emotions were raw but the faith to believe was seasoned.

Tom nodded in agreement. "Jean and I have prayed about who would replace us as small group leaders. I know this may seem unconventional, but we feel strongly it should be Snake and Fauna. Before you state the obvious, let me say I know they aren't married. I thought Snake could use his house and he could lead the discussion and prayer time, while Fauna hosted by overseeing the food and fellowship time. Do you think they're ready for the challenge?"

Rey sat silently contemplating the recommendation. Then he spoke. "It may work. Let me pray about it and talk with Callan. If the Lord gives me the green light, then I'll talk with both and see how they feel. When did you want to step down?"

Jean answered. "Maybe we could handle two more weeks. Our girls will be arriving in the next few days and as much as we want things to remain the same, I know there may be some changes ahead for all of us."

"You tell us what works best for you. We can make phone calls and end it now. That would give you more time with your girls."

"Pastor that may be best," Tom glanced at Jean. "It is difficult for us to step away from this ministry. Jean and the girls must come first right now."

Jean looked at Tom and nodded in agreement.

Callan assured them. "Don't worry. We'll take care of everything and make the phone calls."

"Thank you both. We've taken enough of your time. Let us know where the meeting will be on Thursday. Whenever we're able we'd still love to attend." Tom helped Jean up from the couch.

Callan stood too and took Jean's hand. "Rey, can we all pray before they go?"

Rey nodded his head and reached for Tom's hand. They formed a prayer circle. Rey led in prayer; for peace, for wisdom, for healing, for strength—just as he had done many times before. Only this time the crisis was personal.

Callan and Rey walked Jean and Tom to their car. Rey hugged Tom tightly and said, "I'll call you tomorrow."

Rey took Callan's hand as they watched Tom and Jean back away. They walked back to the house. Once inside the safety of the parsonage Rey broke. Callan held her strong husband around the waist. He wrapped his arms around her and rested his chin on the top of her head. Callan felt the weight of his sorrow.

Through his pain, Rey spoke. "What will we do without her?"

"No. We can believe for a healing. I know it. God will heal her if we ask."

"Callan, people have to die sometime. We aren't meant to live in this world forever."

"I'm just not ready to stop believing for a positive outcome. I can't. Healing is real. It could happen. We must pray for it. Believe."

Rey pulled back his wife and held her at arm's length. His eyes still moist he looked directly into Callan's face. "Death isn't an enemy and it's not to be feared by the Believer."

Callan's eyes pooled with tears. "I won't stop believing for God to heal her. I won't!" Callan cleared her throat and said. "Let's have Snake and Fauna over for dinner in a few days. I'll call the rest of the small group members."

"Okay. I know what I'll be praying about tomorrow."

"I just can't believe it. I can't. I won't."

Rey opened his arms and Callan melted into them locking her arms around his waist. They held each other for longer than usual.

Footsteps echoed down the hallway. Ty slid to a stop on the hardwood floors.

"Are you guys dancing?" Ty smiled and threw his good arm around both reaching full circle with his casted arm. He awkwardly swayed back and forth with them.

□□

The boys and Rey were sleeping when Callan crept down the hallway to the quiet of the family room. She clicked on the lamp closest to the recliner and soaked in the quietness. In 30 minutes the sound of the boys getting ready for school, and Rey preparing to leave for the office, would fill the house.

Callan reached for her iPad and opened the webpage for *The Healer*. She clicked on the owner's name, Victor Darwin. *The Healer* claimed to have the ability to bring spiritual wholeness by means of chanting, prayers and massage—not to mention healings for physical, mental and even sexual abuse. Callan felt chills as she read what she knew were false claims. They held classes at the office to teach students how to contact the spirit world, how to make energy life choices and have a healthy aura. She scrolled through the paragraphs of psychic mumbo jumbo feeling sick in her stomach at the thought of

Samantha Hayes and poor little Baylee being connected in any way to such foolishness.

Callan breathed the name of Jesus as she plowed through the disturbing information. The picture of Victor Darwin was creepy. His hair was shiny and black making his skin look ghostly white. His dark-framed glasses added to his lifeless complexion. Callan couldn't tell from the photograph if he was tall or short—heavy or trim. His eyes seemed to follow her as she maneuvered through the website popping up on each new page.

Callan had seen enough. This place and this man were dangerous—this she felt in her spirit. She laid her hand on her iPad and began to pray in the Spirit. She knew this was not a battle she could win without the help of the Lord.

"Father, I come asking for Your divine intervention. I need You and I need You now. I'm asking, not demanding, not screaming, not yelling…I'm asking my Father. Please destroy the foothold of the enemy and move this evil business out of Hillbrooke."

Callan signed. "This man, Victor Darwin, has even tried to steal your name. You Lord are Healer. The one and only Healer, Jehovah Rapha, the God who heals. Lord, please open the eyes of each person that walks through the doors of that business. Give them the sensitivity of Your Spirit to discern truth from lies, counterfeit from what is real. If the people searching have ever known You even in the slightest way, rock their very being with Your presence in a transforming way."

A wave of emotion washed over Callan as she continued her prayer. "If they have never called on You, make a way in the midst of this evil for them to know truth. Lead them into Your Truth. Your Word says that the weapons of our warfare are not carnal but mighty through You, Lord. And these weapons have the power to pull down strongholds. Destroy the stronghold of lies and sickness and rise up in their place—truth and healing."

Callan continued to call on the Name of the Lord until the burden lifted.

Callan closed her iPad when she heard footsteps coming down the hallway. She knew this was now in the hands of the Lord. She would wait for the Lord to do what He promised in His Word He would do.

A sleepy Ty rounded the corner into the family room and curled up next to his mom in the recliner. Callan slipped her arm around her son and drew him in for morning snuggles. Ty put his good hand on top of Callan's and patted it.

"Mom, when can I go see Baylee again?"

"You like her, don't you?"

"I do—she's nice. But she's not my girlfriend ya know." Ty looked up at his mom to be sure the conversation wasn't going in an unwanted direction.

Callan tussled Ty's hair and gave him a tight squeeze. "I love that you want to spend time with Baylee. I'm proud of you. Maybe I can call Samantha today and set something up. Does that sound good?"

"Yes—for tomorrow okay. I need to talk with her really soon." Ty paused then added with a hint of mischief in his voice. "I have a plan."

Callan moved Ty away from her to look directly into his eyes. "A plan? I'm not sure I like the sound of that."

Ty scooted out of the chair and stood taller than Callan remembered. "Don't worry. I'm working on a good plan. Maybe this is one of my best plans…" Ty pointed into the sky and raised his voice putting all his emphases on the word, "…EVER!" Then he turned and ran down the hallway to his bedroom.

Callan made a mental note to delve deeper into that comment later.

There were shouts coming from Zander and Ty's bedroom. Callan wasn't sure if they were giddy with excitement that school was nearly out for the summer or war was erupting, whatever the case—it was time for intervention.

Callan sighed as she walked to the battlefield just in time to see Zander on the top bunk with his arm cocked back in pitching position, a pair of balled up dirty socks in his fist ready to draw first blood.

"STOP! Come on boys let's not start the summer off like this." She positioned herself in the middle of the room blocking Zander's field of vision. "Hurry up. Breakfast will be on the table in 10 minutes and the bus will be here in 30." Callan turned to Zander and reached up to take his ammunition. He reluctantly released the socks to his mom. She left the room fighting back laughter. These two mischief-makers were the joy of her life. They always had something brewing that kept her on her toes.

After breakfast they rushed outside to wait for the bus, but not before Callan slipped in a kiss on the top of each of their heads. Standing at the door, Callan watched the boys playing at the end of the driveway. Summer would begin for all of them very soon. The bus pulled up and both boys turned to wave goodbye to their mom. Callan blew them an air kiss, waved until the bus was out of sight, and then went back inside the house.

16
Somethings Are Never Easy!

Callan glanced at the breakfast table where her cell phone was waiting. The task before her was not one she looked forward to doing. Calling all those in the small group and reliving the news of Jean's cancer would be agonizing.

Callan picked up her cell phone and made her first call of the day.

"Hi Marilyn. It's Callan. I'm not sure if you've heard about Tom and Jean yet?"

Callan shared the shocking news of Jean Brown's diagnoses— a total of six times. She notified each member of their small group—except for Snake and Fauna.

Callan cried with them. They prayed together, but it didn't get easier the more she told it.

Her last call was to Harold and Esther Smith.

"Hi Esther. This is Callan. Hope I'm not catching you at a bad time."

"No. It's never a bad time for my Pastor's wife to call."

Callan smiled. Esther was old-school. She still held the pastoral family up on a pedestal. She had never once called Rey by his name without tacking Pastor on the front of it. Whenever she introduced Callan it was always. "This is our pastor's wife." It warmed Callan's heart to be treated with such honor. She liked to fly under the radar by not revealing she was connected in any way to the clergy, but with Esther it was always sincere, giving honor where honor was due.

"Esther, I have some disturbing news I need to pass on."

"Go ahead, dear, I put you on speaker phone so that Harold can hear too."

"Tom and Jean Brown stopped by last night to tell us that Jean has been diagnosed with a terminal cancer. The prognosis in the natural doesn't look good." Callan paused to allow this news to resonate. She didn't hear a sound on the other end of the line—not a gasp, oh my, a cry, or a prayer. Nothing!

Callan continued. "Tom and Jean are going to step down from leading the small group. We believe it will be temporary. We should know more later this week sometime as to who the fill-in leaders will be. I'll contact everyone again then. I know this is a lot to absorb. We won't be meeting this Thursday either." Callan paused again to give Esther a chance to respond.

When Esther spoke, it was soft but authoritative. "I read this verse this morning, Psalms 73:26. *My health may fail, and my spirit may grow weak, but God remains the strength of my heart; he is mine forever.*" Esther added matter-of-factly, "Harold and I will pray. We know God is still in the healing business—and we know His ways are high above ours. Thanks for calling us Callan. We'll be praying for Pastor and you that the Lord would lead you in His plan for the small group leader and how to effectively walk with Jean, Tom and the Community Outreach family through this process."

"Ahhh. Okay. I'll call you both later when I know more." Callan was shocked. She didn't even ask them to pray—nor they her. She had saved the Smiths until last, believing they would take it the hardest. Every other call had been weeping, unbelief or stunned silence. With Esther it felt like she was ending a call where they had just talked about recipes—not life and death.

"Callan? Just one more thing." Esther's voice was like a sweet grandma. "Death isn't an enemy. We all fight the good fight—but eventually we *will* finish the race."

"But...what about healing and believing for healing?" There was a bit of fight in Callan's tone. She clicked the phone to speaker and laid it on the table in front of her.

"Absolutely! Believe, ask, pray, plead...then trust...God has a plan."

Callan began to sob—she couldn't speak even when she tried. She could hear Esther's voice, calm and controlled began to whisper. "Jesus...Jesus...Jesus—We love You. We trust You. You are good. You love Your children. You are Master, Savior—Lord of our lives."

Callan could hear the blending of Harold and Esther's voices as they joined in prayer—interceding for things only God, Himself knew. There in the parsonage, at the breakfast table, Callan felt her clenched fists begin to relax. Her hands open. All the fight, all the denial and all the pain she lifted to Jesus. And she sang a new song—only heaven could understand.

□□

Rey just finished his morning prayer time and picked up his phone to call Snake. Rey guessed he'd just leave a message since Snake was working.

Rey's thoughts were interrupted by a second, "Hello? Pastor are you there?"

"Sorry, Snake—yes I'm here. I was expecting voice mail."

"Hey Pastor. What's up?"

"Hey, I'll make this fast. I know you're at work."

"No, problem. I'm a multi-tasker." Snake balanced his cell phone between his shoulder and ear, while he continued typing on his keyboard.

Pastor Rey could hear a soft clicking sound coming through the phone. "I was wondering if you and Fauna could come to the parsonage for dinner on Thursday night."

"Sure. Were you thinking an early dinner before small group?"

"No. It's instead of the small group. The Brown's need to cancel for this week, they received some very bad news regarding Jean's health."

"Oh. I hope it's not serious."

"It's serious. Jean has been diagnosed with pancreatic cancer and she has chosen not to have any medical treatment."

"Pastor, I'm shocked. Of all people—Jean?" There was a moment of silence. "Pastor. I'm sorry I don't know why I said that. No one should get cancer no matter if they're good or bad. I'm just speechless. It's surreal—Jean? How is Tom? Why?"

"Snake, I stopped asking the Lord 'why and why not' a long time ago. I've learned to roll with the ups and roll with the downs—Job 13:15 says—*though He slay me yet will I hope in Him.* I'm choosing to hope and trust—not be in despair or doubt."

Snake relaxed his shoulder and held his cell phone in his hand. "Pastor, I'm gonna need a moment to process this."

"I know—it's a lot to take in, but there's more. I want to ask you something."

Snake repositioned himself in his office chair. He felt like the oxygen in the room was slowly being pulled out. There was no more air to take a deep breath. He tentatively whispered. "Okay Pastor."

Rey cleared his throat more from nerves than need. "Before dinner tomorrow night, I'd like you and Fauna to pray about becoming our new small group leaders. I know this doesn't give you much time. I believe you'll have clear direction before then."

"Okay Pastor. Fauna and I will pray, and we'll talk tomorrow."

"Thanks Snake. I knew I could count on both of you."

Snake sat in his office looking out his wall of windows that gave him a view of the ten cubicles on the work floor. Each of these workers reported directly to him. There was no place to hide. He felt his eyes well-up with emotion. Jean was sick—really sick—maybe even facing death. He thought for a moment of his own mother. How would he feel if it were her? What about the years he had lost because of bad choices? He could never get them back.

Snake picked up his cell phone and called his mom.

"Zak? Hello? Is that you?"

Silence.

"Honey. I know. We heard about Jean." Marilyn heard a soft sigh on the other end. If she could have reached through the phone lines to hold her grown son at that moment, she would have. "It's okay. We're all processing."

"Mom?"

"Yes son."

A tear rolled over the hissing snake tattooed on the side of Zak's face. "I love you."

□□

An empty box sat open on the top of Fauna's desk. The temp-job at the school would be over tomorrow. She needed to pack up the few meager personal items she allowed herself to accumulate over the past few months.

A soft tap on the open door drew Fauna's attention away from the empty box. Isabelle Hayes stood in the doorway of her office.

"Come in, Isabelle. How are you doing?" Fauna thought how the child's face looked—pleasant.

"You're leaving?"

"Yes. My position here was temporary." Fauna glanced at Isabelle before placing a few more items in the box. Was that a hint of sadness, she saw? Fauna stopped packing and kept eye contact with Isabelle. "Someday I hope to have my own counseling center where I won't have the restrictions of a school district telling me what I can and can't say. I want the freedom to pray for people when I feel prayer is needed." Fauna gave Isabelle a wink and smiled.

Isabelle allowed a halfhearted smile to form on one side of her mouth.

"I'm still available to talk with you anytime. You'll just need your parent's permission—of course."

Isabelle still standing in the doorway was silent.

"If your parents will allow it, we have a group at our church for youth. They meet on Tuesday nights. I'm part of the leadership team and I help with one of the discussion groups. It's a friendly and non-judgmental place."

Fauna pulled a card from her desk drawer and wrote on the back of the card. "This is my business card. I put my cell phone number on the back along with the church address with the time we meet. I'd love to see you come. Call me, or have your parents call me, for more information."

Isabelle took the card and pushed it into her front jean pocket.

Fauna took that as a very good sign.

"I'm praying for you Isabelle. I think you are a great girl. I believe good things are about to happen in your life. You just need to trust and open yourself up. Let people in a little bit."

Isabelle awkwardly shifted from one foot to the other but didn't leave. She rested her shoulder on the door frame of Fauna's office.

Fauna took the opportunity to converse with Isabelle. "I've taken a job as a waitress at the little restaurant at the end of Main Street. Do you know the place?"

"Yes. I went there a week ago with this other lady who kinda knows my mom."

"I start work there on Monday. If you stop in, I'll buy you a burger and fries."

"Okay—Maybe."

Without saying anymore, Isabelle turned and walked out of the counseling offices. Fauna followed her to the door and poked her head out into the hallway to see Isabelle swept away in the moving crowd of middle schoolers.

Fauna went back into her office thinking the whole exchange with Isabelle was odd and resumed packing.

17

Yes—I Have A Plan For You.

Snake maneuvered the streets of Hillbrooke in the direction of the church parsonage. His eyes were fixed on the road ahead—his mind was deep in thought. Fauna sat quietly in the passenger seat starring out the side window hypnotized by the passing landscape.

"Are you going to say yes?" Fauna's question broke the stillness. She kept her eyes on the moving scenery out the side window.

Snake blankly stared ahead—non-responsive.

Fauna turned and looked at the side of Snake's face. It was the side without the tattooed serpent. With a bit more volume, she spoke his name. "Snake!"

Startled from his thoughts, Snake glanced in Fauna's direction then back at the road. "Huh?"

Fauna clinched her teeth and sighed.

Snake said. "Sorry. Did you say something? I'm thinking about tonight."

"I know. Me too." Fauna paused for a moment then rephrased her original question. "Do you think being small group leaders is a good fit for us?"

Snake glanced over at Fauna then eased to a full stop at the four-way. "I've been praying about it. Asking the Lord for a positive sign—a scripture, a word from someone—anything that would confirm the direction I should go. I wanted a clear yes or no, but heaven has turned a deaf ear to me right now. How about you?"

"What do you mean—how about me? I'm not gonna be leading the small group. This one is all you. If I understood correctly, Pastor's invitation to me was coffee making and snack prep. I'm good with that even without spiritual confirmation."

Snake examined her face quickly. "You didn't feel insulted by that...did you?"

"No way. I think it's more relief. Anyways...I already help Jean with those things now."

"I know, but how do you feel about us being a team—doing it together?"

Fauna made a contemplative sigh before she spoke. "Fine...I prayed last night too. I don't have a scripture or a verbal confirmation from anyone, but I feel peace in my heart. If the Browns believe in us and Pastor Rey trusts us—I think that's confirmation enough for me."

Snake knew what Fauna said made sense. He just wanted that extra assurance that he was doing the right thing.
He drove on without responding.

Fauna asked. "Do you have an issue with the leading of the discussion and prayer time?"

Keeping his eyes on the road Snake whispered, "Yes." He gripped the wheel tighter with his hands. "I know I can do it— that's not the problem. It's just a bit strange that Pastor Rey would prefer us to others in the group. We are an unmarried couple—*not|even engaged*."

Fauna shifted uncomfortably in her seat and turned her head again to look out the side window.

Snake glanced in her direction looking at the back of her head. The body language and non-verbal communication was thunderous. He spoke cautiously. "I mean, just think of it. Only five years ago I wanted nothing to do with the Lord, Christians or church. Now they are willing to let me…" He paused, "*us…* lead seasoned believers. I guess that part is a little intimidating for me."

Fauna faced Snake, "I understand that, but what about inside. Do you feel peace?" She fought the insecure feeling about their future together and the desire to give Snake the silent treatment for that *not even engaged* comment.
Tentatively Snake whispered, "I do."

Fauna couldn't let that one slip by. "I do? I've been waiting a long time to hear those two words come out of your mouth."

"Not funny."

Snake turned into the driveway of Pastor and Callan's house just in time.

□□

Dr. Hayes focused on the evening news. Samantha and Baylee sat at the table in the family room playing a card game while Isabelle was in her bedroom. It was a typical evening in the Hayes home—minus Baylee screaming in pain and Isabelle slamming doors. Samantha slapped the pile of cards and laughed. Baylee giggled in glee. Stuart glanced back at them from his seat on the sofa and smiled.

The phone rang drawing everyone's eyes to the T.V. screen— no one moved. An evening call usually meant a medical emergency was brewing for Stuart. *Call from Heidi Alden* popped up in the right top corner of the screen.

Dr. Hayes shifted uncomfortably in his seat.

"I'll get it." Samantha said. Passing by her husband she touched his shoulder. "That's the woman I told you about. She brought lunch and helped that day Isabelle ran out of the house. She wants to take Issie out for lunch sometime."

Stuart wasn't involved in the activities of the children and to put his opinion in now might seem strange. Something about this woman made him uncomfortable. He certainly didn't want his daughter befriending an adult woman who acted like a flirty co-ed. Stuart said nothing, keeping his eyes on the TV until he heard Samantha talking in the kitchen. Stuart looked over his shoulder and watched her.

"Hello. This is the Hayes residence." Samantha stayed in script even though she knew who the caller was and likely what she wanted.

"Samantha, its Heidi Alden. I wanted to see if we could get something on the calendar for me and Isabelle to go out for dinner sometime."

Samantha liked the way Heidi got right to the heart of things—no 'how are ya's' to plow through. The only thing better would have been a text message. "Well...I spoke with Issie and she wasn't sure. I think she was a bit uncomfortable seeing that she really doesn't know you." Samantha was on the fence herself and was leaning toward vetoing the whole thing.

"Oh. No problem. I felt we had all made a connection and that Issie could use a friend." Heidi paused then added. "Someone outside the immediate family she could talk with."

Heidi let the words sink in, hoping to play on a mother's need to help her struggling child.

"She does seem to be doing better lately. I'll leave it up to her. Can you hold a minute?"

"Sure. I can wait."

Samantha ran upstairs and talked the situation over with Isabelle. Heidi waited on the phone straining to hear the muffled conversation.

Walking out of Isabelle's room, Samantha resumed her conversation. "Heidi?"

"I'm here."

"She said yes. Would Friday evening work for you?"

"Yes, it would. I'll pick her up about 6 P.M. and we'll do dinner and a movie. Do you have any restrictions on what she watches?"

"I'm sure you know what is appropriate for a fourteen-year-old girl."

A half smile formed on Heidi's face. She knew just the movie. This might just clinch the deal. What kid wouldn't want to watch something their parents forbid? No restrictions here. "I have just the movie picked out. I'm sure she'll love it. See you Friday."

□□

The baggage claim area of the Hillbrooke airport was empty. Tom stood watching the carrousel circle around and around in front of him. His eyes were fixed on the one piece of unclaimed luggage. He glanced at his watch, then the screen that showed the arriving flight schedule. Then back at the red suitcase—it circled the carrousel—all alone. The irony wasn't lost on him.

A gate agent strolled to the belt and removed the bag, pulling it behind him into a nearby office. The conveyor belt stopped. The large area became uncomfortably quiet.

Tom walked a few steps and found a seat that gave him a view of the escalator. The next herd of passengers would disembark soon. His daughters, Debbie and Kim, had thoughtfully arranged their travel to arrive together. He was sure they did that to lessen his load even though the airport was only 45 minutes away.

Tom's phone rang echoing through the baggage area. He pulled it from his pocket and glanced at the caller ID. The word HOME scrolled across the screen with a picture of Jean surrounded by three of the grandkids. She was beautiful.

"Jean is everything okay?"

Jean's voice was strong with a hint of excitement. "Have they arrived?"

"No—not yet. The plane is late." Tom kept his eyes on the vacant escalator. "It should be any minute now. Are you sure you're okay?"

"Yes—of course. I told you I was feeling fine. I could have come along." A hint of disgust was evident in Jean's voice.

"No—it was the right thing for you to stay home. I'm glad you aren't here waiting. It's best you rest up for the girls' visit."

"Fine—I hate it when you're right!" Jean laughed.

A sad smile formed on Tom's face. He loved the sound of her laugh. He fought back emotion. "This gives me some time with the girls before they forget all about me and focus all their attention on the star of the show." Tom gasped. "I see them! They're here. I'll call you back once we're on the road. I love you. We'll be home soon. Bye." He hung up and slipped his cell phone into his pants pocket.

Tom bolted to his feet at the sight of his girls running toward him. He had a momentary flash back to a scene after a school play when the girls saw that he had made it to their performance. That night, so many years ago, they ran toward him with excitement and threw their little arms around his legs shouting with delight, "Daddy, you're here!"

Now, two grown women rushed toward him, but all he saw was those two little girls. He couldn't pick them up, hold them on his lap or swing them in the air anymore—he couldn't even protect them from the pain that had engulfed all of them. They would all walk-through Jean's cancer together…and alone.

Debbie and Kim threw their arms around their father, burying their faces in his chest. They didn't speak. Tom's arms encircled his daughters. They were still his babies.

□□

Zander and Ty stood at the front door yelling. "They're here! Snake and Fauna are here!"

Ty pushed the front door open and held it for their dinner guests to enter. Snake gave Ty's belly a few air punches as he passed by and Fauna kissed Ty on top of the head and gave Zander a tight side-hug.

"I bet you boys are happy school's out now!" Fauna loved kids—especially these two boys. She always took time to acknowledge them. Her efforts did not go unnoticed. Both boys smiled big goofy smiles at the beautiful and colorful lady. Snake was like that young, cool uncle and both boys loved him too.

Callan came into the living room wiping her hands on a kitchen towel. "Boys go play and leave Snake and Fauna alone." The boys shuffled out of the room feeling embarrassed by the rebuke.

Snake watched the two dejected boys leave. "Are you kidding? These two could never be a bother!"

Callan confirmed her orders. "They know we're having a meeting tonight. We've already talked about it. Right after dinner they're off to play video games with the little girl a few doors down. Her name is Baylee. Right boys?"

Ty smiled brightly. "I'm ready to go. Just say the word."

Fauna chuckled. "Well, I'm suddenly feeling very 2nd place." Ty ran back to Fauna and gave her a big one-armed hug. Zander stood in the doorway of the living room feeling very envious of his younger brother's boldness.

"Not 'til after dinner Ty—soon." Callan motioned for Fauna to join her in the kitchen. Snake and Pastor Rey stayed in the living room. The boys followed Fauna like trained puppies to the kitchen with their mother.

Callan stacked the plates, silverware and glasses on the cupboard. "Guys, you want to set the table for me?"

Ty looked at the cast on his arm and shrugged his shoulders.

"Just do the best you can." Callan handed a stack of plates to Zander. Then she gave Ty a handful of silverware to carry. Once the boys were out of ear shot Callan whispered, "Have you guys made up your minds yet about the small group?"

Fauna wasn't exactly sure how to answer. "Ahh…mmm. We only had the car ride over here to talk about it."

Callan yelled from the kitchen at Rey. "Don't you guys say anything important without us! Dinner will be ready in ten minutes."

After dinner Callan called Samantha to be sure Baylee was up to seeing the boys for about an hour. She stood on the porch and watched Zander and Ty run across the neighbor's yard to the Hayes' house. Once they were safe inside the house she headed back inside. The kids had formed a nice friendship—one that didn't require Callan to be with them. It was nice that Samantha allowed them to come over.

Callan came back into the dining room where Rey, Snake and Fauna sat talking casually. With one hand on her hip she sighed. "Okay, the boys are at the Hayes' house—let's talk shop!"

Everyone laughed. It broke the awkwardness that had been looming throughout dinner.

Rey looked at Snake. "I know it's been just a bit over 24 hours, but have you been able to pray about the possibility of being the fill-in small group leader?"

Snake found Fauna's hand under the table and held it while he spoke. "Yes. Fauna and I both have prayed. I hope you don't think me unspiritual to say I didn't get a positive confirmation one way or the other.

Pastor, I do have to ask—why me?"

Pastor Rey didn't answer immediately, but he looked directly into Snake's eyes. Slowly a smile formed on his lips and a laugh almost escaped. "Are you kidding me? Look how far you've come in five short years! You have surpassed many Christians who are twice your age. You love the fellowship of Believers. You love God's Word. I've never met anyone who can witness the love of the Lord like you do. You'd witness to the devil himself—if you met him on the road. You understand the power of prayer and how it can change a life. You live a Spirit-filled life. I can't think of anyone better than you."

Snake sat speechless. He counted Pastor Rey a dear friend, but he had no idea the depth of his respect. He wanted to make a joke to break the emotion welling up in him.

Fauna squeezed his hand tighter. Her pride was easy to see as she looked at the tattooed man sitting closely beside her at the dinner table.

Snake turned to Fauna. "I can only do it, if you'll help me."

Fauna answered him with a smile and a snicker. "I will!"

Snake's eyebrows rose up as high as he could lift them at the "I will!" remark. They both laughed at their private joke.

Rey and Callan looked at each other and smiled a knowing smile. These two weren't fooling anyone. Their love for each other was evident and it seemed for a long time that they were more of one mind than two.

Pastor Rey brought the conversation back to business. "Would next Thursday at your place be too soon to begin?"

"I look forward to it, Pastor."

☐☐

Zander and Ty dashed up the stairs to Baylee's room. They had only been to the Hayes' house twice before, but Ty had called Baylee two other times on the phone. It was a budding friendship about to burst into bloom.

Samantha yelled behind them. "Baylee the Douglas boys are here."

Zander put his hand up to knock on the door, but Ty burst past him opening the door wide before his knuckles made contact. "Ty—no."

"Baylee we're here."

Baylee sat in the chair to the side of her bed. A big smile brightened her face. "Come in—I've been waiting! The game is in the player the controllers are ready—it's on."

The boys each took a controller and sat on the bed. Before Baylee turned on the game she said, "I had a few bad days last week. I really hate being sick."

Ty and Zander exchanged looks. Zander shook his head at Ty.

Ty ignored him. "Baylee. I know something about making sick people better."

Baylee's brown eyes twinkled. "What is it?"

Zander injected. "Hey, we only have an hour. Let's play the game already." He shot a disgusted look at his brother hoping for the impossible.

"I know stories and I have a book that tells all about it."

Baylee asked. "Can I read the book?"

"Sure. I'll bring it next time I come."

"Could you tell me one of the stories?" She was more than politely interested in the stories.

"There's so many I get them mixed up sometimes, but the book has all the stories…and the best part is…"

Zander cut his brother off. "Tyson James—stop it. You know what mom said."

Ty winked at Baylee and held his hand up to the side of his head like a phone and mouthed the words 'call me.'

Zander turned on the game and the annoying music filled the room.

Outside the bedroom door Samantha leaned against the wall listening to the children talk. She thought she would be interested in that healing book Ty was talking about.

□□

Zander and Ty strolled across the neighbor's yard on their way home. Snake and Fauna's car was still in the driveway.

"I'll race ya." Zander got into the starting block pose.

"Wait. Don't say anything to mom about me talking to Baylee."

"You're going to get in trouble if you keep pushing this healing thing. Mom said not to talk to them about it—they won't understand how we believe."

"That's not it Zander. I can't explain it, but sometimes adults just don't get it." Ty pouted.

"Of course, adults get it—they're adults. We're kids. You're gonna get in so much trouble."

"Please, don't tell. I just have ta help her. You can help her too."

"No way. You're not dragging me into this."

"Okay—but please—just wait until I have a chance to tell her about the healing and about prayer."

"Are you crazy? Not everyone believes like us. We're pastor's kids so we have ta believe all that—but her dad's a doctor and doctors only believe in medicine stuff."

Ty ask, "What if I'm right and Jesus wants to heal Baylee? What if all she needs is for me or somebody to pray for her, and what if we gave her the Bible—and she really got healed—what then? You'd be happy I told her—wouldn't you?"

Zander huffed. "Fine, but that's a lot of 'what ifs.' How about this 'what if'… What if mom finds out or Baylee's mom or dad find out? We won't get to play with her anymore."
Ty looked sad as he pondered what Zander said.

Fauna pointed in the boy's direction. "Look who's coming. Did you guys enjoy your time with Baylee?" Fauna yelled from the front porch where she and Snake were saying goodbye to Rey and Callan.

Zander blurted out from across the yard. "I won!" He examined Fauna's face to look for any sign she was impressed with his feat.

Ty gave Fauna a goofy grin. "It was fun." There was a twinkle of mischief in Ty's eyes that was hard for Fauna to interpret— even though she was a trained counselor.

"I know that smile." Callan said. "You're up to something." She shook her finger in front of Ty's face. "I'm watching you. Don't think you're gonna slip anything past me."

Zander looked ready to confess—but Ty grabbed his hand and ran into the house.

18

Do You Know
Where Your Children Are?

The repeated blast of a car horn brought Samantha to the front door. She looked out at the waiting car and was about to motion for Heidi to come in when, Isabelle ran past her like the Flash. Issie yelled back over her shoulder. "It's Heidi for me! Be back later." And she ran to the waiting car, hopped in and Heidi drove away.

Samantha felt uncomfortable with the pick-up. This kind of behavior would be expected from a teenager who just got a driver's license and was on a first date. But Heidi was an adult woman the same age as her. Samantha thought it would have been respectful for Heidi to come in for a minute to talk about her plans for the evening.

The tail-lights of Heidi's car disappeared, and Samantha closed the front door wondering again if she'd made the right choice in allowing this outing to happen.

Heidi glanced in Isabelle's direction when she paused at the four-way stop. "So, Isabelle, I was thinking of trying this little diner downtown. It's kind of rugged but private. They have great burgers and fries. Sound good to you?"

Isabelle wasn't feeling overly chatty or friendly now, but she'd been trying to be more open with people like Ms. Reynolds had encouraged her to be. "Sure. That sounds fine." She spoke in her moody, fourteen-year-old voice.

When they arrived at The Diner on Main Isabelle knew it was the one that Ms. Reynolds said she would be working at for the summer. Heidi opened the door of the restaurant for Isabelle and an aroma of fried foods overtook her senses. Issie cocked her head in every direction searching for Ms. Reynolds. She wasn't there. Then Isabelle remembered that Ms. Reynolds had said she would be starting work on Monday. She felt disappointed but wasn't sure why. She didn't like the counselor or anything—she said out loud, "Who cares?" Then was suddenly aware she allowed the words to slip from her thoughts.

"What? Who cares about what?" Heidi asked as she pulled gently on Isabelle's arm leading her to a table in the corner. "I like this area. It's private."

"Okay." Isabelle didn't resist.

"So, what exactly is it that you don't care about?" Heidi questioned again.

Isabelle shrugged her shoulders and slumped into the chair. "Oh nothing."

"Come on. If we're gonna do this, we need to be open with each other. I'll go first. I don't care that people don't get me." Heidi did air quotes when she said, "get me." Then she added while bobbing her head, "because I know I'm an amazing person." Heidi sat down in the bulky wood captain's chair and scooted it up to the table.

Isabelle sat directly across from Heidi. A slight smile formed on Issie's face. This lady is kinda funny, she thought.

"Come on…spill." Heidi cupped both of her hands palms facing up and made the motion of someone calling you to come. "Come on." She encouraged Issie to tell all.

Issie chuckled then blurted out. "I'm moody and I like it."

Heidi approved. "Don't ya know it! Moody is the best and being angry is better yet. When somebody gets on my bad side—look out! I love getting even. Nobody better do me wrong or there'll be a price to pay!" Heidi threw her head back laughed loudly.

Isabelle asked. "Really? You get even with people—how?"

"It's easy. Just a few weeks ago I leveled the playing ground but good with someone who did me wrong. She deserves whatever she gets for treating me like I'm nothing." A vengeful expression replaced the fun that had been on Heidi's face moments before.

Isabelle felt uncomfortable—a touch of fear crept in. This woman was nothing like Ms. Reynolds. She acted more like those girls in her school—the ones she called 'the noses.' They were always getting into everyone's business. They stirred up trouble between other girls and sometimes guys too.
Isabelle felt more like prey than friend.

Heidi laughed again and said, "Just kidding. You should see your face."

Isabelle wanted out. She wanted to go home. This woman was scary.

"Okay. Let's order." Heidi pointed up at the chalk board across the small diner in the direction of the handwritten menu.

Issie looked down at the table and said. "I'm feeling sick." She put her hand over her mouth and made a fake heave.

Heidi shot to her feet like a cat jumping out of the line of fire. The confidence Heidi spewed moments ago was replaced by someone who had never cared for a sick child a day in her life. "Oh…we should reschedule and do this another time." She waved her hand in the air at the man standing behind the grill. "I need a bag over here. She's sick." Heidi pointed at Isabelle, putting a safe distance between them.

Once they were back in the car, Isabelle kept the bag near her mouth to play the part of someone ready to hurl. Heidi broke the speed limit to get Isabelle back home. In her best attempt at being motherly she said, "We're home, honey." She turned the car off and opened her car door to get out.

"No. It's okay. Thanks for inviting me out. Sorry I got sick. It came on so sudden it may be contagious."

"Yes—you're right." Heidi stayed in the car. "Good thinking. I'll just drop you here and call you next week. We can try again."

"Sure—later." Isabelle bolted out of the car and up the porch steps. She disappeared into the house.

Samantha had a clear view of the front door from the kitchen. "What are you doing home already?" She asked Issie. "You only left a few minutes ago."

The happy girl from a few days ago was gone. Isabelle ran up the stairs and to her bedroom without saying a word, thinking… adults—all of them—I will never trust any of them again. I can't believe she almost drew me in. She's mean. I don't think she even cared about me. Why would she be interested in me?

A soft tap at Isabelle's bedroom door brought a harsh reply. "Go away Mom. I'm fine. I just wanted to come home. I want to be alone."

"What happened?"

"NOTHING!" Issie yelled at the one person she knew was a constant—but still not trustworthy.

"I'm gonna give you 30 minutes, then we're talking—like it or not." Samantha and Isabelle were both surprised by this sudden parental outburst. "I'm running out to the store and when I get home…we talk." Samantha felt for the first time she and Isabelle were having a normal exchange like mothers and daughters who spar back and forth. She liked this far better than being the mother who always took the beating for the sake of harmony in the home.

Samantha pulled out of the driveway and headed to the store. A car pulled into her driveway moments later.

A few miles down the road Heidi rethought how she handled dropping Isabelle off. She wondered, even if the child was sick, she probably should have seen her safely into the house. She never dreamed she'd have such good luck as to see Samantha leave and Stuart home. Heidi shut off the car. She waited a moment in the driveway to freshen her makeup before getting out of the car.

Heidi stood in front of the glass door of the Hayes' house. She tugged on her short skirt and adjusted her low-cut blouse. She wiggled around getting everything in just the right place and rang the doorbell.

The door opened. It was Dr. Hayes.

Heidi smiled warmly. "Hi, Dr. Hayes. I dropped Isabelle off a few minutes ago, but she wasn't feeling well, and I thought I should at least stop back by to check on her before going home." Heidi looked past Stuart to see Isabelle standing at the top of the stairs. "Well, there she is." Heidi stepped into the house. "Are you feeling better, honey?"

Isabelle didn't speak but turned and went back to her room.

Stuart stood at the door completely out of his element. "Would you like to wait for Samantha? She'll be right back."

"Well—sure." Heidi walked into the family room and sat on the sofa. Stuart followed behind her. He reached past her to pick up the remote lying on the couch and clicked off the T.V. "Can I get you something to drink?"

"Wine?" Heidi asked.

"Well…Sure…Yes." He walked into the kitchen and selected a wine from the cooler. He took one glass from the cupboard and set it on the counter. Then he paused and went back and took out one more glass and poured the wine. He glanced back in the direction of the family room wondering what in the world he'd gotten himself into.

Heidi yelled over her shoulder. "You need any help in there?" Stuart came in carrying a glass of wine in each hand.

Heidi reached up and took a glass for herself. "Thank you so much." She said with a breathy voice. "I really need this right about now. That little girl of yours nearly scared me to death." Heidi took a long sip of wine.

Stuart looked puzzled. "What happened?"

"Oh, she didn't tell you? She took sick at the restaurant and was going to throw up. She wanted to come home. I dropped her off but then thought I better come back and make sure she was okay. We never even ordered. I'm starving."

"Oh, I didn't know. Samantha usually handles that kind of stuff. I'll go check on Issie."

"She looked much better when I saw her upstairs. She's probably just tired. How was your day?"

"Aaaaa…fine. And yours?" Stuart responded more out of habit than interest.

"Do ya have an hour? I could tell you all about it." Heidi rambled on making jokes and being very animated. She was pretty sure she saw Stuart smile at least three times. Then his face changed abruptly.

"Samantha, you're home."

Samantha looked at her husband and Heidi sipping wine and suddenly felt territorial. "Heidi, what happened tonight with you and Isabelle?"

"I was just explaining all that to Stuart, I mean Dr. Hayes."

Samantha added. "Isabelle was pretty upset when she got home."

"Yes. She told me she wasn't feeling well. I dropped her off, but thought I better come back to check on her."

Samantha's expression softened. "Yes. I'm going up now to talk to her. It was nice of you to stop by. We won't keep you—I'm sure you've had a long day."

"No. Not really." Heidi sipped on her wine while looking up at Samantha who stood nearby.

This time Samantha held her arm out toward the door. "Well, we have some family business we need to handle right now. It was nice of you to come."

Heidi stood to leave, casting a smile back at Dr. Hayes. "I enjoyed our conversation." Then she looked at Samantha. "I hope Isabelle and I will be able to do this another time when she feels better."

Samantha walked to the door neither confirming nor denying Heidi's hopes. Samantha held the door open and smiled.

Heidi left.

Samantha went directly upstairs and knocked on Isabelle's door. This time Issie opened the door.

"What happened tonight, Issie?" Samantha looked at her daughter knowing something wasn't right. The pleasant girl from a few days ago was gone.

19
Someone Is Listening

The four posters hung on the wall of the Sunday school classroom, each displaying different miracles Jesus performed. Soft Christian music played in the background while Grace laid out the workbooks for her 3rd, 4th and 5th graders. Her back was to the door when Ty and Zander Douglas walked into the room.

"Ms. Grace, we're here early. Do you need any help?" Zander asked.

"Hi boys. Sure. You can put these containers of crayons and pencils on the tables."

Zander finished the task before Ty had a chance to help. Other children began arriving in twos and threes until all the chairs Grace set out were filled.

"Boys and girls, we are going to review the last two miracles we talked about and then move on to this week's lesson. Does anyone have any questions about the lessons we've been talking about over the past two weeks?"

Ty's good arm shot up in the air.

"Yes. Ty?"

"Ms. Grace does Jesus still heal people today? And can kids pray for people to be healed or just adults?" Under the table Zander gave his brother a kick in the leg. "Ouch! Why'd you do that?" Zander kept his eyes downcast.

"Well—Ty, those are very good questions. Let me see if I can answer them one at a time." Grace walked over to the table the children were gathered around and sat down to be at their level. "I do believe God is able to do miracles such as healing today. However, we don't hear of these kinds of miracles so much now—not like in the times when Jesus did his earthly ministry. That said—I do believe kids should pray for each other. God hears them the same as an adult who prays. Did I answer your questions?"

"Well. Yes—but say I knew someone that needs God to heal them. Would it be okay for me to pray for them?"

"Absolutely!" There was an assurance in Grace's voice. "You should pray for people you feel need prayer. You could pray with them anytime you want."
Zander moaned softly.

"Zander is something wrong?"

"No Ms. Grace." He paused then added. "But…as kids should we pray for people when we've been told not to?"

"Did someone tell you especially not to pray for someone in need?"

"Well. Yes—but no. Just not for them in person…"

Ty interrupted. "But kid's prayers do matter. Right, Ms. Grace? We can pray—should pray."

The rest of the class listened with less enthusiasm than the Douglas boys.

"It seems like there may be more here than I know. Let's talk more after class or better yet—with your parents. Does that sound like a good idea?" Zander quickly said, "Yes." Ty didn't answer.

"Okay, if there are no more questions we'll review the healing of the blind man and the healing of Peter's mother-in-law before we hear the story about the four men who brought their sick friend to Jesus."

After the lesson review Grace told the story of the sick man being lowered to Jesus through the roof by his friends. Ty listened with interest while a plan formed in his mind, a plan to bring his friend Baylee to Jesus.

□□

At the close of the service Pastor Rey opened the altar for anyone who needed special prayer. The prayer team lined the front of the church. Tom and Jean Brown along with their two daughters walked as one group to the altar. Esther and Harold Smith stood off to the far left alone. The other members of the prayer team were interceding for the needs of others. The Browns walked towards Harold and Esther. Before they reached them, Esther opened her arms to Jean and they embraced. Within minutes a group gathered behind them, at their sides and even behind Esther and Harold encircling them with prayer. The sound of many voices blended together in petition to the Lord.

Pastor Rey left his place on the platform and joined those who surrounded Jean. More and more people filled the space at the altar until the volume of their voices boomed like thunder. Then it happened, people could no longer stand in the presence of the Lord. At first it was a swaying, then people began to drop to their knees while others crumbled to the floor. No one in that room could deny the Spirit of the Lord was moving in their midst.

Ty Douglas watched from the front pew of the church.

The Douglas boys sat quiet in the back seat looking out the window on the way home from church. It was a short ride home—but long enough for a conversation.

"The altar time this morning was powerful. I don't think I've personally experienced anything like it." The experience was fresh, giving a hint of emotion in Callan's voice.

Rey replied while keeping his eyes on the road. "What if Jean was healed this morning? I pray a miracle is happening."

Callan responded. "I want to believe it. Something happened in that service. Jesus was there. We prayed! Believed! Asked!"

Rey patted the steering wheel keeping beat to non-existent music. "Let's wait and see. We prayed. Now let's wait and see."

"Rey, you should preach a message on healing. Give a whole service to it—have you ever done that before?"

He didn't answer immediately. "No. I don't think I have. I've preached on healings Jesus performed, but I've never connected them to people being healed today. Why do you ask?"

Callan answered. "I don't know…maybe it would be good to hear a message from our pastor on the topic of healing." Callan paused then added. "I mean seeing Jean's illness is known by the church and she's deeply loved by so many—maybe now's the time."

Rey nodded his head slightly. "I'll give it some thought." He knew that the Bible clearly states that we are to pray for physical healing. Healings took place in the Old and New Testaments. Now, however, the topic of healing was difficult. There were many questions that surrounded the subject.

The thought of speaking a whole message on physical healing gave Rey self-doubt on his ability to handle the text with skill. He had prayed for sick people, but he had never seen anyone miraculously healed. He'd heard of people being healed—but he'd never seen one first hand. At least not with the magnitude of blind eyes seeing, deaf ears hearing, limbs being restored, or terminal cancers healed. He couldn't explain nor understand why so few people were healed while many others were not. Why good people die and evil lives on.

Rey and Callan were silent the rest of the way home—each deep in their own thoughts. In the back seat of the car, Zander looked out the window daydreaming. But Ty had listened intently to every word spoken by his parents. Between his Sunday school lessons, the altar time at the close of the service and the conversation between his parents—his plan was taking shape. He believed what was written in the Bible, what he heard, what he felt and what he saw. Ty believed God.

□□

Jean sat in the padded chair next to her bed. Her Bible rested in her lap. She used her feet to swivel back and forth in the rocker. They had lived in this house for six years and never thought before to turn the two chairs in front of the bedroom window to view the lake. These two chairs were rarely used in the past years. Since moving to Hillbrooke, their lives had been busy. Who had time to sit in the bedroom gazing out at a lake? A soft smile formed on her face. The view out the window was breathtaking.

The sun rose in the sky throwing a blanket of warmth over her body. Jean closed her eyes and let the sun warm her face. Tom had left for work an hour ago.

Jean's bedroom door creaked open. Debbie, Jean's oldest daughter, poked her head in. "Mom, you ready for something to eat?"

"I'm not really hungry, but I would love a cup of coffee with heavy cream. You know how I like it—same as you."

"Coming right up." Debbie left the bedroom door opened and walked to the kitchen.

Jean moved the open Bible from her lap to the end table next to her chair. She removed her reading glasses and laid them on top of the Bible, rubbing her eyes gently. She moved her hands to the back of her neck and massaged it while turning her head from side to side.

The atmosphere in the room suddenly changed. A feeling of *being held* brought tears to her eyes. She prayed but not a sound passed her lips. Peace washed over her as she communed with the Almighty.

A few minutes later, Debbie stood next to her mom's chair holding a tray with a cup of coffee and a plate with buttered toast. Her mom's eyes were closed and her lips moving.

"Mom?" Debbie asked in a soft voice.

Jean wiped the few stray tears from her face. "Oh, honey, I was just praying."

"I'm sorry. I can put this down on the foot stool and..."

"No, you're never a bother. When your sister is up I'd like to speak to you both."

"She's up. I heard her in the bathroom." Debbie left the room for a moment.

Jean could hear voices in the hallway. Kim followed her sister into their mom's bedroom. They each took a seat on the bed and Jean pivoted her chair to face them.

"I believe the Lord gave me a word and I want to share it with you both." Jean looked at her daughters. The past weeks had been a strain on the whole family as they came to terms with Jean's diagnosis.

"We've all cried a river of tears and laughed ourselves sick. We've talked about the past and the future. This morning in my Bible reading I read about Elijah at the Brook Cherith and it was like I heard the Lord speak these words to me...*when your brook dries up—what will you do?*" Jean picked up her coffee cup and took a sip. She returned it to the tray and continued.

"Girls, you know how young I was when my mother died. I've shared my story with you many times, and I've sat with other people in grief during the weeks and months leading up to the loss of a loved one, but now it is knocking at our door— our family—me."

Jean felt a wave of emotion. She fought it. Looking into her daughters' faces she knew she had to press on with the word while she still had the strength.

"In life, women are given many different roles to play. When we are cast in a new roll—one we didn't expect and didn't ask for— this is when the quality of the woman can be seen. I have chosen to live my life out as a godly woman." Jean swallowed. "I have endeavored to put God on display for everyone to see—I've always wanted you girls to watch me. What's that saying? It's caught not taught. I wanted you both to watch..." Jean began coughing violently and doubled over in pain. Both girls jumped up from the bed where they were sitting to help. Jean leaned heavily on her daughters as they eased her into the bed.

Kim gave firm direction. "Mom, rest. Don't try and talk anymore."

"I have too. Let me finish my thought then I'll rest." Jean rested her head on the pillow and continued. "In the weeks, months and years to come your roles will continue to evolve but the role of a Godly woman, whatever the circumstances—

that will never change. God is not asking you to be a good person within your giftings or skill package. He is asking you to be infused by the Holy Ghost. He wants to equip you to be something you can't be in your own strength and power. You must rely on Him." Jean's eyes fluttered shut for a moment.

"Mom don't talk like your dying. We're trusting God for a healing." Debbie had hoped her words would have held more authority, but they were halfhearted, and she knew it.

"This isn't meant to be a *parting words* kind of talk. This is hot off the presses and burning in my heart. I must share it with you right now." Jean took her daughters by the hand and held them tenderly. "Without the intervention of a divine healing, you do know my days are few…and I'm okay with that. I am going to live out my life for the Glory of God. Will you both promise me right now that if your brook dries up; you won't allow it to affect your faith? That you will be the godly women I raised you to be in every circumstance. Will you remember this…my girls?"

Debbie and Kim each nodded in the affirmative and whispered in unison, "Yes, Mom." Then they laid down on the bed next to their mother, one on each side of her and placed an arm across her like she had done to them so many times. The roles had reversed—too soon.

□□

Monday morning at 6 A.M. Fauna walked into The Diner on Main. She pulled a clean white apron from a rack in the food storage area. A cup of pencils sat next to a stack of order pads on the counter in the storage room. She grabbed an order pad, put it in her apron pocket and stuck the pencil behind her ear. The owner unlocked the front door and flipped the sign in the window announcing to the empty street that the diner was open for business.

Fauna poured a cup of hot coffee and sat down at the counter while her new boss gave her the laid-back instructions for the day. There weren't many rules except—take the orders and clean the tables. He would keep the stock ordered and food prep areas stocked. She would interact with the customers.

Fauna felt a wave of contentment wash over her. If she had to wait while the Lord put everything in order for her future, she liked this simple place to work until He moved her in another direction. This job gave her income, freedom and people all wrapped up with a nice bow. Fauna whispered, "Thank you, Jesus."

The first customer through the door was a pasty white fellow with black glasses. He was alone. Fauna waved her hand at the empty diner and smiled. "Take a seat anywhere. I'll be right with you."

□□

Callan turned down the side street off Main. She eased her window down, taking her foot off the gas and the car slowed to a crawl. She looked at the old house oddly squeezed between the two newer buildings. She could hear the creaking sound of the porch swing moving in the warm breeze. Wanting to know more about this Healer, Callan pushed the errand she was supposed to do out of her mind. With her friend Samantha in her thoughts, Callan passed by the house and turned around in the driveway of the business next to *The Healer* and parked on the road in front of the old house. She rested her head on the steering wheel and whispered a prayer. "Lord, help me as I venture into this place. I pray for the protection and guidance of your Holy Spirit. Help me find out what I need to know to better help Samantha and her family."

Callan stepped out of the car and walked toward the door of the business. The wood porch creaked with each step she took sending a chill up her spine. The sound of chimes greeted her as she opened the old wooden door of the house. An unseen person called from the back of the business. "I'll be right with you."

While she waited, Callan collected a handful of pamphlets from the display rack on the wall. The office was meagerly decorated, mostly with objects from eastern religions. To some people these artifacts would seem harmless art objects, but to Callan the meaning represented something deeper—a false hope for those seeking help. Callan heard footsteps walking toward her.

She turned and came face to face with Heidi Alden.

"Heidi?" The name came out of Callan's mouth in the form of a question. In her mind she processed the shock of seeing this woman. Callan noticed a man stood in the hallway behind Heidi—she could see it was Victor Darwin, the man from the website, the owner. It was hard to see him in the dim lighting.

Callan breathed the name of Jesus.

Heidi snapped in anger. "What are you doing here?"

Callan felt for a moment like the child who was caught with her hand in the cookie jar. "I-I was just stopping in to see what type of business this was. I picked up a few of these brochures." She held up the tri-folded paper like a fan as proof.

Heidi snatched the brochures from Callan's hand. "You wouldn't be interested in anything we have to offer here."

Callan was shocked. "Oh. I'm sorry. No offence intended. I was just inquiring."

A superior smile formed on Heidi's lips and one eyebrow raised as she spoke. "We don't need the likes of you coming around here. This is a proper business that wants to help people—not use them and then throw them away like trash."

Heidi walked to the front door and opened it. "You're not welcome here." She stood holding the door open with a stern look on her face. The sound of chimes lingered in the air.

Callan walked toward the open door. She paused and looked behind her. The man who stood in the doorway moments ago took a step back into the dark—his form still visible, but not his face. Callan moved forward stepping on the porch. She glanced back over her shoulder and met the hateful stare of Heidi. The door of the business slammed loudly in Callan's face.

Callan was relieved to slip into her car. She turned the key and started the engine. She sighed, "Jesus."

Heidi stood frozen in place by the door. She was trembling from the encounter. Victor Darwin stepped into the reception area. "Who was that woman? She has a seriously bad aura."

"That's the pastor's wife—the pastor I used to work for. Her name is Callan. I hate her, and I hate him. They made my life miserable."

Victor walked over to Heidi and put his hands on her head. He pressed his fingertips into her brow and pushed in a circular motion. With a calm almost whispering voice he spoke. "Think peaceful thoughts…a slow-moving stream…" Victor paused between each descriptive phrase allowing Heidi time to visualize the words. "Trickling water…a crackling fire…soft rain…" Victor's voice was soothing. His hands gently pressed on the sides of Heidi's forehead. "…your thoughts will be clear, and your path will be vibrant. People will pay for what they have done to you and wrongs will be made right—you are in control." His voice drifted off.

BEVERLYJOYROBERTS

Heidi's eyes were pinched tightly closed. Warmth flowed—her heart rate sped up. Heidi visualized Callan's face—she looked hurt when she left. A slight smile curled on Heidi's lips. Victor took her hand and moved with her to the examination room.

□□

Fauna stood at the front door of Snake's house to welcome each small group member as they arrived. Everyone was present except Tom and Jean. The house was filled with lively chatter, but there was a keen sense of Tom and Jean's absence.

Fauna stood between the living room and kitchen and raised her voice over the conversation. "If you'd like something to drink, it's in the kitchen. Help yourself. This is a no-frills kinda house. Any takers on helping me with setting out the food for later?" Fauna went back to the kitchen. A few of the ladies followed her. She assigned them small jobs to finalize the food.

"Okay, ladies—we're done. Let's go join the rest of the group." They returned right at the moment there was a lull in the conversation. It was uncomfortable for a moment until Snake took that opportunity to begin the meeting.

"Thank you all for coming. Pastor Rey has asked me to step in for the Brown's while they are going through a personal battle with Jean's health. Let's open with a few worship songs and then we'll pray."

Snake lead the group. The busyness of the day and the worries of tomorrow faded away as the group drew together as one. The singing ended. The sound of voices blending in praise filled the small room. Then a hush fell, and a single voice spoke.

"Fear is not your friend. Don't welcome it. Don't entertain it like a guest in your home. God has called you. His

192

plan for you is without repentance. Don't give up and don't give in. What He's called you to do—He'll equip you to complete. Don't sell yourself short—God has a plan for you."

The room was quiet. The words spoken under the direction of the Holy Spirit were falling on open hearts.

Snake knew this word was for him. In his thoughts he questioned, finally, could I be moving in the right direction? Is this a confirmation for leading the group or something else? A peace invaded his whole body like a refreshing wave washing over him.

Snake led out in prayer. "Lord Jesus, we come with hearts of thanksgiving. You love us. You encourage all of us in Your Word to *Fear Not*. We know that fear can be crippling to the Believer—keeping us from fulfilling Your plans and purpose in our lives, hindering us from touching those You've called us to love. Father, we ask for Your anointing to be with us as we study Your Word."

Snake paused then added. "Lord, we continue to believe for the healing of Jean Brown. Your Word tells us to 'rejoice always, pray continually, give thanks in all circumstances; because this is Your will for us in Christ Jesus.' Your Word also tells us to come boldly to You and to pray with confidence. It even says that we should ask anything, and You will hear us when we do. Lord, I'm asking and we're agreeing together, please heal, restore and do a miracle in Jean's body, we pray. Thank you, Lord, for hearing our prayer. It is in the wonderful name of Jesus that we pray."

All those present said, "Amen."

"Snake?" Harold Smith had his hand raised like a child in a classroom.

Snake nodded at Harold. "Yes, go ahead and share what's on your heart."

"I also had a word from the Lord come to me this week. I wrote it down wondering if it was for me or maybe someone else. I feel prompted by the Holy Spirit that someone here may need to hear this. Maybe someone will identify with it now—or it may be something that is coming soon. Mine is about fear too, but kinda different." Harold fumbled in his Bible and pulled out a folded piece of notebook paper, the kind from a spiral binder.

The room was silent. All eyes were on Harold as he tugged at the tangled paper. Once open—he read with a soft voice. "...Fear not and don't be afraid, trials come, persecution comes and what is coming to you is to perfect you—not destroy you. Stand strong and don't be overcome with evil but overcome evil with good. This will pass, and when it does, the glory of the Lord will shine forth even to those who persecute God's anointed. You will see with your eyes, hear with your ears and know in your heart—God has a purpose—God has a plan. It is always forgiveness. It is always redemption. It is always eternity. You will see the power and might of the Lord God in this—we will all see."

Snake broke the silence. "That was a powerful word, Harold." He shook his head in amazement. "It was great that you wrote it down. If it's okay with you—I'd like to put today's date on this and watch and see what the Lord is going to do."

Harold took out a pen and wrote the date on the top of the paper. He handed it to Snake, who slipped it inside the front cover of his Bible. The remainder of the meeting flew by ending with a closing prayer and fellowship.

Pastor Rey and Callan tried to fade into the background giving Snake and Fauna a chance to shine. Watching from the sidelines he knew God was faithful—no matter what may come. He held the word that Harold shared in his heart.

20
Face To Face With Evil

Friday morning Heidi unlocked the door to *The Healer's* office. She stepped inside and stood in the spot where Callan Douglas had stood yesterday afternoon. *The Healer* had tried to comfort her with therapy following the surprise attack by Callan, but that encounter ended with more questions than answers. There was a fog in her brain about what happened. The phone rang interrupting Heidi's thoughts. This puzzle would have to wait—she pushed herself to focus on work.

"Peace and wholeness—you've reached the office of *The Healer*— This is Heidi Alden; how may I help you?" She knew the greeting was halfhearted at best.

A male voice answered in a deep, booming voice. It was unsettling. "Yes. This is Russel Palomo. I'm a private investigator hired by a former client of Victor Darwin."

He drew out the word FORMER a bit too long for Heidi's taste. "And *who* is this former client?" There was a hint of mockery in her tone.

Mr. Palomo stayed on task. "I'm calling from Florida. I was hoping to speak with Victor Darwin. Is he available to take my call?"

"Ahhh-mmm. He's not in yet. Would you like to leave a message?"

"Maybe you could answer some of my questions. How long has Mr. Darwin been working in Hillbrooke, Michigan?"

"I've been working here since the *The Healer* opened his practice and that's been over two years."

"Do you know what other cities and states he's practiced in before coming to Hillbrooke?"

Heidi thought for a moment. She knew nothing about Victor before two years ago. It was as if he never existed. She became a bit defensive. "Why are you asking these questions?"

Mr. Palomo didn't answer but asked another question. "As Mr. Darwin's receptionist, have you received any complaints regarding inappropriate behavior with clients?"

"What are you implying?" The shock in Heidi's voice was undeniable. Then she surprised herself by adding, "None—that I know of." There was an intonation of question more than declaration.

The matter-of-fact voice continued. "Is there a third party in the room with Mr. Darwin during physical contact with his clients?"

Heidi momentarily paused while she searched for the exact wording she was looking for. Her tone and attitude had just taken a 180. She was willingly offering information. "With very young clients, a parent stays in the room. Adults are alone with *The Hea*...I mean Victor for their sessions." She swallowed hard and was glad this was a phone conversation.

She worried how this investigator might read her expressions and body language had he questioned her face to face.

"What age would you say constitutes an adult?"

"Ahh—mmm, *The Healer* decides that." Heidi felt a pounding in her chest. She could hear muffled conversation on the other end of the line.

Mr. Palomo's voice boomed through the line. "Would you be willing to testify to this?"

Heidi felt her hands begin to shake. "Listen. I don't know what this is about. I am not answering any more questions." Feeling afraid, she defended *The Healer*. "I've only seen Mr. Darwin doing good for people." Heidi felt conflicted even as the words exited her mouth. This line of questioning stirred up some doubts she had been battling regarding Victor for a while. She'd just pushed them down, but last night—she just couldn't remember what happened and this wasn't the first time.

The missing puzzle pieces were magically appearing, but Heidi swatted them away. The questions Mr. Palomo asked were producing doubt. A wave of nausea grabbed her stomach holding it in a fist. This was all Callan's fault. Why did she have to come nosing around where she didn't belong? Heidi's breathing accelerated.

Mr. Palomo's voice broke into Heidi's thoughts. "I have just one more question, Ms. Alden. Do you personally have concerns regarding Mr. Darwin?"

Heidi slammed the phone down disconnecting the call. She fell back in the office chair behind her. Her thoughts held her captive. What was in that locked room at the back of the house? Why did Victor ask family members to leave the room when he worked on some clients? Her throat went dry and the room closed in on her. She had encouraged everyone she knew to come to him. She had told people about *The Healer's* amazing methods and how he helped people cope with any issue. She promoted him to anyone who would listen.

Heidi let her face fall into her hands pressing her fingertips hard into her throbbing forehead. She inhaled deeply then sighed. In her mind she questioned, what have I done?

"I see you're practicing my relaxation methods." Victor Darwin stood close to Heidi's desk looking down at her. "Are you feeling better this morning? After your healing massage you were sound asleep. You were so peaceful, I hated to disturb you."

Heidi kept her face down. She didn't have a poker face. She didn't respond to Victor's question.

Victor rested his hand on the desk in front of Heidi and leaned in. "Is something wrong? You look like someone punched you in the gut." He tipped his head to the side in thought. "That evil woman didn't come back again and disrupt your peace—did she?"

"I-I'm…it's nothing." Heidi looked at the appointment book on her desk. "You have someone coming in 10 minutes."

"Okay." He turned to leave then stopped. He touched Heidi on the arm. "Are you sure there's nothing wrong? I can fit you in later today for another session."

"No. I'll be fine." A wave of nausea hit Heidi. "I might be coming down with the stomach flu."

"Do you need to go home? Leave if you need to—no need to make everyone sick." Victor backed away from Heidi's desk.

"No. I can stay. The Hayes family has an appointment today and I want to be here for them. Especially Isabelle."

The Healer walked down the hallway. Heidi rested her forearm on the desk then laid her face in the crook of her elbow to keep the tears hidden.

□□

School had only been out for a few days, but the Douglas home was in full-summer melt down. Callan's voice rang through the house like a crazy woman. She had reached her limits. It was the exact moment the straw landed on the camel's back that a stranger pulled into the driveway and got out of her car.

Callan bellowed. "A soft ball in the house! Really? What were you thinking?"

Ty and Zander sat on the couch in the formal living room. Each boy kept his head down not daring to make eye contact or answer the question that hung like pollution in the air.

Callan continued her rant unaware of the woman standing on the porch watching and listening through the screen door.

"How many times have I told you? You have a backyard to throw the ball...not the house...the living room...my picture, the mirror." Callan tapped the top of each boy's bowed head with two fingers. "Well—do you have anything to say for yourselves?"

Silence.

The doorbell rang.

Callan slowly turned her head toward the open door in slow motion. She immediately regretted her momentary loss of control and pushed through with an embarrassed laugh. "Oh. Sorry you heard that—summer's off to a great start. May I help you?"

"Are you Callan Douglas?"

"This isn't really a great time. I'm not interested in buying anything, signing anything or joining any causes. Maybe some other time." Callan walked toward the screen door and placed her hand on the big door moving it slowly toward the stranger's face.

The older woman in the boxy pant suit said. "I'm with Child Protective Services and I'm here to conduct an interview with you. I must be permitted to talk with you here or I'll have to call the police for assistance."

Callan stopped moving the door. "What? Someone reported our family."

"Yes Ma'am. I need to speak to you, your husband and the children."

Callan unlocked the screen door and the social worker stepped in. Callan looked at the badge that was clipped to her lapel. It looked official—the real deal.

The boys looked up from their places on the couch in wide-eyed wonder at the stranger. She flashed a smile at them. Zander looked away. Ty returned the smile. Neither boy moved.

"I'm Ms. Klingburg. Is there some place we could talk privately away from the children?"

"Boys. Go outside for a bit. Stay in the backyard."

Feeling they had received a pardon for their careless behavior, Zander and Ty scurried outside.

"We can sit here in the living room." Callan gestured for the social worker to take a seat on the couch. Callan sat down across from Ms. Klingburg in one of the side chairs. A broken mirror and picture leaned against the wall at the side of the couch.

"Mrs. Douglas, we received a call that someone was concerned that your son, Tyson Douglas, may have been hurt by one or both of his parents. This is in reference to the broken arm."

Callan felt defensive but tried to keep her tone in check. "A police report was made from the incident when we went to the emergency room. I doubt anyone there suspected that my husband or I would break our son's arm, give him a concussion and then drag him out to the ditch to wait for an ambulance. Oh, and also have the forethought to bend the tire of his bike for good measure." Callan knew the sarcasm was mean—but she wasn't feeling very kind at the moment.

Ms. Klingburg looked up over her reading glasses with a stern expression. "Yes. I received those files and reviewed them before coming." She opened the portfolio on her lap, took out a pen and began to write.

When questioned, the mother became defensive and angry— unhelpful in finding closure.

Callan watched the social worker writing and felt exposed. She wondered. Who could have or would have reported them for abuse?

Ms. Klingburg stopped writing, looked up at Callan and asked, "You seemed very angry when I arrived. I saw you hit your children on the top of the head. Is this a common form of discipline?"

"I tapped them. It was a tap. I didn't hit them." Callan crossed then re-crossed her legs.

"What other forms of physical discipline do you use with your children?"

Callan felt uneasy answering anymore of the social workers questions. "I'm going to give my husband a call. He will want to be here for these questions. And you did say you wanted to talk with him." Callan left the room to call Rey at the church. She quickly filled him in on everything. When she returned, Ms. Klingburg was making more notes in the black portfolio she held on her lap.

> *The mother refuses to answer questions about physical discipline without the husband present. Makes me think they want to be sure and keep their stories straight.*

Callan mustered up enough self-control to use her hostess voice. "My husband will be here soon. Can I make you a cup of coffee or tea while we wait?"

Ms. Klingburg looked up for a moment from her writing. "Coffee would be nice. Sugar no cream."

Callan was relieved to be out of the room. She took her time in the kitchen hoping Rey would be home before she needed to speak to *that* woman again.

Callan checked the clock in the kitchen. She couldn't drag this thing out another minute. Then she heard the garage door opening. She sighed and finished plating the cookies, pouring the coffee. Rey walked into the kitchen, Callan motioned to the living room and mouthed—*she's in there.*

Rey went first, and Callan followed him carrying the tray.

Rey extended his hand to Ms. Klingburg. "Hello. I'm Rey Douglas. I hear we are under some sort of investigation for child abuse. Let me assure you there is nothing further from the truth. We'll do everything we can to clear this up ASAP." Rey sat down; Callan put the tray on the coffee table and sat in the chair next to Rey.

Rey noticed the broken mirror and picture on the floor. "What happened in here?"

Callan shook her head and whispered. "I'll fill you in later."

Ms. Klingburg peered over her glasses at Rey examining him with one eyebrow raised. "Good—you're here. Now we should be able to wrap this up. As I was telling your wife, we must investigate all claims of abuse. We left off talking about what forms of discipline you practice."

Rey answered without hesitation. "Our first course of action is explaining the bad behavior by talking things out. The boys respond very well to this. If we feel that they are not responding to talking or everyone's emotions are high, we do a time out in their room or at the dining room table. We've used the one minute per year of age for timeouts; spanking is something we use only as a last resort. As the boys get older we haven't had to use this form of discipline in quite a while."

"When I arrived today, I saw your wife strike your boys on the top of their heads. I was standing over there on the porch. She didn't know I was there." Ms. Klingburg watched for Rey's reaction.

Callan spoke before Rey could react. "I *did not* strike them." Callan held two fingers up in the air—stood slightly to reach the top of Rey's head and tapped him. "This is what I did, only to get their attention—to get them to look up at me."

Rey looked at the social worker. He held up a pillow lying on the floor by his feet. "Would you show me the force in which Callan struck the children on this pillow? Also, was it fingers or an open hand that you saw her hit them with?"

Ms. Klingburg looked away from the pillow. "I couldn't tell all that from over there at the door. Plus, your wife was partially blocking my view."

"It sounds to me like you're unclear as to what you saw."

"I heard her yelling...screaming at the children." The social workers voice was defensive.

Rey, not wanting to alienate or anger the woman further, changed tracks. "We have never come in contact with anything like this before. We consider ourselves good, kind and loving parents. I am the lead pastor at Community Outreach Church and I have on occasion had people upset with me to the point of making false accusations to try and hurt my family and me. This type of accusation isn't a surprise. Recently, there have been vicious rumors circulating that are untrue. Whoever is saying these things about my family is lying."

"I'm sorry Mr. Douglas. Because an accusation of abuse was made, and Ty's arm is broken—we have to follow up. Also, when I arrived today I heard your wife screaming out of control. You must understand I can't in good conscience give this a pass…for the sake of the children."

Rey responded. "Yes. We do understand. Please go ahead and finish the interview. We are both willing to answer all your questions and concerns—to put this to rest."

The distrust on both sides eased up—just a bit.

After a lengthy interview with Rey and Callan, Ms. Klingburg asked to speak with each boy separately. She began with Zander.

Sitting at the breakfast table Ms. Klingburg asked Zander her first question. "Do you feel safe at home?"

Zander could tell his mom and dad did not approve of this woman. They were acting different than normal and for this, he blamed the stranger. She was trying to make him believe his home was not a safe place. He wasn't going to make nice with her no matter how much his dad tried to make everything sound okay. He decided to give curt answers and refused to elaborate on any question no matter how much Ms. Klingburg tried to draw him out.

It worked. She finally gave up on him and asked, "Would you go ask your brother to come and talk to me now." Zander got up and left the room.

Ms. Klingburg jotted down in her notes.

The child (Zander Douglas) was uncooperative and overly protective of his parents. He shows signs of anger that could be associated with abuse; emotional, physical or sexual. I would recommend an interview with a trained child psychiatrist to further investigate the depth of the abuse.

Ty ran in the room grinning. He plopped down at the table and examined the lady with the granny glasses. His eyebrows arched as high as they could go. He lifted his arm with the cast up high and laid it on the table between them. "Are you here because I broke my arm?"

"Yes. That's part of it."

"Do you want to sign my cast?" Ty smiled pointing at the pen Ms. Klingburg held in her hand.

"Sure. I'll put Ms. K with a heart." She proceeded to write on Ty's cast.

Ty examined her work and added. "I can tell you how it happened—if I you want."

"Sure. I'd like to hear what you remember."

"I remember all of it. Me and Zander were riding bikes in the driveway. I hit the rock and flew off my bike into the ditch. My mom prayed. Jesus was there too. I had a headache and they put a cast on my arm at the hospital."

"Ahh—What do you mean Jesus was there too?"

"He was. When my mom prayed—Jesus was with her."

The lady took off her granny glasses and looked across the table at Ty. "Are you talking about Jesus from the Bible? Or do you have a friend name Jesus?" The social worker used the Spanish pronunciation for Jesus.

Ty looked confused. "Who? I'm talking about Jesus. The one in the Bible and yes—He is my friend."

The social worker slipped her glasses back on and wrote in her notebook.

The child (Tyson Douglas) does not appear to have anger issues. However, he does seem to be adversely influenced

toward fantasy and even hallucinates about religious figures
i.e. "Seeing Jesus." This child speaks as if he has a friendship
with said Jesus and believes he has seen him in person. My
recommendation for this child is to see a psychiatrist to delve
deeper into the root of this issue.

I recommend this case stay open until this matter can be
investigated further. Currently, pending the interview of
both children with a child psychiatrist, I believe the
children are safe in the home of their parents.

Ms. Klingburg stood up and walked toward the door she entered 90-minutes before. As she passed through the living room Callan and Rey stood and followed her to the door.

The social worker put her hand on the door to leave, then turned and spoke in a matter-of-fact tone. "I've completed the necessary interviews. You'll receive a formal letter in the mail with the results following my supervisor's review."

"Thank you, Ms. Klingburg." Rey and Callan didn't linger in conversation. They were happy to see this woman leave their home.

As her car backed out of the driveway Callan asked, "Rey, what's happening? Could they really believe we're unfit parents? Could they take our children?" All the pent-up emotion escaped. Callan fell on Rey's shoulder and sobbed.

Zander stood at the opening of the living room paralyzed with fear. Ty pushed past him and ran to his parents. "Mommy. Don't cry. It's okay. We're sorry about the ball and breaking your picture. We won't do it again."

Callan reached down and circled her son's shoulders with her arm comforting him while Rey comforted her.

Rey motioned for Zander to join them. He slowly walked across the room and leaned against the side of one of his father's legs. Rey let go of Callan, dropped down to his knees and put his arms around his sons. "Everything's okay—I promise. If you have any questions about what just happened—you can ask. Mom and I will answer honestly."

Callan hugged the boys—pulling herself together for their sake. After a group hug, Callan fixed lunch and the family sat together at the table.

Ty and Zander had plenty of questions, and Rey and Callan did their best to answer each one honestly.

At the end of the discussion Ty added. "I'm going to pray for Ms. Klingburg. She didn't even know who Jesus is. She asked me if Jesus' name was Hey-Sue."

A smile formed on Callan's lips as she thought. Now that was a perfect ending to this stress filled morning.

□□

Heidi looked up from her desk to greet the first client of the day. It was a man in his sixties—a regular who complained of neck and shoulder pain. Heidi threw out her usual *'peace and health to all'* greeting and motioned for him to follow her to the examination room for men.

As she walked past the two empty examination rooms on her way to the back of the business, she was suddenly gripped with the fact that Victor Darwin used certain rooms for certain clients. He had trained her two years ago that the rooms must be used as follows: adult male, adult female and children. She had no reason to suspect anything peculiar ...*before*...but now she questioned if there was a deeper meaning to the three examination rooms.

The male client followed a few steps behind Heidi. She passed the room where only adult women were treated. Heidi had been in that room many times undressing for a massage. A panic gripped her at the reality of what might be...could be…happening right under her nose and possibly—to her. She wanted to scream, run. She opened the door of the male consultation room and stepped aside for the man to enter.

"You can take everything off from the waist up. You know the routine. *The Healer* will be in shortly. There's a sheet on the table to cover up. Is the room warm enough for you? I can turn on the space heater."

The man said he was fine as Heidi shut the door and returned to her desk.

Heidi picked up the office phone and then placed it back on the holder. She looked at the appointment book in front of her and thought about the next family that would be arriving in less than an hour. She picked the phone back up and dialed the Hillbrooke Medical Clinic. She pushed a few numbers on the keypad and finally was able to speak to a real person.

"Dr. Hayes' office." The overworked receptionist sounded slightly bothered by the call.

"This is Heidi Alden. I'm a patient of Dr. Hayes, and I'd like an appointment as soon as possible."

"What is your medical issue?"

"I'm sorry. I can't talk about it with anyone but Dr. Hayes. It's personal."

Heidi could hear papers shuffling followed by an annoyed sigh. A feeling of insignificance washed over her—like the person on the other end of the line was inconvenienced by her issues.

The receptionist finally said. "Well, I guess we could squeeze you in about 3 P.M."

"Thank you. That will work for me." Heidi felt fragile and vulnerable—two words she would never have used to describe herself—before today.

□□

Samantha Hayes opened the door to *The Healer's* office. Baylee struggled to walk—Samantha hovered at her side trying to be helpful. Isabelle followed behind them and sat down in a huff without acknowledging Heidi.

Heidi glanced up at the family then back at the appointment book in front of her. *The Healer* liked to keep things old school. There wasn't a computer in the office—that she knew of. When Victor was busy with a client, Heidi would use her iPhone to look things up, go on Facebook or send emails. Once she finished her notations in the book she looked up again and smiled.

"Samantha, hello—who will be going first today—Baylee or Isabelle?" Heidi asked.

Both girls looked at their mother for direction. "I think..." She paused to think about it. "...Isabelle will go first since this is her first time."

Victor Darwin walked into the reception area followed by *shoulder pain man.* Victor smiled at the Hayes family then turned to talk to the man. "I think we can up your appointments to three times a week now that you're managing the pain."

The man nodded in the affirmative.

The Healer leaned in close to Heidi and whispered, "The older girl can go in the adult room and put the mother and younger one in the kid's room."

Heidi whispered, "Shouldn't the family stay together?" A rush of prickly fears caused her to shiver.

Victor didn't acknowledge Heidi's question. He walked down the hallway to his office. Heidi watched him disappear and felt his silent reproach. She was glad 'shoulder pain man' stood in front of her desk blocking her red face from Samantha Hayes.

Heidi scanned the appointment book for openings then jotted down a few appointment dates on a card. She handed the card to the man. He pulled a $100 bill from his wallet and handed it to her. She took the money and laid it on the table in front of her, opened the cash box and gave the man his change.

'Shoulder pain man' smiled at the family in the waiting room, "*The Healer* is a miracle worker. I highly recommend him." He gave a nod of approval and left.

Heidi wasn't feeling her chatty self. She stood and motioned for the Hayes family to follow. "I'm going to keep you all together in the family consultation room for your appointment." The Hayes family followed Heidi down the hallway. Baylee struggled to keep up, wincing in pain as she walked. Heidi opened the door to the kid's room and allowed the family to pass by her.

Victor sat at his desk in his office space at the end of the L-shaped hallway. He had a view of the doorway to two of the examination rooms. His eyes narrowed at Heidi's purposeful opposition to his instructions. The defiance felt empowering to Heidi—then petrifying.

Heidi turned back toward the Hayes family. "Isabelle, go ahead and sit on the table. *The Healer* will be in shortly." As she turned back toward the hallway, Heidi shut the door on a sick child, a rebellious teen and an uninformed mother. A moment of doubt washed over her—then she spoke in a whisper as she moved toward her desk, "At least they have each other." The clock on her desk flashed the time. It was 11 A.M.

21

You Only Get One Life— So Live It.

D ebbie, the eldest daughter of Jean and Tom Brown, was able to arrange her schedule to stay for two extra weeks—even more if it became necessary. Kim had to leave a week ago, due to her work schedule. She would be back soon—she promised Debbie.

Jean Brown and Debbie sat in the waiting room of the Hillbrooke Medical Center. The appointment for Jean was a courtesy—she had requested a visit with Dr. Hayes. Her medical care had been turned over to the oncologist a month ago. Debbie could see her mother losing her strength a little more each day. It was a terrible time for all of them, believing for a healing yet preparing for something else.

The nurse stepped into the waiting area to call the next patient's name. Balancing on one foot, the nurse held the door open with her other foot. "Jean Brown." She called.

Debbie helped her mom to a standing position secretly wishing she would have used the courtesy wheelchair the clinic provided in the entry. When they arrived, Debbie had put her hand on the back of the wheelchair and turned it toward her mom, but Jean refused to sit. She walked past the wheelchair into the waiting area. Debbie had to respect her mom's wishes, yet inside she wanted to plead with her to rest, sit, don't push yourself so hard. She let go of the wheelchair, hurried to take her mom's arm and took the first seats inside the door.

Debbie waved in the nurse's direction to identify they were coming. She glanced back at the empty wheelchair in the entryway. Jean stood slowly allowing her body to unfold, then took the first of many steps toward the nurse and the open door. Debbie held her mother's arm and moved at her pace— grateful when the nurse stopped at the first examination room inside the doorway.

The nurse didn't do any of the usual things like weight, temperature, blood pressure or health history. She positioned a piece of paper in the box outside the door and said. "You can be seated in the chairs. The doctor will be in soon."

All the things the nurse didn't do or say, both Debbie and Jean heard in her facial expressions and lack of interaction. *You're nearly dead so I'm not gonna bother you with the stuff we do to for the living.*

The nurse shut the door behind her and the room closed in on Debbie. She tried to lighten the mood with conversation. "Do you feel like going out for lunch later?"

"Maybe. I'll see how I'm feeling when we leave. If we do go out I want it to be a diner that has real hamburgers and fries. It's been a long time since I've eaten anything like that. Maybe even a thick chocolate shake." A smile formed on Jean's face at the thought of such extravagant food.

"Okay, Mom! Let's do it."

The sound of a soft knock drew their attention in the direction of the door.

Dr. Hayes eased the door open. "Good morning! It's wonderful to see you again Mrs. Brown."

"Oh, come on Dr. Hayes—it's Jean. We're way past formalities."

"Yes. I guess we are. So, does that mean you'll call me Stuart?"

Jean nodded her head. "Stuart is a fine name.

"Jean, what can I do for you today?"

"Doctor…uummm…Stuart, I know my prognosis isn't good. I also know that in the event that I die—I'm ready to face what comes next."

Stuart moved uncomfortably in his chair. He didn't like to talk about death or the afterlife. There was no afterlife so why discuss it. He was cynical about life as well. It has little to offer other than what a person decides to make of it—or not. He had always tried to keep medicine and religion separate. He doctored the body and allowed people to seek spiritual comfort from clergy—if they needed that type of comfort. He was feeling this conversation was going nowhere good—for him.

"Stuart, I know I'm dying. I wanted to see you one last time— because God put it in my heart to come."

Debbie touched her mom's arm. "Mom, the doctor's very busy. We can't take his time for this."

Debbie kept her hand on her mom's arm and Jean put her hand over it but continued to look at Dr. Hayes. "There will never be any time in my life or yours that will be of more value to you than the next few moments."

Debbie looked down at the floor. It would be futile to persuade her mom to do anything other than what the Lord had directed her to do.

"Stuart. This will only take a few minutes —may I continue?"

Dr. Hayes' jaw was tight, "Yes. Jean, please do."

Jean took less than five minutes to layout an eternal plan for the ages. It was all about love, disobedience, redemption, a demand for payment, sacrifice, surrender and eternity.

Dr. Hayes listened. His face had softened but remained nonemotionally. When Jean finished, Debbie was wiping tears from her eyes.

Dr. Hayes was not. He asked Jean one question. "Are you angry with God?"

Jean smiled—an essence of peace flowed from her. "God doesn't owe me any explanations. My job is to trust Him. Someday His purpose will be known, but until then I ask—and then accept whatever comes."

Dr. Hayes stood and reached out his hand to take Jean's. "Thank you, Jean, for coming."

Jean stood up slowly and hugged the doctor. She whispered in his ear. "Goodbye." When she released him Dr. Hayes exited the room without saying a word.

Jean smiled at Debbie—there was a beautiful peace on her face. She had completed her mission—obedience felt good. "Honey, I'll take that wheelchair now." Jean sat back down. "My spirit is strong, but this old body is growing tired."

□□

In Snake's private office at Superior Solar Energy, he twisted from side to side in his swivel office chair. He felt nervous and uneasy. Something like a kid who couldn't sit still. He needed to get up and move around. It was senseless to try and write computer programs when he felt anxious. He prayed silently. *Lord, help me focus. I'm a mess today. Help me get my act together and get back to work.* He continued the nervous movement—relieved that his office was private. No one else could see him fidgeting.

The cell phone in his front pocket vibrated which startled Snake, causing him to react by jumping straight up in the air. He quickly turned his head back and forth to see if anyone saw him. Everyone was busy working. He reached in his pocket, answered the phone and sat down at his desk. "Hello."

"Snake. It's Pastor Rey. Have you had lunch yet?"

"No Pastor."

"You wanna meet me at the Train Depot. My treat. Say in about fifteen minutes."

Snake looked at the clock. It was past his lunchtime. "Sure—I need a break from my desk and these four walls. I'm leaving now."

"Okay—I'll be right behind you."

Snake closed his computer and headed for the door. He arrived first at the Train Depot Restaurant, found a table and waited for Pastor Rey. A few minutes later he saw a tall man coming in his direction. Pastor Rey had a goofy smile on his face.

"What's going on Pastor?"

Rey fought a mischievous smile as he slid into the booth across from Snake.

"I know that smile. Something is going on. What have you heard?"

Rey snickered like a little boy with a secret. "Honest, I really don't have any agenda for meeting. I guess it's just the giggles."

Snake looked skeptical. "Really?"

"Yes. Of course." Rey laughed again. "Can't a guy just be happy?"

Snake squinted. "I'm sorry, but this is sorta out of character for you."

"Fine." Rey laughed. "I wanted to meet and tell you what an amazing job you and Fauna did last night at the small group.

You two flowed like two people who had been working together for years. I was just wondering…when's the plan to *put a ring on it!*" Pastor Rey threw his head back and laughed at his own joke.

Snake didn't laugh.

Rey looked across the table at a somber face. Rey knew that his joke didn't ring true for Snake. "I'm sorry. Did I say something wrong?" He caught his breath and asked. "Did you break it off with Fauna?"

"No, but there are no plans to marry."

Rey frowned. The shock was evident in his voice. "What? You mean never?"

There was a long silence before Snake spoke. "Have you forgotten that I have a criminal background?"

"No Snake. I haven't. Remember I was there visiting you in jail. But what does that have to do with marrying Fauna."

"Pastor, how could I ask her to take on my past? It's her dream to open a family counseling center. Who wants their counselor married to a former drug dealer and other stuff that could come out from my past? If you were looking for a marriage counselor or someone to talk to your troubled teen, would you pick the one who choose a person like me to marry? It doesn't really speak to that person's good judgment."

"What? Why am I hearing about this now—for the first time? You've been dating for over a year. You have a clean record. You're off probation. You have a great job and you're active in the church. You even help delinquent boys."

Snake spoke defensively. "You know me. You've had years to develop a friendship and trust with me." He shook his head. "There are people out there who would destroy Fauna if they didn't like her advice or she didn't fix their problems to perfection—they would be vicious. Look how people treated the pastor…" Snake pointed both index fingers in Pastor Rey's direction. "… for reaching out to the poor and the likes of me and that wasn't so many years ago."

Rey wasn't giggling anymore. "Snake, please don't believe that. It's a lie from the enemy to keep you from moving forward. The devil wins, if he can keep you locked up and in bondage from your past mistakes. Brother, you've been set free—you gotta walk in that freedom. You've got to fight the past, not surrender to it."

The waitress stepped up to the table and smiled. "Hey Pastor Rey. Hey Snake. The usual or ya wanna look at the menu." She pushed two glasses of water across the table, then tapped the two menus she held under her arm.

Rey looked at Snake to answer. Snake said, "I'll have the usual."

Rey nodded signifying the same. The waitress walked away snapping gum and doing a few dance steps to the 50's music playing through the diner's sound system.

Pastor Rey looked back at Snake and continued. "Fauna's a great girl and she's not gonna wait forever. Have you discussed this with her? Ya know—she should have a say."

Snake leaned forward like he was about to share a secret. "You know how Fauna is. She would believe it was a non-issue. She doesn't know people like I do—having a convict for a husband would be a disaster—I couldn't bear to see Fauna hurt."

"Have you done any research on the matter? I mean is it unlawful for a counselor to marry a reformed criminal."

"Of course not." Snake answered. "And—yes I know that because I did the research."

"Well, then don't you think Fauna should have a say?"

Snake shook his head in frustration. "This thing has been eating me up. Fauna has dropped more than one hint that she's ready to move forward. I suppose you caught the little inside joke at your table when she emphasized the I WILL the other night."

"Yes, Callan and I thought that might be because you'd already asked her and were waiting to spring the news on the rest of us."

"I wish." Snake looked defeated.

The waitress held two plates waist high in front of her and announced the orders. "Two Reuben sandwiches with fries. Eat up." She placed the plates down in front of the men. "And here's the catsup. See, I didn't forget. Let me know if you want dessert later."

Pastor smiled at her and answered. "You know we will." She scurried off, picking up dirty dishes on her way to the kitchen.

"Let's pray. We can talk more about this later."

Snake bowed his head while Rey prayed for the food— Snake silently prayed for a miracle.

□□

The Healer opened the door to the examination room. Samantha smiled. He brushed past her and moved toward Isabelle. Baylee cowered behind her mother. Samantha could feel her youngest daughter trembling.

Isabelle narrowed her eyes and watched Victor Darwin. She willed herself not to be intimidated by him. She was coming to this appointment because her mother begged her to come. She would give it a try. Ms. Reynolds told her to be more open with people. She had given that crazy woman receptionist a try and that didn't work out so well. Now, this pasty undertaker was trying to play "stare down" with her. Isabelle thought this freak has no idea who he's dealing with. A sly smile tried to form on Isabelle's mouth. She fought it—trying to keep her face and emotions impersonal and under control.

The Healer circled the table. Not saying a word. He looked at her from every side.

Isabelle kept her eyes forward. To follow him with her eyes would be surrendering to him. That she would not do.

The Healer breathed in a low voice, "I'm going to touch your head with my hands to read your aura."

Isabelle put up one arm and blocked his hands as they moved toward her. "The heck you are." She slid off the table and stood. "Isabelle!" Her mother shouted in surprise.

"This isn't right. He's *creepy*, and he's not putting his hands on me." She walked past her mother and out of the room.

Samantha looked at *The Healer* in shock. "I'm so sorry. She's a teenager."

Victor Darwin held up one hand to silence Samantha. "She'll come around when she's ready." He patted the table for Baylee to come.

Baylee held on tighter to her mother a faint cry escaped her lips, "Please mom. I don't want to."

The Healer patted the table again keeping his eyes on Samantha to follow his instruction.

Samantha stood up and lifted Baylee in her arms. She walked the few steps to the table. Samantha stood at the edge of the table, Baylee clinging to her. "Baylee. Relax. It may help. We must try. Don't fight it."

Baylee's body went limp in her mom's arms, and Samantha laid her on the table.

It was a repeat of the first time they came; far away looks and quiet tears.

Following the session, Samantha carried Baylee out of the office.

Isabelle sat in the reception area flipping through a magazine. When she saw Baylee, limp in her mother's arms, she scolded. "What happened to her? Why did you let him touch her?"

There was an empty expression on Samantha's face—emotionally spent—physically drained. Samantha laid $150 on the desk and left without getting her change.

On the way home no one spoke.

□□

Victor walked into the office where Heidi sat. He stood close—too close. He didn't speak. Heidi looked up from her seated position and met his scowl. "You are worthless at recruiting. Everyone who comes with your recommendation is hopeless. You can't even follow the simplest directions. I doubt that family will ever come back after this fiasco."

Heidi tried to explain. "I know that girl. She's not ready to be alone in therapy. I'm still tweaking her—preparing her." Heidi couldn't believe the words were coming out of her mouth. She hated herself—and she hated him.

Victor spit out the words so close to Heidi's face—she could feel his breath. "If they ever come back again—listen to me. I know what I'm doing. The adult room for the girl." He turned and walked away.

Heidi yelled after him. "I need to leave early. I can put the phones on night to answer any calls."

Victor did not reply.

Heidi left anyway.

22

What Are You Afraid Of?

After lunch with Snake, Pastor Rey arrived back at the church. He settled in to put the final touches on his Sunday message. The sermon was part of a trendy series of messages on the Facebook emojis he developed entitled— *How ya feeling?* He had covered the topics; *Thanking God*—In everything Give Thanks, *Enjoying Life*—Judgement is Coming, *Showing Love*—Greater Love, *Losing My Mind*—God's in Control, *Lying in Bed*—Parable of the Foolish Man and *Sleeping*—We don't grieve like those who have no hope. The message for this Sunday would be *Enjoying the Rain*—Endure Until The Test Is Over. Seeing what he and Callan were walking through—these were timely messages.

Rey silently read the scripture text for his message from James 1:2-4. Then he spoke it out loud listening to each word. *"My brothers and sisters be very happy when you are tested in different ways. You know that such testing of your faith produces endurance.*

Endure until your testing is over. Then you will be mature and complete, and you won't need anything."

Rey looked up from his open Bible and noticed the light flashing on his phone indicating a message. He entered his password and listened through the speaker. "Pastor, it's Grace. When you have a moment this afternoon I'd like to speak with you. It's nothing bad. It's just a question about the boys from Sunday school."

Rey wondered. Great, what did those boys do now? If they were disrespectful to Grace, they are going to get a talking to. Why did she wait until Friday to talk to me about this? He sighed and felt his shoulders slump as he hit the intercom button that connected him to Grace's desk.

"Yes, Pastor?" Grace answered.

"I have a few minutes if you want to talk with me about the boys and what happened in Sunday school."

"Okay—I'll be right in." Grace switched the phones to answering machine mode and walked down the hallway past the other pastors' offices.

Rey heard a soft tap at his door. "Come in, Grace."

"Pastor, this shouldn't take long."

"Those boys—what did they do now?" Rey leaned forward in his chair listening attentively to whatever Grace was getting ready to share.

"No—it's not like that. In my Sunday school class, we've been talking about the miracles of Jesus, and I was reviewing the past two week's stories on healing."

Rey was listening, but he wasn't sure why. He nodded his head to let Grace know he was following her story wishing he had a remote control and could push fast forward to the part about the boys.

Grace continued. "This past Sunday, the lesson was on the four friends who took the sick man to Jesus and of course Jesus heals him." Grace looked across the desk at Pastor Rey. "Well, the boys were acting strangely. Zander even kicked Ty under the table for asking a question about healing."

"So far you've said nothing that shocks me!" Rey sighed and remembered the scripture for his sermon was all about tests and trials.

Grace laughed, and Rey liked that she got his humor. "The part that had me baffled was when Ty was questioning whether his—a child's prayer—for people who were sick could be heard or answered by God."

"What did you tell him?" Rey asked.

"I told the class that God hears everyone who prays. Ty seemed happy about that but..." Grace wasn't sure how to phrase the next part. She didn't want to sound like she was accusing Pastor or Callan of doctrinal error.

"Buuuut?" Rey moved his hand in a circle to help keep Grace moving.

Grace mumbled. "Well...he seemed to be under the impression that an adult in his life had told him not to pray for someone who was sick."

"What? That doesn't make any sense. Callan and I pray every night with the boys. We've prayed for people who are sick many times. In fact, just recently, the boys never miss praying for a neighbor child with pain or something."

"Yes, I thought it was strange too, I didn't know if they may have overheard something or had gotten wrong information from someone other than you and Callan. I thought you'd want to know and maybe talk to them. I hope I did the right thing in telling you."

"Of course, you did. I want to know if my children have spiritual questions or are confused about biblical things. Who better to answer those questions than their parents?"

"Yes, Pastor—I thought the same thing."

Rey had an *ah-ha* moment. "I wonder if this has anything to do with Jean Brown's condition. I bet they heard Callan and me talking about it over this past month. I'll talk to Callan and we'll get things cleared up. Thanks for sharing that with me."

As Grace was walking out of the office, stopped and said, "I love Ty and Zander and wouldn't want them to worry or be concerned about the freedom to pray for people in need."

Rey smiled. "Absolutely."

Grace was relieved as she walked back to her desk.

□□

Heidi signed in at the Hillbrooke Medical Clinic. She wasn't feeling as smug this time as she did a few weeks ago. She took the chair nearest the door that led to the examination rooms. How would she ever put this into words? What if they thought she was crazy—making these kinds of accusations? Her heart started pounding in her chest.

"Heidi Alden." The nurse looked past her for the patient. Heidi stood up. They were nearly standing nose to nose.

The nurse released the door to Heidi and motioned for her to follow. They walked past a few rooms then the nurse stopped. "You can drop your things here. I'll check your weight in the hallway over there." The nurse gestured to a location out of Heidi's sight.

Heidi dropped her things in the examination room and followed the nurse to the scales down another hallway. After the weight check, Heidi followed her back to the room where she checked her blood pressure—a bit high, temp—normal, pulse—a bit fast. Then the dreaded question came. "And what brings you in today?"

Heidi thought, should I tell her? She may be more sympathetic than a male doctor. Heidi decided to lie. "I am having problems with my birth control and I need to talk about my options."

"Oh—well okay." The nurse seemed a bit confused but didn't question Heidi. "You may have to wait a few minutes longer today. We've had to *squeeze* people in." There was a hint of disgust in her tone when she put emphasis on the word *squeeze*. Heidi felt the implication—*your problem isn't exactly an emergency!*

Heidi humbled herself. "Thanks for fitting me in. I can wait."

The nurse left with a nod—Heidi was alone. She looked around the small examination room. Her eyes welled up. She had no one. Not one person to walk through this with her—except a doctor she had openly flirted with—but even in her fantasies, she knew he was a stranger.

Heidi stood and walked over to the counter. There was a sink and a few glass jars with things like tongue compressors, cotton balls and long Q-tips. She was looking for a box of tissues. She opened a drawer and found a box hidden away out of sight. She pulled out an ample supply.

"Don't cry—don't cry." Heidi spoke the words in a whisper. Too late—the tears were rolling down her cheeks when Dr. Hayes walked in.

"Mrs. Alden—would you like the nurse to come in?"

Heidi shook her head no. Then with emotion in her voice she reassured, "No. Wait—I'll be okay." She blew her nose, wiped her tears and took a deep breath trying to shake off the emotion.

Dr. Hayes waited—then said. "Mrs. Alden, I can come back in a few minutes, if you want."

Heidi blurted out, "Please stop calling me Mrs. Alden! It's Heidi."

"Heidi, what exactly is the problem today? The nurse said that it was of a personal nature."

"Yes. I-I suspect, but I'm not sure." Heidi stopped. She didn't even know how to put this into words.

"Is this a medical issue?" Dr. Hayes tried to drag something—anything out of the emotional woman sitting across from him.

Tears welled up in her eyes again. She felt like a fool. "Never mind. I think I should go."

"Heidi is someone hurting you?"

Heidi looked at the doctor with a surprised expression.

Dr. Hayes said, "You need to go to the police and make a report if someone has or is threatening you."

"What can I report? I don't have any proof."

Stuart knew better. He knew better than to touch—a crying woman. He stood up and tried to comfort her. He touched Heidi's back with a pat.

Heidi jumped up from the chair and hugged the doctor around the waist laying her head on his chest. She sobbed. Stuart put both hands in the air like he was being held up—he would not embrace her—but he did know he was feeling emotionally drawn to this hurting woman. He felt sorry for her situation— she seemed in danger.

The knock on the door helped Dr. Hayes break Heidi's grip on him. "Doctor is everything okay."

Dr. Hayes opened the door to speak to the nurse. He whispered. "I need the brochure for the Crises Hotline."

"Yes. Doctor, I'll get that right now." She glanced past the doctor and saw Heidi standing and crying.

Dr. Hayes left the door slightly ajar.

"Heidi, I'm unclear exactly what is happening, but I can see you are going through a difficult situation. I'm going to get you a number to call. I can do an exam if there is bruising you want documented."

"No. I'm not in pain. I feel so stupid and ashamed."

The nurse slipped into the room and handed the pamphlet to the doctor and quickly left.

"Here." Dr. Hayes handed the brochure to Heidi. "Read this and *call* the hotline. It's all confidential. You never have to give your name. You may feel more comfortable telling your whole story to someone who you're not looking at face to face. I can write you a script for anxiety."

"Yes. I think I'd like that."

Stuart stood to leave and patted Heidi's shoulder as he left.

She looked up at him with tear filled eyes and mouthed the words. "Thank you."

□□

The Douglas family was nearly back to a normal routine. A week had passed since Ms. Klingburg had stopped by for the surprise interview. There had been no phone calls or letter to silence their concerns one way or another. The CPS system seemed a dark abyss to Callan and Rey. While they knew CPS helped many people, the Douglas family didn't belong there. This was a world they were unfamiliar with and did not want to be drawn into.

Callan was relieved when Samantha called to invite them over again. Samantha wanted Baylee to have some distractions by having the boys over while she needed to talk with Callan. "Come on boys. We're leaving in a few minutes. Gather your games or whatever you're taking."

Ty packed up a few games in his backpack. Zander saw him slip in the kids Bible that Grandma and Grandpa Douglas gave him a few years ago. It was a gift when he first learned how to read. "You can't take that. I'm gonna tell."

"No. Don't. Please—If I we get caught, I'll take all the blame. It's too important."

Zander puckered his lips. "Okay, but you owe me."

Callan was waiting for the boys in the living room. She held a plate of chocolate chip cookies in her hand. "It's always a good idea to bring a gift when you go visit someone." She smiled at the boys.

Ty returned her smile. "I agree, mom. That's a great idea." He winked at Zander who shifted his eyes.

The Douglas family cut across the yards of the two houses between their home and the Hayes. Baylee sat on the porch waiting for her two friends. When she saw them coming she yelled, "Mom, they're coming!" In her excitement, she stood too quickly and lost her balance. She fell with a loud thud on the front porch. Baylee's pain was excruciating, but she knew if she cried out her mother would end the fun before it began. She pulled herself up with the porch railing and examined herself. One knee was bleeding. She held tightly to the wood railing, fighting the pain and the tears that formed in her eyes.

Ty reached the porch first and walked toward her. "Hey— Baylee. You're outside!" He swung his backpack around and with excitement in his voice said, "Wait 'til ya see what I brought." As he walked closer Ty saw Baylee's face. "What happened?"

Baylee whispered. "Don't say anything—if I my mom knows I fell she'll make me go to bed and I won't be able to play."

Ty reached down and unzipped his backpack. He fumbled around a moment, then pulled out an old napkin from a forgotten lunch months ago. He dabbed at her knee to stop the bleeding.

Zander stepped up behind Ty. "Did you fall or something?"

Baylee put her finger to her lips. "Shhhhhh."

Zander blocked Baylee from his mom's view.

Callan glanced in the children's direction. "Hi Baylee. Is your mom inside?"

"Yes. Mrs. Douglas, go on in."

"Come on. You can call me Callan." Callan didn't wait for Baylee to respond. She tapped on the door as she opened it. "Samantha, it's Callan."

Once Callan was out of sight, Baylee hobbled to the seat a few steps behind her. Ty released the tissue to Baylee and she applied pressure to the cut.

Zander was questioning his involvement in the cover-up. "Do ya want me to get your mom? What if it won't stop bleeding?" He looked at Ty and asked. "What if you need stitches?"

Ty put his hand on Baylee's hand. It was the hand that was pushing the napkin against her leg. "I'm going to pray for the bleeding to stop."

Zander jerked his head toward the door then back. "What? You aren't gonna be happy until we are sent to prison. Mom said…"

Ty's prayer cut him off. "Dear Jesus, my friend Baylee is hurt. She needs help. Please help the blood to stop and help her to feel okay again. In Jesus name I pray. Amen."

When Ty opened his eyes, Baylee was smiling at him. "What was that?"

"That's praying. We do it all the time. Jesus—you know him—right?"

Baylee shifted in the yard furniture. "I've heard of him. I've heard people say, Jesus Christ when they're mad. Is that the same thing?"

Zander rolled his eyes. "See, I told you. She doesn't know anything about what we believe."

Ty removed his hand from Baylee's knee. "Check it. Let's see if Jesus heard my prayer."

Baylee slowly removed the napkin. The bleeding had stopped, and a part of the napkin stayed attached to the dry blood. "It stopped. Let's go upstairs and I can put a Band-Aid on it before my mom sees."

Zander and Ty stood on each side of Baylee. She put her arms around each of their waists, and they hobbled up the stairs to her bedroom.

Samantha yelled from the kitchen. "You kids be good up there. I'll come up in a minute to check on you."

Baylee yelled back. "Okay mom."

Once in the bedroom, Baylee sat in the chair next to her bed. "Can you open that drawer? There's Band-Aids in there."

Zander obeyed and pulled a box of Band-Aids from the drawer. He opened the box pulling out the largest one and handed it to Baylee. He passed by her to get the video games set up— grabbing the backpack from Ty, Zander pulled out a video game and dropped the backpack on the floor.

Ty picked up the backpack and hugged it. "Baylee?"

She answered, "Yes." While she applied the flesh colored bandage to her knee.

"I brought you a present. It's used so I hope you don't mind."

"A present for me? Thanks."

Ty dug in the backpack and pulled out the book. "This is a Bible. It tells all about Jesus and how much he loves us. It's kind of a secret so I'm going to stick it under your pillow. When you are alone—read it. We can talk more about it later. If you want to get saved—I can show you how to do that too. The big thing is—Jesus heals people."

Baylee looked skeptical. "Is he like *The Healer*?"

Ty looked surprised and Zander stopped fiddling with the video equipment. "How do you know about Jesus being a Healer?"

"I don't know Jesus—only the one downtown who calls himself *The Healer*." She bit on her bottom lip to stop the quiver. "He hurt me. I don't like him."

Ty looked at Zander and said. "Jesus doesn't hurt people. He makes them better." Ty tapped on the Bible he was still holding in his hand. "All the stories are in here. You'll like them…and you'll like Jesus too." He pushed the Bible under the pillow on the bed and walked over to examine Baylee's knee. "See—Jesus is a kind Healer. He stopped the bleeding, so we can play."

□□

Callan sat on the comfy sofa in the Hayes' family room. From her seat she could see Samantha fixing the coffee in the kitchen. Callan coached her thoughts as she blankly watched Samantha. Take it slow. Keep it causal. Build a relationship before you push in with spiritual things. Wait until she's ready to hear.

Callan's thoughts were interrupted by the smell of coffee near her face. Samantha said, "Here ya go."

Callan reached up and took the solid colored coffee cup from Samantha. It was a pale blue, no frills, just like Samantha. Her beauty became stronger and deeper each time Callan was with her.

Samantha sat on the other end of the sofa and tucked her feet up underneath her. "So, it's been a few weeks since we talked. Is everything going well with you?"

Callan felt conflicted. If this was going to be a true friendship—she needed to trust Samantha with her troubles too. Callan ventured out to a place she had never been before— trusting I someone outside her church. "As a matter of fact, we had a visit a week ago from someone at the Child Protective Services. She came unexpectedly to our door to investigate Rey and me. They were under the impression that we broke Ty's arm."

Samantha listened to Callan while she unconsciously stirred her coffee with a slender silver spoon. She stopped stirring, pulled the spoon out of her coffee and waved it around in the air as she spoke. "How could anyone who knows you think such a thing? I can't speak for your husband. I haven't actually met Rey, yet."

Callan suggested. "We should do something altogether sometime. I'd love for Rey to meet Dr. Hayes. He was so sweet to me and the boys at the follow-up visit from Ty's accident."

Samantha agreed. "We should. I'd like that."

"I'll talk to Rey and you talk to Dr. Hayes and we'll see what we can set up."

Samantha smiled in approval and asked. "What happened with the investigation?"

"We haven't heard. The worst part was the day the investigator came I was having a mom melt down over the boys throwing a ball in the house. She heard the whole thing and that didn't look good for me."

"Surely, they are trained to weed out stuff like that. She must have known it was the exception not the norm."

Callan sighed. "I hope that will be the case when everything is examined. The social worker seemed predisposed to finding fault with us. I'd be fearful this stranger might be capable of doing my family harm if I didn't know who I am and what is true."

Samantha shook her head in disbelief. "I know what you mean. I struggle with believing I'm a good mother all the time.

Since Isabelle is out of school for the summer it's been one roller-coaster ride after another." Samantha threw her arms in the air like she was on a thrill ride. "Stop, I want off."

Callan laughed. At that moment, she felt like she and Samantha were finally pushing past—awkward neighbor—and becoming trusted friends.

As Samantha told her story, she grew more serious. "A few days ago, we went back to *The Healer's* office. I know you warned me not to go. I should have listened. We won't be going back there ever again."

"What happened?" Callan asked because she wanted to be a listening ear to Samantha and she also knew the danger that loomed in a place like that.

"It's really kind of funny. Isabelle told off Victor Darwin and refused to let him touch her. I was secretly proud of her and wished I'd have had the backbone to follow her." Samantha looked out the window next to the fireplace. "I could have followed her, but I didn't. I put poor Baylee through another hopeless and painful session." Samantha swallowed hard fighting the tears welling up in her eyes.

Callan tried to console her. "Samantha, come on. We try to do the best we can for our kids, but sometimes we get it wrong." Callan slapped her hand down on her leg with a smack.

Samantha jerked her head in Callan's direction.

Callan continued in a softer voice. "We just get it wrong and there's not a dog-gone thing we can do about it…except don't make the same mistake twice."

Samantha sighed. "I did make the same mistake twice. But I won't make it a third time."

"Well, I think my work is done here." Callan pretended to get up to leave and then plopped back down. "Can't get rid of me that easy!"

"Callan, there is one thing I've been meaning to ask you about. When the boys were here at one of their visits, I overheard Ty talking to Baylee about healing and prayer. Is that something your family practices?"

Callan wasn't prepared for the swift change of course. She prayed to herself. *Lord, help me.* "Do you remember exactly what he said?" She asked.

"No, not exactly. But, I guess you know—if I'd put my kids through a visit at *The Healer's...*" She hung her head and continued. "...twice. Then you must know I'd like to know whatever you can tell me about the healing Ty was talking about. He sounded like he knew something special and wanted to share it with Baylee, but it was all kind of secretive." Samantha looked directly at Callan and waited.

"Yes. We do believe in prayer and healing. It's a long story. Do you have time to hear about it now?"

"Can't think of a better time than the present! Would you like me to freshen up your coffee?" Samantha picked up Callan's cup from the coffee table and went into the kitchen.

Callan prayed with her eyes open. She looked in the direction of the kitchen, her lips moved quietly, her heart pounded in her chest—she prayed as the Spirit guided her. She knew this was one of those special moments. She held the seed of truth, and she prayed it would land on fertile ground.

23

Pride Messes Everything Up.

D r. Hayes opened the back door and walked into the kitchen. Samantha was putting the final touches on dinner. She looked at her husband and said, "You look beat. Did you have a rough day?"

Stuart stood at the island resting his briefcase on the stool. "You have no idea. It went from bad to worse with people at death's door, feeling the necessity to fulfill their bucket list items all in one day. I'm emotionally spent." He dropped his briefcase by the wall and walked into the family room. He sunk into the couch and put his feet up on the coffee table. He scanned the area for the remote and spotted it on top of the fireplace mantel across the room. He sighed wondering if he dare ask Samantha to come and get it for him. He thought better of that and got up to get it.

Before Stuart could sit back down Samantha stood beside him. "I had a bad start to my day but a great finish."

Stuart looked at her closely. "You look different. Is it a new hair style?"

Samantha shook her head—no.

"Well, something's different. Are you going to tell me, or do I have to keep guessing?"

"Don't be mad!"

Stuart sat back down. "Those three words usually mean I will be mad—what did you do and how much is it going to cost me?"

"It was free."

"I like free."

"Callan came over today with the boys."

"Samantha, I told you I don't know if they are the best people to buddy up with."

Samantha continued despite Stuart's rebuke. "We had the best time and I finally feel like I have a friend—a real friend. She cares about what's happening in my life and the girls too."

"Really. Could you be anymore needy right now?" Dr. Hayes clicked on the TV indicating to Samantha their conversation was over.

Samantha pushed for a few more minutes. "Wait. I didn't even get to tell you the stuff Callan and I talked about today. Someone called Child Protective Services on them. Isn't that just terrible?"

Stuart pushed the mute button on the remote and looked at Samantha. "Not really. They probably did something to deserve it." Stuart watched Samantha's face change from conversational to combative. He continued. "I know Baylee likes the boys and I'm sure the kids are fine, but do you have to be chummy with that mom? Why don't you befriend that other lady? The one who took Issie out the other day seems nice. She may need a friend like you to encourage her." Stuart didn't want to share all he knew about Heidi. If they became friends, it would be better that Heidi share her story and not him.

"You mean Heidi?" Samantha sat down on the love seat. "I have some concerns about her. I don't think she's such a wonderful example for our teenager, and I don't really see myself being close with her."

"Why? You barely know her. Here's what we do know—she picked up our daughter in the middle of nowhere and brought her home safely. She even tried to take her out for dinner and a movie but Issie became dramatic—for whatever reason. When Heidi came back here that day—she was concerned about Isabelle and polite."

Samantha felt defensive. "Well, maybe you should befriend her." She immediately regretted the words as they rolled off her tongue. How did this turn ugly? She had great news she wanted to share with him.

Stuart stood up, walked to the mudroom and slipped his shoes back on. "I'll take my dinner at the diner."

Samantha stood silent. Her pride was hurt. She knew she could stop him if she wanted to, but—she watched him shut the door with a slam.

Issie stood in the hallway looking on. "Was that dad?" Samantha turned back into the kitchen and busied herself. "Dinner will be ready in a few minutes."

□□

Callan sat at the foot of the bottom bunk. She leaned forward a bit to keep from bumping her head. Ty stretched out on his bunk behind Callan. Zander's head hung down from the top bunk to keep an eye on his brother. Rey stood by the head of the bed with his arm resting on the top bunk. "Boys, we wanted to talk to you for a minute before we pray."

Zander pulled up and propped his head up with his hand to get a good view of his dad. He asked. "Are we in trouble?"

"No—not at all. Why would you think you're in trouble?" Rey asked wondering if he'd missed something.

Zander flopped back in his bed. "Just wondering—that's all."

Rey decided not to look for trouble. "I wanted to ask you boys a few questions from the Bible. Do you think you'll get them right?" Ty rolled to his side and sat up in preparation for the quiz. "I'm gonna get them right," he proudly stated. Showing he was up for the challenge.

Rey started with the first question. "Okay. How do you know someone is saved?"

Ty piped in with a loud voice. "I would tell them the story of Jesus—when He was born—when He died on the cross and that He came to save us." Ty paused then added. "And you need to have Him in your heart." He smiled proudly at his mom, who patted him on the back.

Rey asked. "Jesus died on the cross. So, does that mean He's dead?"

Ty laughed. "Oh—no! Three days later he rose again and conquered death."

Rey pressed him more. "Well, what if that person asked you— howl can I be saved or what do I need to do to be saved? What would you tell them?"

Without missing a beat, Ty quoted scripture. "Believe in the Lord Jesus Christ and you will be saved."

Callan gasped. "When did you learn that verse?" A proud smile formed on her lips.

Zander piped in. "That was our memory verse a while ago."

Rey pressed the boys for more. "What do you need to do— just believe?

Ty's voice squeaked a bit louder. "You have to have Him in your heart."

"Yes—but how do I get Him in my heart? What do I have to do to get Him in there?" Ty looked confused.

Rey asked. "What did you do Ty, when you got saved?"

"I prayed! And asked Jesus to be in my heart."

Rey continued to lead Ty with his questions. "How would a prayer like that sound?"

"I'd say to my friend to pray like this, 'Dear Jesus, be in my heart and forgive me for all my sins and everyone's sins and help my friend's family and help him to go to church so if he dies he can have eternal life and joy with you in heaven. Thank-you, Jesus. In your name I pray—Amen.'"

"That's right Ty. Good job." Rey shot a proud smile at Callan.

Zander's head had been dangling over the top bunk looking down at his brother. He pulled himself back up and laid down gazing up at the ceiling he said. "That's too easy, Dad. Don't you have a harder question for me."

Rey put his hand on Zander's head and messed up his hair. "Sure. Here's one for you. How would you pray for someone who was sick and needed to be healed?"

Zander wondered if this was a trick question—what had his father heard? If I answer—I might be in trouble because of Ty— that Ty always gets me in trouble.

Ty jumped in. "I know what I'd do. I'd tell the person not to be scared because God is always by your side and so is His son, Jesus. Cause with Jesus in your heart and if you believe Him— you won't die. You will be alive. Jesus can do a miracle. He can do the impossible."

"Yes, but what happens if the person you prayed for dies?"

"That's okay because they will go to Heaven."

Rey was getting ready to ask another question when Ty said, "Well, let's say a child had cancer and he was eight years old like me. Say he was someone in my class or someone I know in my school. Say one day, I could go over to his house and pray with him. I'd say. 'Dear Lord, help my friend get through cancer help him to survive it and heal his body. Help everyone in the world and anyone in his family who is sick. Help them too. Help him not to be scared and let them feel peace through cancer and heal his body, give him a miracle. In Jesus Name, Amen!'"

This time Rey and Callan looked at each other and smiled. Callan gave Ty a big hug and said. "Ty, I'm proud of you. That is an awesome prayer you prayed. Do you believe God hears your prayers when you pray?"

"Of course. He hears everyone who calls on Him for help."

Rey looked directly at Ty. "But you do know, not everyone gets saved and not everyone gets healed." Callan kept her arm around Ty's shoulders while he processed the information.

Ty answered thoughtfully. "Yes—I guess so. But we still have to ask and lots of times too."

Rey touched Zander on top of the head. "The Bible tells us to ask—keep on asking, knock—keep on knocking."

Ty said. "Huh?" Then he fell back into his bed and covered up.

Callan patted his leg and said, "Okay. Let's pray. Then lights out."

☐☐

Stuart sat at a table facing the door of the Main Street Diner. He glanced up at the large chalk board on the wall to read the specials for the day. He didn't feel like eating. An internal anger stirred within him that he tried to suppress. His heart was pounding as he wondered why he became defensive about Heidi. She's a patient—nothing more. He loved his wife and knew she was stressed. He really did want to be more understanding.

A young lady with long dark hair stood near his table with a pad and pen in hand. She cleared her throat before speaking, "Are you ready to order or are you waiting for someone?"

Stuart took a closer look at the young woman's face and was assaulted by a butterfly tattoo. He tried to divert his eyes and wondered—why do people do that to themselves? His thoughts turned to Isabelle for a moment remembering the permanent damage she had done to her wrist. He glanced again at the chalkboard and said, "I'll have the meatloaf special." Stuart said this at the same moment a woman entered the diner. A cow bell sounded her arrival and all eyes were drawn to the door. Heidi? Stuart was shocked to see her again. He wasn't sure if he had spoken her name out loud.

At the same moment, Heidi saw Dr. Hayes and smiled so brightly at him the waitress pulled back the empty chair at the table for Heidi to sit.

Heidi walked the distance between the door and dining table like it was her debut as a runway model. She stood next to the table and asked. "Are you alone?"

"Yes." Stuart answered the question—without thinking of the implication.

The waitress in a moment of confusion said, "Oh, I'm sorry. I thought you were together."

Ignoring the waitress, Heidi asked. "May I sit with you?"

Stuart nodded, and Heidi sat down across the small table from Stuart. "I'll have the same as he's having." She looked at the waitress and frowned at the tattoo on her cheek. When she looked back at Stuart, he was digging at some dried food on the table.

The waitress said, "My name is Fauna, if you need anything just call. I'll get this order in right away." She glanced around the room at the two other customers sitting at the counter and with a smile in her voice added, "It's a slow night." Fauna walked away in the direction of the open grill.

"Dr. Hayes. I can't believe I would run into you tonight. Thank you for being so kind and understanding today." Stuart kept digging at the crusty spot on the table.

Heidi watched Dr. Hayes as he focused on the dried food. "I can ask the waitress to clean that off, if you'd like."

Stuart glanced across the table at Heidi. "Oh—no. It's fine." Then he brushed away the few crumbs and looked uncomfortably at Heidi. The first few times they had met she was full of life and talkative. This time there was definitely a sadness about her. Right now, he regretted more than ever storming out of the house—so much for anonymity. He certainly didn't want to do counseling with Heidi after office hours across the dinner table. He had just wanted a bit of peace and quiet.

"Dr. Hayes, if this is awkward. I can move to another table." Heidi couldn't believe the words were coming out of her mouth. She moved her chair backwards very slowly keeping her focus on the doctor.

"No, it's fine. It would be silly to move now." Stuart patted the table. "Stay."

Heidi smiled contentedly and scooted her chair back up to the table. "I called that number the brochure you gave me recommended. I spoke with a counselor over the phone. Never in a million years could I believe this…" Heidi's voice trailed off and she glanced from left to right.

Dr. Hayes broke in. "We don't need to talk about it. I'm glad you're getting help."

Heidi fought back the emotion in her voice by swallowing hard. "How are Isabelle and Baylee?"
Stuart gave a one-word answer. "Fine."

"Did they tell you how their time with *The Healer* went today?"

"No—not really." Stuart thought that may have been the news Samantha wanted to share before he became defensive and stormed out of the house.

Heidi looked around the small restaurant wondering how she could draw this quiet man into a meaningful conversation. Then she began to throw her first date questions out at him. She asked him about college, his hometown, his childhood and how he and Samantha met.

Before long something she wasn't expecting happened— they were talking—and laughing. They were both caught off guard when the waitress slipped the dinner plates in front of them and reminded them. "If you need anything just wave. I'll be at the counter. Will this be separate checks?"

Dr. Hayes spoke without looking up from his plate, "Make it one check to me, please."
Fauna nodded and headed back to the counter.

Heidi smiled down at her plate. A warm feeling rushed through her at the kind gesture. She moved the plate of meatloaf from side to side but no matter how much she angled it—it was still meatloaf. She pushed her fork into the soft meat and took a taste. It wasn't horrible. She decided to eat half to not appear ungrateful.

□□

Samantha stood at the door of Baylee's bedroom. "I'm going to shut the light off, are you ready?"

"Can I leave my lamp on for a while and read?"

"Sure. I can get you a book if you need one."

"No, I have one here." She patted the blanket next to her.

"Okay, remember to shut the lamp off when you're done reading."

"Thanks, mom—I will."

Samantha shut the door. Baylee slipped her hand under the pillow and pulled out the Bible Ty and Zander gave her. A book mark was placed near the back of the book. She eased the book opened where the book marker was placed. The name Mark was on the top of the page. She began reading at chapter two. Someone used a yellow highlighter to mark some of the columns.

Baylee read the words through the numbers 11 and 12 then stopped. She reread those two numbers again.

> *"Then, turning to the paralyzed man, he commanded, 'Pick up your stretcher and go on home, for you are healed!" The man jumped up, took the stretcher, and pushed his way through the stunned onlookers! Then how they praised God. "We've never seen anything like this before!" they all exclaimed.*

An excitement rose up in Baylee that this sick man—was now better. And it was all because the man named Jesus—commanded it. Holding the bookmark in her hand she noticed Ty had written other names and numbers on the marker. There was Romans, more in Mark, and some in Revelation.

Baylee looked up each name in the front of the book and found the page number—then the chapter then the numbered line. The first one in Romans talked about believing and confessing that Jesus Christ is Lord. Then more sick people being healed, then a description of what it will be like in Heaven. No more pain. No more tears.

Baylee said the words out loud, "He will wipe away all tears from their eyes, and there shall be no more death, nor sorrow, nor crying..." Her voice cracked, "...nor pain." A soft sob followed as she finished the verse. "All of that has gone forever." She glanced back at the name—Revelation. The chapter was twenty-one and the numbered line was four.

Baylee lifted the bedsheet to her face and wiped the tears from her eyes. She laid the Bible open across her small body. It made a tent over her nearly touching the bed on both sides. She wrapped her arms around the book and thought about *The Healer*— the one her mom took her to. He never made me feel like this. He never said there would be no more pain or tears. He scared me and hurt me. I cried.

A sigh came from deep within Baylee and she said out loud, "Jesus, I believe."

She drifted off to sleep holding the book.

□□

Isabelle sat quietly on the window seat in her bedroom and focused on the darkness outside her window. The long summer day was over. She was feeling alone and gloomy. The bedside lamp cast a soft light around the room. Readjusting the iPad resting on the front of her drawn up legs, she refocused on the movie about teenagers in love and the problems that followed. The earbuds she wore blocked out all other sounds around her.

Isabelle turned her head toward the dimly lit room. A small paper, under her bed, drew her curiosity. She unplugged her earbuds leaving her iPad on the window seat and walked across the room, dropped to her knees and fished her hand around under the bed. Locating the business card, she pulled it out. In bold font, the name Ms. Fauna Reynolds was on the front with an email address. Isabelle turned the card over. On the back, Ms. Reynolds had written down her cell number and the day and time for youth meetings at her church.

Isabelle flipped the card from front to back a few times and thought. Should I call her? I wonder what she'd be like outside of school. Would she really even care to see me? Maybe that school thing was all an act—a show to keep her job. Why would she care about me outside of school? I am nothing to her.

Isabelle's thoughts turned to Heidi Alden. She spoke out loud, "That was an epic fail." Then she thought of the creepy guy who Heidi worked for—*The Healer.* She whispered to no one.

"Perv."

Issie's cell phone was plugged in next to her bed. She stood up; reached for the phone still attached to the charger and texted a message to Ms. Reynolds. *Could we meet? Isabelle Hayes*

Issie balanced the plugged-in phone in the palm of her hand. She waited for a full minute. No reply. Her own thoughts mocked her. I told you she didn't care. She doesn't have time for you. Now you put it out there and she'll mock you for bothering her.

Isabelle laid the phone on the end table and walked back across the room with the ear buds still dangling. On her way back to the window seat, she dropped the business card in the waste basket next to her desk. She plugged her earbuds into the iPad jack and pumped the volume up as high as her ears could tolerate. Lying back down, Issie faced the window nearly in a fetal position. She leaned the iPad against the window frame and blocked out the world. There was a pain in her chest that caused her breathing to increase. It was unsettling—until she whispered the words, "I don't care! I don't care!" Her jaw tensed. Her breathing was abrupt. Through clenched teeth she spoke the phrase one last time. "I don't care!"

Across the room a ping sounded from her phone signaling a received text message.

□□

Samantha stopped at the door of Baylee's room. A soft light framed the outline of the shut door. She eased the door open, tiptoed across the room and reached for the lamp. She paused to look at Baylee. A beautiful child, pain-free for the moment and sound asleep. An open book lay at Baylee's side. Samantha picked up the book and closed it. The title on the cover was *My First Bible* with the words 1st—4th graders written in small text under the title.

Samantha glanced again at Baylee—she was peaceful. She held the book in her hands and wondered. Where did she get this? She flipped the front cover open and read the inscription.

> *To Tyson James Douglas, We are proud you have learned to read. Now—read this book—it holds all the answers. We love you, Grandpa and Grandma Douglas.*

This was the book Ty told Baylee about—the Bible. This was what Callan had told her about. This was what she wanted to share with Stuart. Samantha sat down in the little rocker next to the bed and angled the light toward the book she held. She opened the book and flipped through the pages landing on a page where the words were highlighted in yellow.

□□

Callan knocked on the door of Rey's home office. "Can I come in?"

"Sure." Rey turned his swivel chair away from his desk to look at Callan standing in the doorway.

"When are you coming to bed?" She asked.

Rey looked at Callan who was obviously tired from her day. They both carried the weights of sick friends, false accusations, pastoral needs as well as personal ones. They had tried to project an image of being above such tests and trials—but they weren't. Rey was mindful that humanity was fragile—meant to be loved and cared for.

Rey answered, "I'm right in the middle of something. I'll be coming to bed soon."

"I'm going now. I'm exhausted." Callan closed the office door behind her and called back to Rey. "We can talk in the morning."

Rey turned back to the lap top on his desk and resumed reading the article he had opened on healing. The strong unwavering faith of his children, especially Ty, sent him on a quest.

Over the past few days, Rey had read through the Gospels highlighting the healings and miracles performed by Jesus. It was an amazing exercise for him. There are 3,779 verses in the four Gospels dealing with the miraculous—many of these verses were now highlighted with a yellow marker.

Rey reread the verse in John 21:25 the Message Bible. *There are so many other things Jesus did. If they were all written down, each of them, one by one, I can't imagine a world big enough to hold such a library of books.* He had never given much thought about all the other miracles and healings that Jesus performed beyond the stories recorded. One thing became very clear to Rey. Jesus never performed miracles or healings to draw a crowd, in fact after some miracles, Christ commanded the people not to tell what they saw.

This seemed contrary to what Rey had seen in the past seven years. Some of those with healing ministries seemed showy and flamboyant. Regardless of this, healings and miracles were flowing from God's love to His broken world. The *whys* and *hows* of healing caused Rey to have more questions than answers.

Rey's internet search ran the whole gamut. Websites were out there that proclaimed healing was easy if people would follow certain steps or visit a place. Some sites offered things for sale like holy water or a handkerchief. Each promised an amazing result—Rey thought of the scripture in Jude—*clouds without rain*. These charlatans promised something that steps, places, water and cloth would never fulfill. Other sites claimed God no longer was in the business of physical healings.

Rey's heart was grieved by what he read—he himself had paid little attention to physical healing over the past years—neglecting it and the opportunity for God to show Himself with signs and wonders. He whispered, "Father—forgive me."

Rey turned his computer off and reached for his Bible. He flipped through the Gospels and read a few of the scriptures he had highlighted over the past few days. He found them encouraging and read one out loud. "What God has done before He is able to do again—He is the same yesterday, today and forever." Rey's eyes focused on one of the highlighted stories found in Mark's Gospel, chapter 8. It was simply entitled; *Jesus Heals a Blind Man at Bethsaida.*

He read the story out loud both seeing and hearing the Word. Letting it go deep into his spirit. Rey moved his legal pad next to his Bible and began to write down the points that came to him as he studied the scripture. First, Jesus takes the man away from the crowd to perform this miracle. He wasn't going to put a show on for the crowds. Second, Jesus spits in the man's eyes. Jesus never sets a pattern lest people choose to *follow the pattern* more than seeking the Lord. Third, Jesus asked the man if he could see. Rey thought about this point for a moment. Then he wrote down…This is the only time Jesus asked someone He prayed for if they received their healing. Fourth, Jesus prayed a second time. It is ok to pray for things more than once. It's not a lack of faith, but rather a proclamation of faith. Fifth, healing when instantaneous is a miracle but healing can also come progressively.

□□

Dr. Hayes eased the garage door open. The house was dim with just one-night light glowing from a kitchen outlet. He shut the door quietly behind him and went to the family room. Samantha was upstairs. He could hear her moving around. He chose to watch TV until after eleven hoping not to pick up where they had left off. He wasn't ready to talk—not yet.

Stuart's eyes fluttered open. The last thing he remembered was crawling into bed after 11:30 P.M. He rolled over to see if Samantha was awake. Her place in the bed was empty. She was up—probably in the kitchen. Most mornings, she had a to-go cup of coffee ready for him to take to work. His breakfast usually consisted of a mid-morning health bar at the office.

Stuart slipped out of bed and followed his usual morning routine, then headed down the stairs to face his wife. He had decided during his shower it would be best to tell Samantha about the casual encounter he had with Heidi at the diner. Gossip in a town this size could be unforgiving.

Stuart hesitated in the hallway watching Samantha in her summer robe leaning over the kitchen island reading something on her iPad. She glanced in his direction and smiled. Stuart suddenly felt a twinge of shame for allowing the dinner with Heidi to happen. She was a patient—and a needy one at that.

He stepped into the kitchen and sat down on one of the bar stools. Samantha left her iPad and poured Stuart's coffee stirring in an ample amount of half and half and one teaspoon of sugar. She snapped the lip in place and slid the cup across the counter in Stuart's direction.

"Here ya go. Have a great day at work."

Stuart usually responded with a grunted 'thank you,' then disappeared out the door. No hugs, no kisses were a part of the morning ritual. Samantha was caught off guard when Stuart stood up without taking his coffee, walked around the island and held her in his arms for a moment. Then he gave her a gentle kiss on the cheek leaving Samantha motionless and speechless.

Stuart said. "I want to tell you something, but don't be upset." Samantha held her ground. "Oooo. That sounds ominous."

"No. Not at all. When I left last night, I had a lot on my mind. I went to that little diner downtown to eat dinner and be alone, to think…" He paused and met Samantha's eyes. "When I was giving my order to the waitress, who by the way looked like she was part of a motorcycle gang…" Stuart paused to see if Samantha appreciated his little observation. She didn't. He decided to just throw the truth out there come what may. "Heidi Alden walked into the diner and for some reason the waitress pulled out a chair at my table for her to sit."

Samantha frowned. "Why would she think you were together?"

"I have no idea. Heidi came over smiling and asked if it was okay to sit with me. It was so sad. I couldn't tell her no."

One of Samantha's eye brows arched. "You couldn't or wouldn't?"

"You weren't there. It was awkward and kind of pitiful." Stuart's voice was defensive.

"Stuart, I don't trust her. At *The Healer's* yesterday, it was a fiasco. I can't believe I put poor Baylee through such an ordeal— never again."

Stuart tried to rein it in, but the force of his self-preservation was kicking back. "Okay. Fine! Don't ever take Baylee back there. I just wanted you to hear from me how things happened last night. I didn't want it to be an issue— that's why I'm telling you."

Samantha felt angry. Her heart was pounding, and she knew if she opened her mouth again, she would be inflicting damage that may take a long time to make right. She didn't listen to that inner voice and plowed ahead. "Callan Douglas told me to be cautious when it comes to Heidi Alden. I think she was saying that she's not a safe person. I interpreted that to mean I should be guarded in how much time I spend with her or let the girls spend with her. I didn't think I'd have to be concerned about my husband spending time with her too."

Stuart mentally released the reins. This was not going as planned. He blurted out. "Do what you want! I'm not your social secretary."

"Did you know that recently, someone turned the Douglas family in to Child Protective Services? Who would do something so mean?" Samantha asked the question innocently.

"I am not going to get into a *who's better than who* fight with you between Callan Douglas and Heidi Alden. I am uninterested in either one of these women or their problems. I'm leaving now before this gets uglier." Stuart grabbed his coffee from the counter and yelled back at Samantha. "That's what I get for trying to keep the lines of communication open."

Samantha ran to the garage door and yelled at her husband as he opened the car door. "That's not communication, that's bad behavior on your part." She wasn't sure how much of it he heard, but it felt good to say it, until Samantha turned around and saw Isabelle.

24

Promises to Keep

Tom dangled the car keys in front of his daughter, Debbie. "Don't come back for at least two hours—the longer the better. You've been working hard, and you need a break."

"Dad, I'll go—but promise me you'll call if you need me or anything changes." Debbie finished wiping the kitchen island making sure everything was clean. "Dad, I want you to know that I wouldn't trade what I'm doing for Mom—for anything. I know…" Debbie stopped talking and cleared her throat to push back the emotion. The words were in her heart and she wasn't sure if she could articulate what she wanted to say without breaking down into a puddle of tears. It wasn't a sacrifice to be with them—it was a joy. And in the scope of eternity—it would be a blink of an eye. She cherished— savored every moment with both of her parents.

Tom walked around the island and put his arms around his daughter and patted her back. "I have no words that could adequately describe how much your help has meant to me— us."

"I know Dad. This is all happening so fast. There are days I want to go outside and yell at the top of my lungs for things to slow down." Debbie tossed the dish cloth in the sink and took the keys from her dad. She headed toward the garage. "Remember— call me, if anything changes." Debbie shut the door. She sat in the car for a few moments fighting back the urge to sob. She had to get a grip before venturing out.

Tom walked back down the hallway to the master suite. Jean laid motionless in the king size bed. She was a shell of her former self. It had been a full month of watching Jean decline bit by bit each day—the past week she had been in bed more than out—asleep more than awake.

Tom sat down in the swivel chair near the bed. Lately, he sat for hours at a time in this chair and watched his wife sleep. Sometimes he read and sometimes he prayed. Sometimes his thoughts drifted off remembering better times. Then like a sniper's bullet the thought of a future without Jean would take him down.

At the last oncologist appointment, the word hospice was mentioned. The doctor had given them a folder with all the information. They could call when ready. Following that appointment, Jean put the folder in the kitchen junk drawer and walked away—everyone knew where it was, but no one spoke of it.

Tom swiveled his chair toward the lake and prayed a silent prayer.

"Tom?" Jean's voice interrupted his thoughts.

Tom stood up in a hurry and turned back to the bed nearly falling forward over his chair. "Yes, Jean. I'm here." He wedged himself between the chair and end table moving toward Jean. "Do you need something?"

Jean turned her head and smiled watching Tom fumbling about to meet her needs. "Could you prop me up? I feel like looking out the window."

"Sure." Tom leaned over Jean to move the extra pillows closer to her. He eased his hand behind her back until he was able to lift her with his forearm—gently raising her to a semi sitting position. With his free hand, he propped one pillow behind her shoulders then rested her back against the pillow. "Is that enough elevation or do you want another pillow?"

Jean turned her head toward the window and smiled. "That's fine." There was a moment of silence. Then she thoughtfully whispered. "I'm sorry."

Tom replied quickly, "What could you possibly be sorry for?" His response was too quick. He knew, and she knew exactly why she was apologizing.

Jean looked up at Tom and an all-knowing smile formed on her face. "I'm sorry for what's ahead and I'm sorry I won't be here to help."

"Don't talk like that." He looked from side to side and made a joke to keep from crying. "I don't see any fat lady singing in here. Do you?"

Jean smiled. "No! There certainly isn't any fat lady in here." She cast her eyes downward toward her small frame. Then added, "...are you ready?"

Tom spoke with a half-hearted authority. "I'm *still* believing— for a miracle."

Jean gave Tom an all-knowing smile. "Tom, I've got my miracle."

"What do you mean?" Tom sat down on the edge of the bed. "Do you feel like God is doing something in you— healing you?" Jean smiled. "My miracle is eternal life—that is my promise as a Believer. Even if the Lord did select to heal me right here, and right now—I'd still be facing death in three years, five years, ten years or twenty. God didn't promise me an eternity here on earth. I know where I'm going and I'm at peace." Jean pointed upward and continued. "Tom, I'm ready for my miracle. Are you?"

Tom slid off the bed and rested on his knees. He laid his face on the bed next to Jean. She reached over and stroked his hair. "You'll be okay." It was quiet—then she added. "Promise me—you'll be okay."

Tom found her hand and cupped it in his, then pressed his lips against the top of her hand. In a whisper he uttered, "With the Lord's help—I'm ready. I promise!"

"Tom, can you ask Pastor Rey to come. I have something I want to share with him—alone?"

Tom stood, "I'll call him now."

□□

The sun was coming in through the window filling her room with light and warmth. Isabelle forced her eyes open, rolled over and unplugged her phone. Holding it in her hand, she saw it was 10:07 A.M. She rolled back over gripping the phone with her eyes shut tight. It was that floating time between awake and asleep—she loved summer mornings. No rushing off to school, no fighting with her mom, no going to classes with juveniles— just sleep.

A knock at the door startled her awake.

"What?" She yelled.

"Get up Issie. Don't sleep away the day."

She fussed back. "Why not?"

"I want to talk with you—come down to the kitchen."

A loud sigh of disgust filled Isabelle's room as she swung her legs out of bed. Now she was awake and there was no going back to that twilight sleep. She looked again at the cell phone in her hand. There was a new text message. She didn't recognize the phone number but opened it anyway. As she read the message, she knew it was from Ms. Reynolds. She had responded.

Hi. I'd love to see you. Come by my work anytime and I'll buy you lunch or dinner—whatever works for you. Let me know. I'd like to hear how your summer is going.

Isabelle read the message over three times. She pushed down the excitement that was creeping in. She thought—be prepared to be let down. Be prepared to be disappointed— that's what adults do.

Isabelle got dressed and headed downstairs. She passed by Baylee's room expecting an outburst of screams at any moment. It was quiet. She peeked into the room—Baylee wasn't there. Walking down the stairs she could hear her mom and Baylee talking in the kitchen...and laughing. This was not the sound normally heard in the morning at the Hayes house.

Issie stepped into the kitchen and asked loudly. "So, what's so important?"

Samantha and Baylee were startled and turned their heads to look at Isabelle standing in the kitchen doorway with her hands on her hips. Samantha smiled, "There's something that Baylee and I wanted to share with you."

"I'm not hungry." Isabelle assumed it was food they were going to share.

"That's not it. But there are pancakes and bacon in the warmer, when you are hungry."

"Then what's the big news." Isabelle demanded.

Baylee looked up from her seat at the kitchen island. "We prayed last night. Both of us."

"You what? Is this more of that *Healer* crap?"

An expression of regret flashed across Samantha's face. "No. That was wrong. I'm so sorry. Please forgive me for taking you girls there." Samantha looked back and forth at her two girls.

Baylee smiled and nodded.

Isabelle's expression softened at her mother's apology. She plopped down on the bar stool—two down from Baylee. "I can't take all this mystery first thing in the morning—just come out with it already."

Samantha added. "This is something that Baylee and I both did last night...separately...then together."

Baylee responded first. "I'm not sure what it's called but—we believed in Jesus last night." She smiled at her mom and pointed back and forth. "Both of us."

Samantha looked happy and apprehensive all at once. "Do you want to read the Bible that we read last night?" On the counter was a book. Samantha patted the book in front of her.

Isabelle looked back and forth between her mother and sister studying them. Was she on one of those shows that trick people— punk them? Was this a joke? They did look happy which sparked her interest. Then her good sense got the better of her. She slipped back off the bar stool and started to leave the kitchen. Turning back, she said, "You woke me up for this! You're both nuts." She stomped back up the stairs. Moments later a loud thud reverberated through the whole house.

□□

Callan yelled from the kitchen. "Ty, Zander—Come on, we're going to be late!" She headed for the front door. "We have to go—NOW!"

Rey sat in the car glancing in the direction of the house. He checked his watch for the third time. When he looked up

Zander took a flying leap from the top step of the porch sprawled out like a sky diver. He landed on the cement sidewalk throwing his hands in the air like a gymnast dismounting a piece of equipment. Rey shook his head—it's a wonder we haven't been investigated by Child Protective Services before now. He thought.

Callan held the front door open and yelled at Zander still holding his landing pose. "Have you lost your mind? What are you doing?"

Rey watched from behind the steering wheel, in the air conditioning, with a tight-lipped smile. He rolled down his window. "Come on Zander—in the car."

Ty bolted past his mom ready to leap from the porch like his brother, but Callan pulled him back to safety by grabbing the back of his tee shirt just before he took flight.
Ty cried in protest. "Ah Mom—Zander got to do it."

Callan directed him gently toward the car. "One cast at a time. First, let's get this one off before we have to get a second one."

The Douglas family piled into the car, Rey glanced over at Callan who looked frazzled. "It's going to be fine." He patted his wife on the hand. "Ty will get his cast off and that CPS thing will go away soon. Everything will be fine."

Callan's shoulders rose in the air as she inhaled a deep breath. She exhaled the words, "From your mouth to God's ear." She clicked on her seat belt and pressed her back against the seat to relax. "Sometimes I feel like I can't get off this cycle of high-highs and low-lows. If the Lord is trying to get my attention or teach me something—well, I've got to be the slowest learner in the world, 'cause I'm not getting it."

Rey laughed. "Let's take one thing at a time. Today—right now—it's the cast."

The ten-minute car ride to the doctor turned into squabbling brothers and 20 questions in rapid progression. "Zander's touching me." "Ty's making faces at me." "Is it going to hurt when they take the cast off?" "Can we celebrate with ice cream after?" "Can I save the cast?" "Can we go swimming today?" "What's for dinner?" "Can I go show Baylee the cast and my arm? She's never seen this arm before?" "Can I still ride my bike?"

Rey looked at Callan and smiled. "It really is summer."

"Oh. Believe me I've been living it the past month."

"We're here." Rey announced the obvious. "I heard this Dr. Hayes is a good guy."

Ty answered fastest. "I like him. He's funny and jokes with me. Plus, Baylee is his daughter and she's nice.

The family filed into the Hillbrooke Medical Clinic in a dignified manner—looking more military than chaotic.

In short order, the family was seated in the same examination room they were in just one month before. The ducky sheets and the magical forest—nothing had changed. Rey asked, "Do you think we'll have to wait long?"

Callan began to answer, but she stopped as the door opened and in walked Dr. Hayes.

The doctor glanced around the full room at the Douglas' family.

"Good morning. I'm Dr. Hayes. I assume we're going to be removing that cast today?" He pointed at Ty's arm. He was more business than fun.

Ty smiled. "Yes. I'm excited, but it's not going to hurt—right?" Dr. Hayes smiled at Ty. "I've not had any complaints—yet!" Rey extended his hand to the doctor and introduced himself. "Dr. Hayes. I'm Rey Douglas, the father. We've not had an opportunity to meet, but I hear our children are becoming good friends."

Dr. Hayes turned and gave Rey a dismissive head nod and went to the sink to wash his hands.

Rey sat back down and looked at Callan with a puzzled look. She responded by raising her eye brows while shrugging her shoulders. They watched Dr. Hayes remove the cast. He joked a bit with the boys—then left without speaking to Rey or Callan. The nurse returned and dismissed them with a list of things to look for and exercises for Ty to do with his arm. A recheck was scheduled in one month.

Rey held Callan's hand as they walked toward the car while the boys ran ahead. Rey squeezed Callan's hand. "I thought you said Dr. Hayes was nice. He seemed stand-offish to me, like he had something against us."

"He wasn't like that at our first visit. He joked with the boys. He even gave me his home number to contact his wife. That's how the boys started going over there. Something doesn't seem right."

"Well, I guess anyone can have a bad day. Let's chalk it up to that. No use looking for things that aren't there."

Callan shook her head. "Something was off with him—no question about that." She opened her car door to get in but stopped to speak to Rey across the top of the car. "Whatever it was—it must be you Rey. Last time we came, when it was just the boys and me, he treated us like old friends." She laughed, and it felt good. After the past few weeks, it felt good to laugh.

Callan got into the car still giggling. Rey sighed. "Why not!"

□□

Snake watched Fauna move with grace from table to table taking the orders from the lunch crowd. He sat at the

Formica topped table and munched on crispy French fires. Checking his watch, he wondered if Fauna would get a break before he had to return to work. He waved his hand in the air as Fauna passed balancing four plates of food. "Miss—when you get a chance I need something!" He winked at her and she frowned back.

Fauna finally found a moment to stop and sit down with Snake. The aroma of hot grease hung in the air. "I have ten minutes—let's make the most of it."

Snake smiled and pointed at the table behind her. "Could you hand me that catsup?" Snake quickly patted her hand and said, "Kidding."
Fauna's face spoke silent volumes about the joke.

Snake quickly maneuvered the pending car wreck back on the road and changed his tone. "I never dreamed how hard you worked here. Are you sure you don't want me to put a word in at the Solar plant? The entry level jobs for people with college degrees would pay more than this, and it would be a desk job."

Fauna relaxed. "Believe me, on days like today I'd probably consider it." She glanced at her wrist to check the time.

"I'm going to check the employment link when I get back to the office and see what's open."

"No! Don't. If I get a comfy job somewhere I'll never pursue my dream."

Snake smiled. "Or you could make enough money to pay for your dream."

"I'm saving now. I won't let this dream slip through my fingers. It's going to happen. With the help of the Lord—I will have a family counseling center. I'm going to call it *Healthy Homes*."

Snake laughed. "What happen to *Agape Helps Center*?"

Fauna pushed back her chair with a mischievous smirk and said with a dismissive wave, "That was so last week. Gotta go."

Snake watched Fauna rush off giving customers their checks and picking up dirty dishes. He couldn't believe she would rather work in a greasy diner than sit at a desk in a clean office. Fauna smiled at the people she waited on, laughing and joking as she moved about the small diner. Snake knew exactly why she stayed—people—human contact. She thrived on it.

□□

"Look at my arm! It's so light." Ty moved his arm up and down in slow motion in the back seat. Callan and Rey glanced back at their happy little boy. Ty's mouth ran non-stop with plans for what he would do once he arrived home.

Rey's cell phone chimed notifying everyone in the car that a text message arrived. The phone rested in the cup holder between them. Callan picked up the phone and asked, "Do you want me to read the message to you?"

"Sure. Who's it from?"

"It's from Tom Brown. He says, when you get a chance stop over, Jean needs to speak with you."

Rey frowned. "I wonder what's up with that?"

"Do you think she's…?" Callan's voice was soft almost a whisper.

The back seat suddenly became very quiet. Rey took notice. "I'll drop you and boys off at home and head over there. I'll call you as soon as I know more."

The rest of the car ride home was quiet. Everyone was lost in their own thoughts.

Rey pulled into the driveway and rolled to a stopped. The boys got out of the car and ran for the house. Before getting out of the car, Callan leaned toward Rey and kissed his cheek. "I'll be praying."

Rey backed out of the driveway—his heart was heavy, and his thoughts ran the gamut of possibilities. He shook his head to clear his mind and began to talk to the Lord. The ten-minute drive went by faster than usual.

Rey pulled into one of the extra parking spaces in the Brown's driveway. He took notice it was the same place he and Callan had parked the first time they came for dessert over six years ago. When Tom and Jean had prayed with them at the close of that first visit—it awakened a hunger and passion for more of God. Rey knew he owed this godly couple more than he could ever repay.

Rey walked toward the massive log home, taking notice that Tom stood at the door. He felt a twinge of fear rush through his body. Was bad news waiting to greet him?

Tom welcomed Rey in. "Pastor, thanks for coming, I don't know what Jean wants to talk with you about. She just said to call you."

A wave of relief washed over Rey. "I'm glad you did." Rey followed Tom to the master suite in the front of the house. He glanced at the bed where Jean laid with her eyes closed. He scanned the panoramic view of the lake out the wall of windows and whispered to Tom. "I've never been in here before. It's a breathtaking view."

Tom motioned for Rey to take a seat in the chair that had been moved close to the side of the bed. Rey sat down. He fought emotions welling up in him at the sight of Jean. Last week, when he stopped by, Jean was able to meet with him in the family room for a short visit. She looked weaker and her skin was an ash-grey. Rey took Jean's hand and held it in his. He spoke softly. "Jean, I'm here. It's Pastor Rey."

Jean opened her eyes and turned to look at her pastor. A beautiful smile formed on her lips. "I'm glad you came. We need to talk."

Tom sat at the foot of the bed and listened as Jean shared what was on her heart.

"Pastor, I'm dying." She winked. "I'm ready."

Rey listened.

"I don't want you to misinterpret my death. It's not a loss. It's a win. I have finished my race. I've run the course. I see the ribbon across the finish line just in front of me." Jean reached her hand out feeling for the finish line. "I can almost touch it. It's right there."

Tom sat at the end of the bed holding back the sea of faith filled words that wanted to burst hope into the gloominess of the situation.

Jean breathed slow and deep then continued. "God is using death as a tool to take me from the temporal to the eternal. I'm ready." Jean closed her eyes and her body relaxed.

Rey, still holding Jean's hand, looked at Tom for direction.

With her eyes closed, Jean spoke. "I sense in my spirit that God is going to do a new thing at Community Outreach. He's going to show himself as The Healer—He is the one and only Healer." Jean opened her eyes and looked directly at Pastor Rey. "Be strong. Be courageous. And remember this—you don't need to defend God. He's able to defend himself." Jean opened her eyes and gave Rey's hand a firm squeeze. "I'm going to rest now."

Tom stood and motioned for Rey to follow him. They walked to the family room and sat quietly each processing the words Jean shared through their own filters.

25

God said,
"I Can Work With That."

Callan weeded the flowerbeds around the front of the house while Zander and Ty tossed the baseball behind her. The mail truck stopped at the end of the driveway then moved on to the next house. Callan stood up and dusted the dirt from her knees and removed her gardening gloves.

Zander yelled. "I'll get the mail." He ran toward the road with Ty two steps behind.

"Okay. Watch for cars." Callan stood in the driveway and watched Zander run with Ty at his heels. "Boys! Slow down. Don't run toward the road."

The boys stopped at the end of the driveway and looked to be sure no cars were coming before stepping in front of the mailbox and removing an armload of mail from the box. Zander handed a few pieces to Ty and they both ran back to Callan feeling very accomplished.

The boys passed the mail off to their mom and returned to throwing the ball. Callan took the mail up on the porch and sat down to sort through the things that were important and discard the junk. The electric bill—save, another credit card application—junk, the visa bill—save, an ad for an upcoming political campaign—junk. The next letter in the pile was from the Department of Child Protective Services. Callan felt a twinge of fear creep in. She placed the letter in the save pile and continued sorting the mail. There was one more bill and the rest was junk.

"Boys, I'm going in the house for a minute—you go to the backyard and play." The boys ran around the side of the house. Callan went inside and set the mail on the kitchen counter. She washed the little bit of dirt from her hands that had seeped through her gardening gloves, then glanced back at the pile of mail on the counter. It was still there. She walked past the mail and made a cup of coffee. Finally, with cup in hand, she picked up the letter from CPS opening it carefully—half expecting Ms. Klingburg to jump out of the envelope and choke her.

> *Dear Mr. and Mrs. Douglas,*
> *After final review of your case we are recommending*
> *further investigation…*

Callan gasped and let the letter fall on the counter. "Lord, no." That familiar feeling of fear gripped her whole body. "Lord—why? Why is this happening?"

A door slamming drew her eyes to the family room. Zander asked. "Mom? What's wrong?"

Ty followed with a question of his own. "Are you crying?"

Zander looked scared.

Callan tried to pull it together. When parents fall apart—kids have no safe place. "You boys want to watch TV? I need to call Daddy." Callan snatched the letter and walked to her bedroom and shut the door behind her.

She picked up her cell phone and prayed as she dialed hoping Rey would have his cell phone nearby. On the third ring he picked up.

"Hey, Callan."

"Rey. I just opened the letter from CPS. It's not good."

"Can you read me the letter?"

"I'll try."

Dear Mr. and Mrs. Douglas,

After final review of your case we are recommending further investigation. Currently, we do not deem the children in danger under their parental care. However, we feel it would be in the children's best interest to see the school psychologist for assessment. Pending the outcome of the assessment your file will be closed without prejudice.

It is your right to refuse this recommendation and to seek legal counsel, in which case your file will remain open and you will be placed on a rotation for unscheduled home visits.

Please notify your caseworker Ms. Klingburg with your decision within five business days of receipt of this letter.

Respectfully,

 Mr. Frank Olive

 Supervising Director,

 CPS Hillbrooke, Michigan

An awkward silence followed—Rey contemplated the words of the letter, while Callan sat on the bed frozen in fear.

Callan spoke in a soft voice, "Rey, what should we do? Should we submit to these assessments or fight it?"

In a nervous fashion, Rey tapped his finger on the desk while he spoke. "We have five days to decide. Let's take all five days. Rushing into a quick decision right now won't bring a good outcome. We are emotional—we've got to think of the boys." Rey added a leg bounce to the finger tapping. "I want to seek legal counsel too. I'll call Steve Orvis. He's a family-law attorney. He can give us good advice."

Callan's voice was a whisper. "I feel like I'm losing it Rey… how can this be happening to us? We're good parents."

"Callan—pray! We can't lose hope. The boys are watching us. They need us, and we need to be strong. People face crises every day, and we are no exception—we're going to get through this."

Callan responded. "Pray for—me."

Rey could hear the desperation in Callan's voice. He knew she was the one on the front lines. She was the one who, moments from now, would be back in the trenches. When the call ended she would do her best to act like their home was a safe place and they had the power to protect their children, when behind the scenes, CPS loomed. It seemed to Callan this group was ready to swoop in and remove their precious boys, whisking them away from the security of home and parents.

With his cell phone set on speaker, Rey closed his eyes and prayed. "Lord, we know You are not surprised by what is happening in our lives. This one is completely out of our control—out of our hands. We feel blindsided, grief-stricken and fearful." The phone fell silent for a few seconds—the silence was painful. "…But we know You're in control of this and everything. You're not afraid of the source of these charges. Whoever this person is, whether they are in a place of authority or not—I will do what Your Word tells me to do.

Pray for my enemies and those who despitefully use me." Rey paused. He rubbed his eyes and rested his face in his hands.

Callan agreed with Rey in prayer. It was nearly inaudible, but a few times Rey could hear a broken voice say, "Yes—Jesus." "Help—Us." "We trust You, Lord." "Protect our boys."

Rey continued to pray. "Lord, when troubles come our way— I am encouraged that Your Word tells me—You don't change. You stay the same. You were faithful to us in the beginning and You remain faithful still. You are watching over us. You are still on the Throne."

Rey's prayer changed from a pleading voice to proclaiming. "I choose not to be afraid." He paused then said... "*We* choose to trust. *We* choose to hope. *We* choose to be strong in the face of adversity—kind in the face of anger—honest in the presence of lies. Lord, we know this CPS matter rests in Your hands."

Rey paused and inhaled deeply then exhaled as he spoke. "You've got this one—Callan and I release it to You. We don't want to be the decision makers or the ones holding the reins. Guide us into Your truth. May Your will be done in our lives and each person you bring into our lives—if you bring them—we will be faithful to tell them about Your great love. Your plans and purpose for our lives is without repentance."

Callan agreed with each word Rey spoke. Nodding her head and softly repeated the phase, "Yes, Lord."

Rey continued. "You don't call us and then have a change of heart. We believe Your Word is true. You have called us—You will be faithful to the end. This we know. Your Word tells us that we should not lean on our own understanding but in all our ways acknowledge You and You will direct our path. Lord, we completely and fully trust You, depend on You. We step back and allow, You to lead and we will follow. In the mighty Name of Jesus, we pray. Amen."

Rey felt a freedom he hadn't felt in months. It was like an umbrella that had been blocking him from God suddenly floated away. The full force of God's presence poured down on him. "Callan—do you feel it? It's freedom from bondage. It's the full rain of God being poured out on us."

Callan cried. Not the cry of pity or woe. Not this time. She couldn't put it into words until Rey said it...but she too felt the heavens open as Rey prayed. There was nothing blocking the blessings. Her tears poured out as the presence of the Lord showered her. It felt good. Like water poured out on dry ground—it was saturating.

There was a knock at Callan's bedroom door followed by a soft voice. "Mom, can we get a snack?"

Callan pulled the phone away from her mouth and spoke to Zander. "Sure. Help yourself. I'll be out in just a minute." Placing the phone back to her mouth, she told Rey with a smile in her voice, "I bet whoever typed that letter a few days ago never dreamed it would bring down the glory of God when it was read. You gotta admit—God must have a roaring sense of humor."

"I love you Callan. Now go get those boys a snack."

□□

Isabelle cupped her cell phone with both hands and used her thumbs to type a text message at lighting speed to Ms. Reynolds. *Can we meet today?* She kept the message window open—ready to reply.

The message from Ms. Reynolds popped up quicker than Isabelle expected. This brought a smile to her face as she read.

Working most days. Come to the diner. I'll buy dinner. 6pm tonight? Or any evening...

Isabelle typed her reply. *Yes...tonight!*

She closed the message app and found her mom in Baylee's room sitting in the little rocker beside the bed. Baylee was sleeping. Isabelle curled her finger at her mom motioning for her to come to the hallway.

Samantha laid down the book she was reading and joined Issie in the hallway.

"Mom, can you drive me to the diner at 6 P.M. to meet Ms. Reynolds for dinner. She works there. She invited me and is buying my dinner."

Samantha didn't know for sure how she felt about another adult woman becoming involved with Issie, not wanting a repeat of the Heidi debacle. She envisioned Isabelle getting mad for some reason and storming out of the diner without calling— walking the two miles home. "Let me think about it."

"No mom. I already said yes. I'll just walk or ride my bike."

"No Issie. Just give me an hour to think it over. You can wait that long. It's only 3 P.M. for goodness sake. And does it have to be today? Tomorrow would work better for me." Samantha paused, then added. "After breakfast, Baylee took a turn. It could be a rough night for her."

Issie snapped back! "I'm going."

Samantha tried to reassure Issie. "I'm not saying no—I'm saying wait. I'll tell you by 4 or 5 P.M. at the latest." Issie stormed down the stairs.

Samantha's shoulders dropped as she sighed and followed Issie to the kitchen. "What's the rush? You can't wait a few hours or one day?"

"I won't text her back and say—I can't come. That's embarrassing. She'll think I'm a kid."

Samantha retorted. "You are a kid. And I'm pretty sure your school counselor knows that." She knew her tone was sharp, and her words were sarcastic. The expression on Issie's face was another reminder—her daughter felt powerless in an adult world.

Isabelle's eyes narrowed to slits. "I should have just gone and not even told you." Issie drew in a deep breath and yelled. "You don't care where I am most of the time anyway. Go on back to Baylee. She needs you…I DON'T"!"

Exhausted Samantha blurted out. "Oh, for goodness sakes— get over yourself." She pointed her index finger at her rebellious teen. "I said that I'd give you my answer by 5 P.M. and I will. Remember this—it will be a lot more embarrassing for YOU, if your mom shows up at the diner because you didn't have permission to be there." Samantha turned on her heels and went back upstairs.

Issie watched her mother leave and plopped down on a bar stool—shocked that her usual insolence didn't get the desired results.

A few moments later a scream reverberated through the house, but this time it wasn't Baylee. A fear like Isabelle had never known shot through her whole body with the force of an electrical current. She ran up the stairs entering Baylee's room within seconds. Samantha held Baylee tight against her body. Baylee wasn't moving. Samantha's face was buried in Baylee's neck.

"Mom? What can I do? Tell me what to do."

Samantha didn't respond. She moaned like a wounded animal.

Issie ran back to the kitchen, grabbed the phone from the cradle and dialed 911.

A female voice asked, "What's your emergency?"

With a breathless voice Isabelle pleaded, "My sister...she won't wake up..." without waiting for another question Issie said. "We need an ambulance. Right now! We live at 1115 Lancaster Drive, Hillbrooke. I'll go outside and wait."

"Don't hang up. Are you with your sister? How old is she?"

"No, my mom is holding her upstairs. She's ten years old."

"Can I talk to your mom? Can you take the phone to her?"

Issie followed the instructions of the operator and ran upstairs as fast as she could. When she rounded the corner into Baylee's room, her mom was crying and rocking Baylee back and forth in her arms. Issie couldn't make out what she was saying but Samantha was whispering in Baylee's ear and crying.

Issie spoke to the 911 operator, "Ma'am, I don't think my mom can talk right now."

"Can you check to see if your sister is breathing?"
Issie touched her mom's arm, but Samantha continued to whisper in Baylee's ear—frantically rocking. Isabelle touched Baylee's back but didn't feel any movement. She reached her hand around to feel for air coming out of her nose—she wasn't sure. "I don't know. I can't feel anything."

The 911 operator asked. "Do you have a small mirror in the house? Put it under her nose."

"Yes, in my room." In a robotic motion Isabelle ran to her bedroom. She kept the phone to her ear. She found the mirror on her bathroom vanity and snatched it up. Hurrying back to Baylee's room she pushed the mirror between her mom and Baylee resting it against her sister's upper lip. Two faint circles of white appeared on the mirror. Issie yelled. "She's breathing. She's breathing. Baylee, can you hear me?"

"What's your name—Honey?" The 911 operator asked.

"Isabelle—Isabelle Hayes."

"How old are you, Dear?"

"I'm fourteen."

"You're doing a great job, Sweetheart. Now stay strong and go to the end of the driveway and wait for the ambulance." Isabelle gulped back the tears when the operator used terms of endearment to address her; Honey, Dear and Sweetheart. Her emotions were raw, and tears pushed to be free with the force of an ocean. Taking a deep breath, she ran to the end of the driveway with the phone still pressed against her ear. The operator continued to make 10 second comments.

"Do you hear the ambulance yet?"

Isabelle's heart pounded in her chest. "No Ma'am."

"It should be very soon. They're en route. I spoke with them moments ago."

Isabelle sucked in air through her nose to push back the emotion.

"You're doing a great job—Isabelle. Tell me when you see or hear the ambulance."

"I-I hear it. It's coming." At the sound of the sirens wailing, Isabelle couldn't hold back the tears and she sobbed out. "There're coming."

"Don't hang up, Honey. Not until they are in the driveway."

Isabelle waved her free arm at the ambulance as it came into sight.

"They're pulling into the driveway now. May I go?"

"You did very well, Sweetie. Real good. Bye now."

Isabelle ran after the ambulance that was already at the door of the house, still pressing the phone to her ear.

26
Death Doesn't Mean It's Over

The 12—story medical center was unusually quiet for 2 A.M. Pastor Rey pulled his car in the parking spot reserved for clergy. The August morning air felt warm and musty. He hurried into the hospital through the emergency room doors. His adrenalin kept sleep at bay as he rushed down the familiar hallways of the hospital.

Less than thirty minutes ago, he was startled awake by the ringing of the phone. No one is *ever* prepared to hear that sound in the middle of the night.

Rey stopped in front of the east elevators and pushed the up button. He nervously paced back and forth replaying the events in his mind. The phone ringing, answering with a sleepy voice, then Callan waking up and whispering a prayer—while he thought he pushed down the feeling of panic that was welling up.

Callan had watched, examining his face for the tiniest piece of information as he spoke to the caller. Her expression showed concern as she listened to the emotion in his voice. He ended the short phone call with, "I'll be there as fast as I can."

Rey recalled dropping the phone on the bed. He hurried to fill Callan in, while he slipped on a pair of jeans, tee-shirt and lightweight jacket. Ten minutes later, he was heading down the road on a familiar late-night drive to the hospital.

Rey pushed the up button three more times then looked at his distorted image in the elevator door. He glanced up at the changing numbers showing the progress of the elevator. The numbers clicked down 10, 9, 8, then 7. The elevator stopped. Rey sighed and whispered a prayer. "Please, Lord."

The past six years in Hillbrooke, he had stood by the bedside of the dying. He held the hands of those who grieved the loss of a loved one. Each death hit him hard, especially the ones who died young.

He watched the floor numbers resume 6, 5, 4, 3, 2 and finally the doors of the elevator opened. Rey was surprised the elevator wasn't empty. A man stood leaning against the wall. He looked emotionally shaken with red, swollen eyes.

"Dr. Hayes, how is she?" Rey stepped into the elevator and placed his hand on the doctor's shoulder. He felt the doctor tense under his touch. "Are you here for Jean Brown?"

Dr. Hayes looked up in surprise. "Jean's here?"

"Yes. I just received a call and I'm on my way to be with the family."

Dr. Hayes stuttered. "I-Is she—dead?"

"I hope not." Rey realized his hand was still on the doctor's shoulder. He gave the doctor's arm a friendly pat and moved to the other side of the elevator. Dr. Hayes didn't move. He stood frozen in place. Rey looked at the open elevator door and finally asked. "Are you getting off here?"

Dr. Hayes looked at the floor and replied. "No. I'd like to go with you to Jean's room, if you don't mind."

"I think that would be wonderful." Rey pushed the button for the 10th floor and watched the doors ease shut. The elevator rose to the 10th floor without stopping. Rey hurried down the hallway to room 1005 and eased opened the closed door.

The room was dimly lighted. Debbie stood next to the hospital bed and held Jean's hand on one side and Tom stood on the other side of the bed. His back was to the door. Dr. Hayes followed Pastor Rey into the room. Soft worship music played in the background. Debbie looked up and smiled causing Tom to look back over his shoulder to the door.

"Pastor, she's gone—with Jesus." He still held her hand—not ready for the final separation. He turned back to the bed and fixed his eyes on the woman he had shared life with for over forty years. He shook his head and whispered. "I selfishly wanted more." He turned back and saw Dr. Hayes in the shadows by the door. "Dr. Hayes. Jean spoke highly of you. She prayed for your little girl right up to the end."

Dr. Hayes nodded but didn't speak.

Pastor Rey put his arm around Tom's shoulders and drew him in. "Whatever you need—we're here for you."

"Yes, Pastor. We know."

Debbie added, "It was peaceful. She just took her last breath and it was done. Look at her face. It's like she's smiling an all-knowing smile. She loved that scripture that says, to be absent from the body is to be present with the Lord." Debbie patted her mom's hand. "She's not here anymore. She's with her Lord. Everything she lived her life for—her very reason for being was to share the love of Jesus with others." Debbie glanced toward Dr. Hayes. He stood stock still with his head bowed.

Pastor Rey asked. "Tom, if it's okay with you, could we gather together and pray?"

"Of course, Pastor."

Tom and Debbie released Jean's hands and held hands with Rey. Dr. Hayes held his ground at the door—not moving to join the circle. Rey remembered that first time he and Callan stood in a prayer circle with Tom and Jean Brown at their home years ago. Callan nearly freaked out over the hand holding and spontaneous words of adoration to the Lord.

"Let's pray." Pastor Rey looked at Tom with his head bowed. He was no longer 'Tom and Jean' from now on he would be known as Tom. "Dear Jesus, we need You right here—right now. We lean on You and draw near to You in our time of need. We know You hear our prayers because Your word tells us that where two or three are gathered in Your name You are there. We draw comfort from Your presence. We are comforted by the life that Jean lived in You. This is the assurance we have because we were witnesses to her life. It was a book that was open for everyone to read. She wasn't a mystery, Lord, she knew without wavering that she was *Your child*. Now we stand in the full knowledge of this truth with a peace that passes all understanding." Rey stopped speaking. A holy hush filled the room as the presence of the Lord washed over them—Dr. Hayes stood alone by the hospital room door—feeling but not knowing the presence of a living God.

□□

Isabelle woke up groggy and looked around the unfamiliar room. She allowed her eyes to focus on the bed in the center of the room. Baylee. They were in the hospital. Her mom slept in a chair next to the window seat where she had fallen asleep. Her dad must have gone home for the night. Baylee didn't move. She was quiet. For the first time in her life Isabelle wished Baylee would cry out—at least she'd know she was alive. Issie stood up, walked the few steps to the hospital bed and gently stroked her sister's arm.

The door opened, and a group of doctors walked into the quiet room. Isabelle reached back and woke her mother.

"Mom, the doctor is here."

Samantha bolted out of the chair in a daze and looked at the group of strangers standing in an awkward cluster. The doctor that was the oldest amongst the youngsters extended her hand. "I'm Dr. Kaplan. Are you the mother?"

"Yes. Can you tell me what happened? What made her become non-responsive?" Samantha could hear the demand in her voice and tried to tone it back.

"We have studied Baylee's file." The doctor waved back at the group of doctors standing near the door to include them in the assessment.

Samantha looked past Dr. Kaplan at the group of young doctors. They looked more like children playing dress up with white doctor coats on than qualified professionals.

Dr. Kaplan continued. "And we agree that your daughter should have the double leg amputation as soon as possible. The immediate issue she is having is a reaction to the pain medication. She has been using high doses of pain meds for too long and it is doing damage to her kidneys and liver, if we don't get her off these medications as soon as possible the damage may be irreversible."

Samantha put her hand over her mouth to hold in both the gasp and the spew of words that were ready to fly. She cleared her throat then said slowly. "My husband is a doctor and we'll review your recommendation. When can Baylee be discharged?"

The look on the young physician's face told Samantha what she didn't want to hear. Dr. Kaplan went ahead and said it anyway. "We don't recommend you leave the hospital before the legs are amputated."

Samantha gripped the cold steel bar on the hospital bed. "Thank you. I'll speak to my husband about that."

The group drew closer to the bed where Baylee slept to begin the prodding process. Samantha clinched her teeth and spoke with stern authority. "Don't touch her—let her sleep. She's had a difficult night." Samantha thought that was a reasonable request seeing Baylee was the sick one in the room.

Dr. Kaplan moved closer to the bed while speaking to Samantha. "Ma'am we need to examine her."

Samantha quickly moved around Baylee's bed and stood between the doctor and Baylee. "Do you understand what I'm saying? You may not put your hands on my child. Please leave." A few of the young ones began to head for the door. Dr. Kaplan stood her ground obviously not accustomed to being told what to do by a patient's family member. She moved forward and stood toe-to-toe with Samantha.

It was tense. Samantha didn't back down. Dr. Kaplan finally did. When the doctor reached the door, she turned and said, "I'll call your husband. He's a medical professional and will understand."

Samantha smiled condescendingly and nodded. "Yes. You do that."

Once the door was shut, Samantha extended her hands palms down in front of her. They were trembling.

Isabelle spoke up. "Well played, mom! What's with you being all feisty and in everyone's face lately."

"I don't have any idea, Iss, except..." Samantha patted Baylee's leg gently. "We prayed. Baylee and I prayed. She's not going to lose her legs. I just know it." Samantha walked around the bed and sat down in the recliner where less than ten minutes ago she was sound asleep.

"Mom don't get all weird about that praying stuff. It's creepy. When can I go home?"

"Once I speak to dad, we're all going home and the sooner the better."

□□

Rey and Callan sat at the breakfast table in the parsonage kitchen with heavy hearts and reddened eyes. They hadn't told anyone yet. It was news that most in the church expected, but no one verbalized. The phone rang. It was 8 A.M.
Rey answered with a, "Good Morning."

"Pastor, this is Grace. I've been getting calls at home this morning that Jean Brown passed. Is it true? I didn't want to believe it until I heard it from you. Someone said they saw you at the hospital last night crying. I hate to bother you with this." Rey confirmed the report. "Grace, Jean's with Jesus." There was sniffling on the other end of the phone.

"Grace—we don't have any details yet about funeral arrangements. You can confirm that she did die last night at the hospital, if anyone asks. Let them know when we get the details we'll pass them on to the congregation. I'll be in later, but you can send calls to my cell phone or the house, if I'm needed."

"Oh Pastor. I'm so sorry...for all of us. And Tom. And Debbie. And Kim."

Rey handed the phone to Callan. "Grace. We'll be making a few calls to people from home this morning—the church board and the small group members. Please pray."

"I will, Callan. The Brown's small group will be heartbroken."

Callan could hear Grace blow her nose. "Okay, Grace. Gotta go." Callan hung up the phone then looked at Rey. "So how are we gonna do this? Who do you want to call first?"

With a blank expression on his face, Rey cupped his cell phone. His eyes were fixed on the phone, but he didn't move. He was frozen in thought.

Callan touched his hand. "Rey—you okay?"

He sighed. "I'll call Snake. You can call Fauna." Rey left the table and headed down the hallway to his office. He went in and shut the door behind him and speed dialed Snake.

Before Rey could speak, Snake by-passed the usual greetings, "Oh Pastor, I heard. I'm so sorry. My heart is breaking for Tom. Were you there when it happened?"

"No. She passed moments before I walked into the room... Snake..." Pastor Rey paused. He wasn't prepared for the emotion that kept coming wave after wave.

"Yes, Pastor, I'm here for you—take your time."

"...Snake, I'm gonna need you with me for support."

"I got ya—Pastor. Whatever you need, I'm your man. Should I call Tom?"

"You do whatever you feel led to do. I'm not telling you yes or no. But will you coordinate the information flow with your small group. I thought of everyone that loved Jean—this group would want to take a lead role in covering them—him."

"We would, and we will."

"One other thing Snake. I know this is short notice, but I feel prompted by the Holy Spirit that in 10 days we're going to have a Healing Service at Community Outreach. I know this isn't much warning, but could you design some fliers and posters to promote the service around the area."

"Pastor send me over an email with the details and I'll have something for you to look at by tomorrow. I can print them the same day they are approved. Fauna and I can handle the promotion."

"Thanks Snake. I'll send that email off to you right now."

The two men said their goodbyes and Rey turned on his laptop and began typing.

> *Hey Snake, here are the deals for the flier. Work your magic. Healing Service, prayer for the sick, Community Outreach Church, Friday, August 15th, 6 P.M., Everyone welcome!!!! Include this verse somewhere on the flier. Psalm 103:2-4 Praise the LORD, my soul, and never forget all the good he has done: He is the one who forgives all your sins, the one who heals all your diseases, the one who rescues your life from the pit, the one who crowns you with mercy and compassion.*

Rey reread the details and nodded his approval. He knew the timing was right—even with the death of Jean, faith was alive in him. He believed for the physical and emotional healings for this community. He pushed his laptop away, folded his arms in front of him on the desk and bowed his head. A picture began to form in his mind of the sanctuary at Community Outreach Church. The altar was lined with prayer warriors. The aisles were filled with hurting people—some he knew, but many were strangers. A great cry rose up from those waiting— there were too many to pray for—too many to touch—so many hurting—many were sick.

The urgency of what Rey saw compelled him to pray. Words turned to groans—groans to physical pain as the Lord showed Rey in the Spirit realm what He wanted to do. During Rey's prayer time he moved from sitting at his desk to lying prostrate on the floor of his office.

He pushed himself up from the floor using the chair next to him and sat back at his desk. He pulled the laptop in front of him and began to write his first sermon on healing. He had one Sunday to preach before the Friday night service. "Lord, stir in the hearts of your people—breathe the gift of faith and miracles into those who are in need—into those who are longing to be made whole. In ten days, let it be as the Spirit showed me—You have heard their cry and your ear is not turned away. Touch your children."

☐☐

At 7 P.M. Baylee Hayes was released from the hospital. Dr. Hayes signed her out, against the recommendation of Dr. Kaplan, *The Amputator* as Samantha had begun calling her.

"I hope you told *The Amputator* we aren't considering her suggestion." Samantha looked at Stuart with firm resolve. The two of them had not spoken about the harsh words that passed between them before Baylee took sick. Pushing past their personal pain—they opted to deal with Baylee's physical needs first.

"She's a good doctor, Samantha. She's just doing her job."

"I can't believe you would defend *that* woman. Do you believe Baylee's legs should be cut off?"

Stuart was beat. "Something needs to be done to ease Baylee's pain. We've tried everything. I'll give you a little bit more time to prepare yourself before we make any permanent decisions, but we're going to have to face the reality, and soon, with the fact that our daughter has a degenerative disease that is not improving. It's a terrible thing to lose your legs, but death is far worse, and possible, if we don't make a decision soon."

Samantha didn't reply for a moment—then asked, "How much time do we have?"

"Two weeks to a month, max. Then we will need to make a choice. It may be good to begin now to prepare Baylee for the inevitable." Stuart's voice was serious.

Samantha remembered that in the past Stuart had taken a *wait and see* attitude. This gave her all the time in the world to play around and dabble in whatever she wanted to try to improve Baylee's way of life—but now it seemed Stuart was drawing the final line in the sand. Time was running out. In that moment, Samantha knew the timeline had been given so she could make peace with the inevitable. Stuart didn't strong arm her into a decision right now for only one reason—he loved her.

27
Death Where Is Your Sting?

T he Community Outreach Church was filled with the friends and family of Jean Brown. Rey stood behind the podium looking down at his copy of Jean's obituary. In a few moments he would read about Jean's amazing life in four short paragraphs. These words were lacking, falling short, incapable of giving those listening an adequate description of this amazing woman.

Callan stood next to the piano. Her beautiful voice was like oil poured out as she sang the last verse of *Amazing Grace*.

> *When we've been there ten thousand years*
> *Bright shining as the sun*
> *We've no less days to sing God's praise*
> *Than when we first begun*

While the words resounded through the sanctuary, Rey thought about the life of Jean Brown. He had known Jean for seven short years. No one at the funeral had known her longer, except for her family, yet she impacted so many lives; the folks from Community Outreach Church, Solar Energy and the town of Hillbrooke. Jean was in her mid-fifties when Rey met her. Debbie and Kim had not attended the Hillbrooke public school or played on any sports teams in the area. Jean had not served on social committees or held a public office, but the church was filled with people, even some standing against the back wall. Jean had impacted many lives.

Rey had no idea what this woman had done in secret, without fanfare. She lived a purposeful life. She put Jesus on display— in an exceptional way. Rey estimated more than three-fourths of those attending were people without any connection to Community Outreach Church. He had always known Jean was an amazing woman, but until last night as person after person told his and her story to Tom, Debbie and Kim—Rey had no idea the lives forever touched by one.

A smile formed on Rey's lips as he thought of Jean's kindness, contagious laugh, warm motherly ways and outgoing personality. Rey drew in a deep breath as Callan sung the final phrase of the song.

"I once was lost, but now I'm found. Was blind but now I see."

Eldon Chambers, the worship leader, finished the song with a dramatic piano run up and down the scales. Callan slid the microphone into the stand next to the piano and returned to her seat in the front row.

> *Jean Louise Hampton was born on February 2, 1952 to Ralph and Louise Hampton of Bloomville, Oklahoma. She married Tom Brown on June 27, 1972...*

Rey went on to read Jean's educational accomplishments, the jobs she held, children and grandchildren born to her family. He closed the reading with the names of those family members who passed on before her. Rey laid the obituary aside—it really spoke little about the amazing woman—Jean Brown. That would be his job. For the next forty minutes Rey painted with his words a work of art called—the life of Jean Brown. It was mixed with stories by family members, a video, scripture and two more songs. Rey ended the service with a prayer then took his place at the side of Tom Brown and watched the attenders file past the family members extending their sympathies.

...and it was over—done—final. Life would go on for the Brown family, Community Outreach Church, the small group and the many people who were touched by the life of Jean.

Rey's thoughts were invaded by the scripture that talked about life being a vapor—here then gone. He wouldn't let that happen—not to Jean. The last meeting, he had with her—she was prophetic. Rey believed God had gifted her with spiritual insight before He called her home, and God was on the cusp of doing something incredible.

□□

Rey called a special board meeting. They would meet at his house the evening following the funeral. The board sat around the family room. Callan served a light snack, and then left them alone to discuss the topic of their meeting. Only Tom Brown was not able to attend—for obvious reasons. The others were all able to come on short notice. Rey had kept the details of the meeting to a minimal, opting instead to discuss the issues on the agenda face to face. The board members had changed over the past few years. John Alden, James Fields and Peter Carver had all stepped down leaving Rey with only two original members; Harold Smith and Henry Samson. Both men had stayed loyal to him over the years—James Fields eventually had a change of heart, but he chose not to serve in a church leadership role.

The new board members were Tom Brown, head board member, Steve Orvis a family law specialist and Bud Babin a thirty-something self-made e-commerce businessman. This group of men was a healthy representation of the church both spiritually and economically.

The meeting was ready to commence. Rey cleared his throat and began. "Men, I'm very happy you could meet with me tonight on such short notice. As a church, we have experienced a great loss with the home going of Jean. Tom is home with his daughters and their families. He said to just keep him informed on whatever we discuss—I assured him we would. He belongs with his family at this time."

Steve and Bud nodded in agreement and Harold gave a hearty, "Amen to that, Pastor." Henry jotted something down on the legal pad he balanced on his crossed leg.

"There are two things I need to bring to your attention. First, Callan and I have been under investigation for child abuse. I wanted you to know this as my governing board. I thought it was just going to go away quickly, but evidently, after the home interview some questions about our boy's mental health were raised in direct relationship to our Christianity." Harold gasped. "That's religious persecution."

Pastor continued. "I've talked this over with Steve and he has given us good counsel how to proceed forward and hopefully we can put this behind us soon. We just want it to be over."

Bud Babin jumped in, "But Pastor, shouldn't you fight it? I mean, I have three small children and I don't want the government coming into my home telling me my children are damaged because I take them to church, pray with them and require a certain amount of behavior and respect from them."

Rey replied. "Bud. I hear ya. That was my first instinct too. Then after speaking with Steve, I felt it best not to drag it out any longer. We decided to allow Zander and Ty to be interviewed by the school psychiatrist. You all know these two boys will have no problem sharing how they feel—but please pray. They will meet this week at the school in back to back appointments." Rey paused then added. "I wanted you all to know what was going on in case something about this matter surfaced in the church or community. I could address it from the pulpit, but I don't want to give it more attention than it deserves unless it should become necessary."

Harold Smith chimed in, "I'll support whatever you think is best in the matter, Pastor. What was the other issue?" Harold had a way of keeping the train on the tracks. His comment told everyone—discussion on point one over, on to point two.

Rey fought back an urge to chuckle. He glanced down at the agenda on his lap and bit his lower lip. "Okay then, moving along. The passing of Jean Brown has produced some questions. Most importantly, why wasn't she healed? We all prayed. We all believed. Yet, she died." Rey looked at each man in the room taking in the body language of his spiritual team.

No one spoke. Henry continued to doodle on his legal pad. Bud's expression was one of confusion. Harold pursed his lips tightly and shook his head. Steve massaged his jaw line and looked downward.

Rey spoke. "I know this may sound unconventional, but the conventional ship sailed seven years ago." Rey's words drew their attention. "I feel compelled by the Spirit to have a city-wide Healing Service at Community Outreach Church. It will be a week from Friday." Rey allowed the words to soak in.

No one moved or responded—yea or nay.

Rey continued. "I know this is short timing, but I feel compelled by the Lord that this is the right timing. I need to know you are all on my team. I can't do this alone. I'm going to need a prayer team ready and believing at the altar." Rey skillfully changed from the singular to the plural. "*We'll* need people willing to fast and commit to pray beginning now through the night of the Healing Service."

The men leaned in listening attentively. Rey took notice. He took a breath and added. "Will you stand with me?"
Harold spoke first. "I'm with you, Pastor."
Then one by one each board member spoke in favor.

Harold added. "Pastor, we need to bring Snake on board too. He's a genius organizer and he's motivational too."

"I'm one step ahead of you for once, Harold. Snake will have the flier's ready tomorrow and he and Fauna will handle the promotion. Let's get down to work and organize teams for each of you to oversee."

Following a time of prayer, the men stood to leave, each with their assignments. There was an expectation that God was preparing to do something wonderful.

□□

Samantha lifted Baylee into the car. They had not left the house since Dr. Hayes signed Baylee out of the hospital five days ago. Isabelle had begged her mother to drop her at the Diner on Main to meet Ms. Reynolds. Stuart had called earlier saying he would be working late and not to hold dinner. He didn't plan to be home until after 7 P.M. Samantha had no other option but to pack Baylee up and take her along for the ride. She felt it was Isabelle's turn to have some attention.

Baylee was doing well and could stand a short car ride to the diner and back.

Isabelle turned from her front seat in the van to speak to Baylee. "Thanks for coming. I hope the ride's not too painful for you."

Baylee looked surprised by her sister's concern. "No. It's good to get out. Mom said we'd get pizza on the way back home."

"That'll be fun." Isabelle turned to watch Samantha slip into the driver's seat.

"Everyone buckled up?" Samantha asked.

With a touch of irritation in her voice, Isabelle said, "Yes, mom—let's go."

Samantha drove the two miles to the diner downtown. She eased to a stop right in front of the entrance.

"Mom, not here! Drop me at the corner up there." Isabelle pointed to the corner in front of them. There was a hint of *'can't be seen in the van with my mom'* in her tone.

Samantha fought back a full smile. "This is the drop off and pickup place. Text me when you're ready to come home. And don't even think about walking." Samantha's tone was firm and final. "You call or text me no matter what!"

Opening the front door of the family van, Isabelle nodded at her mom and looked back at Baylee and winked. She slipped down to the pavement and closed the van door. Isabelle stood by the curb, waving until the van turned left at the light and disappeared behind some old buildings.

Isabelle strolled toward the diner stopping abruptly at the door of glass. Her eyes focused on someone she knew sitting at a back table of the restaurant. It was Heidi—with her dad.

Isabelle moved away from the door and stood with her back against the brick wall. The entrance to the restaurant was just a few feet away. A couple opened the door to leave and the cow bell attached to the door announced their departure. The sound of the bell shouted to the patrons—*hey; look at the girl hiding by the door!* Isabelle ducked down and hurried past the store front windows. She stood at the corner of the building contemplating what to do next. She had no problem being confrontational when necessary, but the thought of Heidi…and her dad…at the same table made her sick to her stomach.

Gross!

Her mind raced. Should I text my mom? No. What would I tell her? Should I text Ms. Reynolds? No. What would I tell her? I'm trapped.

Isabelle walked toward the downtown stores as she thought about her options. A black car with darkened windows moved slowly past her. She was able to make out the face behind the wheel. It was a pasty white man with black hair leered out at her. A prickly feeling of panic attacked her body. She thought. Could this get any worse? Glancing back over her shoulder the car was turning around—and it just got worse.

Isabelle stepped into the drugstore, two buildings down from the restaurant. She watched the car pass by the store slowly. The driver's eyes scanning the building. Then the car quickly accelerated. Smoke from the tires curled in the air behind the speeding car. The familiar feeling of 'trust no one' surfaced. Walking around the store, she considered her next move. Walking home— a big fat no to that! Calling her mom—what would she say? She was unable to even formulate a lie in her head for this mess. She looked around the drugstore for a few minutes then peeked back out the front window. No creeps in sight, she walked back toward the diner. Taking a deep breath, she peeked in the corner of the front window. It gave her a panoramic view of the diner. Heidi was gone. Her dad was gone. She decided to risk it and opened the diner door. The cow bell chimed, and all eyes looked in her direction.

Ms. Reynolds waved from behind the counter by the open grill. She patted the counter top in front of her. "Isabelle, sit here. That way I can visit with you while I'm working."

Still feeling apprehensive about what she saw less than 15-minutes ago, Isabelle angled herself up on the stool and watched Ms. Reynolds looking very busy serving the customers of the Diner on Main.

Ms. Reynolds pointed over her shoulder at the chalkboard menu on the wall. "Look it over. I'll be right back to take your order." She hurried to the three tables where people were sitting. She slipped a piece of paper on each table. On her way back to the counter, she picked up dirty dishes from the table where Heidi and her dad were sitting a few minutes before. Ms. Reynolds put the dishes in a bin behind the counter.

Fauna stopped to speak to Isabelle. "How has your summer been? I can't believe school will be starting back up in just a few weeks. I'm happy you wanted to talk."

Isabelle pointed at the table that Fauna had just cleaned off. "Ms. Reynolds, who were the people sitting at that table?"

Fauna asked. "Do you know them? I was wondering about them myself. This is the second time they ate here. I couldn't tell if they like each other or what. Neither one of them wanted to talk to me. With some customers I might as well be invisible." Fauna laughed.

Isabelle liked the 'not in school' Ms. Reynolds. She seemed friendly—free of rules and regulations. "I thought I knew them. That's all." Isabelle glanced up at the menu then said. "My summer has been crazy, just like my life."

"In about 20 minutes this place will be empty. Then maybe we can talk all about what you've been doing—I'd like that. What would you like to eat?" She asked.

As Isabelle gave her order, Fauna yelled each item to the cook standing at the grill. It sounded like that echo game.

"Cheeseburger/Cheeseburger, French fries/French fries." When Isabelle said, "And a chocolate shake," Fauna tapped her finger on the counter. "Oh, I'll make that for you—and I use extra chocolate for my friends!" Fauna winked and smiled as she turned to the workspace behind her and began to scoop ice cream into a silver cup. Fauna poured in the milk and a heavy dose of chocolate syrup. She hooked the cup up to a blender and walked away leaving the machine to do its job. Isabelle's mouth watered.

29

I Am Not Willing That Any
Should Perish. –God

The days leading up to the Healing Service, members of Community Outreach signed up to fast and pray. Each person chose the fast that best fit their life. Rey decided to fast every other day for the whole day. Callan chose to fast every day until 3 P.M. Families were encouraged to come together in the evening or morning to pray together. The church was open from 6 A.M. to 11 P.M. for corporate prayer during the week leading up to the service.

The Douglas family prayed together each night. Zander and Ty caught the excitement of the possibilities. There was little they could do other than pray—still they wanted to be a part of what God would do.

Callan had not spoken to Samantha in over a week. With Jean Brown's death, memorial service and the medical emergency Baylee had, the timing just didn't seem right to try and get together. Callan had hoped to follow up with her. Samantha was at a critical crossroads.

Callan sighed at the thought of a missed opportunity. The busyness of life has a way of turning leaders into followers. Once the leader of her life, she juggled church, school, home and family. A picture came to Callan's mind of a farmer standing behind one of those old-fashioned plows, tilling slowly and steadily. Then the horse gets spooked and off it runs. The farmer who was making straight rows is suddenly flopping in the wind behind an out of control life. Callan whispered out loud, "Life happens. Help them, Lord."

Ty's voice interrupted Callan's thoughts. "Mom, Baylee wants me and Zander to come over for a little while. Can we go?"

Callan looked at Ty with a scrutinizing eye. She suspected the information she was getting was lacking. "Did she ask you, or did you ask her? You know she's only been out of the hospital less than a week."

Ty looked at the floor. "I asked if I could come...but she said, yes."

"But does her mom know she invited you?"

"Baylee said her mom wouldn't care." Ty kicked at the side of the kitchen island while he spoke.

Callan reached for her cell phone on the counter. "I'll call Mrs. Hayes and check."

"But—Mom, I really need to go over there." Ty's voice sounded mournful to the point of alarming. "It's super important that I see her. Please." Ty dragged the word please out for a long time.

Callan could hear the unspoken words...with a cherry on top... in his plea. She fought back a smile as she dialed Samantha's number. "Sorry Ty. I can't just send you down there without calling first. It'll only take a minute to ask." Callan held up her index finger signaling a conversation was close.

Ty crossed his fingers on both hands and scrunched up his face while he listened to Callan ask the important questions. In short order she hung up the phone and with a smile told Ty, "You can go, but only for one hour. We have an appointment later today."

Ty jumped straight in the air and landed with a shout. He ran down the hallway to get Zander. Within 60 seconds the front door slammed behind them and they cut through the neighbor's yard to get to the Hayes house. A yellow piece of paper announcing a Healing Service at Community Outreach Church was folded up in Ty's back pocket.

□□

Ms. Klingburg stood outside the school waiting for the Douglas family. When Rey turned into the school parking lot, the social worker was looking at her watch.

Rey glanced at Callan and said, "That's probably not a good sign."

From the back seat, Ty asked, "What's not a good sign?" Callan answered. "We're a few minutes late—that's all."

Rey pulled into the nearest parking space and the family piled out. As they approached, Ms. Klingburg, who stood near the school entrance spoke with an undeniable irritation, "I can take the boys from here." She held both of her hands out indicating the boys should come to her.

Ty and Zander did not respond to Ms. Klingburg's demand.

Rey replied in a civil but firm voice. "We'll walk them in and wait outside the office during their interviews."

Ms. Klingburg rolled her eyes in disgust. "Fine. But this isn't an interview, it's an assessment. If you want to stay, you cannot interfere in any way."

Callan bit her lip to hold back the mass of words pushing to get out.

Rey responded with an authority and used his 6-foot 5-inch frame to look down at the boxy woman. "You are mistaken, Ms. Klingburg. We are here voluntarily, and we certainly will interfere, if we feel at any time this process is not in the best interest of our children."

Ms. Klingburg's eye brows arched upward. She turned and walked into the school with the Douglas family following behind—at their own pace.

□□

Once the Douglas family had left the building, Ms. Klingburg opened the office door of the school psychiatrist. He was jotting down notes on a legal pad and looked up to see Ms. Klingburg standing with folded arms.

"Well, are the children in any danger—in your opinion?"

The young man in his late thirties met Ms. Klingburg's glare. "I'll have my report ready in a few days and will submit it through the usual channels."

"Come on Doctor. I'm the case worker. Give me something to work with here. If those children are in danger— I need to know NOW!"

The doctor laid down his pen and looked directly at Ms. Klingburg. He frowned at the forceful woman then said, "They are safe. My full report will be ready in a few days."

An audible huff escaped Ms. Klingburg's pinched lips. "Really. You didn't find the children's talk about Jesus a bit— adult driven. Those poor children are being indoctrinated against their will. The parents are religious radicals. Without intervention, these are the kind of kids that grow up to shoot up the school or build a bomb. If this report doesn't show a need for more intervention—well—this one will be on you, Doctor." Ms. Klingburg slammed the door behind her.

The doctor watched her leave then returned to writing.

> *The assigned social worker, Ms. Klingburg, seems unduly connected with the Douglas family. Her demands against them seem personally driven by something that may have happened in her own life rather than in the Douglas family.*

Ms. Klingburg left the meeting room at the school with a clomping sound echoing in the hallways. By the time she reached the exit doors, her jaw and fists were clenched. As she crossed the empty parking lot toward her car, she noticed a yellow piece of paper rolled up and placed between the side mirror and the driver's door. She eased the paper out and unrolled it.

The flier was an invitation to a Healing Service. Ms. Klingburg wadded it up in a ball and was ready to hurl it into the school yard when she opened the paper again and reread the invitation. It was the church where Rey Douglas was pastor.

Ms. Klingburg smoothed out the paper and thought for a moment if she should walk the poster back into the school and wave it in the face of that Doctor. Instead, she unlocked her door and slipped into the front seat. A smile formed on her face as she laid the yellow flier on the passenger seat. She opened up her calendar and jotted down Friday 6 P.M. Community Outreach Church. If no one else could see what she knew, then she would get the necessary information herself. She snorted a sigh of relief.

30

Mirrors Have a Way
of Reflecting.

P osters for the Healing Service were in almost every store window in Hillbrooke—thanks to Snake. Storekeepers found it hard to say no to the man with the hissing serpent tattooed on his face. To those who knew Snake, the tattoo had ceased to exist, but to a stranger it was intimidating, if not outright frightening.

Callan drove through the downtown area on her way to the box store at the edge of town. She spotted no less than ten of the bright yellow signs announcing the Healing Service on Friday. She pulled her car into the parking lot and saw the store was unusually busy for an August afternoon. Grabbing a stray cart from the parking area, she headed toward the store entrance. Another yellow poster announcing the upcoming service at Community Outreach was displayed on the window going into the store. Two women stood by the poster—Callan pretended to read the poster from a short distance away.

One of the ladies said, "This ought'a be a hoot, the best show in town." She poked her friend. "Are you gonna go?"

The other woman looked confused and replied. "It's kinda sad to think people are sick and would go to something like this. It's just hype." The woman paused for effect. "And no, I won't be going." The two women turned abruptly and almost ran into Callan's grocery cart.

Callan could feel her face turn red. One of the ladies looked at her and said. "Are you okay? You look like you're having a heat stroke." They didn't wait to see if Callan needed help, they looked at each other and walked away.

Callan pushed her cart into the store. She felt conflicted as she mulled over what she'd just heard. She hated to see the sacred service they were praying and fasting for reduced to a spectacle, a carnival side show. She was 100% on board with Rey's decision to have a special meeting focused on healing and even having it open to the community, but now that their business was plastered all over town on bright yellow posters, she was having her own second thoughts. This was not the first time she heard chatter about the crazy people at Community Outreach Church. Callan felt a bit like someone had pulled back the curtains on a personal and private moment to ridicule and mock what she held precious.

Her own feelings about praying for people who were sick and believing for their healing had evolved since she received the baptism in the Holy Spirit, yet she still battled with how those who didn't believe as she did would view her.

She pushed her cart a few more steps thinking about what had happened outside the store. Passing by a row of full-length mirrors, Callan saw her reflection. Right then, something unexpected happened. She stopped in front of the mirror and began to laugh. Speaking to her reflection—she said, "Old nature don't you try creeping in—there is no soft place for you to land here." Callan pushed her cart past the mirrors with a satisfied smile. In her heart, she declared, the Spirit has never disappointed—not once. If Rey believes, then I will stand with him. God has a plan to do something exceptional, supernatural and miraculous. I will be obedient. I close my ears to naysayers. I will trust and believe what God's Word says.

□□

Stuart was home when Samantha and Baylee arrived with pizza. Samantha yelled into the family room to Stuart. "You want to have pizza with us?"

He yelled back. "No thanks."

Samantha left the pizza on the counter and walked into the family room where a documentary held his interest. "You got your work done fast. I wasn't expecting you until at least seven."

Stuart answered without looking at Samantha. "Things moved fast without any interruptions." Stuart continued to give the television his full attention.

Samantha could sense something wasn't right, but she chalked it up to the scare they all had last week with Baylee in the hospital. Baylee sat at the kitchen island with a big piece of pizza on her plate. For that moment, Samantha was able to push past all the stuff that had happened in the past year. In this moment, she sat next to her baby girl enjoying a slice of pizza while Isabelle visited at the diner with a good person— she hoped.

When the text came into Samantha's phone *Come get me*, she was glad Stuart was home to watch Baylee. It had been almost two hours since Samantha had dropped Issie off at the diner—so she took that as a positive sign that the visit went well.

The family van rolled to a stop in front of the Diner on Main. Issie bolted out the door waving to the building behind her as she opened the front door of the van.

"Did you have a good time with Ms. Reynolds?" Her mom asked.

"She's nothing like I remembered her from school. She's— like a friend. We talked and laughed so much." Issie's voice drifted off.

Samantha glanced over at her. "So, why the sad face?" Fourteen was too young to hold back what Isabelle has seen. She wasn't sure what she should do about seeing Heidi and her father together at the diner. She glanced over at her mom driving and thought. How could I put one more thing on her? Watching her mom at that moment made her think. She almost looked normal—not tired and beaten down like she had been most of the past year. Maybe I should talk to my dad first?

Samantha made another stab at conversation with her daughter. "Did you see anyone you knew at the diner?"

Isabelle snapped her head toward her mom and questioned. "Why do you ask that?"

When Samantha stopped at the four-way by their house, she took her focus off the road and looked directly at Issie. "Why so defensive? I was just wondering if you saw any friends from school. I'm not insinuating anything."

Isabelle looked out the side window pondering her next move. Just as Samantha turned the car into their driveway Issie blurted out. "Mom, I saw Heidi at the diner...and Dad sitting at the same table. I didn't go in. I went next door to the pharmacy and walked around for a few minutes then when I went back, they were both gone."

Samantha pulled the van into the garage. "I'll talk to dad about it. It's best not to assume anything. I'm glad you felt you could tell me. I'm sure it's all very innocent. You should never burden yourself with that kind of stuff." Samantha stayed calm and cool on the outside, but inside was another case.

□□

Heidi had not been herself since the realization that *The Healer* was not all he claimed to be. Sitting at the desk in the reception area she fingered through the pamphlet with testimonials and claims about *The Healer*'s extraordinary feats. Heidi read the material over with her nostrils flaring in disgust. She clenched her jaw and began to grind her teeth together as she contemplated her life. I have to get out of here, but where? What am I going to do? I feel like I'm on a sinking ship with no escape route. Her eyes darted around the small waiting room area. She once felt safe and secure in this place—now she jumped at every sound and worried for each young patient.

Heidi slipped her index finger to her mouth and began chewing on the side of her fingernail. She scolded herself, "Don't start biting your nails again!"

"And who are you talking to?" Victor stood close to her and she nearly jumped out of her chair. How does he do that? She wondered.

Heidi tried to busy herself with the few papers on her desk. She didn't look at Victor but answered his question. "Just talking out loud."

Victor leaned in close. "How many clients do we have today?"

Heidi leaned away from him as she ran her finger over the ledger with the day's appointments. "It looks like we have three coming in today."

Victor's voice became stern. "You do know that something has to change if we're going to keep this place open." Victor placed his open hand on top of the appointment book. "You think about whether you want to keep working here or not. If you want to keep your job, then start recruiting patients or I'll be looking for another employee."

Heidi had not looked directly at him in weeks. When she glanced up at his face she felt like his eyes were drilling holes into her soul. She quickly looked away. The thought of better days working with Pastor Rey Douglas as her boss flashed in her memory.

Victor turned and abruptly left the reception area. Heidi heard his office door slam shut. She sat frozen with fear. This was not a safe place. If only he would fire her, then she could collect unemployment, but if she left then she'd have nothing. A desire to pray and ask the Lord for help stirred inside of her. She pushed it down telling herself—no don't go there. Don't be weak-minded. She opened her phone and began to search the classified ads.

The front door of *The Healer's* office opened, and four police officers rushed in. Heidi let out a gasp at the sight. She stood up not sure what was happening—was there a fire? Was the whole street being evacuated? Then she saw one of the officers resting his hand on the gun strapped to his side.

"Ma'am, please sit down and don't move. We are looking for a Victor Darwin. Is he here?" The officer speaking eased his gun from the holster.

Heidi sat down. She pointed toward the hallway—unable to speak.

The first officer drew his gun and moved slowly down the hallway making hand motions to the two officers behind him. No one spoke. One officer stayed behind with Heidi. She heard the words boom from the back of the house. "All clear."

"Ma'am was he here today?" The officer's voice was loud.

Heidi was numb with fear. She found her voice. "He was here. Literally moments ago, is his car gone?"

"Do you know the make and model?"

Heidi's expression spoke volumes before the words came from her mouth. "It's a black one with dark windows."

The officer with his hand on the gun pulled a piece of paper and laid it on the desk. "This is a search warrant; please stay seated while we search the premises."

"What? Why?" Heidi picked up her phone to make a call.

"Ma'am put the phone down. We're going to need to question you before you make any calls."

Heidi chocked back the tears. "Am I in trouble?"

"That depends on what you knew and when you knew it."

Heidi began to tremble. She wondered if she could be guilty of some crime because of something Victor did. If necessary, she'd tell everything she knew…and more.

Within a few minutes, the police officers had removed a box that looked like medicine bottles, some with liquid and some with pills, two computers, a stack of video tapes and some video equipment.

Heidi watched the items being carried out by the officers. She began to gag and reached for the wastebasket under her desk.

□□

With an extra loud voice, Baylee yelled for her mom.

Samantha entered the room a few moments later—slightly out of breath. "Is everything okay?"

"Oh—yes, sorry mom. I just have a big favor I wanted to ask." She held a folded piece of bright yellow paper in her hands.

"What's that you have?" Samantha drew closer to the bed and sat next to Baylee who sat propped up with pillows.

"Ty gave this to me and I really want to go. This is for me—I just know it!" She handed the folded paper to her mom.

Samantha opened it and recognized that it was the same flier that she'd seen all over town. "Baylee. Do you believe this is actually possible?"

"Mom, you've taken me to every crazy kook out there some medical and some not. This is what I'd like to try."

Baylee pulled the Bible out from under her pillow. She and her mom had not talked about it since that day she went to the hospital. She opened the Bible to the story about the man whose friends brought him to Jesus to be healed. "Mom, I can't go alone. I need someone to take me. Could we all go? Our whole family."

"Oh Baylee." Samantha held the paper in her hand and smoothed out the wrinkles. "I don't know. It's just a few days away."

Baylee sucked her lips in and bit down, then slowly released them. "I heard you and dad talking about my legs and maybe getting them cut off." She pushed herself into a full sitting position and swung her legs out of the bed. She sat hip to hip with her mom. "Could we just give Jesus a chance before the doctors take them?" She patted the top of her legs and looked at her mom. "Please mom—take me? I can't get there without you."

Samantha gulped back the emotion that welled up in her chest. "Let me think about it."

Samantha walked downstairs and placed the flier on the counter. She now had two things to speak with Stuart about. She purposefully let some time pass before talking to Stuart about what Issie saw at the diner. At that moment, her emotions were high and the ability to think and speak rationally was certainly compromised. Had she come in *hot* for the Heidi discussion, she knew it would not produce good results—for anyone.

Samantha touched the poster on the counter, leaning in she read every word—location, time, event and scripture. She pushed the poster away and sat down at the island. She prioritized things in her mind. When Stuart came home tonight, they would need to talk privately. She told herself, "One thing at a time, Samantha!"

Samantha's phone pinged. It was a text message from Stuart. *Another late night don't wait dinner.*

Samantha held her cell phone and twisted her mouth to the side contemplating her next move.

□□

Rey and Callan loved Hillbrooke. They had seen miraculous things in their lives personally and in the lives of those around them. Neither of them dreamed how far the Lord would stretch them both spiritually and socially. The infilling of the Holy Spirit had changed them forever. Religious terms like the Word, fasting, prayer and the altar were once spoken casually, but now, each one represented a foundational pillar where the Holy Spirit was building the man and woman of God.

Now, a new pillar was taking shape—healing.

□□

The Hillbrooke International Airport was packed with stranded summer vacationers. The thunderstorm that rolled through knocked the schedule off one day with flight delays and cancellations. Debbie and her family left ahead of the storm, but Kim and her husband's travel arrangements were the day after the storm. Tom watched his youngest daughter fade out of view as she passed through security. He waved one last time, unsure if Kim could see him. Turning to leave, he knew, this marked the beginning of his life forever changed— today he would begin life without Jean. Tom struggled with his emotions. They were fresh and surfaced at the oddest of times. Tears streamed down his face as he walked past summer travelers happy for the last weeks of vacation before school resumed.

Tom passed through the automatic doors into the humid August day. He encouraged himself to take another step forward. I'm on a journey not of my own choosing. There will be lots of detours but no short cuts on this journey through grief. God has a plan and purpose for my life—I'm not alone.

Tom reached his car and touched the handle to unlock the doors. Once inside the car he said out loud, "Lord, I can't do this without you. Help me!"

□□

It was 5:30 P.M. The afternoon sun was hot and the air musty. Samantha looked again at the text message Stuart sent earlier in the day. *Another late night don't wait dinner.*

Samantha thought—working late my foot. A second look at the text message caused her breathing to speed up and threw the cooling off period out the window—rereading the message poured gas on the smoldering coals and a full inferno erupted. "Isabelle, come here." Samantha had her purse over her shoulder with the car keys in her hand when Issie strolled into the kitchen. "I need to run a short errand. I hate to ask you, but please stay with Baylee until I get back."

Isabelle responded mute of emotion. "Sure." Turned and went back upstairs.

Samantha shut the door behind her and considered whether to go to the clinic or the diner. After chewing it over she decided the diner. What good would the clinic do, if Stuart was there it would be—just as he said? She hoped he wouldn't be at the diner. She hoped Issie was wrong about what she saw. Still, the girl knew her own father and Heidi too. That could not be refuted. But why were they at the diner—together? Maybe there was a good reason and maybe not. Samantha couldn't stop her thoughts from going to dark places.

She wished she could pray like Callan had prayed with her. That brought peace. She picked up her phone to call Callan—then laid it down on the passenger seat. She decided to give a try—best she could. "God, remember me? I told you last week I believed in You. I'm hoping that means we can talk. Will you help me? I don't want to be unreasonable…or untrusting…or stupid! Amen—I guess that's the right ending. So, I need direction. Amen!"

Samantha pulled into the parking lot behind the Diner on Main. There were only four cars there and one of those was Stuart's. Samantha pulled the van next to Stuart's sports car and stepped out. Walking toward the back entrance she whispered again. "God, help me." She put her hand on the door and opened it slowly—afraid of what she might see.

From the narrow hallway, she could see Stuart. He was facing the front doors with his back to her. He sat alone. Taking a deep breath, she approached him from behind and placed her hand on his shoulder. "Imagine meeting you here." She tried her best to keep her voice upbeat.

Stuart jerked around at the sound of Samantha's voice and stood asking. "Where are the kids? Who's with Baylee?" His face looked startled and caught all wrapped up into one expression.

Samantha sat down across from Stuart and answered. "Issie is with her. I didn't expect to be gone long and surprisingly Issie didn't even resist the idea."

Stuart looked past Samantha toward the door at the front of the restaurant. "What are you doing here?"

Samantha smiled. "I guess I could ask you the same thing seeing that you are having…" She pulled out her phone and read Stuart's text message. *"Another late night. Don't wait dinner."*

Stuart replied quickly. "The diner is close to the office. I drop in here sometimes for a quick meal. Then back to work." Stuart's tone was defensive.

The waitress walked toward Stuart and Samantha's table and set two glasses of water down. "Well, hello Mrs. Hayes." The waitress kept her focus on Samantha. "It's nice to see you again."

Samantha responded. "Ms. Reynolds. It slipped my mind for a moment that you worked here. Isabelle had a wonderful time with you…" She paused then added. "…a few nights ago, when I dropped her off."

Stuart wasn't a mathematician, but he was able to piece together this small equation. The puzzle pieces came together in his mind, he looked at Samantha's all-knowing smirk.

Samantha gestured across the table at Stuart. "Ms. Reynolds, I don't believe you've met my husband. This is Dr. Hayes." Samantha looked at her husband and said. "Ms. Reynolds is Isabelle's school counselor. I told you about our meeting a few months ago. She's the one who first saw the tattoo on Issie's wrist. We owe her a lot."

Stuart realized a moment too late that his mouth was hanging open in an awestruck way. He quickly pinched his lips together and forced a head nod in the waitress's direction.

Samantha continued. "Isabelle had a wonderful time talking with you." She looked at Stuart while she spoke to Fauna. "She told me *all* about it."

Stuart took a sip of water. Then tried to take control of the runaway train—he looked at Fauna. "I'll have tonight's special." Fauna wrote it down and looked in Samantha's direction.

Samantha smiled at Fauna. "I'm not staying. I just stopped in to speak with my husband for a moment—maybe another time."

Fauna turned to leave the table and noticed a woman walking away from the entrance of the diner.

Samantha turned her attention back to Stuart who sat back in his chair—a bit cocky. "You know I'm not one to play games." Samantha kept her eyes fixed on her husband. "You know, and I know, that you've met Heidi at this diner at least once for dinner. You want to tell me what's going on?"

Stuart's smile was mocking. "Then why all the cloak and dagger stuff? If Isabelle saw me here with someone, she should have just come in and talked to me. It was only for a moment. Ms. Alden is a patient and saw me sitting here alone and asked to talk to me. Before I could say no, she'd pulled up a chair and was rambling on about some issues I'd spoken to her about in the office." He shot an accusatory look in Samantha's direction feeling he'd made a good case for himself.

"I don't really care why or how it happened—it just can't ever happen again." Samantha tapped the table with the palm of her hand while making her point.

"Samantha, you knew when you married a doctor that I'd have patients approaching me in the oddest places. You've seen it before when you've been with me. It's awkward for me and if the patient is emotionally hurting—they often don't take subtle social cues. I hope you can see that's what happened here the other day."

"Are you saying she's a stalker? Is she dangerous to you or us?" Samantha leaned forward. Her questions were sincere.

Stuart relaxed. "To tell you the truth—I'm not sure. I keep directing her to seek help outside the clinic for her issues. They are beyond my scope of specialty."

Samantha frowned. "Well, that's not comforting. We allowed our teenager to be alone with her. Thank goodness Isabelle had the wherewithal to recognize Heidi wasn't a safe person and ended it, even though she pretended to be sick."

Stuart shifted in his chair, then leaned forward resting his arms on the table.

In a low voice, Samantha spoke. "Stuart, you have to be careful. Callan warned me that Heidi wasn't a safe person."

Stuart responded with sarcasm. "Well, Callan isn't privilege to doctor patient confidentiality. Besides that, your friend, Callan, may have some issues of her own."

With a frown, Samantha replied. "What do you mean? Did Heidi say something negative about Callan or her family?"

Stuart was silent.

"I've seen both Heidi and Callan in action. I've no trouble choosing whose team I'd want to play on." There was a confidence in Samantha's voice that was unrecognizable— even to her. "I need to get back to the girls. I came to warn you to be *very* careful. Even in a mid-size town like Hillbrooke—people can talk. Relationships here are like a tangled web." Samantha glanced in the direction of the counter at Ms. Reynolds. Stuart's eyes followed. She looked back at Stuart and said, "Case in point!"

Stuart looked away sheepishly as Samantha pushed her chair back to leave. "One more thing, Baylee wants the whole family to go to a healing service at Community Outreach where

Callan's husband, Rey, is the pastor. I think we should go. Baylee doesn't ask much."

Stuart lifted his glass to his mouth and took a long sip of water. He set the glass back on the table and narrowed his eyes. "I'm sorry, but I'm not going to any church and especially not the church of *those* people. But I won't stop any of you from going. When did you say it was?"

"It's Friday. The poster is right there in the window." Samantha turned toward the front door and pointed at the yellow poster taped to the window next to the door. Across the street a car was parked—it looked a lot like the one Heidi Alden drove. Samantha turned back to face her husband and repeated her warning. "Be careful Stuart. I know you want to help—but sometimes it can be dangerous. As a doctor, you of all people know— cancer needs to be cut off before it attacks the whole body."

"You're talking medicine with me?" Stuart chuckled as he watched Samantha leave.

Ms. Reynolds watched from behind the counter, and Stuart immediately regretted humiliating his wife.

31

Great News

Grace prayed in the quiet of the church office. Her work was done. The phones were quiet. The pastoral staff was in the sanctuary praying for the upcoming healing service. Her heart was ready for whatever the Lord had for her, Community Outreach Church and those who were sick and hurting. She whispered, "Lord, meet the needs of the people. Move on their hearts to come. Stop all fear and anything that would hinder them from coming. Heal the sick, bind up the broken hearted, set the captives free." Her stomach rumbled loudly, and she rubbed it gently. She glanced left and right to be sure no one was within ear range. She took a long sip of water from the water bottle on her desk.

The desk phone rang, and Grace swallowed the water before answering. "Hello. You've reached Community Outreach Church. This is Grace speaking."

"Grace, this is Tom Brown. Is Pastor available?"

"He and the staff are in the sanctuary praying for the service tomorrow. Would you like me to get him or you can leave a message?"

"Sure. Give me his voice mail."

Grace put Tom on hold and sent the call to Pastor Rey's voice mail. Following the mailbox greeting from the pastor, Tom left his message. "Pastor Rey. Give me a call. I have an amazing piece of news that I want to share with you. God is good."

□□

Rey hit the flashing light on his desk phone. It was Tom Brown's voice. After listening to his message, Rey picked up the phone and called him back. On the fourth ring a breathy voice answered. "Hey Pastor. I was on the treadmill. I'm so glad you called me back so soon."

"What's going on? Your message sounded intriguing." Rey leaned back in his office chair and looked up at the tongue and groove wood ceiling of his office.

"I heard from the president of Superior Solar Energy. He's been extremely concerned since hearing about Jean's illness and passing. He called me into the office today to let me know the company is donating $100,000 in Jean's name for a memorial of my choosing. They met in a special meeting while I was out of the office and the board of directors approved the donation. I'm giddy with excitement."

Rey leaned forward and rested his elbows on the desk. "That's awesome. Do you have any ideas yet what you want to do with the money?"

"Not yet. I wanted to pray about it, of course, but also see if you had any ideas. I know it will have to be something that touches the lives of hurting people. That would have made

Jean so happy. Her goodness will continue through this memorial. I wanted to give you some time to think about it. I know when the right thing comes along—it will ring true in my heart."

Rey agreed. "I believe that too. There are all kinds of foreign mission's opportunities and home mission's projects right in Hillbrooke. I'll dig a little deeper and get a list of ideas for you to consider. This is a beautiful investment with eternal dividend."

"I'll see you early tomorrow night for the pre-prayer service."

"Looking forward to it and anticipating what the Lord will do."

□□

The Diner on Main was empty. Fauna wiped down the last table and dropped the dirty cloth in the bucket of soapy water under the counter. She glanced at the cook who was sitting on a wooden stool next to the grill swatting at flies with a rolled-up newspaper. Fauna watched the cook for a moment. It was amazing how he sat with his back straight and slowly lifted his arm to take a swing. He never stood up or leaned forward—not even a bit.

Fauna chuckled to herself that this was the sort of thing that occupied her mind of late. She sat down at the counter and sipped an icy Coke while she watched the clock tick down the last hour of her shift. She thought about Snake's offer to put in a good word for her at the solar energy factory where he worked. She struggled in her mind if it would be a compromise—or would it? She could set a goal of two years—save her money, then open a counseling office or even do weekend counseling out of the church. Maybe there were financial backers she could find to get the business off the ground.

The cow bell on the diner door reverberated through the quiet eatery. Fauna slipped off the stool to greet the customer. She said before looking up, "Take a seat anywhere." She heard a low familiar laugh and jerked her head up. It was Snake. She waved her arms in front of her at the empty diner. "As you can see we have unlimited seating."

"Can you sit with me?" Snake asked.

"Sure. I think we'll be closing up in about 50 minutes...or less."

"I had someone call me today about a reference for you."

"For what? I haven't filled out any applications for work— I've been having mixed emotions about possibly going back to the middle school, if they asked me. But, school starts in less than a week. I'm thinking they have their team in place by now."

"Well, maybe not. It was the school that called and wanted a personal reference. They asked me a lot about you. How would you feel about going back?"

Fauna leaned back in her chair pondering the idea. "Surprisingly, I'm feeling a bit apprehensive. The school job keeps me in my profession, but with so many restrictions. I guess I'll see which way the Lord leads if an invitation is actually given." She breathed deeply then changed topics. "On another note...are you ready for the healing service tomorrow night?"

"Yes. How about you?"

"Whenever I've prayed about it—there is a stirring in my heart that God is about to do something big. I don't know what to expect—but I know He is about to do something wonderful."

Snake shifted in his seat. "What if nothing happens? What if nobody comes? Have you considered that possibility?"

"That's not the scuttlebutt I've been hearing at the tables from the lunch and dinner crowds. There's a buzz, a curiosity, some who feel hopeless and have nothing to lose. I have no doubt the church will be filled with all sorts of people."

Snake whispered. "Lord, build my faith. I know I'm a bit of the glass half-empty kinda guy."

"You are not! You're loyal, faithful and true."

He snorted a laugh. "You make me sound like a companion dog."

Fauna rolled her eyes and laughed. "Well, you are sorta."

"Speaking of companions—I've been struggling with making decisions about our future—you and me."

Fauna reached across the table and touched Snake's tattooed hand. "Whenever you're ready—I'm not going anywhere."

Snake met Fauna's eyes and swallowed. "I'm almost ready— just wanted you to know that."

Fauna held back the emotion. "That is good to hear—very good to hear." The cow bell announced a group of loud teenagers coming in the door. "Back to work for me." She leaned in and whispered. "They look like big tippers too." Fauna laughed. "Did you want to order something before I wait on them?"

"Just a Coke…and fries."

Fauna winked at the tall man—feeling a sense of security she'd never felt before.

The TV in the corner of the diner flashed the words across the screen—BREAKING NEWS IN HILLBROOKE, MICHIGAN. Snake saw it first. "Fauna—turn up the sound on the TV." She found the remote behind the counter and clicked it in the direction of the screen. The sound filled the room. The reporter stood outside a business a few blocks from the diner. In the background police were exiting the building with boxes and computers.

The newscaster reported, "This is the office of *The Healer*. Channel 6 News uncovered an ongoing investigation with the Florida department of justice and the Hillbrooke Police Department who were jointly investigating improprieties in the dealings of Victor Darwin—owner and operator of the office of *The Healer*. There are similar stories surfacing from both Florida and Alabama where Mr. Darwin used the alias Alan Fallow and Dallas Solomon. Darwin's business was meant to help people manage pain and emotional issues, but instead the owner, Victor Darwin, is alleged to have drugged, spied on female patients while they undressed and, in some cases, allegedly assaulted them."

The reporter pointed over her shoulder to the front of the business. The police were escorting a female from the house. "Behind me, you will see the receptionist for the business, Heidi Alden, being led out by police. We are told that she is cooperating but considered a person-of-interest. Mr. Darwin is unavailable for comment and a warrant has been issued for his arrest. There will be a full report tonight on News at Eleven. We'll keep you posted as new details become available. This is Heather DeFranko, Channel 6 News." Two side by side still shots filled the television screen; one of Heidi Alden from her Facebook page and one of Victor Darwin from *The Healer's* website. The local programing returned, and Fauna lowered the volume.

The teenage patrons turned their focus back to loud talking and roaring laughter. Fauna walked back to Snake's table and sat down. "I just saw that lady in here a few nights ago—it was the night Isabelle came in. She seemed distraught and was talking to Dr. Hayes. His wife came in here last night and we talked. It was odd and uncomfortable. Me knowing another woman was with her husband two other times." Fauna stopped. "Okay. I'm stopping now. This is sounding very gossipy—sorry. That poor woman! Who knows what terrible things she's experienced and witnessed. All of this going on right under our noses in Hillbrooke."

Fauna stood up. "See, that's why we need a real counseling center in town." She walked across the diner to the table of loud teens. She pulled her pad and pen from her apron pocket. Turning back to Snake she called. "Can you wait until my shift is over? I'd like to talk more."

Snake nodded and took another sip of his Coke.

□□

Heidi sat alone in her apartment. No lights on, no candles burning, only the glow of the 24-hour news channel that reported the breaking news in Hillbrooke, Michigan. Heidi's name on the national news—like a common criminal—it was over for her in Hillbrooke. She had no reason to stay—unless. She picked up her cell phone and scrolled through the recent calls. Finding the doctor's cell number, she sent a quick text.

I'm leaving Hillbrooke.
There is nothing for me.
Can I see you one last time?

Stuart pulled his cell phone from his pocket and checked the text message that just arrived. The number seemed familiar. He read the message and knew immediately—it was Heidi. He texted back his reply. *Yes—I'll let you know when and where.*

When Heidi read the reply, she put her hand on her heart and sighed. She never dreamed he would reply so quickly. Maybe all was not lost.

□□

Samantha didn't say a word but stepped in front of Stuart's view of the television. He leaned to the left to try and see past her— unaware of her purposes. He finally stopped stretching and looked at his wife.

"What are you doing?" He asked with a confused look on his face.

"I wanted to be sure I had your full attention. I think I have it now." Samantha picked up the remote and clicked off the television.

"Why'd you do that?" Stuart tried to reach for the remote, but Samantha placed it behind her back.

"This will only take a minute. Tomorrow night is that healing service. It starts at 6 P.M. It should last at least ninety minutes maybe longer—I don't know exactly. Callan wasn't sure when I called to let her know we were coming."

"We?" Stuart questioned.

"Well, I'd hoped it would be—we. Will you come—for Baylee?" Samantha's voice had a pleading tone.

"I told you before—you go. Have fun. Try not to be too disappointed. I have a very good grip on reality and I don't need any false hope to string me along through life."

"Okay. We're going. I'm going to ask Isabelle to go with us too."

"Yeah—good luck with that!"

Samantha headed upstairs. She thought her chances might be better with Issie, if Baylee did the asking. Samantha walked into Baylee's room surprised to see Isabelle sitting in the chair next to the bed. Samantha sat down on the other side of the bed putting Baylee between them. "Baylee, dad doesn't want to go with us tomorrow."

Baylee looked worried. "Do you think it will still work without him? The story said his friends took him to Jesus. I can't think of anyone closer than you, Dad and Issie."

Issie looked at her little sister. "Do you want me to go with you?"

"Please, Issie would you go?" Baylee asked.

Isabelle shrugged her shoulders and said, "Sure—I got nothing better to do on a Friday night."

Baylee pushed her head back into her pillow. "That's it. Tomorrow Jesus is going to heal me!"

Isabelle shot a look of concern at her mom. Samantha looked stressed as she tried to reason with Baylee. "You know—we don't understand anything about Jesus really or how things are done. Let's go with an open mind but be prepared to learn. Maybe healing comes in steps."

"Mom, that's not how it happened in the Bible. Jesus saw that those friends were willing to take the sick man to Him and He healed him. He'll do it for me too. I just know it."

"Baylee, I don't want you to be disappointed—that's all. Let's go and see what it's all about. I'll—we'll take you."

Isabelle looked upset. "I'm going to bed." She looked at Baylee as she left the room. "I hope tomorrow is everything you wish it to be."

"I already believed. Jesus is going to heal me—tomorrow night. Right mom?"

Isabelle ducked out the door before Samantha could answer, but Baylee kept her eyes on her mom. Samantha nodded and said. "I believe He will."

32
The First Miracle

The day that the leadership of Community Outreach Church had prayed for had arrived. They had fasted and believed—with faith unwavering—God would meet with and heal the sick in body and the sick in spirit. The prayer team assembled at the altar. A mournful cry rippled through the front of the church. It was soft, barely audible, and then the volume increased filling the sanctuary as the prayer warriors interceded for things unknown.

Following the cooperate prayer time, Pastor Rey spoke to the prayer team, "We only have a short time before people begin arriving. I want the first miracles to come start here among us tonight. Let's get in groups of 3-4 and pray for one another's needs. Share, but don't take too much time. Make it quick and let God do the rest."

The groups began to form. Pastor Rey, Callan and Grace formed one team. Harold and Esther Smith with the Samson's formed another group. The two newest board members Steve Orvis and Bud Babin along with their wives formed another group. The other pastoral staff "the young ones," gathered together.

Fauna and Snake joined with Tom Brown to form the last group. The groups began to share their needs quickly and the prayers ascended.

Zander and Ty watched it all from their seats in the front row. Ty reached over and took Zander's hand and with his head bowed, he prayed. "Heal Baylee tonight. Take away the pain. Help the bones grow straight. Help her family. Thank you, Jesus. Amen." Zander shook his hand free from his brother—but not before Ty said Amen.

□□

Samantha looked at the pile of outfits on the bed. She frowned and thought what does one wear to a Healing Service? Blue jeans and a tee shirt just didn't seem proper and a dress seemed too formal. Samantha settled on a black pair of pants and a lightweight blue cap sleeved sweater. She pulled the matching sweater off the hanger that went with the shell in case the air conditioning was cold. She stepped back from the full-length mirror in her walk-in closet and gave herself a once over. She tipped her head and shrugged her shoulders remembering she was a novice at all things church related.

There was a knock at the bedroom door. Samantha yelled from the closet, "Come in."

Isabelle opened the bedroom door and scanned the room for her mother.

Samantha poked her head out of the closet. "In here."

"Mom. I hope this is okay for church." Isabelle opened her arms and did a quick spin to reveal a teen appropriate outfit. "I realized when I was getting dressed that I've never been inside a church in my entire life. Kinda crazy—right? I've seen church scenes in movies and on television and I think I nailed it." Isabelle chuckled at her comment.

Samantha smiled nervously—Isabelle seemed happy. "I can't say I've been in many churches in my lifetime either—except for weddings and funerals."

Baylee limped into the room. Her face grimaced with pain. "Can we go now? I need to go now."

Samantha bent down in front of her. "Are you sure you're okay to do this? Do you want something for the pain before we go? Just to take the edge off."

"I can't Mom. I'll be sleepy. I need to be awake. Can we go?"

The three Hayes ladies headed down the stairs. Baylee leaned against her mom. Each step brought a moan of pain.

Samantha left Baylee by the garage door and stepped into the family room. "Last call. You want to join us, Stuart?"

Stuart kept his eyes locked on the television screen and replied. "No way. What you're doing to that girl is a shame! I won't be part of it."

Stuart listened for the garage door to close. He stood up crossing the room to look out the window. He watched the van circle around the horseshoe drive and pull out onto Lancaster Drive.

He took his phone from his pocket and sent a text message.

☐☐

The crisp fall air brought a cool evening breeze. Callan, Rey, Zander and Ty sat in the front pew of the church sanctuary. Every Sunday these were their seats—but this wasn't Sunday. It was Friday night. The night of the special Healing Service and the sanctuary was full. The atmosphere was electric. There was an excitement and expectation in the air—something was imminent.

The worship leader, Eldon Chambers, led the congregation in an upbeat rendition of an old song, *Whose Report Will You Believe*.

He sang the first phrase alone, "Whose report will you believe?"

The worship team echoed, "We shall believe the report of the Lord."

The congregation joined in. "His report says, I am healed His report says, I am filled. His report says, I am free. His report says, VIC-TO-RY!"

A shout rose up after the word victory and roared through the sanctuary like a marching army! The song was repeated two more times. The people who were able were on their feet with their hands lifted in surrender. The people's shouts sent a surge of faith through the sanctuary.

Eldon sang alone, "Are you healed?"

The worship team responded, "Yes—we are!"

Eldon sang, "Are you filled!"

The team answered, "Yes—we are!"

Eldon asked in song, "Have you got the victory?"

Everyone yelled in unison, "Yes—we do!"

Pastor Rey could feel the presence of the Lord engulf him, breathing life into his Spirit man. He was energized as he drank in the presence of the Lord.

The worship time ended. The volume of praise increasing like the thumping beat of a drum. The sound of it shook the place.

As quickly as the voices soared, a hush followed.

One voice rose above the rest with a prophetic word. Tom Brown proclaimed, *"Do you have a need? Are you confused, discouraged, disappointed? Is anxiety robbing you of peace? Are you lonely? Are you sick? Do you need a miracle? He is your Jehovah Rapha—the God who heals. Your problems are not too big for Him. He is a Wonderful Counselor. He is the Prince of Peace. He is Mighty God. He is everlasting Father. He will never leave you—He will not forsake you. Bring your need to Jesus. Come! Taste and see that the Lord is good!"*

At the back of the sanctuary a middle-aged woman in a business suit sat. Her face was stern, her eyes darting around in skepticism. A black portfolio lay open in her lap. Her hand rested on the pad of paper with a pen ready to write. She observed everything happening in the meeting.

□□

Pastor Rey had moved to the place behind the pulpit while the prophetic word was spoken. When Tom's voice went silent, Pastor Rey spoke.

"We are a forgetful people, and the Lord is reminding us that when we have a problem He is the answer. Whatever your need may be, call out to Him." Pastor Rey encouraged the people to remember what the Lord had done for them.

The voices of the congregation increased in volume. The people shouted out to the Lord all that He had done for them. Pastor Rey stood quietly, allowing the presence of the Lord to wash over him. He felt a confirmation in his spirit—this special healing service was Spirit led. It was God ordained.

In his heart a fresh word burned. He looked out at the faces of his church family. There were many he didn't know. There was hope and anticipation. He prayed silently. *Lord may Your will be done. Holy Spirit have Your way in this place tonight.*

□□

Pastor Rey gripped the sides of the podium, leaning forward he read the first line from his notes. His voice was slow, deliberate and broken with emotion.

"Jesus became human—that he might be—a sympathetic— High Priest. Touched—with the feelings—of our infirmities." He paused, looked out across the congregation. The eyes of the people were locked on him— the expectancy was palpable. Pastor Rey knew the stories of many in attendance. He knew their infirmities—some were seen—some unseen. Life and death hung in the balance. His heart was breaking.

33
Do You Believe In Miracles?

Baylee sat close to her mother on the church pew. The pain pulsated through her legs sending signals to her brain that it was time for pain medication. She stifled the urge to cry out in pain coaching her mind to wait—soon, they would bring her to Jesus.

Samantha, Isabelle and Baylee sat halfway back from the stage. The seat selection had been her mom's idea. Baylee couldn't see over the people in front of her nor could she prop herself up on the pew to see above the sea of bodies that blocked her view. She leaned her head against her mom's shoulder and breathed deeply.

Samantha wrapped her arm around Baylee's shoulders and softly rested her arm around her daughter's small frame. As the music stopped the voices of the people cheering grew quiet. Baylee listened to a single man's voice speak from among the many people present. She could hear people agree with the words of the man and some people were crying. Then it was Ty's dad who stood up on the stage. She tried to focus on his words, but she couldn't understand. When Ty told her stuff—she understood that, and when she read the Bible Ty gave her, she understood that too—well most of it. With her head resting against her mom, Baylee rolled her eyes and thought, grown-up talk—bla-bla-bla.

□□

Samantha listened intently to Pastor Rey as he spoke. She could feel the weight of Baylee resting against her side. There was a battle in her mind whether she should stay or go. The idea of going home and facing Stuart, and the sheer knowledge of what faced Baylee, kept her firmly planted. She prayed silently. Jesus— give Baylee this miracle. Do what that man said and be her true Healer.

□□

Isabelle sat on the other side of Baylee squirming in her seat crossing and re-crossing her legs every few minutes. While the tall man on the stage was speaking, she scanned the faces of the crowd and spotted Ms. Reynolds sitting near the front. The man next to her was huge. He turned his head occasionally and Isabelle saw a fierce tattoo on the side of the man's face. It was a snake tattoo and seemed to move even when the man's head was still. Isabelle would look away and her eyes would be drawn back to the moving serpent like a high-powered magnet. She couldn't decide if she was totally creeped out by it or impressed. The tattooed man was far more entertaining than the one yakking up front.

□□

Pastor Rey looked out across the sea of faces. He was compelled to press on. "I don't claim to understand healing. To be honest— I've prayed for more people who haven't been healed than those who have. That statement is true only if we choose to understand healing as an instantaneous restoration of a person to perfect health. I'm not sure that's how God looks at healings and miracles—but that's how we often do." Rey glanced over in Tom Brown's direction. His face was hard to read. Rey wondered what Tom might be thinking at this very moment. It was only a week ago Jean said her earthly good-byes.

Rey ran his finger over his notes on the pulpit locating his next thought. "I can't think of a more perfect healing than eternal life or a more marvelous miracle than to be transported from this life to the next."

Tom Brown agreed. "Yes. Amen."

Rey felt a surge. "Still, God's word gives us the hope of physical and emotional healing in this life because of Christ's death and resurrection. We are instructed to pray for the sick and ask for their healing. Jesus is our example of this in the book of Mark, chapter eight, verses 22-26."

Baylee looked up at her mom like she had received a secret clue and whispered her new revelation. "Mark is a book and the numbers are chapters and verses." Baylee reached for the Bible in the pew pocket in front of her.

Isabelle watched Baylee and did the same. Isabelle began fingering through the pages.

Baylee found the book, chapter and verses Ty's dad was talking about and pointed out the title of the story at the same time Pastor Rey said it.

"This is the story of the Healing of the Blind Man. Most of us are familiar with this story, but for those who may be visiting with us, let me give you a recap." Pastor Rey told the story from the Bible. He reviewed the different types of miracles that Jesus preformed such as; nature, restoring the health of those sick, the casting out of demons and rising people from the dead.

Rey prayed in his heart as he pressed forward—let this truth find fertile ground. "Christ healed many blind people during His earthly ministry. Four of those miraculous healings are recorded in detail in the Gospels. It should be noted that Jesus never relied on a formula for healing. Sometimes healings came by His command, by His touch or because someone touched Him. And in this story, he even spit." Rey looked out at a few raised eyebrows following the word—spit. He could sense an apprehension from the unchurched that the spitting portion of the service might be coming.

Rey proceeded. "If Jesus would have used only one consistent formula can you imagine how people would constantly try to reproduce that today? This should remind us that it is never about formulas, but all about God. Please take note, the birth of this miracle relates to people who didn't have a need—bringing someone who did have a need, to Christ."

Rey could see Harold and Esther sitting near the front with their eyes closed and lips moving. He could feel their prayers as he pressed on. "This is the mandate for all believers. We are called to be involved in bringing those in need to Jesus Christ. In the first part of this story the response of Jesus is surprising. In verse 23 it says, *He took the blind man by the hand and led him outside the village.* Why would Jesus walk the blind man outside the city?"

Rey allowed the rhetorical question to resonate. "God separates us from the crowd because He often does His best work, on and in us, when we are alone with Him. This scene shows the compassion of Christ for the blind man. Also, it reveals the blind man having confidence in Christ. He didn't ask Jesus, where are you taking me? What will happen when we get there? No—he showed confidence in Christ!"

Rey slapped his hand down on the pulpit. "What if we simply held the hand of Jesus and relied on Him to lead us step by step?"

Heads snapped to attention all over the sanctuary. "I love what follows – Jesus does something totally unexpected! Has God ever done something for you and you just didn't have a clue what was going to happen next? It was a "suddenly"—a surprise! God told a married couple in their 90's, Abraham and Sarah, that they were going to have their first child—*surprise!* God told a coward by the name of Gideon that he had been chosen to lead the armies of Israel to victory—*surprise!* God told Samuel to anoint the youngest son of Jesse's family to be king—*surprise!*"

Isabelle leaned across Baylee to whisper to her mom. "Do you know any of those people he's talking about?" Samantha shrugged her shoulders.

Rey stepped away from the pulpit and paced back and forth. "I love when God surprises us! No one was more surprised at what Jesus was doing than the blind man. Once outside the city, Jesus places both hands at the back of the blind man's head." Rey acted out the process. "Here the blind man must of thought— this is it—Jesus is about to heal me with that special touch of his. Nope—instead the blind man hears a familiar but unwelcomed sound; it starts in the back of Jesus' throat." Pastor Rey made the sound of someone clearing their throat getting ready to spit—but stopped short of expectorating.

Rey could see shocked looks as he continued. "And Jesus proceeds to spit in each of the blind man's eyes!" Rey paused and threw both arms in the air and wiggling his hand yelling, "SURPRISE!"

A soft chuckle rippled through the crowded room.

Rey fought back a smile. "It doesn't matter how you try and explain it away—in the time of the Bible as well as now, spitting on someone or being spit on by someone was unacceptable and insulting." Rey followed up this statement with a biblical history of the need to be cleansed after being spit on. Then he asked the question. "Why would Jesus spit in this poor man's eyes?"

The people waited to hear—what explanation could this pastor give for such an insulting act. Rey answered his own question, "If you haven't heard anything else I've said tonight—hear this. Jesus is steering us away from formulas for healing. He was cursing the blindness—spitting in the very eye of it."

Rey felt passionately about what he was saying. He could feel his heart beating with each word he spoke. "Then a strange thing happened. It's the only time in the ministry of Jesus where he did this. He asked the man; *do you see anything?* The blind man responded. *I see people; they look like trees walking around.* The question some may have following this scripture is—was the healing incomplete?"

Rey pointed out across the sea of faces and yelled. "NO! Jesus was revealing two important truths to us. Healing can be progressive and at times we must pray more than once. Another question that is raised is—does repeated prayer for the same need show a lack of faith?"

Another question followed by a thoughtful pause. This time Rey clapped his hands loudly and walked to the left side of the platform. "NO!" He said. "We must repeat the same supplications not twice or three times, but as often as we have a need, a hundred even a thousand times. ... We must never grow weary in waiting for God's help."

Baylee looked up at her mom. The questioning look in her eyes said everything. Samantha leaned in close until her lips touched Baylee's ear and whispered. "There are no formulas to follow. Let's wait and see."

Rey walked the few steps back to the pulpit and glanced at his notes. He read Mark 8:25 from his text. *"Once more Jesus put his hands on the man's eyes. Then his eyes were opened, his sight was restored, and he saw everything clearly."* Rey looked out at the people. "I love that phrase *once more*. You may grow weary seeking God for your need, and Satan may whisper this lie. 'God doesn't care about you.' 'Nobody cares about you.' 'Look at your life—God has allowed you to suffer in pain both emotionally and physically—HE DOESN'T CARE!'"

Isabelle leaned forward in her seat. The pastor had captured *her* attention. His words were reeling her slowly in—the hook was almost set. It was like he had invaded her most private thoughts.

Rey pointed out into the sea of people and Isabelle felt his stare. "God is saying to you, bring it... *ONCE MORE* I bring it to ME; sickness, a broken marriage, addiction, unsaved loved ones, rebellious teens, loneliness, heartache, trouble at work."

Rey paused and looked to the back row. He couldn't see the faces clearly, but the Holy Spirit was leading him. He pointed over the heads of the crowd in the general direction of the back of the church and said. "You think God doesn't know what happened to YOU as a child. He knows, and He cares. Don't take it out on others—His healing is for you, today. RIGHT NOW!"

A pen fell from the hand of an older lady in the back row of the church. It rolled out of sight. The lady didn't try to recover it. Her hand laid open and empty on the portfolio in her lap as tears formed in her eyes.

Rey voice boomed with authority. "ONCE MORE— BRING IT." Then his voice became soft. "Bring it to Jesus."

Eldon Chambers came to the keyboard and began to play softly.

Rey continued. "Prayer team come and line up across the front. We're going to give each one who wishes to be prayed for an opportunity. There are teams of two waiting to pray with you for whatever your need may be. This is not limited to physical healing. Come and ask the Lord once more."

Eldon played the keyboard softly in the background as Pastor Rey gave his invitation. "The blind man needed a touch from Jesus, but there is another story about a woman in need who pressed through the crowds to get close enough to touch the hem of Jesus' garments. She didn't let anything stop her from touching Jesus. Tonight, whatever your need may be— come to this altar. Press through the crowd and ask one more time."

Eldon led the congregation in a song. The prayer team lined up across the front of the church facing the people. Callan stepped into the main aisle to direct people for prayer. People began to fill the aisle. As quickly as they came, Callan sent them for prayer. The need was greater than they had anticipated, but the people waited. They waited for their turn.

Near the middle of the sanctuary, Samantha watched. Baylee watched. Isabelle felt drawn to move. She turned toward her sister and mother. "Can we go now?"

Samantha responded. "Can you wait for a bit? I don't want to go home yet."

"No mom. Can we go to the front?" She used her head to point at the altar.

Samantha stood up. "Yes. Yes."

Baylee's face was sad. "I can't do it mom. I can't stand in the line." Tears began to roll down her cheeks.

Samantha picked up her ten-year-old daughter like a toddler and edged her way down the pew to the center aisle. There were many people in front of them, but they waited.

Ty and Zander watched from their front row seats. Some people came up quickly and left just as fast. While others lingered, not wanting to leave—knowing something amazing was happening at that altar.

Pastor Rey stepped off the platform with a small glass bottle in his hand. He walked to where Callan was standing and took her hand. They began praying for people standing in line. They would pray for the next person in line then send a few people to pray with the teams at the altar, and then they would pray for the next person in line. This happened over and over until Callan looked up to see Samantha holding Baylee like a sleeping child. Baylee's head rested on her mom's shoulder and Isabelle stood close to her mother's side.

The picture of this family proved more than Callan could endure. Tears pooled in her eyes and spilled out. Her voice was broken with emotion. She looked at Rey, "This is Samantha Hayes our neighbor and her daughter Isabelle." Callan laid her hand on Baylee's back, "And this is Baylee—Ty and Zander's friend. The one we've been praying for at night." Callan felt a touch on her arm. She turned toward the touch to see Ty worm his way into the group.

Baylee wiggled down from her mom's arms and stood next to Ty.

"Baylee are you ready for Jesus to heal you?" Ty asked.

A wave of faith washed over Rey and Callan. Rey knelt on one knee and looked down at Baylee. "Baylee, I'm going to touch your forehead with a drop of this oil and then we're going to pray and ask God to heal you." Rey looked at Samantha and asked. "What exactly is wrong with her?"

Samantha was crying. "It's a birth defect that has stunted the growth of her legs causing her fierce pain. She's facing the amputation of both legs, if something doesn't change."

Callan dropped down on her knees to be face to face with Baylee. Rey touched Baylee's forehead and began to pray. The sounds of movement in the far corner of the sanctuary grew louder increasing in volume. Rey prayed louder speaking over the sound of a roaring wave crashing against a cement embankment. "Dear Jesus, Baylee needs Your touch. We come asking for Your help. We have no certain words to say or rituals to perform—we come, we ask, we believe You are able, we trust You." The sound of a building collapsing from the force of a tsunami bellowed in Rey's ears as he asked. "Heal Baylee's legs right now in the name of Jesus I ask."

Ty stood behind Baylee resting his hand on her shoulder. He prayed out loud after his father, "Please Jesus—heal my friend."

Something happened in that little circle—it played out in slow motion—yet instantaneously. The silence after the storm filled the sanctuary and the sound of knuckles cracking was all anyone could hear in the deafening silence. One bone cracking then another and another echoing through the quiet.

Baylee began to cry repeating the words. "It's happening. I feel it. I feel it. I feel it."

Right before their eyes, Baylee stood taller than before—she moved her legs and began to draw her knees to her chest one at a time releasing them and then repeating the exercise again. She whispered at first, "The pain is gone!" Then she said it again three more times, each time her volume increased.

"The pain is gone!" "THE PAIN IS GONE." "THE PAIN IS GONE!"

Samantha's face revealed shock. "What's happened? What's going on?" She collapsed into the nearest pew her whole-body trembling.

Isabelle watched with saucer sized eyes. Not speaking—just watching.

Ty yelled. "Jesus healed you! He healed you! I knew He would!" He began jumping up and down. He grabbed his mom's arm. "Look. Look. Jesus did it. He did it!"

The once straight line of people waiting for prayer turned into a mass pressing in to see what had happened. The prayer team moved forward to see.

Fauna saw Isabelle and reached for her. Isabelle did not resist the hug. The physical touch of her school counselor broke down whatever resistance was left, and Issie held Fauna like a drowning person would cling to a life preserver. Fauna leaned in close and whispered into Isabelle's ear—watching another miracle taking place inside her arms.

Ty took Baylee's hand and began walking back and forth in front of the church. It wasn't showy. It wasn't boastful. It was childlike faith—on display in all its innocence and faith.

Callan sat down next to Samantha and embraced her trembling body, quietly speaking to her as the Spirit directed. The prayer team began ministering to those in line.

Pastor Rey felt a tug at his shirt sleeve and turned around and looked down at a small woman with a portfolio tucked under her arm. "Ms. Klingburg, you're here!"

This was a different woman, then the one Ray saw just days ago. Her eyes were wet from crying and her voice was humble. "Pastor Douglas, I was wrong about you. I came tonight hoping to find something to bring your family down and destroy you." She fought with the emotion in her voice and swallowed. "But what you said. In your message—how I could you know? Then this…" She pointed at Baylee, then moved her hand in the direction of the altar where people were still praying. She put both hands over her heart and added, "…He healed me too!" Ms. Klingburg wiped a tear. "I had so much pain, blamed so many people and judged so many families through my own pain." Tears spilled out from behind her glasses. "Lord, forgive me."

From that moment on, there were only believers in the sanctuary of Community Outreach Church for they had all been witness to an undeniable miracle.

34
…Too Many Too Count

The healing service was over—only the prayer team was left. Pastor Rey and Callan sat in the front pew still basking in the presence of the Lord. Snake walked over and sat next to Rey. Rey reached his arm around Snake's shoulders and bear hugged him.

"Snake, we were witnesses to a miracle." Rey corrected himself. "—another miracle."

"Pastor, there were too many to count tonight." Snake held a folded piece of notebook paper in his hand. "A few minutes ago, I dropped my Bible and this note fell out. I believe it's for you, Pastor, from the Lord." Snake smiled slyly and handed the note to Pastor Rey. Snake walked away.

Rey unfolded the paper and noted the date at the top of the page. He began to read the word that Harold Smith had written before the first small group meeting at Snake's house. …Fear not and don't be afraid, trials come, persecution comes and what is coming to you is to perfect you—not destroy you.

Stand strong and don't be overcome with evil but overcome evil with good. This will pass and when it does the glory of the Lord will shine forth even to those who persecute God's anointed. You will see with your eyes, hear with your ears and know in your heart—God has a purpose—God has a plan. It is always forgiveness. It is always redemption. It is always eternity. You will see the power and might of the Lord God in this—we will all see.

□ □

It was past 11 P.M. when Samantha pulled the van into the driveway on Lancaster Drive. The garage door closed behind them and Isabelle was the first one out of the van. She threw open the mudroom door and burst into the family room where Stuart sat in the same place they left him less than four hours ago. Now... everything had changed, nothing was the same.

"Dad." Issie stood in front of the television. "Dad—you won't believe it!"

"Isabelle, stop yelling. What's the emergency? I was ready to call the police. Where have you been?" Stuart stood up and looked toward the kitchen for Samantha. He held his tongue for now, but she would hear plenty once the kids were in bed. How dare she worry him!

Samantha stood by the mudroom door with a glowing smile.

Stuart looked back and forth between his eldest daughter and his wife. "Where is Baylee? What happened? Is she sick—hurt?" He frowned then spoke with anger in his voice. "Samantha, wipe that stupid smile off your face and answer me."

The garage door slammed. Stuart focused on the doorway from the kitchen to the mud room anticipating Baylee's entry. Baylee moved with ease past Samantha. Mother and daughter wore matching smiles. With her arms open from side to side, Baylee proclaimed. "Dad...Jesus healed me." She stood straight and tall. She did one big jump straight up in the air to rid any doubts that her statement wasn't true.

Stuart drew his lips inward and bit down. His lips began to quiver. "What? Who?" He took one step toward Baylee and she ran to him, throwing her arms around his waist. She buried her face into her father's side. Stuart pushed her back slightly and dropped down to his knees. He hugged her. While holding Baylee tight, Stuart glanced up at Samantha standing across the room. Her eyes were red and swollen. He looked at Isabelle who had moved from the family room back to the kitchen. Her eyes were the same.

Isabelle said. "It was a miracle—with no spitting and Pastor Rey only asked once."

Stuart looked confused by the statement. He questioned. "Did this happen at that church meeting?"

Samantha nodded. "I took Baylee to six professed healers, but Healer #7 was the true healer. He heals the body, mind and soul."

Stuart stood up raising Baylee up in his arms. He held her at arm's length for a moment, then drew her in and hugged her tightly. Her healed legs dangled pain-free.

"It doesn't hurt when people hug me." She giggled with glee.

Samantha joined the hug. Stuart looked at Isabelle and nodded his head beckoning her to join the family hug.

Isabelle stood by the kitchen island with a blue scarf in her hand. She asked. "Mom is this yours?"

☐☐

Snake and Fauna walked to their car following the healing service. The excitement of the night was alive in them. Snake clicked the keychain to unlock the doors and asked, "Are you hungry or do you want to go directly home?"

Fauna clicked on her seat belt and suggested. "We could go to the drive through and take it back to my apartment."

"Sounds good to me." Snake headed toward the fast food restaurant on the way.

After a quick stop at the fast food chain, they headed to Fauna's apartment on the other side of town. Snake took an unexpected turn.

"Where are you going? It's late." Fauna added a yawn to prove her point. "...and the food's gonna get cold."

Snake slowed down in front of a weathered gray house one block off Main Street downtown. "I just had a thought and wanted to drive by this old place."

It was dark, but the light on the covered porch was bright enough to show the police tape circling the building. A new sign was posted on the wooden front door that read, OUT OF BUSINESSAVAILABLE FOR LEASE. The crudely carved wood shingle that said, *The Healer* was gone.

"Why did you want to see this creepy place?" Fauna's voice sounded with disgust.

Snake's voice smiled as he spoke. "God has a crazy way of repurposing things that no one else finds value in. Remember, that's what He did with me." He looked over at Fauna in the dim light.

Fauna found Snake's hand and squeezed it. "He repurposed both of us—for His purpose."

Snake pulled away from the empty house and Fauna glanced back over her shoulder until the house was out of sight.

35

One Year Later

The old house on Main Street received a fresh coat of deep red paint with mossy green trim. The front door was painted a dark charcoal gray. Three months ago, the house was painted causing people to guess what the new business in Hillbrooke would be. Some guessed it would be a year around Christmas store—until the new sign was installed announcing the *Hillbrooke Family Counseling Center*.

Fauna chose the name. She wanted to keep it simple—nothing trendy or fancy—kinda like her. She walked up the front steps of the counseling center and slipped her key in the door. She eased the door open. The smell of lavender greeted her. The seating area to her left was arranged in a U-shape with one sofa and two love seats. Square end tables flanked the sofa. Each table held a decorative lamp. An oversized square coffee table sat between the two love seats with a candle covered by a glass globe for the centerpiece. On the walls were vinyl art decals, four to be exact, each one was a scripture verse.

To the right of the door, the seating area opened to a small resource library. The original design for this 1903 house probably used this area as a small parlor for greeting guests. The three walls were lined with book cases holding volumes of books to help people going through grief, divorce, addiction, marital issues, child rearing concerns and numerous other resources. The books were made available for education and motivation.

Fauna stood at the door, taking in her dream come true. Her eyes landed on the first scripture visible when people opened the door. It was an abbreviated version of Isaiah 9:6.

...HIS NAMES WILL BE:
AMAZING COUNSELOR,
STRONG GOD,
ETERNAL FATHER,
PRINCE OF WHOLENESS.
HIS RULING AUTHORITY WILL GROW,
AND THERE 'LL BE NO LIMITS
TO THE WHOLENESS HE BRINGS.

This verse had proven true in Fauna's life. Now, she had a front row seat watching God pour out his *unlimited wholeness* to those who entered the doors of the center. She witnessed people coming who were alone, lost and hurting—but when they left—they were found. The pains of this life were being soothed by an Amazing Counselor, Strong God, Eternal Father and the Prince of Wholeness.

Today, the center was closed. It was dedication day. The business was three months successful. Fauna propped the door open to finish carrying in a few more loads of supplies for the open house. Her hand touched the small plaque secured to the inside of the door. The plaque hung at eye level allowing everyone leaving to know this…

THE HILLBROOKE FAMILY COUNSELING CENTER IS
DEDICATED TO THE MEMORY OF
JEAN BROWN—WHO RECEIVED HER MIRACLE.

Fauna ran her fingers over the raised letters on the plaque, and the embossed sketch of Jean Brown. If it wasn't for Tom Brown believing in her dream, none of this would have happened. It was in Jean's memory that he donated the money for the counseling center.

The night of the healing service when Fauna, Snake and Tom Brown formed a prayer circle—they each shared what they believed the Lord would do in their lives. That night Fauna asked for prayer. "It's a dream—I've held in my heart for a long time. I know it can only happen if God provides a miracle for me." She said the words the same as she might have said any crazy impossible thing; like walking on the moon or being president of the United States. She said, "I want to open a family counseling center to help people in crisis—find wholeness."

That night following the service, she knew it was strange that Snake drove her by this very house. Now she knew that God was already at work. First, God moved in Snake's heart, giving him the courage to move past the "what ifs" and into the "my God is able." Within one week of the healing service—Snake asked Fauna to marry him and she accepted with an emotional, "YES!"

A few weeks later while Fauna was planning the wedding— Tom Brown met with them. He presented them with the check for $100,000 toward a counseling center in

Hillbrooke. The two-month engagement ended with a fall wedding at Tom Brown's house on Deer Lake. The fall colors were a beautiful backdrop to a perfect wedding.

Pastor Rey performed the wedding. He joked with them at the rehearsal saying, "I now pronounce you Mr. and Mrs. Snake." Snake had changed his name as a troubled teen from Carl Fields to Zak Parker, but Fauna didn't care—she took the name Snake chose. They would be known as Mr. and Mrs. Zak Parker.

Snake's parents were there, James and Marilyn Fields, along with his sister and brother-in-law, Emily and Kota Edwards. Snake's young niece was the flower girl and the ring bearer was his nephew who was barely walking. It was an informal wedding with family and the small group members in attendance. They did a potluck dinner with cupcakes instead of a formal wedding cake. It was exactly what the couple wanted and all those present wished them the best.

□□

Fauna returned to the counseling center conference room with her arms loaded with the last items from the car. She carefully arranged the paper plates and cups along with the cookies, potato chips and sandwiches on the conference room table. She heard the door open in the waiting room and glanced at her watch.

A familiar voice called her name, "Fauna, I brought the napkins." Snake said.

Fauna stepped into the hallway and said, "I'm in here."

Snake met Fauna in the conference room and laid the napkins on the table. He watched his wife scurry around preparing for her special day. The dedication and open house would begin with a prayer of dedication by Pastor Rey. Then

Fauna would say a few words. The center would be open for two more hours for people to come and go as they wished.

In the conference room, Snake and Fauna heard a loud bang. Ty Douglas ran into the waiting room—his brother in hot pursuit. Ty took a tumble over the end table and landed on the love seat. The coffee table centerpiece crashed to the floor. When Callan surveyed the damage—she stood frozen at the door profusely apologizing.

Fauna picked up the broken arrangement and replaced it with three magazines. She fanned them to fill-up the vacant space. "Problem solved!" She winked at Ty as she carried the broken centerpiece to the back of the house.

Callan snapped her fingers at the boys and said, "Sit. Don't move from those seats until I come back." She followed a few steps behind Fauna apologizing all the way.

Baylee and Isabelle came in and sat across from the boys. The freedom Baylee once had with the boys was now being replaced with adolescent awkwardness. Baylee had grown four inches making her taller than both boys. Ty was fine with it, but Zander, who was the same age, was not!

Samantha joined the women in the conference room and Isabelle soon followed her mom to where the other ladies were gathered. She wasn't going to be sitting with the children.

Samantha asked. "Isabelle, did you show Mrs. Parker your new...and last tattoo?"

Isabelle rolled her eyes and huffed. "It's not like I'm getting tattooed on purpose." She realized Mrs. Parker was covered in tattoos and tried to back track. "Well, that's not what I meant. I'm sorry." Then she stuck out her wrist for all the ladies to see. On the wrist of Isabelle's left arm a very delicate lace patterned tattoo looked like a bracelet. "I got this to cover up the word—you know the one." She turned her wrist over to show them the word HATE was swallowed up by the lacey pattern. The ugly word was no longer distinguishable. The new tattoo had changed ashes to beauty and mourning to joy.

Back in the reception area of the center, Rey struck up a conversation with the doctor. "Dr. Hayes." Rey began.

Dr. Hayes stopped Rey. "Remember—it's Stuart. We're way past those formalities."

"Yes, I guess we are. I just wanted to thank you again for clearing things up with CPS. Of course, Ms. Klingburg had a lot to do with that as well. Callan and I are finally respectable parents again!" Rey gave a heartfelt laughed.

Stuart still carried shame for the part he played in reporting Rey and Callan to CPS. He had been deceived and manipulated. He had crossed the line of professional behavior with a patient. Sympathy unchecked can become a quagmire. That was exactly where Stuart found himself a year ago—wading through a destructive mucky swamp.

The night of the healing service he had texted Heidi to stop by to pick something up. Samantha had warned him to be careful. His intentions were honorable—he thought he knew better than his wife. He had the number of a crisis group where Heidi could get help. The moment she stepped into the house—he knew he was coloring outside the lines, but he allowed his sympathy for someone hurting to overshadow his common sense.

Heidi interpreted the invitation to mean more than picking up information. Dr. Hayes escorted her to the door. Being the person Heidi was, she purposefully left her scarf behind. From that moment on he knew—she was not to be trusted—in anything she said or did.

After the police cleared Heidi of all wrong doing in the matter of Victor Darwin, Heidi tried to contact Stuart again. He told her of the miraculous healing of Baylee and the dramatic change in Isabelle. Dr. Hayes credited both to the Lord, to the prayers of Rey Douglas and the church called Community Outreach. The phone went dead.

Stuart was sad that Heidi rejected the help he offered. She chose a different path. A few months after Heidi disappeared from Hillbrooke, the news reported Victor Darwin was arrested in Arizona. He had opened a new clinic and within one month his receptionist reported improprieties to the police.

□□

The Hillbrooke Family Counseling Center was filling up quickly as the members of Snake and Fauna's small group arrived. Harold and Esther Smith, the Samson's, Tom Brown, Emily and Kota Edwards, Snake's parents, James and Marilyn Fields, and the members of the Community Outreach Church board were all there.

Pastor Rey called everyone together in the waiting room to start the dedication. The people stood shoulder to shoulder in the small room. Tom Brown stood on one side of the Pastor and Fauna on his other side. Pastor Rey prayed a prayer of dedication. After he said, "Amen"—Pastor Rey continued. "I now dedicate the Hillbrooke Family Counseling Center in the name of the Father, the Son, and the Holy Spirit. May it be a beacon that draws people into truth. A welcoming place for Jesus—*The True Healer* to transform and restore what the locusts have eaten. I dedicate this ministry to the glory of God. Amen." Rey turned to Fauna and nodded.

Fauna shared. "Thank you all for coming. I can honestly say that I love each of you. My heart is full. For a girl who mostly raised herself and without any role models growing up—looking around this room today, I can only say, God gave me more than I could have ever hoped. He gave me family." Emotion choked off her words. She swallowed hard and finished with, "Now go and enjoy yourselves— Stay as long as you want...but not too long!" Fauna laughed, and the atmosphere changed from quiet and respectful to relaxed and friendly.

Over the next few hours people came and went from the counseling center. Fauna was able to talk to potential clients and greet families who experienced what Pastor Rey talked about in his dedication. These were the ones who were in the process of being transformed and restored. These families had met *The True Healer* and their lives were forever changed.

Ms. Klingburg walked through the center doors and greeted Fauna. She slipped her a piece of paper. "Here are two more families who could benefit from your services. Especially the parenting classes."

Fauna hugged Ms. Klingburg and gestured toward the back of the house. "There are refreshments in the conference room. We can talk more later."

The two-hour open house moved quickly and soon Snake and Fauna began cleaning up as the last guests exited. With an arm load of leftovers in tow, Snake left the center calling back to Fauna. "Promise me you're coming right behind me."

"I promise. I have one more thing to do." Fauna stood at the door ready to flick off the lights. She paused and ran her fingers over the metal plaque on the door. She read the words out loud. "The Hillbrooke Family Counseling Center is dedicated to the memory of Jean Brown—who received her miracle."

Fauna placed her hand over Jean's picture and whispered. "Me too Jean. Me too."

The End

Discussion Questions

Pastor Rey Douglas came face to face with attacks from the enemy in his ministry and in his home. How do you respond to spiritual attacks when they come? Are you prepared or reactionary?

Callan Douglas has grown spiritually since we first meet her in *Hillbrooke New Beginnings*, but she still battles with things from her past. Did you identify with her when her old nature tried to resurface? How do you handle similar situations?

Tom Brown's world is shaken off the axis with the news of his wife's illness. Have you ever walked a similar path? What helped you on your journey through grief?

Heidi Alden is consistent if nothing else. Do you know anyone like her? Did you ever feel sorry for her life choices and situation? How would you reach out to someone like her—or would you?

Snake (Zak Parker/formerly Carl Fields) is carrying a heavy load trying to sort through what's best for the one he loves. He believes, if he and Fauna marry that his past will destroy her future. What does this say about Snake's character? Do you think Snake's concerns were valid or imaginary? Why or why not?

Fauna Reynolds has been pushed into a box by the school system's code of conduct. Was she right to disobey? Might she have acted differently if her job was not short-term?

In this book, Isabelle is a typical teen that only cares about herself, but as the book evolves so does Isabelle's inner strength. What were some of the snap decisions she made that showed she was wise beyond her years? Could you have done that at fourteen?

Heidi Alden believed *The Healer* was helping her, but her actions towards others proved otherwise. What scriptures can you recall that support what Heidi was experiencing? James 4:17; 2 Timothy 4:3; Galatians 6:7

The friendship between Samantha and Callan was sweet and evolved slowly. Do most friendships between women happen like this? How soon would you disclose your trusted confidences with another?

When Samantha takes her daughters for treatment with *The Healer*, she seems blinded to the fact that she is dabbling in something that is evil. Do you think people like Samantha, who are spiritually uninformed, are becoming more the norm, or are they the exception?

The healing service at Community Outreach Church ended with a supernatural healing. How does physical healing compare with the healing of a lost soul (salvation) or the miracle of Jean Brown (eternity)? Do Christians tend to place more value on the seen than the unseen working of the Spirit? Why or why not?

Do you look at death the same way as Jean Brown? Is death a miracle—a win or do you view death as—a loss?

□□

Dear Reader,

Thanks for taking the time to read Hillbrooke The Healer. Please take a minute and let me know how you liked the book. I'd love to hear from you. You can contact me at *beverlyjoyroberts@gmail.com* or leave a book review on my website at

<u>*www.beverlyjoyroberts.com*</u>.

If you liked this book, I hope you will share it with someone.

God Bless.
Beverly Joy Roberts

"Come to me, all who are tired
from carrying heavy loads,
and I will give you rest."
Matthew 11:28 (GW)